Eva Ibbotson

MADENSKY SQUARE

PAN BOOKS

First published 1988 by London: Century

This edition published 2017 by Pan Books
an imprint of Pan Macmillan
20 New Wharf Road, London N1 9RR
Associated companies throughout the world
www.panmacmillan.com

ISBN 978-1-5098-2190-7

1 3 5 7 9 8 6 4 2

A CIP catalogue record for this book is available from the British Library.

Typeset by Ellipsis Digital Limited, Glasgow
Printed and bound by CPI Group (UK) Ltd, Croydon, CR0 4YY

Visit www.panmacmillan.com to read more about all our books
and to buy them. You will also find features, author interviews and
news of any author events, and you can sign up for e-newsletters
so that you're always first to hear about our new releases.

MADENSKY SQUARE

I woke in such a good mood this morning.

There was a dress floating about in my head; almost ready, almost there. Cream silk, the skirt trimmed with tiers and tiers of rough cream lace and the bodice tuckered, but unadorned except for a single rose. When I went to sleep I wasn't sure about the colour of the rose, but when I woke I knew it had to be cream also: a self-coloured rose, a little passé, almost blowsy.

'Dresses come to you like songs come to Schubert, Frau Susanna,' a customer said to me once, and I was so pleased, idiot that I was, that I undercharged her quite badly for the evening cape I was fitting.

But it wasn't just the dress that made me happy. Even before I opened the shutters I knew that the bitter wind from the east had dropped at last and spring had come.

I got out of bed and caught sight of my reflection in the mirror above the chest of drawers, and it was all right still . . . even in the strong light of early morning it was all right. I'm thirty-six but I could have worn it, the rich cream dress with the bell sleeves cut on the cross and the silken rose. It wasn't for me, of course, it was for the shop, but I could have carried it off.

'From what strange ingredients you have fashioned your beauty,' someone said to me once. 'A mouth too large, a forehead too broad, the cheekbones of a Bohemian peasant . . . Still, one must concede the eyes – and the hair. Yes, certainly one must concede the hair.'

Actually it was not 'someone' who said this. It was Field Marshal Gernot von Lindenberg and he is not 'someone'.

For a moment I saw in the mirror what he had seen, this fierce and ageing man, holding my face between his hands. Then I blinked and was confronted by a woman with fair hair and blue eyes, entirely ordinary, no longer young.

I live above my shop in a small square in the Inner City. The bells of St Stephen's Cathedral ring the hours for me and it's only twelve minutes' walk to the opera (all distances in Vienna are measured from the opera!) yet it's so quiet and contained one could be in the country. My bedroom and the bathroom I insisted on putting in (to the amusement of the workmen) face the court-yard at the back where I have planted what is possibly the smallest pear tree in the Austro-Hungarian Empire, but my sitting room and kitchen – and the salon of the shop of course – look out on Madensky Square.

And I was right about the spring! Leaning out of the window, still in my kimono, waiting for the water to boil for my coffee, I could see the water sparkling in the fountain, see the sunlight glint on the brass head of Colonel Madensky, somewhat beset by pigeons. The air was warm, and the smells that in the winter only come fleetingly from shops and doorways drifted voluptuously up-wards: fresh bread . . . vanilla . . . saddle soap.

From the moment I saw the square I knew that this was where I wanted to live and have my shop. We have everything, you see: a fountain, a statue, a café – even our own small church. True the fountain in the centre has only one tier and no one on it could actually be said to *writhe*. When I first came here, eight years ago, I rather wished for stone heroes with rippling pectorals or god-desses with cornucopias and serpents in their hair. But our fountain just has Saint Florian, the patron saint of fires (and of fire engines), a gentle person holding a stone bucket with which to extinguish any flames that come his way. The church, whose little graveyard turns the west side of the square into a garden, is consecrated to him. It's like a country church, our St Florian's: white painted, with an onion dome. Inside there are no skeletal relics of martyrs gruesomely draped in silver filigree and pearls; no swirling Baroque altarpieces to bring the tourists flocking with their Baedekers –

only a carved wooden Madonna whose infant really looks like a baby, not like some attenuated adult laid like a log across her lap. I know all the graves in the churchyard. The Family Steiner (with geraniums), the Family Heinrid (with urns), the Family Schmidt, overgrown and neglected, but wild harebells have seeded themselves in the grass.

The east side of the square is protected from the busy, narrow Walterstrasse by five chestnut trees; and set back from them, turning away from the traffic and facing inwards, is Colonel Madensky on his plinth. I would have liked him to be an equestrian statue – it would have been roomier for the pigeons – but the Colonel, it seems, was not important enough to rate a horse.

He fought in the Italian campaigns and perished at the Battle of Solferino, a troublesome battle where everyone lost everybody else. The Emperor lost his commanding officers in the fog, the officers mislaid their troops and Austria lost Lombardy and Venice. Madensky was a kind man, they say, who wanted all his soldiers to have dark moustaches and gave free hair dye to those unfortunate enough to be fair. You can see that in his face; the desire that things should be the same as each other and not difficult.

Leaning out, I could see the sign of my shop. I didn't know what to call it when I came here so in the end I decided just to use my Christian name: Susanna. And it worked! 'Meet me at Susanna's', people say now, or 'Go and see Susanna; she'll know what you need!'

There are only three shops in the square, all on the south side – on my right, an antiquarian bookseller, on my left, a saddler. I'm in the middle – double-fronted, painted in shining black and gold, and very beautiful!

Opposite, at the café on the corner of the Walterstrasse, Joseph was setting out tables and chairs on the pavement, and that above all is a guarantee of spring. The Café Strauss isn't a literary rendezvous: you won't find Jeritza holding court there on the way home from the opera or Hugo von Hofmannsthal penning an ode. To get twenty people into the Café Strauss is quite an achievement, but Joseph's eggs-in-a-glass are famous and the recipe for his mother's poppyseed kipferl dates from the Turkish siege.

Still opposite, but on the other side, next to the church, in the green stuccoed Biedermeier house where the Schumachers live, Lisl, the maid, was hanging her feather bed out of the attic window. Then she vanished and I knew she had run downstairs to give breakfast in bed to Frau Schumacher who is expecting her long-awaited son. There are six little girls in the Schumacher household: Mitzi and Franzi; Steffi and Resi; Kati and Gisi – but the new baby will be a boy. No one believes that God can disappoint Herr Direktor Albert Schumacher yet again when he so desperately needs an heir for his timber business in the Gurtel. Lisl, who is convent educated, has promised to signal to us as soon as the child is born. If the news is good, she'll hang out a white towel, if it is bad, a black apron.

'Like Theseus and his sail, Frau Susanna,' she explained.

Everyone calls me Frau Susanna, not Fräulein, though I have never been married. My surname, which is Weber, seems only to appear on invoices and delivery notes.

But I was waiting for the event that always heralds the day's true beginning in the square and now it came. The door of the shabby apartment house directly facing me was opened by an invisible hand and a low-slung black dog with a purse round his neck appeared, descended the steps with an air of extreme self-importance, and turned into the Walterstrasse. Till he has fetched the *Neue Freie Presse* for his owner, the concierge, Rip is abstracted and unsociable, but once the moist newspaper has been laid at her feet he gives himself to the affairs of the populace, sitting in his doorway and deciding what may be allowed to happen and what must be prevented. He has the large, square-muzzled head of a Schnautzer and the tail of a muskrat, but his dreams, like his little legs, are Napoleonic.

By the time I'd made my coffee and carried it back to the window, the procession of choristers shepherded by Father Anselm had left the presbytery beside the saddler's and was passing the fountain. St Florian's only has a sung mass once a week so the choirboys the Father trains also sing at other churches. Sighs of sentiment often follow these sweet little boys in their scarlet coats and navy breeches, but I don't sigh. I'm too busy watching Ernst Bischof, the star pupil, whose rendering of Mozart's *Exsultate Jubilate* reduces the congregation to tears, and who is a fiend. And sure enough, as I watched, the charming child kicked out savagely at the shins of the boy next to him. The day Ernst Bischof's voice breaks, Frau Schumacher and I are going to give a great party with champagne.

And now came the regulars who use the square as a passageway, taking a short cut through the alleyway of pleached hornbeams beside the churchyard towards the Ringstrasse trams.

Professor Starsky had changed his brown velour hat for a battered straw, beneath which his wispy grey hair spread out like an aureole. He comes past every morning and he's usually carrying something in a brown paper parcel: a lizard with lung trouble or a tortoise that has expired inside its shell, for he is a Professor of Reptile Diseases and people send him their stricken pets from all over the Empire. Seeing me leaning unsuitably like Rapunzel from the window, he raised his hat.

'Good morning, Frau Susanna.'

'Good morning, Herr Professor. What is it today?'

He held up the parcel. 'A stump-tailed skink. From a man who keeps a pet shop in Bolzen.'

Three years ago I found the Professor standing sadly in the churchyard where his wife is buried, and brought him in for a cup of coffee. Last summer, sheltering in my shop from a sudden rainstorm, he proposed to me.

'I wouldn't expect you to love me of course,' he said, 'an accomplished, beautiful woman like you. But I have a house as you know, and a villa on the Grundlsee – and of course I wouldn't bring work home –' and here he'd touched the leg of a pickled chameleon protruding stiffly from its wrappings – 'not if you were to do me the honour.'

It was a nice proposal; I refused it nicely and we remained friends.

After Professor Starsky came the English Miss, striding to the Volksgarten to exercise her setter bitch. In her heather-mixture tweeds, high breasted and long-legged like her dog, she is a sight so splendid that for a moment she brings life in the square to a halt. Joseph put down the cloth with which he was wiping his tables and stared; in his Biedermeier house, Herr Schumacher left his six daughters at the breakfast table and hurried to the window. And Rip descended the three steps from his doorway, quivered, advanced . . . and recalled himself to sanity, for the bitch, like her owner, belongs to the unattainable world of myth and dreams.

The clock of the cathedral struck seven, and a minute and a quarter later our own St Florian's followed suit. Now I could see Gretl, my sewing maid, turn in from the Walterstrasse between the chestnut trees with my breakfast kipferl and a jug of milk. Time to begin the day.

As I turned from the window I heard again the sound that for the past weeks has become as much a part of our lives as the plashing of the fountain or the bells of the church: the sound of someone practising the piano. It comes from the top floor of the apartment house directly across from me – from the smallest, shabbiest attic flat – and it goes on relentlessly from morning to night. Scales first, dozens and dozens of them; chromatic scales, scales in octaves, arpeggios . . . Then etudes by Chopin, by Czerny, by heaven knows who; Bach preludes, some pieces by Liszt . . . and of late a Beethoven sonata broken off suddenly in the last movement. Never in my life have I heard anyone practise so continuously or with such strength, and the strange thing is, I don't know who is playing. We watched the piano being hoisted into the house and a thin, stooped man with greasy sideburns – very eastern looking – goes in and out, but once I thought I heard the music after I'd seen him go out across the square.

I listened for a little longer. Then I dressed and pinned up my hair – after which I climbed the stairs to the attics and went to wake Nini.

*

It is not actually my business to wake my chief assistant. She should wake of her own accord and be at her machine by seven thirty, but Nini is a passionate Anarchist and spent the previous night at a revolutionary meeting in the suburb of Ottakring. She went in high-heeled white kid sandals which cost her nearly three weeks' wages and in an ostrich feather boa borrowed from the shop, and why I put up with this I really do not know.

Most of my sewing is done by outworkers, but I keep two girls full time in the workroom behind the shop. Gretl, who sleeps out, is a little packhorse of a girl, willing and stupid. She runs errands and does the hems and picot edgings and her life centres round her fiancé and his fire engine, a prima donna of a machine now threatened with mechanization.

Nini is another matter. Her stitches are as small as mine, her taste is unerring, and though she is really too thin to model I allow her into the salon to show the clothes.

She was just waking, stretching . . . extending one foot from beneath the coverlet. A foot whose elongated El Greco toes were caked with blood.

This made me immediately and justifiably angry.

'Will you once and for all not go on marches in unsuitable shoes? I will not have blood-stained people touching my fabrics and modelling my clothes.'

Nini looked at me reproachfully. She is nineteen-years-old and could be my daughter – but this is not a line to pursue.

'It was the anniversary of the Garment Workers' Strike in Yaroslav,' she said. 'We went right along the Danube Quay and everyone supported us like anything.'

'No doubt I shall get another visit from the police soon. When you're actually imprisoned perhaps you'll be satisfied.'

'There is no progress without suffering,' murmured my chief assistant. She rose in her shift and limped to the wash stand. Black tousled hair, ferocious Magyar eyebrows, a beak of a nose – and an unnaturally long neck which makes every movement memorable.

'Oh, it isn't the suffering. I'm sure you'll enjoy that. It's the head lice,' I said – and Nini flinched.

But of course I understand. Oh, I mock, I despair as this girl who spends ten minutes removing a spider from the bath plans to assassinate archdukes and put the bourgeoisie to the sword, but I understand. She wants a better world for the poor and oppressed – and she wants to look pretty while she's getting it – and don't we all?

I found Nini when she was modelling for Paul Ungerer's life class in his atelier off the Schottenring. She was sitting resolute and naked on a cane chair, her black hair hanging over her back, one leg stretched out and her behind too close to the stove which was one of those black capricious beasts of the kind that killed Emile Zola.

Paul Ungerer is a conceited fop who wears a black velvet beret and carries on like Delacroix, but his wife is a good customer of mine and I had promised to drop off a skating dress that she had ordered.

The students were drawing the model and Paul Ungerer was striding round the studio being sarcastic when there was a thud; the chair on the dais had fallen over – and the model lay in a dead faint on the draped, plum-coloured velvet.

Nini's thighs were checked in red and white where the cane had bitten into her skin, and the burn on her behind was serious. I told Paul Ungerer what I thought of him, which pleased the students and took Nini home.

I meant only to feed her up a little, but her mother, it turned out, had been a seamstress. (The father, who had deserted them, had been some kind of clothes-prop hussar, all sabres and *sapkas* and wind. A Hungarian, of course!)

Oddly, it was her Anarchism which made Nini such a good model. For when you are modelling clothes it is no good being ingratiating, and this slightly mad grisette gliding past some bourgeois burgermaster's wife, flashing contempt from her black eyes, could reduce the poor lady to a state of abject longing for whatever garment she was showing.

*

Usually I go straight down after breakfast and open the shop, but today, because of the spring I lingered to talk to my pear tree.

My courtyard adjoins that of the bookseller, Augustin Heller, whose ancient and irregular shop juts out into the Walterstrasse. Heller is old and spends the day reading the antiquarian books which people, much to his annoyance, sometimes insist on buying before he has finished them. Last night his eleven-year-old granddaughter, Maia, came on a visit and had now escaped into the garden in her nightdress.

'Don't you *really* want to go to Madagascar?' I heard her say. 'Really don't you, Mitzi? When you die don't you want to have girdled the earth?'

She's an intense girl, raven haired: a bibliophile and an adventuress.

'No, I don't,' came the voice of poor Mitzi, the eldest of the six Schumacher girls. 'When I die I want to have baked the best gug'lhupf in Vienna.'

The salon of my shop is yellow and white like the inside of a daisy. The drapes in the windows and the curtains framing the long mirrors are the colour of newly picked lemons (that yellow isn't even remotely egg-like) and the walls are ivory and match the alabaster bowls in which I keep fresh flowers. My carpet is grey, the chairs and sofas are upholstered in oyster velvet, and on the low tables I don't just keep fashion magazines but also ashtrays so that the gentlemen who come and trace the imagined contours of their wives and mistresses in the air will feel at home.

The workroom is a different matter. I'm short of space and it hums like the engine room of a ship. The two machines at which the girls work are by the french windows which lead out into the courtyard, the cutting-out table takes up one wall, the wardrobe the other. The racks which hold the bales of cloth stretch tier upon tier almost to the ceiling, and every pincushion and box of tailor's chalk and measuring rod has its place.

Between the workroom and the salon are two fitting rooms:

very calm, very private, but sumptuous and canopied like the tents of Suleiman the Great.

This morning all was well. The salon streamed with light. In one window was a brown velvet street dress with black frogging which looked back to winter; in the other, a green-sprigged muslin with which I'd wooed the spring. Nice dresses both of them, but nothing to the dress that had overcome me in my sleep – the rich cream dress with the self-coloured rose which soon now would bring the traffic to a standstill as besotted women came and pressed their noses against the glass.

I was just unlocking the door when Old Anna, the flower seller, came across the square towards me.

'I've got something for you,' she said, putting down her basket. 'Kept them specially . . .'

She had violets from Parma, jonquils and daffodils from the southern slopes of the Dolomites – and a bunch of tiny flowers not much longer than my thumb which she put into my hands.

'Knew you'd want these,' she said, flashing her golden tooth.

Wild cyclamen. I picked them with my mother in the woods above the Danube, in the Wachau where I was born. To me, as a child, they were almost people: the petals like the pricked ears of leprechauns, the sturdy, silver-dappled leaves like shields.

I can remember so well how Vienna looked to me then, when I was Sanna, the barefoot daughter of the village carpenter. The Kaiserstadt, the Imperial City, heart of the Empire. How it beckoned and shone, how clearly I saw it all: the Kaiser in his golden uniform, waving a white-gloved hand as he drove in his golden-wheeled carriage from the Hofburg to his Summer Palace of Schönbrunn . . . The elegant people parading down the Prater Hauptallee, the marble hall at the opera with its glittering candelabra . . . And now that Vienna is a real place with clattering dustbin lids and foolish dogs, I love it even more. It was a hard road that led me to this shop, this square. I let no one help me, not even the man I love, but since I came here I have woken each morning thinking: I am here where I want to be. This is my place.

I don't believe the rumours that Joseph in the café across the road occasionally retails: that there are plans to widen the Walter-strasse and pull down part of the square. Not even Herr Willibald Egger, the Minister in charge of 'City Development' would be as crass as that. Yet as I was arranging the cyclamen in a bowl on my desk, I felt a sudden longing to record . . . to retain . . . my every-day life here in Madensky Square. I shall remember my tragedies, my follies and my joys – everyone remembers those. But what of the ordinary things, the little happenings? What of the 'dailiness' – who has a care for that?

So now at the end of this first day of spring I sit at my window and begin my journal. I shall try to keep it for a year and I shall write it to remind myself . . . but also I shall write it so that per-haps one day the person for whom I live – no, *at* whom I live since you can't live for someone you will never see – might find it and say, 'Ah yes, I understand. That's what it was like in a dress shop in the Inner City. That's what it was like at Susanna's . . .'

April

If there is one man I really and truly hate it is the Russian impresario, Serge Diaghilev. Why couldn't he have kept his glamorous ballerinas and exotic designers in St Petersburg? Why bring them to Europe to torture poor hardworking dressmakers like me?

At ten o'clock this morning, Frau Hutte-Klopstock, the wife of the City Parks Superintendent, handed me a magazine and said she wanted to look like Karsavina in *The Firebird*.

'Something diaphanous, I thought,' she said. 'Shimmering . . . in flame or orange.'

Frau Hutte-Klopstock is healthy, she is muscular; she is sportif and athletic. A small glacier in the High Tatras has been named after her and of this one must be glad. But, oh God! Karsavina!

I led her into the fitting room where her double, a wire dummy padded by Nini with three whole packets of wadding, confronted her, but without dimming her ardour.

'My sister saw them in Paris – the Ballets Russes. She says they were unbelievable – the exoticism, the colour! So she said why don't you ask Frau Susanna to make you something like that and here I am.'

It's the most difficult thing we do, as dressmakers: take a client's fantasies and bring them slowly, patiently, to the point where they cease to be absurd. It took me half an hour to turn the diaphanous flame into a soft shell pink, to suggest that her husband, the Park Superintendent, would feel more comfortable if the flowing silk georgette was draped on an underskirt because the problems of the ballet are not quite the same as those of eminent ladies attending functions in the town hall. Not that it makes much difference; next month she'll be back wanting to look like Sarah Bernhardt in *L'Aiglon*.

My next customer was easier to please. Leah Cohen's requirements are simple. Any dress I make for her must be expensive, it must be seen to be expensive, and it must be more expensive than anything that could possibly be worn by her sister-in-law, Miriam.

I had conceded seed pearls on the collar and cuffs and a trellis of silver embroidery on the bodice. Now, however, she begged for sequins.

'No, absolutely, no,' I said, pinning the sleeves of the emerald moire. I have dressed Leah for seven years and we are friends. 'I have my reputation to think of.'

'But it's a bar mitzvah – my cousin's boy, I told you.'

'I don't care if it's the circumcision feast of the Shah of Persia, no one leaves my shop looking like a parakeet. I'll frame the bill if you like and you can wear it as a brooch to show Miriam, but sequins, no!'

She laughed then, but almost at once, most disconcertingly, her eyes filled with tears.

'Oh dear. I don't know what I shall do without you,' she said, groping for her handkerchief

'He's still thinking of going, then?'

Leah nodded. 'I'll never forgive that Theodor Herzl. Ever since Heini read his book he's been insane. Who on earth wants a Jewish state? What am I supposed to do in Palestine with all those dreadful people?'

'They say the Arabs are very courteous and friendly.'

'Oh, it's not the Arabs – I don't suppose they'll take any notice of us. It's the other Jews . . . awful ghetto people from the slums of Poland.'

I tried not to smile. 'Perhaps it won't happen. It's not so easy to pull up one's roots and your husband will miss his patients.'

She shrugged. 'I know; he's mad. The best doctor in Vienna and he wants to grow oranges. Oranges! You should see the fuss when I serve fresh fruit at table. He has to have an extra napkin because of the juice, and a special silver knife and finger bowls all over the place – and even then he spends ten minutes in the cloak-room afterwards scrubbing his hands.' She dabbed her eyes and sniffed. It's bad enough having to die and go to heaven without starting on the Promised Land.'

I shut the shop between two and four. Gretl, who only lives ten minutes' walk away, goes home to lunch but Nini (and I don't quite know how this happened) has lunch with me.

Today, however, we sat in silence while my assistant glared at me over her goulash. I was about to take a cab to the von Metz palace and deliver the grey grosgrain day dress I had made for the old Countess – and of the Countess von Metz, Nini does not approve.

I remember so well the first time the Countess's carriage drew up in front of my shop. Nini wasn't with me yet so no muttered *la lanterne* from the workroom spoiled the excited, not to say servile, welcome of Gretl, holding open the door. The carriage was ancient, the manservant who let down the steps seemed scarcely able to walk and the Pekinese he deposited on the ground was both incontinent and blind, but the quarterings on the carriage door professed a lineage which went back to Charlemagne.

If I had known then what I know now I would have shut the door resolutely in the face of the disagreeable old woman who followed her dog into the shop. The Countess von Metz is short and squat with a face like an imperious muffin and a purple nose. That first time she stayed for an hour and made me take down every single roll of material I possessed while her Pekinese, cowering under one of my draped tables, made a puddle. When I had finished the dress she'd ordered, she quibbled for six months about the bill and eventually sent her manservant with half the sum she owed me and what she declared was a valuable Chinese vase.

Since then she has never once paid me a fair price for my work and in the last year has sent in a collection of bric-à-brac by way of payment for which the pawnbroker in the Dorotheergasse, shaking his head, scarcely gives me the price of the cloth. And yet I continue to dress this unpleasant, pathologically mean and ugly old lady. Why? It's not easy to explain . . .

The von Metz palace is one of the smallest in Vienna, ancient and dark. It's in a suburb overtaken by industry; the north side abuts on to a warehouse and in most of the rooms one needs a light on at midday. The Countess has sold or pawned everything of value: only the white and gold stoves, of which in winter far too few are lit, are still beautiful. She herself is served by a handful of decrepit retainers who are too old (not, I think, too faithful) to leave. She has no husband, no known lover in her past and her only brother, an army colonel, has long been dead. In this gloomy palace this ancient, none too clean lady lives entirely alone, her only 'treat' a monthly summons to a meal at Schönbrunn where the Emperor, Franz Joseph, is known to keep the worst table in Europe.

But the Countess von Metz loves clothes. She loves them pointlessly, passionately, for their own sake. Today as I walked through the fusty dark salon towards her boudoir she was waiting with glittering eyes and as I unwrapped the dress her swollen, mottled hands passed in benediction across the ribbed silk.

'I wish to try it on,' she said imperiously.

'Of course, Countess.'

Her creaking maid arrived; the Countess waddled to an embroidered screen and presently emerged. The maid was dismissed and the old lady stood in silence before the cheval glass. In all the rooms of the palace there was no soul who cared for this old woman; no one whose glance would linger on her for an instant; even her dog was dead. Yet as she peered and turned and stared into the mirror, she might have been a girl of nineteen preparing for the ball that was to seal her fate.

'There is one bow too many,' she announced at last.

I had seen it already. We had arranged for a row of small grey velvet bows to run down the underskirt from waist to hem. There were twenty-four of these: the arrangement was expected and symmetrical, but the last bow did just crowd the eye a little.

I bent down, snicked the thread, removed the bow.

She nodded as I removed it – the tiny bow on the underskirt of a dress which no one would ever see in a house to which no one ever came. Then she sighed with satisfaction and turned once more to gaze at herself with rapt attention in the glass. And that, I suppose, is why I continue to dress the Countess von Metz.

After my visit to the Countess I felt in need of consolation so when the shop was shut I cleared the table in the workroom and began to cut out the cream silk dress which had come to me in my sleep. It's a beautiful moment when the material spills out of its bale, voluptuous yet orderly, and one sees in its folds, as in a mirror, the finished form. I'd bought it from an old merchant whose grandfather had travelled the ancient silk route from Antioch through Merv to Samarkand, and on across the desert into China.

He'd told of the women running back and forth in their padded trousers with baskets of fresh-picked mulberry leaves for the worm princelings which spin the priceless silk. For they are the most delicate of creatures, these caterpillars; they cannot abide the smell of meat or fish, loud noise distresses them and they must be protected rigorously from draughts. Even the Empress of China is not too proud to work in the silkworm sheds.

The stories the old merchant had told were all there in the material – and indeed in its price! This will be the most beautiful dress I have ever made but it may just be the most expensive!

Ah, but how fortunate she is, the unknown woman out there, kissing her children goodnight, perhaps, or pulling on her gloves to go out to dinner and not knowing that soon, now, she will be impelled by an irresistible force towards my shop – and the dress that will set a seal on her happiness.

I worked for a couple of hours. Then suddenly I was tired and fetched a jar of apricot preserve out of my store cupboard and went across to visit Frau Schumacher.

Lisl admitted me and, knowing me well, took me first to the room where the little girls lay in their brass beds, ready for the night.

The four youngest in the first room were already asleep. Their nightdresses were white and their coverlets were white and they gave off a sublime smell of talcum powder and Pear's soap. I walked slowly along the row, feasting my eyes.

Gisi, the baby, whose bed still had bars, her mouth greedily fastened round her comforter . . . Kati, her hair just grown long enough to plait, turned even in sleep towards the baby who by day she pushed and pulled and carried with ruthless maternalism . . . The quicksilver Resi, always in motion, falling out of trees, getting jammed in railings – and now twitching like a greyhound even in sleep . . . and Steffi – the family beauty, lying immaculate on her back. All the little girls are blonde and blue eyed, but Steffi has turned the basic Schumacher ingredients into something that turns heads.

In the next room the two older girls were still awake. Franzi was lying on her side, chewing her pigtail, and though I smiled at her I went quickly past her bed because I knew she was telling herself a story. She is the nervous one who lives in her head; not quite as pretty as the others but the most imaginative.

Mitzi, the eldest, was sitting up in bed holding a heavy book and looking worried.

'What is it, Mitzi?' I whispered. 'What are you reading?'

'It's about Patagonia.' Her sweet, plump face was puckered as she peered at a swirling map of mountains and fjords. 'Maia lent it to me.'

'I thought she wanted to go to Madagascar?'

'That was last week,' said Mitzi. She sighed, and my heart went out to her. If there ever was a domestic soul, a Spirit of the Hearth, it was Mitzi Schumacher who begged to be allowed into her mother's kitchen as other children begged to go to the Prater, but Maia held her entirely in thrall.

Frau Schumacher was on the day bed in her room, crocheting a shawl for the expected son; as welcoming as always, but looking very tired.

'My dear, how lovely to see you! You always do me good . . . just to look at you! How that blue brings out your eyes!'

'Ah, but you should see the dress I'm making!' I launched into a description of the rich cream dress. 'I'm just hoping nothing'll go wrong on the stock exchange – it'll take a millionaire to buy it!'

We spoke lightly for a while, but when the baby suddenly kicked, almost causing Frau Schumacher to drop her crochet hook, our eyes met in a look of serious speculation. Was this the kick of the future head of A. Schumacher Timber Merchant and Importer – or was it not?

'Have you decided on the names yet?'

Frau Schumacher nodded. 'Ferdinand Anton Viktor,' she said, rolling the names off her tongue.

'And if it's a girl?'

'Oh please, Frau Susanna, don't even mention it. I don't know what I'd do. Last time Albert was away all night and so drunk they had to bring him home in a laundry basket . . . well, you know. And you couldn't have had a sweeter baby than Gisi.'

'She's adorable. They all are.'

'Well, I promise you, if it's another girl he'll go quite mad. He hardly takes any notice of the two youngest even now. I doubt if he's picked them up since they were born.'

I must have looked fiercer than I intended, being uniquely ill-fitted to regard the birth of a daughter as a misfortune, because Frau Schumacher now felt constrained to defend her husband.

'It's the business, you see. The doctor told him again that I mustn't have any more and if this one's not a boy, Albert'll have to take in his brother's boy from Graz.'

We fell silent considering Herr Schumacher's deeply masculine world. The yard with its mechanical saws, the carts rumbling across the cobbles, the sheds piled high with planks of beech and sycamore and elm . . .

'He's not a very nice child, his brother's boy. The last time he came he emptied all the water out of the girls' aquarium and stamped on the goldfish. But the midwife says I'm carrying high – that's a good sign, isn't it?'

I put my arms around her, laid my cheek against hers. 'It'll be all right, Helene. Whatever happens, it'll be all right; you'll see.'

*

As I crossed the square, half an hour later, the unknown pianist was still playing. I stood for a moment, listening. It puzzles me, the way he plays: the strength, the vigour – and then suddenly the break in certain passages. I've seen the man with the sideburns a few times but he looks too tired, too dejected, to produce such a torrent of sound.

I'll have to be brave and ask the ill-tempered concierge. Frau Hinkler has a deformity of one shoulder which makes it necessary to excuse her greed, her spite and her incompetence. She also has Rip. I suppose it's part of the infinite wonder of the universe that the nastiest woman in Vienna should have the nicest dog.

Each year I can't believe that there ever was such a spring! I can't believe that the hyacinths in the Schumachers' window boxes were ever so vivid, the buds on the lilac beside the churchyard gate ever so fat! The blossom on my pear tree was surely never so exquisite; never showered my courtyard with such abundance. Well this at least is true! My pear tree – I am certain of it – is ready now to produce an actual and undoubted pear!

With the end of Lent approaching, my customers seem to go a little mad. They call in incessantly to make certain that the outfit in which they mean to dazzle the congregation on Easter Sunday will be ready, and to order new ones for the regattas and garden parties that are to come. Frau Hutte-Klopstock (but I expected this) wants to go to the City Parks Associations Summer Ball looking like Isadora Duncan dancing barefoot to Beethoven. I wasn't cross with her, however, because she told me of a disaster that had befallen Chez Jaquetta. Jaquetta, whose fashionable shop in the Kärnterstrasse is so stuffed with gold bird cages and hanging baskets that you can't turn round, has done her best to make life difficult for me, and the news that a treble row of green pom-poms with which she had seen fit to decorate a client's bosom had been eaten by a cab horse outside Sacher's was balm to my soul.

'No blame attaches to the animal,' said Frau Hutte-Klopstock. 'It simply mistook them for brussels sprouts.'

The first tourists are beginning to arrive. Poor things, you see them trailing round the Kunsthistorisches Museum behind their guides or rushing in and out of Birth Houses and Death Houses or houses where Beethoven is supposed to have poured buckets of water over himself. The Danube is a particular problem for foreign visitors: a yellow-grey river skirting only the northern industrial suburbs.

'Someone ought to sue that Johann Strauss,' said an exhausted American lady sinking into my oyster velvet chair. 'The Blue Danube indeed! Though I suppose you can't blame him for the dead cats.'

Did they tell you that it's only blue when you're in love?'

'They did,' she said grimly. A nice woman. Nini modelled the green-sprigged muslin for her and she bought it on the spot.

I've only been able to work on my rich cream dress in snatches, but there's no doubt about it, it's going to be my masterpiece!

I was woken on this glorious Easter morning by a timid ring on the doorbell of the flat. Outside stood Mitzi Schumacher in white organdie, holding out to me a straw-filled basket.

'Mama said I could show you our eggs. We did them all ourselves – well, except Gisi. We helped her.'

I admired Mitzi's own egg, decorated with multi-coloured bows, and Franzi's, garlanded in leaves. Resi, the one who is always upside down or falling out of trees, had approached hers with such energy that she had cracked the shell and covered the cracks with yellow zig-zags, like lightning.

'But there are six of you and seven eggs. Whose is the seventh?' I asked.

Mitzi beamed. 'It's for the new baby.' She handed me an extremely virile egg, very hard-boiled looking and painted with a bright red railway engine from whose funnel there erupted fierce black puffs of smoke. 'Papa said we should do a train because boys like them best.'

'Girls like trains too, Mitzi.'

'Yes. But Papa is a good man and he works hard so God will bring us a brother,' said Mitzi. And then leaning confidentially towards me: 'We all have new ribbons for our hats. You'll see in church. Mine's blue to match my sash. It matches exactly!'

St Florian's on Easter Sunday is an unforgettable sight. It was hard to believe that two days earlier I had come in to see Our Lady wreathed in black, Father Anselm in inky vestments, and the very stones impregnated with the sorrow of the crucifixion. And today pasque flowers spilled out of vases, the altar glowed with gold, and white-petalled stars of jasmine wreathed the Madonna's head.

Everyone in the square seemed to be in church. Old Augustin Heller, who almost never leaves his book shop, sat beside his raven-haired granddaughter in her sailor suit. Maia's head was bent reverently over her missal, but between its pages I distinctly saw the indented contours of a map.

In the same pew as Heller was my neighbour on the other side, Herr Schnee. The saddler is a crusty man who seldom speaks, but is always willing to be helpful if it is deeds not words that are required. I confess that I often envy him his clients: gentle carriage horses, spirited trotters, not one of whom wants to look like Karsavina in *The Firebird* or Isadora Duncan in bare feet. Beside Frau Schumacher, like crotchets in a descending scale, bobbed the heads of the six little girls . . .

Father Anselm proclaimed the resurrection. Ernst Bischof (who the day before had stoned a ginger tomcat sunning itself on the sacristy wall) sang the *Gloria* as though lowered down from heaven for the purpose. And as the service drew to a close, I steeled myself to waylay the vile-tempered concierge, Frau Hinkler, and ask her who it was that played in her attic flat.

I had known she was in church because I had seen Rip outside on the pavement. Fastened to the pretty wrought-iron gate that leads into our churchyard is a notice. It says: DOGS NOT ADMITTED - and Rip knows that this is what it says. Father Anselm, who is so young that his Adam's apple still juts out above his clerical collar, did not put up this notice; nor – I am entirely certain of this – was it countenanced by God.

But Rip – a law-abiding Austrian animal – never enters the

churchyard and lies with his head between his paws, only emitting occasionally the despairing sighs of those who wait.

I had risen to my feet and was about to accost Frau Hinkler as she stumped down the aisle when I was hailed from behind by Professor Starsky. The Professor had taken great trouble with his toilette. His tussore suit was scarcely crumpled, his tie unspotted by hydrochloric acid – but his eyes were troubled.

And understandably, for the story he told me as we moved out into the sunshine was a heart-rending one. A ferocious anti-vivisectionist lady had arrived at the university on a tandem and had released three hundred white rats and two cages of guinea pigs from the zoology lab.

'And she took my terrapins,' said the poor Professor. 'There was another lady on the back and they took the whole lot away in a bucket and dropped them in the fountain. The ducks have made mincemeat of them of course. And I wasn't going to dissect them, Frau Susanna – there would have been no point in that. I was only measuring the effect of mashed spinach on their rate of growth.'

By the time I had comforted the Professor and invited him to supper the following week, the grim Frau Hinkler, with Rip at her heels, had disappeared into the apartment house and shut the door.

My closest friend in Vienna is Alice Springer. She's three years older than I am, gentle and funny, and though she talks almost without stopping she never seems to say anything wounding or indiscreet. Alice sings in the chorus of the Volksoper – a hard life of dirndls and um-pa-pa – and I regard this as a shocking waste because she has a real gift for millinery. Hats come to Alice like dresses come to me and she has total recall for any hat that has ever caught her interest.

She's not a person to complain, but I think of late things have been hard for her. Though she's so pretty – one of those nut-brown women whose eyes and hair have the same russet tint, she's nearly forty and recently there's been a tendency to put her in the second row, often with a hay bale or a milking stool. And from there, as everyone knows, it's only a short step to the back row in a grey wig with the village elders and a spinning wheel.

I usually pick her up at the theatre and we go and have a spritzer at the Café Landtmann. Tonight I was early enough to use the ticket she'd left for me, and so I was privileged to see the whole of a new production from Germany called *Student Love*. Alice was in the second row again, holding huge steins of beer aloft because it all took place in Heidelberg, and about the operetta itself I prefer not to speak.

At the same time people were enjoying it. I noticed particularly a very fat man in the same row as me. He had bright ginger hair parted in the middle and a round red face which clashed with is moustache and it was clear that he was very much moved by what was going on. During the song about the fast-flowing River Neckar he sighed deeply, during the duet in which the nobly born student and the impoverished landlady's daughter plighted their troth, he leaned forward with parted lips, and during the heroine's solo of (strictly temporary) renunciation he was so overcome he had to mop his face several times with a large white handkerchief.

When it was over I went backstage to fetch Alice, who was just lowering what looked like the mossy nest of a Parisian chaffinch on to her curls.

'Oh Alice, what a marvellous hat!' I said when I'd embraced her.

'Yes, it's good isn't it? I got it at Yvonne's. But listen; there were three straws in her window, all with identical brims: big ones. One trimmed with roses, one with mimosa and one with cherries. Imagine it, Sanna, *exactly the same brims in every case!*'

I too was shocked. How can anyone think that roses, mimosa and cherries can all be treated in the same way? For roses the brim must be wider, softer; mimosa (about which I'm doubtful anyway – one so easily feels one is in the presence of a hatchery for miniature chickens) needs to be wired on with a lot of greenery, and cherries really only work on a boater. You have to be quite rakish and impertinent when wearing fruit.

It was a beautiful evening; the scent of narcissi came to us from the Volksgarten and the waiter, who knew us, found us a quiet table, for together Alice and I are inclined to unsettle unattended gentlemen. As Alice poured our wine and mineral water she chatted cheerfully enough, but I know her very well and I thought she was worried.

'How is Rudi?' I asked – and I was right, the trouble was there.

'He's so *exhausted*, Sanna. So tired and grey – and he just works and works. And that wretched wife of his doesn't even feed him properly! I have to cook goulash for him when he comes and that isn't fair. It's wives who should cook goulash; not mistresses – we have so little time.'

'She's become a vegetarian, I hear?'

'Yes, but not the kind that eats proper vegetables – just the kind that has gherkin sandwiches sent to her room while she prepares talks on Goethe's Nature Lyrics. And there's a court case coming up, did you know? The university is suing her: she broke in at night and let out hordes of rats and mice. You can imagine how Rudi feels – one of the most respected solicitors in Vienna having to beg a colleague to defend his wife.'

'So it was her? I did wonder. Poor Professor Starsky lost all his terrapins.'

'If you knew what a saint Rudi was, Sanna. If anything happens to him . . .' She blew her nose.

As a matter of fact I did know what a saint Rudi Sultzer was. I've never been surprised that this balding, bandy-legged solicitor has for so many years held Alice's heart. Rudi Sultzer is an Atlas who supports uncomplainingly an enormous, dark and over-staffed flat in the Garnison Gasse, a villa in St Polten to which he never has time to go, and a wife and grown-up daughter who despise him because he reads cowboy stories and likes to play cards.

'I expect I'm being silly,' said Alice. 'Rudi's only forty-five – he's absolutely in his prime.' She shook off her fears. 'Now listen, Sanna, when you were out front tonight did you see a very fat man with ginger hair sitting in the same row as you?'

'Yes I did. He got very carried away – in fact I thought he was going to burst into tears.'

'That's him. He comes almost every night.'

'Is he in love with you?'

'No, no; not at all. He's a pork butcher from Linz – charcuterie particularly. His name is Ludwig Huber. He came first with the Meat Retailers' Outing and they came backstage and we got talking. He looks a bit gross but he's sweet really. And listen, Sanna, because this could be big for you. He's very rich – owns a whole chain of shops all over Lower Austria. His wife died two years ago and he's getting married again. And I told him that no one could make the bride's trousseau except you!'

'But why is he buying the bride's trousseau? Is she an orphan or something?'

'Her family's very poor. Genteel but without a kreutzer, so he's offered to see to all that. You can charge him a *lot*. They say he's as hard as nails in business but he's very chivalrous with women. You'll be able to twist him round your little finger.'

'What's the bride like?'

'I haven't met her. She's supposed to be pretty and very young. But listen, that's not all. Who do you think is going to be the bridesmaid?'

I shook my head.

'Rudi's daughter! Edith!'

Alice was very pleased with the effect of this announcement. 'You mean the Bluestocking? Are you serious?'

'That's right. Apparently she and Fräulein Winter were at school together. And I've told Herr Huber that the bridesmaid's dress must be designed together with the bride's so Edith will be coming to you as well!'

I considered this. 'If she's as plain as you say, I'm going to have a problem.'

'Well she is plain. Very. And the most awful prig. Rudi says she was a taking little thing when she was small but then her mother started making her into a Wunderkind and that was that.'

I had never met Edith but I knew a lot about her. I knew, for example, about the night on which she had been conceived.

In the spring of 1891, a young solicitor named Rudi Sultzer found himself sitting, at a public lecture in the university, next to a high-minded girl named Laura Hartelmann. Nothing would normally have followed from that, but Rudi had that morning finished the last pot of raspberry jam made by his mother before she died. The consumption of jam made by people who subsequently die is a traumatic experience and Rudi had loved his mother, a witty and beautiful woman who troubled him little for she was Czech and preferred to live in Prague. His eyes, during a pause in the discourse, filled with tears and Laura, always impressed by suffering, offered comfort.

They married, and owing to Laura's passion for Goethe they went to Weimar for their honeymoon. There the bride retired to her bedroom (which overlooked a statue of the poet), put on a calico nightdress and for an hour read from the Master's *Trilogy of Passion* while her new husband waited down below. Then she closed the book, opened the door, and in her high, clear voice called out 'You may approach me now, Rudi!'.

Rudi, to his eternal credit, approached her – and nine months later, Edith was born.

Nevertheless, the strain of being married to such a high-minded woman began to tell on Rudi quite early on. Coming from a hard day at the office he would find a notice pinned to his wife's bedroom door. *Silence, Frau Schultzer is reading Faust*, was the sort of information she liked to convey and while it was meant for the maids rather than for him, Rudi (who was also smaller than his wife and had worldly tastes like *food*) soon realized that he was not worthy of a woman who not only understood Goethe but also Schopenhauer, Leibnitz and the *feuilletons* in the *Wiener Tageblatt*. And when his little daughter also began to quote from Goethe and to give her toys away to the poor, he began to 'approach' my dear friend Alice.

'I think Rudi would be terribly pleased if you could make Edith look nice,' said Alice, looking at me appealingly. 'For all she's been brought up to be such an intellectual snob, he's fond of her.'

Alice loves the Hof Advokat Herr Doktor Sultzer very much. For the past eight years she's made for him a secure retreat in her little apartment in the Kohlmarkt and asked only the basic courtesies that any woman has a right to expect from her lover: a new dress now and then, a bracelet. No one in the Sultzer household knew of her existence yet she shared, if anybody did, his life.

'I'll do my best,' I said.

But since the task was clearly going to be a formidable one, we poured our second glass of spritzer in different proportions. Less soda water and much more wine . . .

May

The first of May means different things to Nini and myself. For me it means lilies of the valley sold on every street corner in the city, and the certainty of summer to come.

For Nini it means Labour Day. Though Anarchists are not supposed to join organizations, being committed to spontaneity and freedom, she is so anxious for the revolution that she condescends to march with the Marxists. Today this caused a problem.

'They've given me a red flag to carry – quite a big one, but it's a proper scarlet: well, you know. I was going to wear my rose-pink muslin because it's so warm, but red and pink. . . I suppose one *can* make it work, but it's tricky. It'll have to be my damask skirt, I suppose, and the broderie anglaise blouse.' Her Magyar eyes slid in my direction. 'I was wondering about your cameo brooch . . . ?'

She never goes off on these jaunts without my feeling a distinct pang. Sometimes the police are idle and quiescent – at other times they suddenly turn fierce.

The newspaper Rip carries each morning to his owner has been full of information about which one tries to be excited: that they have abolished pigtails in China, that Kaiser Wilhelm is displeased with the British, angry with the Russians and not exactly delighted even with us. That the Giant Wheel in the Prater has got stuck again . . .

But the candles on our five chestnut trees are showing white, the English Miss has left off her tweeds and strides past in smocked Liberty lawn – and the rich cream dress is finished! It's in my window and it's a triumph. Sister Bonaventura in the convent made the silken self-coloured rose herself as though she knew the task was too important to be given to a novice, and the luscious cascades of lace foam down the skirt just as they did in my dreams.

Leah Cohen came yesterday and admired it so much that I was afraid she was going to buy it. It is shatteringly expensive, but her husband's medical practice is flourishing and with the threat of a glorious new life in the Promised Land hanging over her head, she deserves it. I could have sold it to her in a minute, but I didn't. There's no one I like better than Leah, but she isn't the right person for that dress.

The Countess von Metz has sent me a rusty implement which she says is a valuable dagger from the Turkish siege and the pawnbroker says is an outmoded tool for pruning fruit trees. It was accompanied by a note summoning me to her palace to bespeak a new two-piece which I shall ignore. Enough is enough.

We have found out who is playing the piano!

Nini returned safely from her march but with a flea. One of the few skills that her father, the Hungarian hussar who abandoned her and her mother in the slums of Budapest, had time to bequeath his daughter was an ancient method for hunting fleas. One strips naked and stands on something large and white – a tablecloth, a quilt cover – holding a cake of moistened washing soap. The flea becomes confused or perhaps a little chilled and hops down on to the white surface – whereupon one whacks him with the soap, impaling him on the sticky surface.

We had finished supper. I was sitting by the window, drinking my coffee. Upstairs in the attic, thumpings and poundings indicated the progress of the hunt. Then there was a shriek, the sound of running footsteps, and Nini appeared in the doorway, wrapped in a towel.

'Oh, quick, Frau Susanna. Quick, quick – bring your opera glasses and come upstairs!'

I fetched the glasses and followed her.

Nini's attic is almost level with the top floor opposite. They must have moved the piano: the shutters were open, the lamp had been lit.

I put the glasses to my eyes.

I'll never forget what I saw, framed in the circle of the lenses as if on a lighted stage. The piano, bare, black, with the lid propped up, two candles in the sconces . . . No other furniture that I could see: no pictures on the wall, the gas mantle uncovered on its bracket.

My eyes travelled across the piano and down . . . further down than one would expect, to take in the thinnest, the most pathetic-looking creature you could imagine. A boy, scarcely ten years old, perched on two battered books. His black hair fell across his face, his skinny legs hung down towards the pedals that were out of sight. And all the time as I watched, this miniature creature's hands moved with undiminished vigour across the keys.

I handed the glasses to Nini. 'Yes,' I said. 'I see. That explains it. That's why he suddenly breaks off. There are places where he just can't reach.'

'It's a shame!' said Nini indignantly. 'It's exploitation. It's worse than sending children down mines, shutting him up like that all day.'

'Can one *make* someone do that? From the outside?'

But I too turned from the window with a frown. It was too vivid, that image: the meagre undernourished child carrying like a hump his arbitrary talent.

Long after Nini had gone to bed I went on adding imagined details to what I had seen . . . The child's frail neck rubbed by the rough collar of his blouse; the dusty neglected room; the sad man with the sideburns, shouting, correcting . . . The pressure, the obsession . . . the total absence of a woman in their lives.

A child should grow up slowly, peacefully, in an unemphasized happiness. Poor little Count of Monte Cristo. His seemed a desperately unenviable fate.

After this, the waters closed over my head.

I don't know the name for these attacks: depression, despair, panic . . . I only know that there's nothing to be done; they just have to be lived through. I used to curl up under my quilt, trying not to exist, but now I walk. I walk all day through the city and out of it and by the evening the worst of it is over.

Nini knows by now. She looked at me sitting on the edge of my bed and said: 'I'll cancel the Baroness Leitner. The others I can deal with' – and I nodded, and put my clothes on and went.

Where I go seems to be arbitrary for I'm hardly aware of what I'm doing yet I never find myself in the old city passing beautiful churches or lovely parks. Nearly always I cross the Danube Canal and then the Danube itself, tramping on through the ugly industrial suburbs, and turn to the east.

Everything that was bad for the city came across this desolate Eastern Plain. The Huns came to pillage and slaughter, and the Turks to pitch their tents before the city walls. The wind here blows straight from the *pusztas* of Hungary; there are no romantic taverns as there are in the Wienerwald; no packs of cheerful hikers tramping through the beeches. The people here are poor and incurious, harvesting their maize, keeping their geese. I could have walked to Budapest, wringing my hands, and no one would have turned his head.

'You should get help,' Alice said to me when she found me once curled up in a darkened room. 'There are so many doctors who understand these things. Vienna is full of them.'

That's true but I don't want any help. My attacks are not mysterious or causeless afflictions like Job's boils. I deserve them. They are entirely just.

I was born in the Wachau, in the shadow – or rather in the sunshine of the rococo monastery of Leck. Glorious Leck with its famous library, its green and gilt and strawberry pink church, its serene arcaded courtyards; its devout and scholarly monks.

My Leck though was different. A small cluster of ochre houses shaded by linden trees; little gardens in front, a hayfield behind. The people who lived there were servants of the monastery: the groundsmen and masons and gravediggers whose wives and daughters, when the monks had visitors, were called up to polish the inlaid floors or work in the kitchens.

It was a stable community and a contented one. My father was a master carpenter: the monks thought highly of him; he earned good money and my mother could stay at home and tend the garden and the goats and hens. We had a trellis on the front of the house with apricots and peaches, then came the little garden: zinnias and sunflowers grew in ours, and raspberries and neat vegetables in careful rows. The garden ended in a green kept grazed and springy by the geese, with a small stream crossed by wooden planks – and when you looked up there was the splendid, curling, glittering building like a magic mountain built for God.

My father was stern, fair; very much a man concerned with his work and the work of other men up at the abbey. But my mother . . . !

My mother believed in God and I believed in my mother. She was fat and fair and smelled of beeswax and vanilla, and she was the only person I can remember who thought it was absolutely all right to be happy.

'There now, look at that!' she would say of the speckles on a bird's egg, the splendid swirling pattern made by the apricot jam as we poured it over the nuts and breadcrumbs to make our strudels. When she washed my hair, rubbing egg yolk into the scalp and drying it off in the sun, she would brush the tendrils round my fingers so that I could feel the spring in the curls and tell me how lucky she was to have such a pretty daughter and that I would certainly grow up to be good because being pretty and good went hand in hand.

(Up at the monastery an old lay brother who worked in the library told me once about Sappho who long ago lived on the island of Lesbos in a valley filled with hyacinths and roses, and made up songs. She had a daughter, Kleis, with hair as yellow as torchlight.

I wouldn't change her for all the gold in Lydia, Sappho wrote about her, and she tried to find her an embroidered head band from Sardis, and chided her when she felt sad. He was an innocent monk and I was an innocent child and it seemed to me that he was describing my mother and myself. And also – I promise there is no hindsight here – that he was describing the daughter that I would one day have and love in just this way.)

Well, I had a long time really. Almost twelve years of baking bread and picking fruit and sewing by lamplight. And of laughing – goodness how we laughed at our idiotic jokes, my mother and I.

She died suddenly of a stroke. I came in from school and the doctor was there and she was dead.

It sounds strange but after the first months of shattering grief I managed quite well. She'd endowed me so richly, you see. I knew how to cook and bake and care for the animals; the monks sent gifts, I was proud to look after my father.

Then Aunt Lina came from Geneva to look after us.

She was my father's half-sister and she was a Calvinist. I've met people of the same faith since and many of them were gentle and kind, but she was a fanatic. My mother lived with God: she baked lebkuchen for Him at Christmas and wove pine branches into Advent rings. She dressed me in my prettiest dress on His birthday and when He rose from the dead, we filled the house with flowers and roasted our best goose.

Aunt Lina dealt with God's shadow. With Lucifer, with sin . . . There were many aspects of sin: sloth and waste and pride. But the worst of course was lust . . . sex . . . and this she saw personified in me aged thirteen. How that woman battled! She scraped back my hair and it burst from its skinned pigtails into its uncontrollable curls. She dressed me in black calico and heavy boots and tried to flatten my breasts – but it was no use. She couldn't blacken my teeth or dim my eyes and the boys still came and whistled outside in the field on summer evenings.

I was a good pupil at school; there was talk of my staying on and training to be a teacher, but I didn't want that for I already had a vocation. I was going to go to Vienna and make beautiful clothes. It beckoned more and more with every wretched year that passed: the Kaiserstadt, the Imperial City – but I was seventeen before I got away and then I went like a foolish girl in an operetta, eloping with a young lieutenant stationed in the little town to which I went each day to work as a sewing maid in an orphanage.

He was good-looking and friendly and undemanding. Simply being alive, that was enough for Karli. He didn't persuade me to run away: he just said, 'I'm going to Vienna; they're sending me on a course'. Then he held out his nice, strong brown hands and said, 'Come with me?' and I came, just like that, in the clothes I stood up in.

We spent a month together in an attic behind the fruit market. Leaning out of the window we could see the green dome of St Charles' Church and the fashionable people driving across the square to concerts at the Musikverein. I was in love with the city and a little with him.

'You don't have to do anything you don't want, Sanna,' Karli said, the first day. 'You're so young.'

But by then I did want to . . . I wanted to know, to be part of the mystery. I was grateful to him too for setting me free. The loss of my virtue, that cataclysmic event, took place pleasantly on a Sunday afternoon with the market women outside, crying their wares. An important day, but in line with the other important days of my childhood: the day we killed the pig; the day the crib was brought out for Christmas.

Then Karli's course finished and he was transferred to a garrison in Moravia. He left me all the money he had and hugged me and said he'd be back. Perhaps he did come back, I don't know. When I found I was pregnant, I moved to the cheapest room I could find, above a draper's shop in Leopoldstadt. Even so the money barely lasted three months.

My daughter was born in the House of Refuge on the seventh of April 1893. I was just eighteen years old and penniless, and the nuns who nursed me through the puerperal fever that followed her birth arranged for her adoption.

If I hadn't been so ill I think I would have retained my sanity and fought for her. For in the moment of her birth I knew beyond any doubt that I was the right and proper person to bring her up. But then the fever came and through it the quiet voices of the nuns, endlessly repeating what they believed to be right. I must be sensible; I must think of the child. They had already found for her a home that anyone would envy.

'You must make the sacrifice,' they said.

So I made it. I turned my back on the legacy of courage and *Lebensmut* bequeathed by my mother; I broke the chain.

And this is why even now I sometimes walk like a madwoman out of the city. Why, too, I don't seek out kind doctors who might help me. I gave away my daughter. Let them cure me of that!

Today Alice's pork butcher, Herr Huber from Linz, came to the shop. He ordered a full trousseau: a wedding dress, two evening gowns, day dresses, a travelling cloak . . . 'And perhaps a negligee and such things; you will know, Gnädige Frau,' he said shyly.

We settled down to business and spent a very useful half hour. I asked for something on account and an idea of his price limits, and it was clear that however hard-headed he might be about charcuterie, where Magdalena Winter was concerned he was generosity itself. The only stipulation he made was that her trousseau should be completed a week before the wedding, which was to take place in the Capuchin Church on the fifteenth of October.

I must say I liked Herr Huber. True he was gargantuan, his thighs spread like tree trunks across the chair, his stomach bulged like a tympani under his waistcoat. But the contrast between his ginger hair and crimson face was somehow endearing, the small brown eyes were bright and alert, and the pride he clearly took in being well turned out was touching. The butcher's brown and white checked suit was immaculate, his spats gleamed, and the handkerchief with which he periodically wiped his perspiring face was of the best linen and spotless.

'Will Fräulein Winter help you with the business?' I asked.

'No, no! Absolutely not!' Herr Huber's eyes widened with dismay at the thought. He was buying for her a villa – well away from the contamination of his factory – which he now described to me: pepperpot towers, gables – and in the garden a wooden shrine to the Virgin carved in oak.

'She is very devout, you see. An angel . . .'

It now became evident that Herr Huber was going to tell me the story of his life so I went to the workroom to tell Gretl to bring coffee and to fetch Frau Hutte-Klopstock's dress which still lacked button loops. When I have some sewing in my hand I can listen to anything.

Herr Huber had been born into charcuterie. He remembered the animals coming into the yard behind his father's shop in a village on the Hungarian border.

'He was the best butcher in the province. One stroke and it was all over; no animal ever suffered at his hands; and he taught me. It's very good for the muscles, slaughtering.' Herr Huber paused to sprinkle Hungary water on to his handkerchief and wiped his face. 'The business was quite small but everyone knew him. My father's *gyulai* had just so much paprika in them; not a spot more, not a spot less, and people came from miles away for his jagwurst. Then he got gallstones and the operation went wrong. I was fifteen; I had my mother to think of, and two sisters. So I took over. And I had a talent, Frau Susanna. You'll know I'm not being conceited because it's clear you have one too.'

The young Ludwig Huber became a connoisseur of charcuterie. He travelled by post bus to Italy to study the richer, more voluptuous sausages of the south.

'I can't tell you how I felt when I saw my first mortadella. It was in Turin, in a little shop by the Duomo. The marble white splodges of fat . . . so round and unashamed, and then the brilliant green of the peppercorns against the pink . . .'

By the time he was twenty-one he had moved to Linz, acquired his own slaughterhouse, and soon afterwards a second shop across the Danube. He pioneered a newer, creamier leberwurst . . .

'People often seem to smile when I tell them my profession,' said Herr Huber. 'To titter, as though wurst was funny. But I can't explain to you how interesting I find it. The endless variations in a salami . . .'

He looked at me anxiously, wondering if I too was going to jeer.

'We are both artists, Herr Huber,' I said firmly. 'You begin with an animal and make it into a beautiful sausage. I take a piece of cloth and make it into a beautiful dress. God may have meant animals to live unslaughtered and women to go unclothed, but life hasn't turned out like that and you and I must do our best.'

'Ah, Frau Susanna you understand,' he said.

And I did. I was also relieved – for a man who can stand transfixed by the beauty of a mortadella is not going to be indifferent to the sensuous qualities of velvet or the fall of a hem. Fräulein Winter would choose, but Herr Huber would pay – and when a man pays I like to please him.

By the time his wife died, Herr Huber had his own slaughterhouse, a factory working entirely to his specifications, a pleasant house with a balcony overlooking the Danube, and seven shops. Frau Huber had not seen the poetry of charcuterie, but she kept the books and enjoyed their prosperity and consequence, and her death left him very lonely.

Then last autumn he'd come to Vienna thinking he might rent a shop in the Inner City. It was a big step, but he felt he still had it in him, being on the right side of forty. He'd seen a property that looked promising, but there were certain problems.

When in doubt Herr Huber, like the rest of us, turned to God. He'd gone into the Capuchin church in the Neuermarkt and asked God whether he should rent 167 Augustinergasse and God had said no. The access at the back was poor and the drainage doubtful.

Then just as he was about to rise to his feet, Herr Huber had beheld a vision.

'A vision,' he repeated. 'There is no other word for it, Frau Susanna: a vision.'

Magdalena Winter was in white, she was in a state of rapt devotion and as she walked down the aisle past Herr Huber in the almost empty church, she smiled.

'At the Lord Jesus of course, not at me. At her thoughts . . . But I cannot tell you . . .'

Herr Huber, however, did tell me. Of his involuntary pursuit. Of the days spent hovering outside the apartment where she lived. Of at last making himself known to her mother. Of the unbeliev-able bliss, the incredulity when he discovered, after months of patient courtship that, given certain conditions, she would marry him.

I happened to be looking up from my sewing as Herr Huber, in his slow dialect, pronounced the words 'certain conditions' and I did not like what I saw. His red face had flushed to an even deeper crimson and a feverish exaltation glittered in his round, brown eyes. What kind of 'conditions' did a penniless girl lay down for marriage to a rich man in his prime?

To conceal my disquiet I asked about the bridesmaid and her mother. Had Herr Huber met the Sultzers?

Herr Huber had. 'Frau Sultzer is a most intelligent woman. She has an amazing mind.'

'And Edith?'

Fräulein Sultzer is very clever too. She is studying Anglo-Saxon at the university. The epic of *Beowulf* in particular.'

'Could you describe her at all?'

There was a long pause while Herr Huber once more had recourse to the toilet water and the handkerchief. His brow was furrowed and I could see him straining to supply me with an encouraging fact.

Then his frown cleared. 'She doesn't have whiskers,' he pro-nounced. A last dab with the handkerchief, and then he added, 'Yet.'

I have just made a complete fool of myself. I went to see Alice to tell her about Herr Huber's visit and on the way back I thought I saw across the width of the Kärtner Ring a figure that I recog-nized.

Yes, I was sure that I knew that soldier in the uniform of the Bohemian Dragoons with his slow gait and clumsy boots. I even thought I could smell across the heads of the fashionable crowd who promenaded there, the whiff of the raw onions that nothing can prevent Corporal Hatschek from chewing when he is off duty. And my heart raced, excitement coursed through me – and I lifted my skirts ready to hurry across the road.

But the Ringstrasse is wide, the hansom cabs are never in a hurry. By the time I'd reached the other side there was no sign of him.

I'd imagined him then. Conjured him up out of my deepest need. It's not the first time that I've run across the road like a homesick child towards this onion-chewing corporal and found he was a mirage. Well, so be it. There is only one cure for what ails me, and thank heaven I have it in abundance. Work.

They've let him out, the little Count of Monte Cristo, the walled-up piano-playing child. It was early evening and I had just shut the shop when Nini called to me:

'Look, Frau Susanna. He's down in the square!'

A small dark-suited figure, a Goya dwarf, had appeared, framed in the doorway of the apartment house. There was an air of bewilderment about him: he was like the prisoners in *Fidelio* who blink at the sudden light.

Then he moved stiffly out into the square, now golden in the last rays of the setting sun. There was no one else with him and he had nothing in his hand: no ball or spinning top or hoop. When he reached the fountain in the centre he stopped, but he didn't bend his head to search for fish or touch the water or run his fingers along the decorations on the rim. He simply stood there, and I realized that he had absolutely no idea of how to play.

This was not a child; it was an unnaturally compressed adult. One sees them sometimes in Flemish paintings: tiny burgermaster's daughters, their heads caught in vice-like ruffs; their small plain faces unutterably grave. Velasquez painted them at the Spanish court; knee-high infantas, imprisoned in silk.

I watched for a few minutes from the window. Then I went out into the square.

Close to, it was worse still: the white face, the dark clothes, the air of 'otherness' which clung to this non-child. His black hair under the cap was long and greasy; the meagre neck unwashed.

No use putting one's arm round such an old, old soul. I felt that if I asked his name he would stamp his skinny legs and vanish into the ground. So I gave him only the greeting we'd used, passing each other, in the country when I was a child.

'*Grüss Gott.*'

The child that was not a child did not reply. He only looked at me: at the blue ribbon threaded through the flounce on my skirt, at the forget-me-nots tucked into my belt, at my white blouse . . . His black and eastern eyes, too small, too melancholy, stayed on my face as I looked down on him.

Then he laid one arm across his narrow chest; the other vanished behind his back. His feet in their dusty shoes came together – and in silence he gave me a perfect concert master's bow.

The Baroness Leitner came to order a travelling suit. Her husband is going to America on a diplomatic mission and she is to accompany him. She insisted on trying on the rich cream dress, and it fitted her too. I thought it only fair to warn her, though, that it was not a very practical dress to take on a journey – very crushable and not at all easy to clean.

After she left, saying she would think it over, I saw the girls look at each other in puzzlement. It's true that I need to get the money back that the dress cost me. True, too, that the Baroness only *slightly* resembles Frederick the Great. But I know that out there, somewhere, is a woman whose life will be transfigured by this dress and until she comes I have to wait.

Meanwhile I have a new client. We were having lunch when the phone rang down in the workroom.

'It's the Hof Minister's wife – Frau Egger. She wants to come this afternoon.'

'Tell her five o'clock.'

I wasn't as gratified as I should have been. Hof Minister Willibald Egger, who has crawled and schemed his way to the top of the Civil Service, is a most unpleasant man who delights in pulling down beautiful old buildings to improve 'mobility' and 'traffic flow'. Nobody believes that he is greatly concerned with the problems of the Viennese cab driver. What he wants is to achieve ennoblement or have a street named after him. So far a Willibald Egger-gasse has eluded him, but the rumours that cause poor Joseph such distress all emanate from Egger's department of 'Development'.

'You shouldn't dress his wife,' raged Nini. 'He's an absolute swine. Do you know what he does? If the lunch isn't ready the second he comes in from the ministry, he picks up a great cow bell and rings it and rings it till the poor girl rushes in with the soup. The maids have to line up every Saturday to have their fingernails inspected and he bullies his coachmen so much that they've had five in a year. Not to mention the Nasty Little Habit.'

The news that Herr Egger had a Nasty Little Habit reached us in a roundabout way via a girl called Lily who works in the post office and is currently enjoying his favours. Or rather she is receiving them; she doesn't seem to be enjoying them very much. Unfortunately while she told Nini that the Habit existed, she did not tell her what it was, and this I must admit I found unfair.

Frau Egger, when she came, wanted me to make her a military cloak. I did not at this point groan aloud because dressmakers who groan when they feel like it do not stay long in business, but my spirits sank. No week passes but some Hausfrau who has attended a passing out parade or a bandmasters' rally arrives, convinced that a sweeping arc of cloth with epaulettes will turn her into a figure of glamour and romance. No use explaining that hussars do not have bosoms, that the rakish swirl of their cloaks depends on a virtual absence of behinds . . . ?

'Perhaps a modified version,' I suggested to Frau Egger, but I did not expect to get my way too easily. With her long, pale face and tombstone teeth, the Minister's wife uncannily resembled those breeding ewes that get stuck in ditches, resisting with mindless obstinacy all efforts to set them free.

I went through to the workroom to fetch some loden cloth and give the bad news to the girls. When I returned Frau Egger was laying a set of buttons down on my desk: brass buttons, big ones, with a curious design – an owl, its head transfixed by a lance and a motto consisting of a single word: *Aggredi*. I have reason to know something about Austrian military uniforms, but these I had never seen.

'I found them in a box in the attic,' said Frau Egger. 'They're not my husband's – he's never been in the army though he behaves as if . . .' She broke off shaking her head. 'But I thought they'd look ever so nice on the cloak. Realistic.'

'Frau Egger, these are genuine army buttons. To clean them you need a button stick and brass polish and a special brush. Even an experienced batman can take an hour to polish buttons.'

'But they're so pretty, aren't they? I looked up *Aggredi* in the Latin dictionary. It means "Charge!" Like in "Charge!" or "Attack!" or "Advance!"'

About this something would have to be done. I have my reputation to think of, and cannot have my clients wandering down the Kärntnerstrasse with pierced birds on the bosom, and labelled 'Charge!'.

I began to sketch a design for a cloak that Frau Egger would regard as military, but would in fact be nothing of the sort. She nodded and at first seemed pleased, but soon she grew restless. Her eyes roamed to the door of the workroom, she kneaded her gloves, picked up an ashtray. And when Nini came with samples of braid to show her, she stared at her fiercely.

'Is that the girl who throws bombs?' she said when Nini had gone again.

I raised my eyebrows, a thing I'm rather good at.

'I mean, is she the Anarchist? The one who wants to murder us all in our beds? Because I wonder if I could have a word with her in private? I think she knows a girl who's a friend of my husband's.' Here the poor woman flushed crimson. 'A girl he's taken an interest in. Lily, she's called.'

My heart sank. Wronged wives can never quite believe that one is powerless to help them. 'If you'd just have a word with her, Frau Susanna,' they say. 'If you'd just tell her what it's doing to me and the children.' There is no one to whom a woman in that state will not turn to: a window cleaner, a dustman . . . anyone connected with the hussy who ruined their lives. I understood now why Frau Egger, whose clothes showed all the signs of home dressmaking at its most dire, had come to me.

'I'm sorry, I'm afraid that's impossible; Nini is just going out on an errand. Now about the collar . . . I would suggest a contrasting fabric in a darker tone. How about velveteen – or would you like to use fur?'

'Why did she look at me like that?' said Nini later, putting away the unfortunate buttons.

I told her.

'Poor soul. But honestly I don't think she's got too much to worry about. Lily really doesn't like him very much – it's not just the Nasty Little Habit – it's that he's so horribly mean.'

They let the little Count of Monte Cristo out most evenings now. He always walks slowly down the steps while Rip looks on, and goes to stand by the fountain. He still has no toys and he still doesn't play with the water or go anywhere else.

I try not to get involved. I don't really understand what is happening in those bare rooms across the square and I'm afraid of becoming indignant at what is being done to him; the endless hours of practising, the unhealthy, imprisoned life. But I'm not musical enough to understand if it's justified. Perhaps this pathetic shrimp is touched by greatness, but it's hard to believe.

All the same, some evenings I can't bear the sight of the lonely black speck by the fountain and I go across and have a few words with him.

His name is Sigismund and I smiled when I heard that, for they were the mightiest kings of all the kings of Poland, the Sigismunds, ruling over the country when her borders stretched from the Black Sea to the Baltic. The sad man with the side whiskers is his uncle, and they walked almost all the way from Galicia with enough money for the hire of a piano and six months in Vienna for the child.

'And after six months they go,' said the detestable concierge. 'Though mind you, they're not Jews like I thought. There's a crucifix in his room and the boy's got one round his neck. Not that Poles are much better.'

I'd noticed that too: the wooden cross hanging on a frayed piece of string between the lapels of his grubby shirt.

His mother is dead, but I didn't need the concierge to tell me that.

'There's someone in the shop asking to see you personally. A corporal. A man of the people,' said Nini approvingly. 'He smells of onions and he won't see anyone but you. Shall I ask him to go away? He can't possibly be going to buy a dress.'

I couldn't speak for a moment. I'd been right then. It was Hatschek. He was back in Vienna.

Nini was looking at me with her head on one side. She was saying something. Asking me if I was all right. 'I'll tell him to go. It's just that he's been here before, I think. His face seemed familiar.'

'No, don't tell him to go. Send him up here.' And as she continued to look at me curiously, I said curtly: 'You heard me. Send him up.'

But I didn't want him to come too quickly. I wanted to spin it out, the moment till I saw Hatschek with his broad, stupid face, his dogged blue eyes, his cauliflower ears. I wanted a respite before I smelled the onion, felt the rough red hands. And I rose quickly and went to the mirror to make sure that my curls fell as I wanted over my forehead, that the bow which fastened the neck of my blouse was perfectly tied, for how I look to this illiterate Bohemian peasant matters more than I can say.

'Frau Susanna!' He had entered, clicked his clumsy boots together, tried to salute – but this I do not permit, and moving forwards I took his hands in mine.

'Hatschek!' Not kissing Hatschek on both cheeks is always difficult but I managed it. 'I thought I saw you on the Kärnter Ring last week, but when I crossed the street you'd gone. Was it you?'

'Aye. We've been in town these ten days past,' he said in his thick Bohemian accent. 'But we weren't alone. Only this morning we were alone again.'

As he spoke I feasted my eyes on him. For Hatschek, you see, is Mercury, the Winged One, the Messenger of the Gods. If they wanted to fetch me up to Paradise it would be no good sending the Archangel Gabriel. Nothing in white with wings, nothing gold-limned in sandals would interest me. It would have to be Hatschek or nothing, for he alone has the key to the only heaven I care about.

I offered him a cup of coffee which he refused. He said how smart the shop was looking and I said yes, business was good.

Only then did I ask: 'How is he, Hatschek? Is he well?'

'Aye, he's well enough in himself but they plague him at the War Office. He's been there the past week shut up with those obstinate old duffers in the Ordnance Department, but it's all talk – no one will equip the men properly. If they had their way we'd still be fighting with broadswords.'

How we hated the Ordnance Department, Hatschek and I. The promises, the lies, the evasions. The graft which stopped supplies reaching the field regiments when at last they materialized. There were two deep furrows etched into my lover's forehead, put there by the Ordnance Department.

'He said, tonight, if you can.'

'If I can.' It is a polite fiction which we like to maintain: that one day I would be too busy to visit the Field Marshal Gernot von Lindenberg when he comes to Vienna.

'He's at the Bristol?'

Hatschek nodded. From his tunic he took a slip of paper with a room number. Then he clicked his heels again and left.

I was never really an adolescent, a *Backfisch,* prinking and dreaming before the mirror; my Aunt Lina saw to that.

But when I go to the Hotel Bristol I go a little mad. I take out every dress I own, I put it on, I take it off. I wash my scrupulously washed petticoats and dry them (but they are never quite dry in time) and press each and every invisible bow again and again. No one else is allowed to do this, but my strange behaviour (for I am not a woman who normally fusses about clothes) now attracted the attention of Nini who observed that I appeared to be going out.

But I can't snub her. I can't snub anyone on days like these. If I met the detestable Herr Egger, the Minister of Development with his Nasty Habit, I would throw my arms round him and call him Little Brother like people do in Russian books.

When I had tried on everything in my cupboard, I went down to the salon and took the rich cream dress out of the window. I swear to God that I had not intended this and even now at the eleventh hour I struggled. But not for long. It was inevitable, inescapable – the conviction that the woman whose life was going to be transfigured by this dress was . . . me.

Ah, but it was a marvellous dress! It fell exactly into the folds I had dreamed of that April morning; it knew exactly where to cling and where to let go. The silken ruffles brushed my throat, the hem whispered under its lightly held burden of *point de Venise*.

'My goodness, Frau Susanna – you look . . .' Nini, about to embark on one of her customary compliments, broke off. Then suddenly she reached for my hand and kissed it.

She is growing too perceptive, this mad Hungarian child; she begins to share too much.

I shall never forget my drives to the Hotel Bristol. In winter there are violets pinned to my muff; the snowflakes drift past and I think of Anna Karenina, but I am luckier than she because her happiness was paid for by others whereas any pain this liaison causes me is my own. In the autumn the chestnuts lining the Ringstrasse send down their bronze and russet leaves . . . But now, in May, the slanting sun turned the laburnums into a shower of gold – and it was all for me, the beauty of the evening: my Royal Triumph.

The Triumph lasted till I alighted at the Bristol, walked across the richly carpeted foyer, smelled the cigars from the Smoking Room – and then there was a moment of panic, for after all any kind of disaster could have overtaken the Feldherr von Lindenberg since the early hours of today.

But it was all right. I gave the name I always gave, the porter handed me a key. No smile of complicity, no recognition though I was here less than two months ago. The Bristol isn't intimate like Sachers; no naked archdukes come whooping out of the Salles Privées. Here is complete discretion, anonymity. No wonder the nice fat English King Edward liked it best of all the hotels in the city.

My room was perfect. I could see over the roofs to a garden with a swing and pond with pin-sized children who should have been in bed. I took off my hat and put it on the hatstand. I sat down on the bed.

There is no waiting like this waiting.

Then came the knock on the door.

'Enter!'

He entered.

Why him? Why this one man of all the men who have courted me? He is fourteen years older than I am and God knows I am not young. He looks like a weatherbeaten eagle, tight-lipped, uncompromising, no softness anywhere in the clean-shaven face. Why a soldier when the whole paraphernalia of army life is repellent to me, why a landowner when I secretly share Nini's dislike of the ruling class?

And why a man who can never marry me and whose wife, the delicate and largely absent Elise, is the object of our continuing concern?

Field Marshals of the Austrian Army are usually princely, glamorous or in their dotage. Gernot von Lindenberg was none of these. Rumour had it that the Kaiser had insisted on his promotion so that he could send him to interminable disarmament conferences and diplomatic missions which were doomed before the entourage ever left Vienna. To the bumbling, ancient Emperor, Gernot was wholly loyal while privately groaning at his narrow-mindedness. If the Crown Prince had lived, my lover might have taken pleasure in his work: he and Rudolf had been friends. As it was he endured the frustration and monotony of the conference table and escaped when he could to manoeuvres in obscure and lonely places or the work on his estate. Yet he had not chosen the army, any more than he had chosen the high-born Elise von Dermatz-Heyer whose family estate bounded his.

'Why, Gernot?' I asked him once. 'Why always duty, duty, duty?'

'Perhaps because I don't think it matters. Duty . . . inclination . . . whatever you start with there are years of grinding work to be filled in before you die.'

From what he didn't say rather than what he did, I sensed his despairing pessimism, his conviction that the corruption, the inefficiency and bumbledom that pervaded the army and the court would land us like an overripe plum in the lap of Kaiser Wilhelm of Germany, whom he loathed more than any man on earth.

Now he came towards me. He doesn't smile much, my protector. When he does one side of his mouth flicks upwards briefly, more in sardonic comment on the idiocy of the world than in amusement, but he has a way of doing something to his eyes which even after twelve years of intensive study I have not identified. We took each other's hands, didn't kiss . . . looked. I thought I saw further ravages played by his foul profession on his face. Then: 'Do you like my dress?' I inquired conversationally.

His steel blue eyes roamed over the creamy folds of silk, lingered in the places where I had arranged for the eye to linger. He stepped back to study me more carefully as I turned slowly round, came face to face with him again.

'Yes, I like it.'

Then he said that lovely thing – the thing that women the world over see as the fulfilment of their labours; their just reward.

'Take it off,' said Field Marshal von Lindenberg. 'At once, please. Take it off!'

When I became Gernot's mistress I changed. I'd been a babbler, but I had to learn discretion and I kept the secret of our liaison from everyone I knew. Alice guessed, I think, but her own affair with Rudi Sultzer was conducted so quietly and modestly that I knew she could be trusted. I learnt to wait – it was often weeks between one meeting and the next, and the best part of summer he was away on manoeuvres. Oh, those manoeuvres which took place in some unspeakable corner of the Empire: Ruthenia, Moldavia . . . on a forlorn and dusty plain. Some of the soldiers' girlfriends followed them there, but not I. Gernot was fanatical about the need of officers to conduct their lives with decorum. It was not Elise who imposed on us the iron secrecy in which we moved – she was in any case involved in a constant pilgrimage round the spas of Europe – it was his obligation to his men.

What changed most, though, was my attitude to God. I went on going to church because I needed Him and I felt, too, that it would be hard on Him to be left only with the virtuous who are frequently so odd. But I didn't go to confession – how could I confess the 'sin' which had dragged me back to life and happiness after I gave up my child? I knew I was doomed to hellfire and of course I minded, but my preoccupation with life after death was not quite the usual one. I thought of the Last Trump, the open graves, the skeletons rising and seeking out their loved ones with whom to float upwards to eternal life.

But who would come for us, the women in the shadows, the mistresses? For on this most important day the proprieties would have to be observed, I understood that. It was the Frau Professorinen, the Frau Doktors and Frau Direktors who would be claimed by their spouses. Alice understood that it was with the musty bones of Frau Sultzer clasped in his arms that her Rudi would ascend to Paradise. And I, of course, knew that the hand of my protector, which even in life has a skeletal touch, would reach for the bones of the woman he had married: the high-born Elise von Dermatz-Heyer who had brought him a useful forest and straightened out an untidy bulge on the borders of his estate.

But the Last Trump was not yet!

*

We lay in bed holding hands. Unnecessary one might have thought in view of what had passed, but not so. I asked after his wife who, even if I knew her, I would not be able to hate, for her son had died when he was five months old and her daughter, now grown up, was a plain and unattractive woman with a discontented face.

Gernot reached out to the bedside table for his cigars. The fact that I can exist in a cloud of tobacco smoke may explain the hold I have over him.

'She's left Baden-Baden. The waters were the wrong temperature or there wasn't enough sulphur, I forget which. So she's gone to Meran. There's a splendid crook there who charges a thousand kronen to keep people sitting up to the neck in radioactive mud while eating grapes. He owns a vineyard of course.'

'And the conference in Berlin?'

His face darkened. 'A fiasco, naturally. Wilhelm will drag us into a war, there's no doubt of it. A purposeless war for which we are entirely unprepared.' He shook off his thoughts and commanded me to prattle.

My lover's curiosity about my shop is outstanding. This complex, busy man listens like a child to nursery rhymes while I describe my customers and the life of the square. So now I told him about the new dress that Leah Cohen had ordered for the races at Freudenau: more expensive than her sister-in-law's but able to be worn for planting oranges if the worst came to the worst, and of the Polish wraith opposite whom I'd had to *show* how to pat a dog. I told him about the letter Herr Schumacher's brother had tactlessly written, urging the claims of his goldfish-slaying son even before the birth of the new baby, and of the mishap that had befallen me when I took the Countess von Metz's Turkish dagger to the pawnbroker.

'Poor old soul; she must be the meanest woman in creation.'

But he is surprisingly kind about the Countess for he knew her many years ago when she kept house for her brother, the Colonel of some obscure Moravian regiment in a distant garrison town.

Only when I described Frau Egger's cloak and the strange buttons did he grow restless and frown.

'An owl pierced with a lance . . . damn it, that rings a bell, it'll come to me. God, my memory; I'm growing old!'

This, however, was a barred area. Some six years ago the Field Marshal decided to renounce me on grounds of age and decrepitude and instructed me to get married. I was still in awe of him then and for weeks I allowed myself to be taken out by an extraordinary number of men, collecting several offers of marriage and quite a few other offers before I put my foot down.

Gernot had propped himself up on one elbow, moved one of my curls to a different part of my forehead. It was probably my imagination but when he spoke I thought there was a trace of anxiety in his voice.

'Did Frau Egger say anything about her husband? His activities?'

I shook my head and – unwisely perhaps – launched into an account of the Minister's entanglement with Lily from the post office and the Nasty Little Habit. 'And I must say, Gernot, I cannot help wondering so *very* much what it might be?'

Gernot's suggestions, as I had expected, were exceedingly creative, but presently he said: 'Susanna, have you ever thought of moving on? Getting a shop in the Kärntnerstrasse or the Graben?'

I shook my head. 'No; the square's just right for me. I don't want to be in a place that's fashionable. I like to stand out. Anyway, I could never afford the Kärntnerstrasse rents – not for a moment.'

'My God, you obstinate, idiotic girl, how many times have I told you that I want to help you? God knows, I'm not rich but—'

'No, Gernot. You know how it is with me.'

'You and your damned pride!'

'Perhaps it's pride. I don't know. But I have to be . . . someone who has asked you for nothing. The only person, perhaps.'

'And what of me? What of my wish to render you a service?'

'The service you do me is to exist.' I began to elaborate this theme, one of my favourites, and presently he stopped raging and decided that it was after all not necessary for him to finish his cigar.

It is my pride to have wasted many of the Field Marshal's best Havanas.

I have seen the dreaded tandem!

Frau Sultzer arrived on it this morning, bringing her daughter Edith to be measured for her bridesmaid's dress.

Their arrival created a certain stir. Rip entirely lost his sang-froid and danced barking round the machine as it wobbled to a halt; Joseph in the café stood with his mouth hanging open.

Frau Sultzer dismounted from the front of the machine, her daughter Edith from the back. Two briefcases were unstrapped from the carrier . . .

And my admiration for Rudi Sultzer leapt to new heights. He might not have 'approached' his wife often, but he had 'approached' her.

On this wonderful May morning, Laura Sultzer wore a musty brown skirt with a swollen hem which undulated like a switch-back and a knitted cardigan under which the sleeves of her blouse bulged in a way which made one wonder if she had secreted some of her rescued rats. Her nose was sharp and long, the thriving hairs which covered her chin and upper lip ranged interestingly from white to grey to dusty black, and as she came towards me I caught the musty odour one encounters when opening ancient wardrobes.

But my business was with her daughter.

Edith was shorter than her mother, with bad skin and be-wildered grey eyes behind the kind of spectacles that Schubert would have discarded as out of date. She looked anaemic, and beneath the bobble-fringed tablecloth she seemed to be wearing, I guessed at her father's bandy legs.

I asked the ladies to sit down and offered Frau Sultzer some fashion magazines which she refused with a shudder. 'Thank you, we have brought our own reading matter,' she said.

The briefcases were then unpacked. Out of hers, awesomely stamped with the initials L.S., Frau Sultzer fetched a volume of Schopenhauer and a propelling pencil. Out of Edith's – a bulging and distressed-looking object of paler hue – she took a volume of *Beowulf*.

'I feel I should inform you that my daughter is entered for the Plotzenheimer Essay Prize in Anglo-Saxon studies,' she continued, 'so I would be grateful if you would keep her fittings as brief as possible. It is imperative that she wastes no time.'

'Her fittings will be exactly as long as necessary, Frau Sultzer,' I said.

I then led Edith away, removing *Beowulf* from her nervous clasp, and while Nini measured her, I tried to think what I could do to make this unprepossessing lump into a pretty bridesmaid.

The first step was obvious.

'Fräulein Edith, if I am to dress you properly, one thing is essential. A proper corset.'

She stared at me, her short-sighted eyes widening behind her spectacles. 'Oh, no, I couldn't! Mama would never permit it. She doesn't approve of them. My underclothes are made by a lady who comes to mother's Goethe readings.'

'Yes, I can see that. But I really cannot sew for someone whose bosom has to be looked for every time they come. It needn't be anything very tight or constricting. I'll give you the name of an excellent woman in the Graben: she's not expensive.' I wrote a name on a piece of paper and handed it to Edith. 'After all, there's no need to trouble your mother; just mention to your father that I insisted on a foundation garment. I'm sure he's aware of the existence of such things.'

Edith shook her head despairingly. Her light brown hair was full of dandruff, but I refrained from suggesting a good shampoo and raw liver sandwiches for it was clear that the Bluestocking, at the moment, could take no more.

'Anyway, no one will look at me,' she said, 'not with Magdalena as a bride.'

'Anyone I dress gets looked at,' I said firmly, but I was curious about Magdalena Winter and Edith answered my questions freely enough.

Magdalena and Edith had attended the same school since they

were seven years old. From the first it seemed Magdalena had been spared the traditional disasters of childhood: chicken pox, acne, braces on her teeth. Not only was she beautiful, she was exceedingly devout.

'She always said she wanted to be a nun. Always. But of course when you look like that . . . All the same, we were very surprised when she accepted Herr Huber.' Edith broke off, flushing. 'I don't mean . . . I mean, Herr Huber is very kind. He called on us and brought us a salami, but we're vegetarians and Mother gave it to the poor. Only, Magdalena had a lot of offers and some of them were very grand – and she'd refused them all.'

I tried to visualize this paragon. 'Is she dark or fair?'

'Fair. Almost white. In the nativity play she was always the Virgin Mary and her hair sort of rippled out over her blue mantle. People just gasped.'

'And you?' I asked the Bluestocking, 'what were you in the nativity play?'

'Oh, I was a sheep,' said Edith. 'I was always a sheep.'

Back in the salon, Frau Sultzer was still bent over her Schopenhauer, occasionally pencilling a *Yes!* or an *Indeed!* into the margin.

How sad for poor Schopenhauer to have died before he knew how absolutely Laura Sultzer agreed with him.

I had intended to see the bride and the bridesmaid together but Herr Huber had sent a message to say that Fräulein Winter was unwell. She had a chest infection and the doctor had advised her to stay indoors. Since there was a great deal of work to be done on her trousseau I'd suggested that Nini and I go round to her house with some samples, and as soon as lunch was over, the butcher appeared in his new canary-yellow motor to drive us to where she lived.

Magdalena's mother was the daughter of an army officer who had fought at Königgratz; her father was a taxidermist at the Naturhistorisches Museum who suffered from chronic asthma and had been retired early on a shockingly inadequate pension.

'The elephant seal at the top of the main staircase is his work,' said Herr Huber, steering his motor down the Wipplingerstrasse. 'A very able man.'

Magdalena had two younger brothers, twins of ten who were destined for the army. They had fallen behind at school and now had to be coached for the Cadet Corps.

'I'm taking care of all that, of course,' said the butcher. 'I regard it as a sacred trust.'

He left us at the entrance to the Kreuzer Hof and we made our way through an archway into a sunless courtyard and up an outside staircase to the third floor. The smell of sauerkraut and drains accompanied us; on the dank, arcaded passage that ran right round the building, aproned women with crying children filled buckets at the communal taps.

Frau Winter opened the door to us, mumuring a brave lie about it being the maid's day off. The tiny parlour was spotless and every surface was covered with crocheted doilies or anti-macassars or lace-fringed cloths. There were pictures of the Kaiser, of the murdered Empress Elisabeth – and one portrait of an army officer whose insignia I fortunately recognized.

'Ah, the 3rd Light Cavalry! The corps that fought so magnificently at Königgratz.'

Frau Winter's pale eyes lit up. 'Yes. That's my father. The boys are going to join his old regiment. They *have* to!'

In her voice I sensed her desperation, the endless fight against the poverty and squalor by which she was surrounded. No wonder Magdalena had felt obliged to marry a wealthy man.

The twins now appeared, clicked their heels, bowed. With their cropped flaxen hair, light blue eyes and sturdy physique they were every recruiting officer's dream.

'Go and tell your sister that the ladies are here,' Frau Winter ordered – and to the faint, unheeded sounds of inquiry from the taxidermist behind a door, we were led to Magdalena's room.

It was an extraordinary place. All the rooms were dark, for Frau Winter had placed the thickest netting between herself and the communal passage outside, but Magdalena's room, which had only a small high window, was crepuscular. One felt as if one were in an aquarium or deep below the sea.

'Oh!' Nini beside me had given a little squeak, her hand touched mine for reassurance – and no wonder.

All round the room – on the shelf above the bed, on the chest of drawers, on the small table, there stood glass jars and inside each of them something white and sinister appeared to float. Curled up embryos? Pickled organs? Had we strayed into some kind of mortuary?

Then our eyes grew used to the gloom and we could see that they were figures made from wax: little doll-like models of martyrs and saints.

'Do you like them?' came a voice from the bed. 'I made them myself.'

Magdalena rose and stood before us in her dressing gown and I forgot the waxen puppets and simply stared. Both Herr Huber and Edith Sultzer had described Magdalena as beautiful, but nothing had prepared me for what I saw. The girl was tall and slender; her loose hair rippled to her knees, her curving eyes were the colour of lapis lazuli.

'The ivory brocade you bought from Seligmann?' whispered Nini.

But I was ahead of Nini. I had already cut the brocade into panels floating down from the shoulders, drawn the back ones into a train . . . had wired the top of the bodice so that Magdalena's throat came out of the cloth like a lily from the stem.

'I'll show them to you,' said Magdalena, and moving gracefully over to the chest of drawers, she took down one of the glass bottles and handed it to me. 'That's Saint Lucy; she's one of my favourites.'

The doll in her waxen grotto was holding in her pink-tipped hands a velvet cushion on which rested her gouged-out eyes.

'This one's Saint Nepoumak,' she went on. 'He's got the rope round his neck, ready to be thrown in the river. And the one next to him is Saint Katherine. She was broken on the wheel, that's why she's in two parts like that. Though she joined up later.'

It was impossible to stop Magdalena as she moved tenderly among her friends: Saint Eulogius holding his severed head, Saint Agatha covering her cut-off breasts; Saint Cecilia smothered in her bath . . . I think she would have spent all afternoon showing us her treasures, but I now said firmly that it was time we got down to work.

At once the life, the animation, went out of the extraordinary girl. She replaced Saint Futurosa in his hair shirt and sat down obediently on the bed like a child getting ready to listen to a tiresome teacher.

I don't think I've ever been so disconcerted. Magdalena nodded politely while I sketched what was possibly going to be the most beautiful wedding dress ever made, she acquiesced in my design for a Renaissance evening gown in cloth of gold; she agreed that a cloak of midnight-blue street velvet would become her.

But she was bored. Unmistakably, unconcealably bored.

Walking back to the shop, taking deep breaths of fresh air, Nini and I tried to make sense of what we had seen. For it seemed that Edith was right. Magdalena had indeed turned down a number of offers from men who'd been quite as prepared as Herr Huber to help the family. There'd been a handsome army captain who wanted to take the boys down to his estate in Styria, a young banker with a house in Paris . . .

'Of course we're grateful to Herr Huber,' Frau Winter had said as she showed us out, 'though I'm glad my father's not alive to see her marry into trade.'

If it was pressure from her family that had made Magdalena agree to a rich marriage, her choice of suitor, clearly, was all her own.

Alice continues to be worried about Rudi.

'He still looks so wretchedly tired,' she said when I met her at the Landtmann. 'That awful wife of his has got this gaggle of females called the Group. They come to the house and listen to her rabbiting on about Goethe, and the maids spend hours putting things on pumpernickel – you know how literary groups love to *eat* – and when Rudi comes in they just lift their heads and look at him like cows. I must say, Sanna, it seems to me so *wrong* that a man should have to endure all that just because he sat next to someone the day he'd finished his dead mother's raspberry jam.'

I agreed. It's always struck me as grossly unfair that men have to carry lifelong burdens on account of some brief and arbitrary accident, and I told Alice about my bank manager, Herr Dreiss.

'He went to Budapest to see his brother and they went to a café where the gypsies were playing. Proper ones, you know, with all those czembaloms and things. And there was this girl from Wiener Neustadt at the next table: the most boring girl with buck teeth – he'd never have looked at her ordinarily – and by the next morning they were engaged. Just because of the gypsies. She has a baby every year and she's brought her mother and her aunt to live. You'd think he could so easily have gone to some other café. Even in Budapest there must be a café where you don't get yowled at by gypsies.'

At this point we got so depressed that we decided to boost our spritzers with a couple of schnapps, and I asked Alice about Magdalena's headdress.

'I want to use freshwater pearls braided into her hair and then take them up into a circlet to hold the veil. Only I'm not sure how to do it without getting that ridiculous pill box effect.'

Alice nodded and took the pencil from me. 'You need that very soft wire they use for aigrettes. Yvonne has some – I'll get it for you. Then you twist it like this . . .'

She drew exactly what I wanted and I thanked her. 'You're wasted on operetta, I've told you before. God meant you for a milliner.'

She sighed. 'He certainly didn't mean me for an ageing village maiden yowling in a dirndl for forty kronen a week.'

The schnapps came. We drank it and felt better, and Alice inquired about Edith.

'Actually I don't quite know what to do about her. It seems an extraordinary choice, to have her as an only bridesmaid. I can put her into moss green crêpe, a princess line and all that. Play safe

. . . But I'd like to do better for the poor Bluestocking. Always a sheep in the nativity play and that dreadful briefcase full of *Beowulf* . . .'

For a moment I shut my eyes and tried to shake my mind free of all preconceived notions about Edith Sultzer. I can do that sometimes and get a kind of instant cameo of a person's essence. It doesn't last long, but it gives me a clue and I design to that.

I had forgotten about the schnapps. What flashed before my closed eyes was a bedroom with a french window leading out on to a verandah which overlooked a wide grey river. Inside the room was a large and tumbled bed and on it a plump Edith Sultzer in black lace underwear bounced up and down.

'What's the matter?' asked Alice.

I stopped giggling and shook my head. 'Nothing,' I said, and explained. 'It'll just have to be the moss-green crêpe.'

June

I thought it was the full moon that woke me; I'd left the shutters open, for today was the first day of summer heat. It was two o'clock in the morning and even in the busy Walterstrasse the traffic was stilled; yet something had disturbed me.

I slipped on my kimono and went through into the kitchen to warm some milk. The moonlight was very bright: Saint Florian with his bucket was white as alabaster.

Then I heard the stamping of horses and saw a carriage standing by the Schumachers' front door. The doctor. Some time tonight, then, the child would be born – and I leant out on the sill and prayed that the baby would be strong and well.

My baby was well. She was perfect. They shouldn't have given her to me to hold, but she was born at night when the sister who was in charge of the ward was absent – and the young novice gave her to me.

So I held her.

As soon as she lay in my arms I knew for certain that I was going to keep her and I told her so. I felt well and strong and entirely without doubts and I spoke to her calmly and sensibly, for my joy was so overwhelming it needed the discipline of extreme politeness.

'There is, for example, the question of your Christian name,' I said to her as she lay and snuffled in the crook of my arm. 'You see, Sappho called her daughter Kleis and I would very much like to call you that. Only I don't think it would go well in German? So I wondered if you'd care to have my mother's name? Would you like to be called Elisabeth?' I asked my baby. 'Would you care for that?'

And she opened her eyes.

We talked most of the night, my daughter and I, and in the shadowed ward the young novice who had brought her to me moved about her work.

The next day the sister came back and was furious. Babies destined for adoption should never be given to the mother to hold. By this time my temperature had begun to rise, and it rose and rose in the next days while half-comprehended figures in black habits sponged my forehead, felt my pulse and mouthed again and again their terrible, sincerely held beliefs. I must be sensible . . . I must sign the papers . . . I must let go.

I had puerperal fever. Most of the time I was delirious, but when I became aware of my surroundings they gave me laudanum because I screamed for my baby and upset the other patients.

Some time during those days, my daughter vanished.

I was ill for a long time. Puerperal fever kills more often than not, but I was eighteen and had been healthy all my life. I got better and they sent me down to their convalescent home in Klagenfurt where I sat in the sun with the other Fallen Women and stared at the Worthersee. After a month the doctor said I was fit for work and the nuns found me a job in domestic service in Vienna.

My employers had a big apartment behind the stock exchange. I slept in a windowless cupboard, rose at five-thirty and worked without a pause till nine at night. But it wasn't the work that was the problem. I was prepared for that. It was my employers' detestable sons, Alphonse and Franz, young men-about-town with incipient moustaches and ridiculous dandified clothes who regarded the maids as entirely available and thought they were honouring me with their favours.

I bit and scratched my way through my three months there. Then one morning I found my employers' newspaper and in it an advertisement for a seamstress in the teeming textile quarter north of the Hohermarkt.

I worked for Jasha Jacobson for three years. He came from Russian Poland and ran a typical sweat shop – overcrowded, noisy, ill-ventilated. I knew nothing about Jews: their religion, their habits – being there was as strange to me as if I'd gone to work in an Arabian souk. We worked unbelievably long hours and my pay was low, but I've never ceased to be grateful for my time there. I learnt everything there was to know about tailoring: choosing the cloth, cutting, repairing the ancient, rattling machines. At first I was a freak – a *schickse* set down in the midst of this close-knit immigrant community – but gradually, I became a kind of mascot. People passing smiled and waved at the blonde girl sitting in the window beside the cross-legged men sewing their button holes. And I was never molested – I might have been a girl of their own faith by the care they took of me.

When Jasha realized that I was serious about wanting my own shop, he began to take me about with him. I met an old Tunisian who did goldwork and his crippled wife who showed me how to handle sequins and beads. Lacemakers, leatherworkers, pedlars from Flanders and Normandy . . . I got to know them all and know them still.

After three years I asked Jasha for a reference and left. There were tears in his eyes when we said goodbye, but he was glad to see me go because his nephew, Izzy, his heir and the apple of his eye, wanted to marry me. Izzy had been rotted by education and lent me books by Tolstoy and Dostoyevsky which I fell asleep over after a twelve-hour day. Jasha knew I had no intention of accepting the boy but it hurt him to have a member of his family who would consider marrying out of the faith.

With the reference Jasha wrote for me I got a job in a fashionable dress shop in the Herrengasse. I started in the sewing room, but soon I was modelling and helping with the designs, and at the end of two years the proprietress hinted at the possibility of a partnership, for she was getting on in years. Some of the customers befriended me and they had brothers, cousins – even fathers – who were very willing to take me out. I began to go to the theatre, to the opera; to meet writers and painters. Listening to their talk in the cafés, I became almost educated. And I learnt how to behave like a beautiful woman, which is not the same as – but more important than – being beautiful.

By this time I was sharing a flat with Alice: three rooms and a kitchen in a pretty, arcaded courtyard behind the Votiv Church. We'd met at Yvonne's, both staring at the same hat: a green straw with parrot tulips and a navy-blue ribbon which we both decided not to buy! We got on well from the start – I don't think I've ever laughed so much as I did with Alice, nor seen so many operettas!

So within five years of leaving the House of Refuge, a penniless girl without a future, I had an excellent job, a home, a circle of friends.

I don't know when I stopped daydreaming and decided to act. But one day at breakfast I said:

'Alice, I'm going to get her back. I'm going to find my daughter. Can she come here?'

And Alice, who alone in the world knew my secret, jumped up and put her arms round me and said, 'Yes. Oh, yes, yes, *yes!*'

At four a.m. the doctor's carriage was still outside the Schumachers' house and the windows blazed with light.

Oh, let it go well for her, I prayed – she's so tired, poor Helene – and let that pompous husband be good to her whatever the outcome.

Should it take so long, a seventh child?

It was one thing to decide to bring my daughter home, another to find her.

The sister who had been in charge at the House of Refuge had been transferred; the other nuns would tell me nothing. The deed was done, the child had a good home. As I beseeched and pleaded, they suggested I go to confession and purge myself of impure desires.

I went to the Ministry of Home Affairs and was transferred from room to room. At last I found the place where the adoption records were kept – and was met with a blank refusal. The files were confidential; there was no question of my seeing them.

'I'm afraid it's impossible, Gnädige Frau. It's the regulations. There's nothing we can do.'

They went on doing nothing, a thing that Austrian civil servants are very good at, for week after week. I kept going to see if a different clerk might be on duty; I implored, I wept – and still, implacably, they answered 'no'.

And yet I didn't lose hope. Now when I drove out with one of my escorts, I looked at Vienna with new eyes, noting fountains which would amuse her, alleys where she could bowl her hoop. I found myself staring at a poster of the Danube Steamship Company, searching the timetable for river trips which would not keep her from her bed too late. Once, quite by myself, I went to the Prater. Sometimes I think that of all the days of my life, that's the one that I'd most like to have back: the day I tested the dappled horses of the carousels, travelled the magic Grottenbahn, sailed high over the city on the ferris wheel with my imagined daughter.

And I began to dress a doll. There has never, I do assure you, been a doll like the one I dressed for my daughter. Alice made her hats, but the rest – the evening gowns of faille and lace, the sailor suit, the nightgowns and bed jackets and capes – I stitched in the evening. The doll was my flag nailed to the mast. While I dressed her, I still had faith.

Then one day in July my luck turned. Going yet again to the records office I found a new clerk: an unattractive young man, spotty, with a big Adam's apple, too much hair cream.

I began again, pleading, asking to see this one entry – the one referring to the adoption of a daughter born to Susanna Weber on the seventh of April 1893.

He listened, looked round to make sure that we were not overheard, asked what I would be prepared to give.

All the money I had, I said, also whispering. Everything I possessed – and I almost tore from my throat, then and there, the necklace that I wore.

But of course that wasn't what he wanted.

It was a long night, the night I spent with him in a cheap hotel behind the Graben – oh Lord, it was long. But he played fair. The next day he brought me a copy of the entry I had asked for. A baby girl born on the seventh of April 1893 to Susanna Weber, spinster, had been adopted on April the twenty-third by Erich and Sidonie Toller of 3, Nussbaumgasse, Hintersdorf, Salzburg. Herr Toller's occupation was given as 'water engineer' and I remember being cross about that. Surely they could have done better for my daughter than a water engineer?

So now I was ready. I had been saving up my annual holiday, and on a perfect late summer's day, with the doll packed in a special box, I set off for Salzburg.

Everyone knows what Salzburg is like. Very pretty, a little absurd. The Mirabelle Gardens, the Fischer von Erlach churches, the castle high on its hill. And Mozart of course. Mozart whom the inhabitants ignored and who now brings the tourists flocking.

But if you drive round behind the castle you come to a green and pleasant landscape which has nothing to do with the fashionable shops and the crowds. Here there are fields of clover, little streams and prosperous villages in which people who work in the town have built pretty villas with well-kept gardens.

Hintersdorf was one of these. There was a main street, a few quiet side streets running out towards the fields.

I had booked into a pension in Salzburg. Now as I alighted from the bus I was suddenly terribly afraid. Not that I couldn't bring her back with me – I knew I could do that – but that she would be less than I had hoped, strange to me. Other . . .

Oh God!

I walked down the lane and found the house. Low, yellow stucco, in a big tree-shaded garden. There was a wooden table under a walnut tree and a swing in the branches of a cherry.

And she was in the garden.

It is becoming very hard to write but I had better finish now.

She was exactly as I had known she would be. Her face, wide-mouthed, sweet and funny was the face from which all others departed at their peril. She was fair, plump and golden-skinned; her thick hair was braided, but loosely so that the ends curled into fat tendrils the colour of corn. She wore a blue dirndl with a crisp white blouse and a dusty pink apron; her socks were white as snow and the ribbons which fastened her pigtails matched exactly the colour of her dirndl.

It was like looking into the mirror, like being six years old again but better. She was prettier than I had been, for her eyes were brown. I could see that from where I stood, half concealed by the trunk of an acacia – and I thanked Karli, my long-forgotten lieutenant, for this gift. They were quite lovely, the brown eyes in the fair and golden child.

I had come as she was preparing for a party. Three stuffed animals were propped against cushions on the ground – a bear, a donkey and an elephant, and everything needed for their adornment lay to hand: bird cherries for earrings, necklaces of threaded berries, rings she had woven from the stems of grass.

'You must be patient,' she said to the animals, lowering a necklace over the donkey's head. 'It takes time to make things fit.'

Her voice was sweet and clear, with a trace of the local accent which would go, as mine had done, in the city.

After the necklaces came the earrings, causing problems with the elephant.

'You'll be pleased to look so smart when you get to the King and Queen,' she told him. 'You'll be glad you didn't wriggle. And remember, I have to get dressed too.'

I watched and watched. I looked at the child, into her, through her. She was gold, pure gold. Then slowly I dragged my gaze away and looked at the house. Neat white curtains, an espalier peach against the wall; petunias and begonias in the window boxes; bantams strutting in a wire enclosure.

My eyes roamed, searching and searching for something that jarred; something I disliked.

Nothing. My prettily dressed yet untrammelled daughter played in perfect contentment in a country garden with her well-loved toys. So I would have dressed her, so I would have wanted

66

her to play. From my child there emanated above all that strange, unspectacular, almost never-encountered thing: a quiet, self contained and peaceful happiness. An ordinariness which is in fact so extraordinary, so unbelievably rare.

Then a woman came out with a glass of milk on a tray and a plate of biscuits and my daughter looked up and smiled.

The child had not noticed me, but the woman saw me. The resemblance must have been very striking for she knew me at once. She didn't scream, she didn't faint – she walked very carefully, slowly to the table and put down the child's milk. Then she grasped the side of the table and held on. Just held on.

It doesn't matter what she looked like. I try not to remember her, but her face went with the house . . . with the garden . . . with what she had made of the child.

So I turned and walked away. I was being good, you see – and as a matter of fact, it nearly killed me.

After all, I did not keep watch with Helene. Suddenly exhausted, I went back to bed just before dawn and was woken by Nini shaking my shoulders, worried because I was late for the shop.

'It's bad news, I'm afraid,' she said.

I sat up quickly. 'Helene Schumacher? Something's wrong.'

'Yes. It's the black apron not the white towel. Another girl.'

'If that's your idea of bad news I'm sorry for you,' I said furiously. I ran and bought a dozen red roses from Old Anna, and sent them round with Gretl.

'Lisl's been crying,' she said when she returned. 'Her eyes are all red. And the little girls looked like corpses, going off to school.'

'Herr Schumacher, no doubt, is in mourning,' I said grimly. 'He went off first thing, even before breakfast. Just stamped out of the house with his umbrella.'

As the black apron collected more and more sympathizers my ill temper increased. I snubbed Joseph in the café when he referred to Herr Schumacher's 'misfortune' and was rude even to poor Professor Starsky when he paused outside my shop to shake a commiserating head.

Reports of Herr Schumacher's progress through the day did nothing for my state of mind. He had been seen in the Golden Hind at lunchtime, already considerably inebriated. There was a second sighting on the terrace of the Hotel Meissner. By early evening he was said to be in the Central having been assisted there by his dentist and his bank manager who'd stayed to join in the grief and lamentation.

I was unpinning my hair, ready to go to bed, when there was a knock at the door of the flat and Lisl, the Schumachers' maid, stood there with swollen eyes.

'The Gnädige Frau begs if you'll come and see her for just a moment.'

'Now? Tonight? Surely she's too tired?'

'No – she particularly said tonight if you could manage. Herr Schumacher is still away.'

'I'll come at once.' And then: 'The baby's healthy, I understand?'

'Yes.'

I put up my hair again, fetched a shawl and followed her.

Frau Schumacher lay alone in the big brass bed. Her kind, plump face was grey with fatigue and swollen with tears. In a bassinet in the corner of the room lay the baby in its muslin tent.

I went straight to the bed, took her hands, kissed her. I'd stitched a little bonnet for the baby weeks ago and laid it on the counterpane.

'Congratulations!' I said. 'A healthy baby, Lisl tells me.'

'Yes.' Then the tears began to flow. She felt for her handkerchief, dabbed, mopped. 'I don't mind having another girl. I *like* girls. I would have *seventeen* daughters and it wouldn't bother me. Why should it matter whether they have that silly thing between their legs? It only causes trouble. Either they have to have somewhere to put it and if they can't find anywhere they start their stupid wars.'

I had never heard Helene talk like this, but I pressed her hands warmly to show how entirely I agreed.

'And the baby's beautiful. I love her. I tell you, Frau Susanna, as soon as I held her, I felt such love. She has violet eyes and the most perfect arched eyebrows. She's a real personality. The girls love her too. But my husband . . . well, as soon as he heard it was a girl he just went out and Lisl tells me he was at the Meissner by lunchtime, quite drunk, and all his cronies commiserating. It's his pride, of course, that's all it is. He never took any notice of the last two – he never held them once or wanted to be near them. So what's going to happen now?'

'Well, she'll just grow up with the others, surely, in the best possible home. Your husband doesn't have to trouble with her if he doesn't want to. She'll have enough love from you and the girls.'

Frau Schumacher shook her head and lay back on the pillow. 'It's not my fault,' she murmured. 'The doctor explained that. It's not my fault and it's not his; it's just a thing that happens, but Albert'll never see that.' And she began to sob again.

I went over to the bassinet and pulled aside the curtains. The baby lay deep in sleep. She had a beautifully shaped head, a warm peach-coloured skin, a retroussé nose.

Then she turned her head a little and I saw that one cheek was entirely covered by a livid crimson birthmark.

I let the curtain fall and returned to the bed.

'Your husband doesn't know?'

She shook her head. 'He just marched out of the house as soon as he heard it was a girl. I wouldn't let the doctor tell him – I wanted to do it myself. But now I can't . . .' She began to cry again. 'It's awful how much I love this child already and I cannot bear it if he . . . if . . .'

'You must tell him as soon as he comes in.'

'Frau Susanna.' She raised herself up on the pillow. 'Would *you* tell him? That's why I asked you to come. He admires you so much. "If Frau Susanna wasn't a virtuous woman you'd have to look to your laurels", he keeps on saying. It's that first moment when he turns away from her or rages and says God is punishing him. I didn't mind with the others, but I cannot *bear* it for this child.'

'Do you know where he is?'

69

'No I don't, not for certain. He was at the Central about seven because someone saw him, but he may have moved on.'

'Don't worry, I'll find him, and I'll tell him. Just rest now; just sleep.'

Herr Schumacher was not in the Central. He had been there and the proprietor remembered him well, and the party of sympathizers with which he'd been surrounded.

'Seven daughters, poor gentleman,' he said – and recoiled from my basilisk glare.

He was not in the Blue Boar either, but in the Regina the trail grew warm again. An inebriated gentleman, supported by two friends, had lurched past half an hour earlier, asking the passers-by what he had done to deserve his fate.

'He went on about goldfish, too. Someone had killed his goldfish,' said the landlord. 'He went off towards the Graben. You could try the Three Hussars.'

And in that ancient hostelry full of antlers and oak panelling I found him. He was sitting between his faithful henchmen, the bank manager and the dentist, the centre of a veritable Pieta. Herr Schumacher's moustaches were limp with grief, glasses and a half empty bottle of wine littered the table. The dentist's heavy hand lay on the stricken father's arm; the bank manager's pince-nez glittered as he shook a commiserating head.

'Good evening.'

'Frau . . . Susanna!' Herr Schumacher recognized me, tried to rise.

'Herr Schumacher, I have just come from your house.'

'Eh. . . what?' Tipsily he pulled out a chair which I ignored. 'Is there anything wrong? My wife's all right?'

'Physically she's all right. Emotionally she's not. She is very much upset.'

'Well, yes; anyone would be. I'm very much upset . . . my friends are too.' He waved his arm at his companions, knocking over a glass. 'I'll have to take in my brother's boy from Graz now. It's a disaster; its—'

I now lost my temper.

'Herr Schumacher, you make me ashamed to be a human being. Your daughter has a large birthmark on her right cheek. It is a serious and permanent blemish with which she will have to live. Your wife is exhausted and wretched – and you sit here like a sot; drooling with self-pity and drinking with your so-called friends.'

'What . . . ? What did you say?' He sat down heavily. 'A birthmark? A big one, you say.'

'Yes.'

The dentist had now grasped the nature of the calamity. 'Hey, that's terrible, Schumacher. Terrible! Not just a girl but disfigured!'

'Dreadful, quite dreadful,' murmured the bank manager. 'You'll have her on your hands all your life.'

Herr Schumacher shook his head, trying to surface from his drunkenness. 'You say she's healthy?' he demanded. 'The baby?'

'Yes, she's perfectly healthy. In fact she's a very sweet baby otherwise. She has the most distinguished eyebrows.'

'Still, if she's got a strawberry mark no one'll look at her. Or rather everyone'll look at her!' The dentist, still bent on consolation, tried to put an arm round Herr Schumacher's shoulders.

The arm was removed. Herr Schumacher rose and managed to stay upright. 'Idiot!' he spat at the dentist. 'Half-wit!' He opened his mouth very wide and jabbed a finger at one of his back molars. 'Do you see that tooth? You filled it a month ago and since then I've had nothing but trouble! Every time I drink something hot it's like a dagger!'

'Come, come Schumacher,' said the bank manager. 'He was only trying to—'

Herr Schumacher swung round to confront his comforter.

'And you shut up too or I'll knock you down. I'm surprised you've got the nerve to look me in the face! Two per cent on a simple loan with collaterals! Two per cent!'

He threw some money down on the table, staggered to the coat rack, jammed his hat on his head.

I had kept the cab waiting. The night air revived Herr

Schumacher, but only partially, as he alternated between threats to knock down the bank manager and the dentist, and inquiries about his daughter's health.

I had intended to leave him by the front door but Lisl looked at me so beseechingly that I accompanied him upstairs.

'Where is she?' demanded the new father, blundering into the bedroom.

'There, Albert.'

Herr Schumacher strode over to the cot.

'Lift her out!' he bade me – and I took the swaddled bundle and carried it over to the light.

'Give her to me!' he commanded.

Frau Schumacher and I exchanged glances. He was still not entirely steady on his feet. I motioned him to a chair, laid the baby across his lap, and stood by in case of accidents.

Herr Schumacher stared intently at his daughter's face. I had placed her deliberately full in the light and the livid mark showed up very clearly.

Then he began to talk to her: 'Well, well, my pretty, that's nothing to worry about! No, no, that's nothing to bother you and me. You just wait till you're riding with your father in a great carriage through the Prater.' He bent down, laid one finger on the blemished cheek and began to make the foolish, clucking noises that drooling women make to little children. 'We'll have such times together, you'll see! We'll take a sailboat down the river and I'll show you how to catch fish. And on Sundays we'll go out to tea at Demels – just the two of us!'

And while he inexpertly joggled and tickled his youngest daughter, the blessed baby just lay there without a murmur, accepting it all – and presently Herr Schumacher informed us that she had little fingernails, his mother's nose – and eyebrows.

Frau Sultzer's court case is coming up next week. The university is suing her for trespass and damage to property – and indeed the rats she has released all over the building *look* damaged. Those that have been seen, appearing from time to time in the Academic

Board Room or the cloakrooms, have that wet look which is never a good sign in rodents, and their pink eyes are glazed and dull.

Unfortunately, her notoriety has gone to Frau Sultzer's head. Notices saying *Silence! Frau Sultzer is reading Schopenhauer* have been replaced by notices saying *Silence! Frau Sultzer is preparing her defence.* Actually, the person who is preparing her defence is poor Rudi, along with the lawyer he has called in and to whom he is paying a lot of money, but the Group is very much excited by the whole business and the lady who accompanied Laura on the back of the tandem on the historic ride to the university is much grieved that she is not appearing in court also.

But Alice, when we met in Yvonne's hat shop, was radiant. True, Rudi still comes home to rooms full of women with salad hanging out of the corners of their mouths; true, too, that the lady who makes Edith's underclothes has started on that Croatian cross-stitch in black and red that high-minded women go in for, so that he has to hide his pyjamas. But at the end of July Frau Sultzer is taking Edith and the Group to St Polten where they will go for walks and listen to her Appreciating Nature, and Rudi has pleaded pressure of work and will stay behind.

'I've been so worried about him,' said Alice, at the same time lowering a dazzlingly beautiful black tulle hat clouded in polka dot veiling on to her curls. 'Last time he came he was so exhausted I thought perhaps we shouldn't make love. In fact I suggested it.'

'I expect he thought that was a bad idea?'

Alice turned her head away in the hope that the hat would be less becoming from the side, but it was not. 'He thought it was a perfectly terrible idea,' she said and smiled into the mirror. 'But now everything will be all right. I'll soon get him completely well again, you'll see. Can't life be absolutely *marvellous* suddenly!'

She then took the exquisite hat to Yvonne, a shrivelled old charlatan who is nevertheless the best hatmaker in Vienna, and returned shaking her head.

'Thirty kronen for a handful of tulle – she's mad!'

'Let me lend you the money, Alice; please. It looks so marvellous on you.'

'No, Sanna, it's sweet of you but I'd rather not. Anyway, who needs a black hat in the middle of summer?'

Magdalena is better. Herr Huber brought her for a fitting in his canary-yellow motor, and with the kind thought of saving Edith from the back of the tandem he picked her up at her house and brought her too.

The contrast between the two girls was almost painful. Magdalena drifted in, a rosary dripping from her fingers; slender, willowy, dressed in white. Behind her came Edith with her bad skin, her dandruff-covered hair, her extraordinary spectacles.

But what upset me was the way Herr Huber looked at his fiancée. Naturally I had expected him to be very much in love, but the adoration, the humble yet frenzied worship, worried me. I wish I understood this marriage.

Of course Magdalena is very beautiful though I admit I felt a little disconcerted as I welcomed her. Not because of the rosary, though I do not have many clients who bring rosaries to their fittings, nor by the absent look in her deep blue eyes, but by the fact that at eleven in the morning in a dress shop in the Inner City, she was wearing her lovely, rippling hair loose almost to the knees. You can of course design for these Ophelia-like girls who model themselves on the English pre-Raphaelites, but it had been my intention also to consider occasions like the Meat Retailers' Outing, or afternoon tea with Herr Huber's sister in Linz.

I left Edith in the second cubicle while I draped Magdalena in Seligman's brocade. By the time I reached the Bluestocking with the toile for the moss-green crêpe, she had been waiting for some time in her unfortunate underclothes and I had no right to be irritated by her bulging briefcase lying on the velvet stool, but I was.

'You could leave your case outside, Fraulein Sultzer. It would be quite safe.'

A sort of gulp issued from the Bluestocking and her pale lips twitched into a nervous smile. Then she snatched the briefcase and began to empty out the contents. A black and tattered copy of

Beowulf, an Anglo-Saxon dictionary, two note books . . . and something rolled in tissue paper which she put into my hands.

I unrolled the package. Inside the tissue was a well-made and very serviceable corset.

'I spoke to my father,' said Edith, flushing, 'and he said it was all right. So I went between lectures.' She looked up at me appealingly. 'My mother doesn't know.'

I was extremely pleased and told her so. For a moment I even wondered if I could do something quite fundamental to make her into an attractive girl. If I changed her spectacles . . . if I gave her raw liver sandwiches . . .

No, not even then.

I have not dared to write this down before for fear of tempting the gods, but I have been watching my pear tree very carefully and I think I can now say that this autumn I shall have an undoubted, a long-awaited and actual pear.

Today it rained and my two least favourite clients came to the shop.

I have made Frau Egger a good cloak: brown loden cloth edged with braid in a darker tone, and frogging.

'Horn buttons would definitely work better, Frau Egger,' I said, laying them against the material. 'The others are far too heavy.'

But she still wanted the military buttons. She wanted the buttons with an owl's head pierced by a lance and the word *Aggredi* repeated twelve times on her bosom, for the cloak is double-breasted.

'We'd better postpone a decision till the final fitting,' I said.

But the final fitting won't, alas, be final, for Frau Egger has ordered a skirt in the same material as the cloak. I'm under no illusions that it is my brilliant dressmaking that attracts the poor woman to my shop. She is still desperate about her husband's affair with Lily from the post office; still determined to speak to Nini and find out what is going on. And the absurd thing is that her panic is quite unnecessary. Lily, quite unprompted, has jettisoned the Minister: pomposity, meanness, Nasty Little Habit and all.

'She told him it was because she didn't want to hurt his wife,' said Nini, 'but it isn't that at all. He's just a horrible man.'

No sooner had Frau Egger left than the Countess von Metz's creaking carriage drew up before my door and the detestable old woman alighted, unexpected and unannounced, and stumped into the shop.

'I have sent for you twice,' she said imperiously. 'I desire you to make me a coat and skirt.'

'When you pay me for the last two dresses I have made for you, I shall be pleased to attend you, Countess.'

The Countess ignored this. 'Wasn't that the Egger I saw coming out of your shop?'

'Yes.'

'Really, I don't know why you dress that dreary middle-class sheep. Her husband is an abomination. He's just turned poor old Baron König out of his house. Some rubbish about widening the street to improve traffic flow. A lot of drunken cab drivers and nouveaux riches in motor cars – why should they flow?'

I repressed the disquiet I always feel when the Minister's activities are mentioned, and picked up Frau Egger's buttons to return them to their box.

'Good God,' said the Countess rudely, peering at the buttons through her lorgnette. 'The Pressburg Fusiliers! A useless lot – they were stationed near my brother's regiment in Moravia. Disbanded in '84 and good riddance! What on earth are they doing here?'

'A customer brought them.'

'Well, she has no right to. Goodness knows what my brother would have said, turning army insignia into playthings.' And as I kept silence: 'I thought a dark green broadcloth or needlecord, perhaps? A flared skirt and a fitted jacket with a peplum – very simple but with bishop sleeves. Your sleeves are always satisfactory, I admit.'

I didn't answer, picked up my account book.

'A lot of people won't wear green. After green comes black,

76

they say. But I don't care for that. Black came to me from the cradle. My mother died when I was two, then my sister, then my aunt. And my brother, of course, but that was later. No, I'm not afraid to wear green.' She hit the floor with her cane. 'You are aware that the dagger I sent you was worth far more than the grosgrain dress? It is a valuable antique.'

'It's a pruning knife. Ask the pawnbroker.'

'The pawnbroker! I give you the treasures of my household and you take them to a pawnbroker! If you are unwise enough to sell, at least take them to a proper antique dealer who knows his job.'

But I wasn't going to be provoked and went on with my accounts.

'Well . . . perhaps I might have made a mistake about the dagger.' Her purple nose twitched with longing for the workroom with its bales of cloth. 'It so happens I have one or two interesting things I could let you have. My brother's cigar box, for example.'

'Countess, those things are no good to me. I can't pay my bills with them. Why don't you go to Chez Jaquetta in the Kärnterstrasse? She may be honoured to dress someone of your rank for nothing.'

'Chez Jaquetta! Are you out of your mind? I wouldn't dress my parrot at that place. Her workmanship's shoddy and she has as much taste as a kitchenmaid. Good Lord, she put the Baroness Lefevre into puce satin covered in dead birds. Ortolans, hundreds of them, hanging on with their beaks. When the Baroness sits down it's like a charnel house: bones breaking, feathers flying . . .'

Defeat. Total defeat. I knew it even as I felt my face crease into an entirely involuntary smile. 'It so happens I have a length of bottle green broadcloth; it's the end of a roll . . .'

It's impossible, reprehensible . . . something must be *done* about the deep and unadulterated joy that courses through me when people speak ill of Chez Jaquetta.

That her activities in the university might have made life difficult for her daughter does not seem to have occurred to Laura Sultzer.

77

I'd been to the town hall to pay my rates and was taking a short cut through the gardens when I saw Edith Sultzer sitting on a bench. She was reading a book and eating a large raw carrot, and I was about to pass her when she looked up and showed her pale gums in a smile of such friendliness that I felt compelled to stop.

'How sensible of you to take your lunch out of doors.'

'Yes, I . . . I used to eat in the university canteen but since my mother . . . since she let out the rats . . . the other students aren't very nice. Not that I have many friends there anyway. I don't mind. I'm too busy with my studies.'

I asked after the Plotzenheimer Prize Essay and heard that it was going well. The deadline was the end of August, but Edith thought she would get it done in time. Her topic (suggested by her mother) was: 'Seventeenth-Century Comments on the Epic of *Beowulf* with Special Reference to the Contribution of Theophilus Krumm'.

'You know, I have to confess that I've never really read *Beowulf*,' I said. 'What's the actual story?'

Edith then told it to me and it sounded good. There was a brave knight, a monster called Grendel whom he slew, and in due course another hazard in the form of Grendel's mother who was even nastier than her son.

'But of course we don't read the actual poem very much,' explained Edith. 'We read what people have *said* about it.'

As I got up to go, it occurred to me that Edith might have some information on a problem that was troubling me, namely Magdalena Winter's hair.

'You see, it's not easy to design clothes for a grown-up woman who has her hair hanging down her back. Do you know why she wears it like that?'

Edith nodded. 'Yes, I do. It's because her hair belongs to Jesus. Only she calls Him The Christ.'

'I see. But surely it could still belong to Him even if it was coiled up and pinned?'

The Bluestocking looked troubled. 'Magdalena has a very special relationship with God,' she said.

'So I observe.'

I'm afraid things are going badly for the poor little Count of Monte Cristo across the way. His uncle is out every day trying to find someone to hear the child, but he is not a prepossessing figure and no one, so far, has shown the slightest interest in his Wunderkind. It is only in the evening when his uncle is back that Sigismund comes out into the square. Perhaps they are afraid that if no one is left to guard the piano it will vanish. Not so unlikely, it is only hired and their meagre stock of money is getting very low.

'Another couple of months,' Frau Hinkler says, 'and then they'll be off back where they came from, and good riddance.'

Meanwhile a new figure has entered my life. She sits on a woolly cloud staring down at me; a dark, angry-looking woman who resembles Frau Wilkolaz, the Polish lady in the paper shop who suffers with her nerves.

This gloomy angel is Sigismund's mother and she is not pleased with me. She doesn't think it is enough for me to say 'Grüss Gott' to her child of an evening when I feel like it. She wants me to take proper notice of him, to care for him and invite him to my house. True, I have shown Sigismund how to pat Rip, I have introduced him to General Madensky on his plinth and explained about the hair dye and the moustaches.

But though he stands and looks at my shop like a starveling in a fairy tale, I have not invited him into my house – and it is this that the Polish lady on her cloud does not think good enough. She wants me to bake vanilla kipferl for him in my kitchen, to stitch him a shirt and tell him stories, but she is destined to be disappointed. If I cannot have my daughter I won't make do with substitutes – that I promised myself when I lost her all those years ago.

Tonight, as Sigismund stood by the fountain, I saw on his skinny, unwashed leg two weals as though made by a cane or ruler.

'What are those, Sigismund? What happened?'

He looked down without much interest. 'My uncle hit me.' Of course; on the leg . . . Never on the precious hands, never a box on the ear.

'Why?'

He shrugged his ancient shoulders. 'He wants me to play the Waldstein Sonata because it looks difficult and people will think I'm clever. But the chords in the last movement are not possible.'

All Poles have to learn the language of their conquerors. Sigismund's German is correct and formal, but he speaks in a low throaty voice so that sometimes I have to bend down to hear him.

'You're too young to play the Waldstein?'

He looked up and his hands came forward, stretched on an invisible keyboard.

'I am not too *young*,' he said. 'I am too *small*.'

Edith was right. Magdalena's hair *does* belong to The Christ. She confirmed this herself as she stood in my fitting room in her wedding dress.

Till I became steeped in mortal sin I was a good Catholic and even now I would be lost without the consolations of the church, but this annoyed me.

'What about Herr Huber? Doesn't it belong to him a little?'

Magdalena turned her beautiful sapphire eyes on me, more puzzled than offended, and regretting my sharpness I said:

'You see, your headdress has been designed to be raised above your braided hair. If you're going to wear it loose I shall have to think again. But do you really want to look like a bride in an Italian opera?'

Magdalena fingered her rosary and said she would ask. 'That's a good idea. Your mother would be able to advise you. Or perhaps you have other relatives?'

'Oh, I wouldn't ask my mother. The Blessed Virgin will advise me. Or one of Them.' She looked up at the draped ceiling of the cubicle and I remembered her tender conversation with the wax puppets under glass.

'The saints, you mean?'

Magdalena nodded. The thought that she is a little crazy has of course occurred to me before – yet with her brothers she is said to be practical and kind, and when you can get her to fix her mind on her clothes her suggestions are often quite sensible. And after all, if more people discussed their hairstyles with the saints one might not see so many bedraggled birds' nests or listing chignons. Even when carrying their eyes in front of them on cushions or tied to wheels, the saints always look neat and seemly.

Meanwhile Herr Huber – there is no doubt about it – has become our friend. He has sent round a kaiserwurst the size of Odin's thigh and Alice (whom he admires inordinately as a hierophant of the sacred art of operetta) is awash in wiener wurstl.

To facilitate his courtship he has taken a room at the Astoria and only goes down to Linz two days a week to supervise his business interests there. God, who was so unenthusiastic about 167 Augustiner Strasse, has approved entirely of 14A, The Graben, which Herr Huber is turning into a temple of charcuterie. Even so, he has time on his hands, for the Winters' flat is so small that he doesn't care to sit there too long of an evening, and he has made it clear that his car and his company are entirely at our disposal.

So old-fashioned is Magdalena's mother, so obsessed with what she imagines to be genteel behaviour, that Magdalena is allowed out with her future bridegroom only in the presence of a chaperon. Middle-class girls in Vienna really do not any longer behave like this and I can't help wondering if it is partly Magdalena's own wish. Since the Winters have no maid it is Edith who has been called in to accompany Magdalena on her outings with the butcher. Laura Sultzer strongly disapproves of this arrangement: Edith should be at home studying for the Plotzenheimer Essay in Anglo-Saxon studies, not riding round in canary-yellow motors with pork butchers about whom neither Goethe nor Schopenhauer had anything to say. But Edith seems quite happy to act as duenna and waddles heroically beside the affianced couple, clutching her briefcase and engaging Herr Huber in the conversation which does not readily fall from the lovely Magdalena's lips.

'Is it true that the Hungarians put donkeys in their salamis?' I heard her say, blinking anxiously at Herr Huber through her spectacles.

And the butcher's soothing reply: 'It is true. But it doesn't mean that the Hungarians are wicked; only that they make good salamis.'

I have not been particularly good this week. I have visited no sickbeds, I was cross with Gretl when she knocked over the box with Frau Egger's ridiculous buttons. And yet – and this shows how mysteriously and marvellously God goes about his business – on Saturday afternoon I found myself sitting beside Hatschek in a carriage bound for a hunting lodge in the Vienna Woods – and Gernot.

My lover had borrowed the house from a colleague who had gone to America in pursuit of a rich wife. We were to have the evening together, and the night. A whole, entire night, for which I had packed a whole and moderately entire nightdress, but I wore the rich cream dress I had worn the last time at the Bristol. So much of love has to do with remembrance.

I love driving with Hatschek. It is from him that I learn those details of Gernot's life that he regards as trivial or uninteresting. It is from Hatschek that I hear the tributes paid to him by his men, the intrigues and dangers that he has to face. They had just returned from Serbia, as part of the delegation supposed to undo the harm we had done by annexing Bosnia and Herzegovinia – a move Gernot had consistently opposed.

'He wouldn't let anyone give him a bodyguard, neither. Just walked round the slums in mufti, saying he had to know what people were thinking. Well, I could tell him what they were thinking. They were thinking how to murder every Austrian they could lay hands on, the swine.'

Even more then the Ordnance Department, we hate the Serbians, Hatschek and I.

We passed Mayerling in its dark circle of trees. They've pulled down the hunting lodge in which the Crown Prince shot himself and his mad little mistress, and built a convent now filled with mourning nuns, but I don't know why. Rudolf had a good life and a good death, surely, with silly, loving Mitzi by his side?

Gernot was waiting by the door. In spite of his gruelling time in Serbia he looked extremely fit.

'Ah, I see you have decided to be beautiful.' He kissed my hands, then the self-coloured silken rose on my bodice, a gesture I found unsettling.

'Do you object?'

Not exactly. As long as you keep it up. I can get accustomed to you looking like the Primavera. It's when you suddenly think of something sad and turn into a potato-picking peasant in one of those dark Van Goghs that I get unsettled. After all, maybe I can have her for life, I think then – not everybody wants to go to bed with potato-picking peasants. And then you giggle and we're back in the schoolroom: a *Backfisch* preparing for her first dance . . .'

'I *never* giggle,' I said sternly, unbuttoning my gloves.

We had supper in a panelled room, served by Hatschek and watched by the heads of about four hundred chamoix on the wall. As we finished our meal it began to rain, but my suggestion that we should now go out and smell the fragrance of the woods was badly received.

'Your hair smells of larches,' said Gernot, 'I've told you before . . . So there's not the slightest need to go plodding about in the rain.'

In the bedroom there were more dead chamoix, a stuffed trout under glass and a bearskin. Also a vast and marvellously solid bed.

I disappeared into the dressing room, took off my clothes, put on the nightdress.

'Ah, delightful!' said Gernot, surveying me through his monocle. 'Might one ask why you have dressed again?'

'It's because we have a whole night. I'm establishing permanence . . . status.'

A mistake. The bleak, closed look came over his face. The furrows made by Macedonia and Serbia and the idiocies of the General Staff deepened on his brow. 'That's why I'll be consigned to hell – because I didn't force you to leave me. You could be a happily married matron with a cupboard full of nightdresses.'

'But not like this one.' It was high-necked, long-sleeved, exceedingly demure; it was just that the material was not very thick. I walked into his arms, fashioned my hair into a tent for us both . . . 'You know I like it best like this; I like having to re-create our love afresh each time. I like being on my mettle.'

A lie, but a good one. And that's so odd – these lies that feel so right. Laura Sultzer never lies, so I suppose she is good and Alice and I are bad. As though we wouldn't change it in an instant – all the glamour, the 'romance' of being a mistress for the humdrum and honourable job of being a wife.

I asked after Elise.

'She's in Aix. An oto-laryngological complaint has been diagnosed.'

I have never discovered what, if anything, ails Gernot's frail and high-born wife. Only a slight dryness in his tone when he speaks of her wanderings betrays Gernot's possible doubts – but as far as I am concerned she should pursue her health with the utmost rigour and determination. Let her hang from stilts in the lake at Balaton and let the jets of water play over her pale, thin legs; let her emerge from the baths at Ischl powdered in salt. May she walk up and down the pump room in Marienbad sipping her sulphur water – and may she soothe herself afterwards with waltzes and cream cakes, for when she is absent I can see Gernot.

'And your daughter?'

'There is hope of an engagement to a whiskery young man in the Diplomatic Corps. Myself, I doubt if he'll come up to scratch, but Elise is working on it.'

My lover's fatherhood is a frail plant. He now indicated that he was no longer prepared to discuss his wife and daughter and we retired to bed.

Outside the wind was freshening; the scent of wet earth came to us through the open window.

How good love tastes in the country!

It was in a place very like this that I first met Gernot. Though 'met' is not quite the right word. I was somewhat mad, walking – sodden – through the countryside and slightly off course for the Danube.

At one level of my mind I must have known that throwing yourself into the Danube is not a good idea: the currents are unreliable, the bridges full of policemen and drunks. But it was the day I had seen my daughter playing under the walnut tree and left her and I wasn't particular about ways and means; I just wanted to get away from the pain. So I started walking.

I never went back to the pension in Salzburg to pick up my case. Wearing only a light cloak and carrying the doll in her box, I set off down a long dusty road, across a stream, blundered along footpaths – and found myself in a neighbouring valley.

Here there was a lake and I stopped to throw the doll into the water. I watched her float and bob in her plaid travelling suit, losing her tam-o-shanter before she sank at last into the reeds. After her, I threw the red evening cape, the lace-trimmed skirts, the blouses, Alice's pretty fragile hats.

But not myself. With the obstinacy of the deranged I had fixed my mind on the Danube and I trudged on in what I believed was the direction of the city.

By nightfall I was in a wood and it had begun to rain. I found a forester's hut and lay there for a few hours, and then I stumbled on again. The rain had grown heavier; my hair was streaming, my cloak torn.

By midday my legs simply stopped working and I sank down against a tree. What happened next was that someone tried to shoot me. Not deliberately; he was aiming at a boar. I had collapsed in the grounds of Count Osterhofen's shooting box in which Gernot (reluctantly because the sport was poor and the Count stupid) was staying for informal discussions on some point of foreign policy.

But I didn't see him then. I came round to find a soldier in the rough grey of a corporal's field uniform staring down at me. A round face, huge ears . . . and for the first time – bringing me back to consciousness – the smell of the raw onions that Corporal Hatschek loved to chew.

The dogs were called off. Huntsmen in green hats arrived. A litter was fetched. I hadn't in fact been hit, but no one believed I could walk.

The Count, fair and moon-faced, looked concerned. 'Such a beautiful girl to come to this,' he kept saying. It was generally assumed that I was either dead or deaf.

Then a grim-faced, clean-shaven man, thin to the point of emaciation, appeared and took charge of the operation. He wore a loden coat but his superior rank and authority were evident at once.

I was carried into the house – a gloomy place surrounded by trees – and up to a bedroom. Warming pans were brought; the housekeeper removed my clothes.

'She's not a common girl, look at those underclothes,' she said to the maid.

They brought me hot soup which I drank. Then a doctor came with a syringe. Although I was supposedly about to end my life, I minded the prick of the needle.

I woke the next morning in a clean nightgown, my hair brushed. I had a memory – or was it a dream? – of a thin, grim-faced man coming in once with a candle.

All that day they questioned me: the housekeeper, the doctor, and the fair-haired Count who owned the house, but I shook my head and would tell them nothing. I knew that if once I began to speak I couldn't stop, and I thought, too, that if I spoke I would realize afresh what I had done: parted for ever from the only person I could really love.

On the second day I tried to get up, and looked for my clothes which they had taken. It was then that they sent for Gernot von Lindenberg.

'You can leave when we know of your circumstances,' he said. 'That you have a home to go to and people to care for you.'

'I have a place to live. And a job. At least I had.'

'Very well. My servant goes to Vienna tomorrow with some papers. He will escort you – but first you must tell me how you came here in this condition.'

'No.'

'Yes.'

He then introduced himself formally, giving himself his full rank and title. 'So you will be aware that anything you say to me will by treated in the strictest confidence.'

'Please don't make me . . . It would be of no interest . . .'

'You are mistaken.'

He sat there some way from the bed in a hard-backed chair and waited. Just waited.

I held out a long time. The clock ticked, the wind blew and rattled the shutters and still he sat there. Midnight struck . . . Then suddenly I began to talk.

Strange, that. The strangest thing of all, almost, that to this austere, grim-looking man whom I had never set eyes on before and never expected to see again, I gave the whole story of my daughter's birth, her loss, the agony and depressions . . . the sudden hope and joy as I realized I could care for her. I told him things I could scarcely remember myself: the woman in the next bed in the House of Refuge saying, 'Her skin is the colour of apricots'.

I told him about Sappho who had chided her daughter for anticipating grief, and how every child I'd seen for six long years had been her: every little girl bowling her hoop in the park, every waif in a painting looking out of the canvas at the world.

By now I was crying so much that I don't know how he

understood me, but he seemed to. Then I told him about what happened three days ago. How I'd seen her and she was everything I'd dreamed of . . . and how I let her go.

'You acted rightly.'

The quiet words goaded me into a rage that almost transcended my wretchedness. 'Do you think I care? Do you think that helps?'

He didn't answer. Then he said something so strange that at first I thought I'd misheard. 'I envy you.'

That stopped me. '*What?*'

His head was turned away from me towards the one candle that burnt in the room. 'I had a son. He died when he was five months old. He *died,* but I did not grieve as you grieve now.' Then in an entirely different voice: 'Tomorrow you may go home – on one condition.'

'What is that?'

'You know, I'm sure. That you give me your word not to take your life.'

I gave it. I had no wish to spend my days in a hunting lodge shut in by gloomy trees.

The next day Hatschek took me back to Vienna. Even with the Count's excellent horses it was a long drive and Hatschek used it to inform me of the Field Marshal's importance, position and stature. This embraced, of course, his military exploits in places of which I had never heard, and his decorations – but in Hatschek's eyes depended also on more arduous and less spectacular feats. Going without food once for eight days, getting proper horse blankets out of the obstinate bumblers at the Ministry, telling the Archduke Franz Ferdinand where he could put his plots. The Marshal's wife and daughter were scarcely mentioned. Hatschek's passionate loyalty lay only with the man.

When I got back I found that von Lindenberg had done his staff work. Alice knew what had happened and was waiting with a meal. My employer had been told I would be returning to work a few days late. My suitcase had arrived from the pension in Salzburg.

So I resumed my life. The anguish went on, growling away, sometimes suppressed, sometimes getting me by the throat, but as the months passed I could attend to my work and even my pleasures, except on those sudden black days which even now I have not outgrown.

And as the months passed, beneath the anguish there was another and entirely discreditable emotion. Chagrin? Irritation? Surprise? How could the Feldherr von Lindenberg, who had sat by my bed throughout a long night, so entirely forget my presence?

For he made no attempt at all to get in touch with me. A formal inquiry, even a note acknowledging the letter of thanks I sent him would have been appropriate, but he made no reply.

Odd how they can exist side by side: anguish and pique.

Almost a year had passed when a tall, narrow-faced, angular young woman walked into Madame Hermine's shop, and with her a man in his forties dressed in mufti: dark suit, a bowler hat, a monocle.

The young woman was Fräulein Charlotte von Lindenberg and the man her father, the Field Marshal, who (most unaccustomedly as it turned out) had decided to buy her a dress for her birthday.

He seated himself, his daughter consulted with Madame Hermine. Three dresses were brought out.

'You had better see them on the model,' said the Field Marshal.

I had been tidying the racks, keeping my back turned, though I had recognized him at once. Now I was told to go and change.

I came out first in the red silk with the fringed shawl. I'd learnt my job well of course and I knew how important it is to sell the dress, not only to the lady but to the gentleman who pays for it. So I passed carefully and quite close to the Field Marshal, and let him see the low-cut back, and hear the delicious frou-frou of the skirt. The next dress, too, I modelled meticulously, showing the tight-faced daughter how, if one picked up the skirt with the left hand the underskirt glowed a shade lighter, like the inner petals of a delphinium. But of course it was the third dress, the black velvet that he wanted her to have – men always want black velvet. It had a boat neckline and by leaning forward I was able to show her (and a little also to show the gentleman who was paying) how it was cut exactly to the point where you could see the swell of the breasts begin. Not that she had breasts, poor girl, but that was not my fault.

She chose the black. Madame Hermine was pleased – it was the most expensive. The next morning Hatschek came for the first time with a note inviting me to supper at the Bristol.

Did I know that first time? I don't know . . . yes, of course I knew. Not the full extent, but . . . yes, I knew. My satisfaction at my successful seduction technique was, however, short lived.

'I decided to give you a year,' said the Field Marshal, walking naked to a painting of the Archduke Franz Ferdinand and turning it to the wall. 'I didn't want to take advantage of your state and so on. But then I decided nine months was enough. I'm going to buy a dress like that for you. It's wasted on my daughter.'

'No. I don't want presents. Not from you.'

Later he repeated that strange thing he'd said in the shooting box. 'You can't imagine how I envied you when you lay there so wild and distraught and desperate.'

'*Envied* me?'

He sat down beside me and pushed the hair from my face.

'To have felt anything so intensely, so utterly. To be so open to sorrow. I've never felt anything like that, Susanna. It's what we all want, to be entirely open to life.'

And under the sheet my toes curled with happiness because he'd said my name.

I have just met Rudi Sultzer and somehow I can't get him out of my mind.

Laura's court case came up today. She was fined five hundred kronen and ordered to keep away from the university in the future. Everyone says if it hadn't been for her husband's standing in the profession, the penalties would have been much more severe.

Needless to say the Group regards the outcome as a personal triumph for Laura. They were all on the steps of the courtroom as she came sweeping out, dressed to kill in a belted calico sack with which the lady who does Croatian cross-stitch had clearly had her way – and taking no notice of Rudi and the lawyers who had conductcd her defence, they bore their whiskery heroine away.

I had been to see one of my outworkers who lives round the corner from the courtroom, and drew level with the building just as Rudi and his colleagues took leave of each other and he was left alone at the bottom of the steps.

I did not expect him to recognize me. I'd met him once at Alice's, at the beginning of their relationship, when I called in unexpectedly, not knowing yet which were his 'days'. He was sitting in his shirt sleeves, his hair rumpled, unabashed but a little shy, and the happiness he had just experienced was in his face.

Now, eight years later, I was shocked by his appearance. He was stooped, his suit seemed to be too big for him; he looked as weary as a man of eighty. Then he raised his hat, greeted me by name – and smiled.

The effect was extraordinary. The mischief, the sense of fun that Alice so loved in him were instantly there. Behind the gold-rimmed pince-nez the blue eyes were alert and amused.

'The corset was successful?' he inquired.

'Very successful.'

'My daughter admires you tremendously. I must thank you for your kindness to her.'

He had replaced his hat, we were about to separate when, moved by some extraordinary impulse, I laid my hand on his arm.

'I'm so glad that Alice has you,' I said. 'So terribly glad!'

As soon as I had spoken I was aghast. I have always kept silence about Alice's affairs: only perfect discretion has made our friendship possible, and now in a public place in broad daylight I had made this highly personal remark.

But Rudi Sultzer had ceased to be Atlas. His shoulders straightened and he looked at me with a quite extraordinary gratitude as though I had given him a marvellous and unexpected present.

Then very distinctly, he said: 'She is my only happiness.'

*

It was a mistake to take Sigismund across to the churchyard, I see that now. Tonight I came in late and found a bunch of flowers on my doorstep.

The bunch was small and not in its first youth, and I recognized the piece of string with which it was tied. I'd last seen it round Sigismund's neck supporting his crucifix. I recognized the flowers too: three withered geraniums from the grave of the Family Steiner, a spray of lilies, somewhat slimy at the stem, from the urn on the grave of the Family Heinrid, an acrid-smelling aster from the wreath of a recently interred councillor and (already quite dead owing to their touching frailty) the harebells that I had pointed out to the child with a particular excitement.

Tomorrow I shall send Nini over with a new ribbon for his crucifix. I'll have a word with Father Anselm too – that impoverished pair across the way have enough problems without a charge of grave robbing!

'Can you smell the limes?' I'd asked the boy when I took him across, and he'd lifted his white face obediently to the dark bole of the tree and sucked in air like someone taking medicine.

From where inside him does he make his music, this sad, old child? Can you be a musician without being a person? Is there no one in this city who can tell me that?

On Sunday the Schumachers asked me for a five o'clock *Jause*. We had it in the garden under the lime tree which grows in the churchyard, but leans over the wall to shade their lawn. Mitzi, all by herself, had made vanilla kipferl and there were linzer schnitten and an iced and marbled gug'lhupf.

The little girls had changed out of the muslins they wore for church and romped in their pinafores, but however busy they were with their games the four eldest came back again and again, like members of the Imperial Guard, to surround the canopied perambulator in which the newest Schumacher lay in state.

'Alfred is completely besotted by her,' said Frau Schumacher, pouring chocolate for me into a rose-sprigged cup. 'He insisted on that pram and you wouldn't believe what it cost. It's English – a Silver Cross.'

'Well, she's a bit special, you must admit,' I said. 'Those eyebrows!'

Helene's face softened at my praise. 'Yes, and she's so *funny*! So dictatorial! If you take the bottle away from her she gives you such a *look*! But Albert really has no sense – it's a wonder she isn't sick the whole day long the way he jiggles her and rocks her and tickles her stomach. And he's invited practically the whole of Vienna to the christening.'

'When is it to be?'

'On the twentieth of August. Albert wants to get it over before he goes to fetch his brother's boy from Graz.' Her voice had taken on a sombre note, for the goldfish slayer was to join the household early in September. Then she laid a hand on my arm. 'I won't press you again, but if you ever feel like changing your mind, there's no one we would rather have for a godmother, you know that.'

'Thank you . . . I'm very touched, Helene, but—'

'That's all right, my dear. I don't want to pry into your feelings. I just thought I'd tell you that we still feel the same as we did when Gisi and Kati were born.'

Oh, why can't I? Why not for this baby who surely will have enough to bear? My daughter is eighteen years old: if I had ever 'had' her I would now be learning to let her go. And yet I still can't, even in this formal and ritualized way, be a mother to anybody else.

'What is she to be called?' I asked. 'Have you decided?'

Helene smiled as at an excellent joke she was about to share. Then she called to her girls: 'Mitzi! Franzi! Steffi! Resi! Come here!'

The four eldest came at once.

'Tell Frau Susanna what names Papa likes for the baby.' Her plainly named Viennese daughters began to giggle.

'Donatella,' said Mitzi.

'Galatea,' said Franzi.

'Leonarda,' whispered the shy and ravishing Steffi.

'Graziella,' said Resi.

'But which?' I asked. 'Which one is she to have?'

'All of them!' cried the children in chorus. 'Every single one!'

'He went to the Kunsthistorisches Museum with a notebook,' said Frau Schumacher, shaking her head. 'He spent all Sunday there looking for inspiration.'

'Well, he certainly seems to have found it,' I said.

Later I took Frau Schumacher to the shop to choose material for a summer dress. Mitzi had gone to play with Maia who was spending Sunday with her grandfather, and it wasn't long before we heard Maia's bossy voice coming over the courtyard wall.

'We're going to make a yurt. We're in the middle of the Gobi desert on our camels and we've missed the oasis so we have to camp here.'

'Can we make a fire and cook something nice?' begged Mitzi.

'No, of course we can't! We have to crouch inside and chew raw yak meat. There's going to be a terrible sandstorm – a fire would blow out straight away.'

'That Maia!' snorted Helene. 'Last week she wanted Mitzi to be an Inca and sacrifice a llama. She's a real bully, that girl.'

A bully, yes, but a visionary too. At Mitzi's age I too would have made yurts.

I have just had the most extraordinary interview with Frau Egger, the wife of the Minister of Planning.

Her cloak is almost finished. She came this afternoon for a final fitting and it looked very nice, but she still wanted the military buttons with the owl's head, the lance and the motto saying *Aggredi*. I can see that in the sight of God it really cannot matter if one of my clients parades down the Ringstrasse labelled *Charge*, but it matters to *me*, and I was about to argue when, to my horror, she clutched my arm and her eyes filled with tears.

'Please, Frau Susanna . . . could I speak to you for a moment? In private?'

I tried to refuse. Nini was out at the lacemaker's, but I was in no doubt that it was Lily from the post office that was on Frau Egger's mind.

'I know you're busy,' she went on, 'but I won't keep you and I'm desperate. I'm simply desperate!'

With considerable reluctance I took her up to my sitting room and fetched the bottle of eau de vie I keep for special customers.

'I shouldn't, I know,' she said, draining her glass at a gulp. 'I don't usually drink spirits, but I'm so unhappy and I thought if I can't speak to the Anarchist girl myself perhaps you'd ask her to give a message to Lily?'

'Frau Egger, I honestly don't think you have anything to worry about. I'm sure that—'

'Oh, but I do, I do. You don't understand, I have *everything* to worry about.'

She held out her glass with a trembling hand and I filled it again, but with misgivings. My eau de vie is made by Gretl's uncle who owns an orchard in Bregenz, and consists of almost neat spirit through which an apricot or two has briefly passed.

Frau Egger was really crying now, grinding her handkerchief into her eyes.

'It's dreadful, quite dreadful. I'm in despair.'

I made another attempt to console her. 'Nini *assures* me that Lily is no longer interested in your husband. She has given him up.'

'I know! I *know* she's given him up, that's what's so terrible! My cook's sister-in-law works as a chambermaid in the Hotel Post where my husband used to take Lily. The walls are very thin and she heard Lily tell my husband that she didn't want to see him any more because I was a good woman. "Your wife is a good woman", she heard Lily say, "she takes soup to the poor and I don't want to hurt her any more". But I'm *not* a good woman, Frau Susanna. I only take soup to the poor because the cook always makes too much and really there's not a lot you can do with soup. If your girl told Lily that, would she take my husband back, do you think?'

'Frau Egger, I don't honestly think Nini could tell her that.'

'Oh, but she must! She must! She must implore Lily not to give him up. And if she could tell Lily that he expects all sorts of advancements after the November elections. Ennoblement is not out of the question.'

She gulped down her second glass of spirits and, fumbling about in her reticule, pulled out a very pretty gold-link chain.

'My husband is not very generous,' she said. 'Men don't often think of these things but if the bomb-throwing girl could give this to Lily . . . just to show her that I really don't mind. That all I desire is my husband's happiness. There's a bracelet that goes with it if she wanted it.'

I was by now extremely harrowed, but it seemed necessary to bring the poor woman down to earth.

'I really don't think it would work.'

'Oh, but it must work. It must!' Before I could stop her she had reached for the bottle and poured out a third glass of brandy and tipped it down her throat. 'Of course if it's not that . . . if it's not me being good, and the soup . . . I mean, if it's my husband's Little Habit, then she must tell Lily that one gets used to it. Really. Well, almost.'

I removed the bottle and put it away in the cupboard, but it was too late. Frau Egger was now definitely drunk and the marital despair of a lifetime poured from her.

'You see, it's all right for you, Frau Susanna. You're beautiful and I don't suppose you've ever had to . . . not year in, year out, with someone you don't like. And of course my parents said I was lucky when Egger asked me. He appeared from nowhere and Father helped him get a job as a clerk in the Ministry – and I was on the shelf. But I didn't realize how it would go on and on . . . Every Tuesday and Friday after lunch it has to be. His doctor told him twice a week is the right amount and everything Willibald does is as regular as clockwork. While I thought there might be children I could bear it but now I don't know what to do. If I say "Let's do it in the dark", he says, "Come, Adelheid, you're not as ugly as *that*" – but of course that's not what I mean. It used to be easier because we had such an excellent organ grinder down in the street.

A real musician. I used to pay him to come and play under the window in the afternoons when Willibald was home. Strauss waltzes mostly. I could manage while he played Strauss. Johann, of course . . . and Josef too. Not Eduard so much; Eduard's waltzes are too sad. But of course the neighbours didn't like it and then the organ grinder went away.'

Frau Egger blew her nose and looked round for more brandy, but in vain.

'Then he took up with Lily . . . Oh, it was wonderful; you can't believe it, Frau Susanna! For months he didn't come near me and he was almost good-tempered. It was like being born again. I started embroidering a footstool cover in *petit point*. I used to love embroidery when I was a girl, but after my marriage I couldn't seem to settle down to it. And now it's all over and there he is again with his white stomach and his Habit. I should have known,' she wailed, beginning to cry again, 'I should have known that nothing good could ever happen to me.'

As a result of this conversation I have decided to be noble. Frau Egger shall have her buttons. Let no one say that I put my professional reputation before compassion to a deeply stricken soul.

July

Last Sunday Herr Huber took us on an outing to Linz to show us the villa he is buying for Magdalena, and to introduce his fiancée to his two sisters, maiden ladies who have an apartment on the ground floor of his old house beside the Danube.

I have always been fond of Linz: a splendidly solid town where the walls always seem thicker than anywhere else, the beds more solid, the pretzels on the café tables larger. It seemed to me absolutely right that Herr Huber's empire should have its centre there.

'I would be most grateful for your company,' Herr Huber had said to me. 'You have such excellent taste and Fraulein Winter is so young. There are decisions to be made about the furnishings and I don't want to burden her.'

Alice too had been invited, but a mentally defective producer had decided to put four live Lipizzaners into *Wienerblut*, which meant extra rehearsals, and it was Magdalena, Edith and myself who set off at daybreak in the butcher's car.

Magdalena, disdaining a motoring veil, sat beside her fiancé, her hair a considerable driving hazard, but there was one most encouraging sign. On her lap she held a large brown parcel securely tied with string.

'It's a present for the house,' she volunteered – and at her words a look of the purest joy passed over the butcher's face.

We stopped for the *Gabelfrühstuck* without which Herr Huber would not have expected to get through the morning, and by midday had reached the villa, twelve miles out of Linz, which was to be Magdalena's home.

It stood alone in a copse of evergreens. Built by a master

builder for his own use, it was adorned by no less than three pepper-pot towers, any number of gables, a porch and a conservatory. In the garden, which was of the romantic kind containing nothing that is edible, we could make out, between two dark cypresses, a bird table with fretwork eaves and elaborately carved legs.

The house had just been vacated by the workmen; ladders still stood about; there was a smell of new paint.

'Well, my dear, do you like it?' said Herr Huber. He never touches his fiancée, but the tenderness in his voice is overwhelming.

'Very nice,' said Magdalena.

She thought the Bohemian chandelier he had installed in the hallway was 'very nice' too, and that he should do exactly as he liked about bringing the drawing room carpet from his house in Linz. Her knee-length hair in ravishing disarray after the drive, still clutching the parcel which she made no attempt to unpack, Magdalena wandered through the empty rooms, as patently uninterested in her new home as she had been in her wedding clothes.

In the dining room I took pity on Herr Huber. The notebook he had brought to write down his bride's suggestions remained empty; the lines on his forehead increasingly resembled those of a bloodhound who has lost the scent.

'I must say, I think a French chintz in maize or dark honey would look lovely in those windows. Swagged, and with a fan edging . . . and the material repeated in the upholstery of the chairs. With a pale grass-cloth on the walls you'd bring the sunshine right into the room.'

I babbled my way through into the study, offering wine-coloured velvet to offset the mahogany panelling, and we went upstairs, Magdalena still carrying the parcel about whose contents I became increasingly curious. A favourite vase? A clock inherited from the army officer? And what was delaying her? Surely a housewarming present should be unpacked at once?

In the first of the spare bedrooms I became quite carried away, suggesting a Dutch look to match the blue and white tiles on the stove; in the second I effortlessly conjured up an Indian bower with parrots on the wall and curtains of printed cotton from Rajasthan.

In the master bedroom, however, with its window looking out on to the lawn and the bird table framed in dark trees, my inspiration faltered. It was possible to imagine anything except the Hubers' bridal night.

But my sudden silence didn't matter, for it now became evident that Magdalena was nowhere to be seen.

'She's gone outside,' said the Bluestocking with a nervous gulp.

'I expect it was the smell of the paint,' I said quickly, seeing Herr Huber's face. 'New paint often makes people feel unwell.'

We followed her out into the garden.

'Look, she's over there by the bird table,' said Edith. 'And she's taken the parcel.'

Not knowing whether Magdalena wanted to be alone, we hesitated, but at that moment she turned, her hair rippling in the light, and beckoned to us with a friendly, almost welcoming gesture, and we set off across the lawn.

I should have known, of course. It wasn't a bird table, it was a religious shrine, a crucifix hanging from the fretwork eaves. And Magdalena had unpacked her parcel.

'Look!' she said, and pointed to the figure she had released from its wrappings and placed between two candlesticks. Not Saint Lucy with her gouged-out eyes, not the breastless Saint Agatha . . . Quite a cheerful-looking saint and one that was new to me. The bald Saint Proscutea who had shaved off her hair to avoid marriage to a heathen, and wore on her waxen pate a slightly rakish wreath of thorns.

In her own way Magdalena had taken possession of her future home, and I was very much relieved.

Herr Huber's old house in Linz was a very different affair. Solid, old-fashioned, with a verandah that ran the length of the first floor, it stood right on the towpath, square to the river, with a garden full of fruit trees and vegetables at the back. As he led us upstairs and out on to the balcony we could lean out and almost touch the horses as they pulled the heavy barges along, watch the tugs hoot on the wide grey river, or look across to the vineyards and gently rolling hills on the other shore.

'Oh, but it's beautiful, Herr Huber,' said Edith – and proceeded to quote from Goethe. I had, of course, expected this – it was not to be hoped that the Master had failed to pen some lines on the significance of running water and its effect on memory, loss and time. But the ode was short, and when I took her out to look at the garden so as to give Herr Huber some time alone with his fiancée, I found the Bluestocking's thoughts surprisingly similar to mine.

'I was wondering whether Magdalena wouldn't be happier here than in the villa,' she said. 'I mean, it's so friendly here and there's always something to look at . . . the river and the towpath, and the town all around one. So safe . . .'

'Yes, I wondered the same thing, especially as he can't sell the house anyway because of his sisters. But Herr Huber thinks that Magdalena shouldn't be so close to his factory – those are the chimneys over there. And the slaughterhouse is just across the road on the other side of the landing stage.'

'Well, of course, slaughterhouses are wicked,' said Laura Sultzer's daughter dutifully. 'But it does mean he would be able to get home in the middle of the day; she'd see him more.'

'If that's what she wants.'

Edith threw me a startled look. 'Oh, surely; he's so terribly *kind*.'

We returned to the house to get ready for lunch which we were to take with Herr Huber's sisters in their apartments on the ground floor.

'I wanted to order a meal for us all at the Ferry Hotel – they keep an excellent table, but I couldn't disappoint my sisters,' said Herr Huber.

And indeed the man who could have disappointed the Fräulein Hubers would have had to be made of steel. Much older than their brother, frail, and beautifully dressed in the bonnets and shawls of forty years ago, they welcomed us with twitters of intense friend-liness. Fräulein Marianne, the elder of the two, was very deaf and carried an ivory ear trumpet; Fräulein Louisa, who was only slightly deaf, acted as her sister's conduit to the world.

While Marianne made sure that no draughts, on this hot sum-mer's day, had pierced the double walls of their drawing room to trouble us, that the chairs we sat in were to our liking, Louisa ran back and forth from the kitchen to confer with the cook – and presently we were led to the table.

Sunday lunch in Linz is a serious matter. It was clear that this occasion had been the topic of conversation for weeks past. The lace tablecloth was exquisite, the gold-rimmed Meissen dinner service a family heirloom.

Grace was said and the first course passed without incident. An erbsen suppe made with fresh garden peas, in which griess knockerl floated, served with croutons of bread deep fried in butter.

Then came the entrée.

'We did think of a roast goose – we have one just ready to be killed and beautifully plump,' said Fräulein Louisa, 'but then we thought coming from Vienna you'd like something that's special to Linz.'

The cook now arrived with a gigantic, steaming platter. As it was set down the sisters looked anxiously at Herr Huber who scrutinized its contents, gave a nod of approval, and tucked his napkin more securely into his collar.

This hurdle safely over, the ladies beamed at us.

'A Linzerschmankerl!' said Fräulein Louisa. 'You won't find it anywhere else.'

I found this easy to believe. In the centre of the dish was a piled-up circle of rindfiletspitzen, the marbled flesh enveloped, but not obscured by a rich dark sauce. Then came a ring of kidneys, each embedded in its halo of perfectly roasted fat. Moving out-wards one came to the rolled-up slivers of ox tongue, alternating with sawn-off segments of thigh bone filled with dollops of creamy marrowfat – and after that stretching away in concentric circles, the roast potatoes, the semmel knodel, the rings of onion fried to the colour of caramel.

Each one of us was now served. Horse radish was handed separately, as was the red currant jelly, the spinach, the crusty bread . . .

'Oh, dear!' The exclamation, quiet and desperate, came from Edith Sultzer.

I had quite forgotten; so had Herr Huber. Both of us were speechless, and it was Magdalena who lifted her head and said calmly:

'Edith never eats meat. She is a vegetarian.'

An assassin leaping through the window with a revolver could not have caused more distress! By the doorway, the cook covered her face with a plump hand and as Fräulein Louisa yelled the dreadful information into Fräulein Marianne's ear trumpet, the ladies fell into a litany of self reproach.

'How foolish of us!'

'We should have asked!'

'We're so out of touch here, you see.'

'I could make an eierspeise,' said the cook.

But at the thought of feeding a valued guest on scrambled eggs, the ladies plunged into even deeper distress. Topfen Palatschinken were mooted, a spinach roll . . .

I now decided to intervene.

'Fräulein Sultzer,' I said, laying a hand on Edith's arm, 'I have long been meaning to speak to you on the subject of your diet. In my view you are seriously anaemic; I'm experienced in such things and I assure you that there are signs. If you could force yourself to swallow just a few mouthfuls of meat – if you could overcome your disgust – I'm absolutely certain that you would feel the benefit.'

The butcher, who had risen to console his sisters, sat down again. 'It is true, you know,' he said in his deep, comfortable voice. 'It is red meat that makes good blood.'

'Oh, but I couldn't . . . My mother . . .'

'Your mother's vegetarianism is noble,' I said firmly. 'We

honour her for it. But sometimes a principle has to yield to expediency. After all, you have your work to think of. The Plotzenheimer prize and *Beowulf*. You have no *right* to let yourself get run down.'

'Perhaps just a mouthful of the Filetspitz?' suggested Herr Huber. 'There's nothing to distress you in a filet; it's a very calm meat, that. You needn't finish it.'

Edith's anxious, myopic eyes went back and forth between us. 'Well, perhaps . . . if you think . . . if it's for my work.'

She took up her knife and fork, cut off a piece of filet, put it in her mouth. Herr Huber was right; there wasn't anything to distress her, and she swallowed it, speared another piece, and swallowed that also. When the filet had gone she looked surprised and began on the kidney, and this too proved undistressing for she finished it, embedding fat and all. Her spectacles steamed up, a flush appeared on her face, and she turned her attention to the rolled-up slivers of ox tongue . . .

There is nothing like a narrowly averted disaster for making a party go with a swing. As Edith began to scoop the marrow from the bones, the ladies laughed and clapped their hands, enchanted to have saved a soul from the perils of inanition; Herr Huber told stories of his early days; the wine flowed . . .

We returned to Vienna by train. When Herr Huber, who had business to attend to in Linz, dropped us on the station platform, loaded with baskets of flowers and fruit which the sisters had insisted on picking for us, Edith thanked him with such warmth that he was quite embarrassed.

'Na, na,' he said. 'Linz isn't like Vienna. No one's intellectual here. My sisters almost never read a book.'

'But they were so kind,' said Edith. 'So terribly kind. I liked them so *much*.'

As the train drew away, it was the Bluestocking who leant out of the window and waved, while the lovely Magdalena sat back in her seat and closed her eyes.

*

Alice has great plans for her summer idyll with Rudi. She is cleaning the flat from top to toe and has made an extra-thick cover to put over her canary so that Rudi can sleep in the day if he wants to – and she is going to cook.

'Seriously, I mean, Sanna. Proper health-giving things. Egg custard . . . and brawn and things like that to build him up.'

We decided to go to a new department store, which stays open in the lunch hour, to buy saucepans.

'Those double ones with water underneath because I do find it difficult to remember what's on the stove when I'm with him.'

And we did indeed set off, but unfortunately we entered the store through the lingerie department where Alice came face to face with a French slip in pale blue lace which was so obviously the thing to wear while cooking egg custard that it would have been absurd not to buy it.

'Oh dear, I do feel guilty,' she said as we came out. 'But he really likes me in blue and I can always put a bowl over an ordinary saucepan, can't I?'

I left her at the turning to the Kohlmarkt and went on down the Graben – where I ran straight into Frau Egger. She was wearing the cloak I had made for her – and the horn buttons I had originally suggested!

'Oh that's much better, Frau Egger. But why did you change them?'

She looked furtively about her. 'It was my husband,' she said, lowering her voice. 'He was so angry, you wouldn't believe it! It seems the buttons I found were very rare; they're from an early British regiment before the Napoleonic wars, even. They ought to be in a museum, he said.'

'I didn't know he was an expert in such things.'

'No, I didn't either. But then, there's not much one knows about men, is there? He particularly asked if I'd got all the buttons back from you. But I did, didn't I?'

I nodded and took my leave. As a matter of fact one of the buttons had rolled under Gretl's machine when she knocked over the box and we'd found it two days ago. But I didn't feel I deserved another visit from the poor sheep and anyway I was curious. Who was right: the Countess von Metz or Herr Egger?

Gernot could have found out for me – but the summer manoeuvres are upon us and heaven knows when I shall see him.

Tonight Sigismund came out into the square and stood by the fountain as usual. I waved from the window, but I had a lot to do and I didn't go down. Usually he stands there for a quarter of an hour or so, but tonight he was still there after half an hour, after three quarters of an hour, just looking up at the window. At nine o'clock he still stood there, and at nine thirty . . .

I was angry by the time I reached him, but not for long. In the hot summer night he was shivering as if frozen to the marrow.

I knelt down beside him. He's nearly eleven years old, but a head shorter than an Austrian child of that age. 'What is it, Sigismund? Are you ill?'

He shook his head.

'Come, tell me. Are you frightened?'

A half nod. I wondered if his uncle had been beating him again. But it wasn't that: his uncle was missing. He hadn't returned home.

'It's not so late, my dear. He'll come.'

The child shook his head – a slow movement to and fro, like an ancient soothsayer's. Then in that husky, scarcely audible voice, he murmured something that I didn't catch.

'What, Sigismund? What did you say?'

He moistened his lips and repeated the word.

'Cossacks,' he whispered. 'The Cossacks have got him.'

Oh, God, what was this?

'Nonsense,' I said briskly. 'There aren't any Cossacks in Vienna. I tell you what, we'll go and sit on Joseph's terrace and have a cup of hot chocolate. Then you can watch out for him and before we've finished, there he'll be.'

I took his hand which grasped mine like a vice. On the crowded terrace where people were enjoying the warm dusk there was one free table.

'Would you like a cake? A piece of strudel or an Indianerkrapfen?'

He repeated 'Indianerkrapfen' though I'm not sure he knew what it was, but when I ordered only one he frowned. 'Will you eat a cake?'

'No, Sigismund. I'll just have chocolate.'

'Then I will not have a cake either.'

I don't know where he got his idea of etiquette from but it was very deep. I ordered two eclairs and he ate his without skill, getting cream on his face – but always watching, watching . . . My face, then the street for his uncle, then my face again.

'Where did your uncle go, Sigismund?'

'To find someone who will give me a concert. If I can play in a recital then I can make some money for the rent and perhaps have some lessons. My uncle can't teach me any more.'

It seemed a forlorn hope that anyone in this city of aspiring prodigies would offer a concert to this ill-kept child.

'He goes every day, but no one will hear me.'

I don't know what I would have done if his uncle hadn't come. Would I have taken the boy home, bringing at last a smile to the face of the irritable angel on her cloud? Probably not. I'd have knocked up the loathsome concierge and told her to mind the child while I went for the police.

At all events he came just as we had finished: a pathetic, dusty figure, his gaunt face creased with exhaustion.

I cut short his thanks and asked Joseph to bring him a glass of wine and an omelette – and when he had eaten he sent Sigismund to bed and told me his story.

Sitting opposite me with his melancholy side whiskers and unwholesome breath, Jan Kraszinsky was not an appealing character, yet as he spoke I felt pity for him for he had been forced by others – by his sister's idealism, his nephew's talent – to leave his native land, his job, the security he craved.

It began in Preszowice. Sigismund's uncle pronounced the name of this obscure place on the borders of Russian Poland with a deep hunger: a straggling row of houses on a white dust road, a church . . . a school.

His parents worked a smallholding outside the little town, but Jan wanted to get away from the bleakness of the land, the frost-bitten turnips . . . He wanted a white-collar job, safety – and after his parents' death he found it as caretaker of the Preszowice school.

'It was a good position. I had my own little brick house in the schoolyard and a woman came to cook my meals.'

Jan had a younger sister, Ilona, whose ambitions were very different.

'She was beautiful. You wouldn't think it to look at the boy, but she was. She had red hair and a fine singing voice.'

Ilona went to Warsaw. Soon she was working in cabaret, and carried along on the tide of the Polish Freedom movement.

'How I hate all those words,' said Kraszinsky, sipping his wine. 'Freedom, Unity, Liberation . . . To me they mean only one thing: people lying in their blood, corpses hanging on gibbets . . . death.'

At a concert ('Chopin, of course,' said Kraszinsky bitterly) Ilona met a young music student who was deeply involved in Pilsudski's plans for an uprising against the Russians. They fell in love, went to live together, and Sigismund was born. But Ilona's lover couldn't keep out of politics. Twice he was arrested and released. Then in 1905 came Pilsudski's revolution, its failure – and the dreadful retribution of the Russians.

With her lover, two other Polish patriots and the four-year-old Sigismund, Ilona fled back over the border to Galicia. One night she arrived with the child and asked Kraszinsky to hide the insurgents in Preszowice.

Sigismund's uncle shrugged with the ingrained despair of the Slavs. 'Where do you hide someone in Preszowice? To cross a road is to meet three people who ask you where you are going.'

Ilona had left her lover and his friends in the forest. Now as her brother remonstrated with her she said: 'Take the boy, then; I beg of you. Take him and I'll come back for him as soon as we've found somewhere to go.'

'What could I do?' asked Kraszinsky now. 'She was my sister.' He paused to dab his eyes with a dirty handkerchief. She put the child down and went out through the back of the school, through the maize fields to find the others who were hiding. But the boy followed her. Later I found him gone. He was so small – as small as a beetle – but he followed her.' He looked down at his glass. 'It shouldn't have happened. The Russians had no right to cross into Austrian territory, but it's all forest to the east of Preszowice, and who is going to tell the Cossacks that they can't ride where they choose? There weren't any shots – they used their sabres – so we didn't know for a while; not till we found the bodies. The boy was sitting by his mother with his knees drawn up – not crying, just waiting. Waiting for her to wake up . . .'

'Oh, God!' It was my turn now to shiver in the heat.

'We don't know how much he saw, but he didn't speak for a year.'

Then the local landowner sent down a piano for the school and Sigismund climbed on to the piano stool . . .

'I tried to give him a violin, I could have helped him better with that, but it was the piano he wanted. When he was away from it he still didn't speak much, but when he was playing he was all right.'

So for the next five years Sigismund sat on the *Encyclopedia of World Art* and played. The villagers brought him sheet music from the market; the schoolmaster taught him a little, and an old Professor from the Lvov Academy of Music gave him some lessons till he fell ill and died. Then last year the people of Preszowice decided to raise what money they could and send the child to Vienna. It was clear from the way Kraszinsky spoke that they, like he, felt no particular pride or pleasure in the child's talent. It was simply something that had to be dealt with, like a multiple birth or a freak harvest.

'And I came with him,' he said now. 'What else could I do?'

I ordered another glass of wine for him. 'Yes,' I said. 'I see. And tonight? What kept you so late?'

'I was trying to get an interview with Van der Velde.'

'The impresario?'

Kraszinsky nodded. 'Meierwitz refused to see me, so did Niklaus. The Dutchman was my last chance. I went to his office but they said he wasn't in, so I went out to his villa in Hitzing. A beautiful place . . . a long drive and high gates with stone pillars. The maid wouldn't let me in – she said he was away from town. But I waited . . . I waited all day by the gates. I thought I would throw myself down on the gravel in front of his automobile, I was so desperate. It was evening before he came and then the chauffeur got out and said he would call the police if I didn't go away.'

'Is that what you want for Sigismund? A concert? Is he ready?'

Kraszinsky shrugged. 'I tried all the music academies at the beginning. Probably it would be best for the boy to be with good teachers and postpone his debut . . . I don't know. But no one would see me there either. If the doorman didn't throw me out it was one of the secretaries. They only see a poor Pole with a foreign accent and funny clothes.' He stretched an arm across the table in a gesture of despair. 'I only want them to hear Sigi. Is it such a crime to want that? Is it so wicked of me to ask it?'

Yes, of course it's wicked. To be talented and still alive in Vienna is unforgivable. Ask Mozart, ask Hugo Wolf . . . Ask Gustav Mahler who died six weeks ago to the unctuous lamentations of the men who hounded him.

But my mind was on something else. On Van der Velde, to be exact. Meierwitz and Niklaus I only knew by their less than savoury reputations, but Van der Velde I had met. Van der Velde I had, in fact, once known quite well.

I decided to go to the opera.

This was nice of me: a sacrifice. It was *Tristan and Isolde*; the last night of the season and the last appearance of the veteran soprano Motte-Ehrlich before her retirement, so all Vienna would be there. Not just the fashionable world, but critics and agents and impresarios.

But if I felt daunted at the prospect of all that darkness and sadness on ramps, there was someone who was pleased. Up there on her cloud, the Polish wraith (now red-haired and not resembling at all Frau Wilkolaz in the paper shop) looked down at me and smiled.

Of the families who had offered me, whenever I cared for it, a place in their box, I selected Peter Konrad and his wife. Konrad owns a large department store in the Mariahilferstrasse with a flourishing dress department. He's always been helpful to me in my work and I thought a little professional gossip in the interval wouldn't come amiss.

'Of course, dearest Susanna,' said Konrad when I telephoned him. 'I'll be enchanted. In fact you've saved my life – Marie has gone on to the Attersee with the children; they've all had chicken pox and needed the mountain air. Being envied by all the men in Vienna will make up for four hours of High Germanic screeching.'

There are not many Wagnerians in the rag trade.

I decided to wear black velvet, cut very low, with a small train, and gardenias in my hair.

'Ah, you mean dressing against the season,' said Nini appreciatively. 'While everyone else is all frothy in muslins and organza.' She paused, eyeing me tentatively. 'And The Necklace?'

I nodded. It was The Necklace which would turn this somewhat banal outfit into a triumph, but the topic is taboo between us. I have told Nini that my diamond necklace is a fake and she has raised her iconoclastic Magyar eyebrows and disbelieved me.

I never wanted presents from Gernot. I don't know why this is – I took them readily enough from my earlier admirers, but when I found out what being in love really meant, I became difficult. I wouldn't let him buy me jewellery or lend me money to start my own shop, and I made my own clothes.

'I don't want any wages of sin,' I said, teasing him, 'I like sin and no one is to pay me for it.'

Not quite true, but my struggles in the confessional were not his business.

'And what of me?' he said furiously. 'Would it hurt you to consider my feelings in the matter?'

But seeing how serious I was he acquiesced. For five years he only bought me flowers. Then one snowy December day a week before Christmas, a messenger arrived with a box from Cartier's in Paris. 'You will accept this,' said the accompanying dictatorial note. 'You will not, please, make me any scenes.'

It was a bad moment. Gernot is not rich; I envisaged a small forest sold, a farm sacrificed. Each time I wear this necklace I am transformed.

Peter Konrad came to collect me. From his startled look before he began to pay the routine compliments I saw that my toilette was effective, and I was glad of it because I had work to do.

We dined first at Sachers and he told me all the gossip of the trade. Chez Jaquetta, I was happy to hear, was borrowing too much, expanding too quickly.

'And you, my dear? You're doing well?'

'Yes. Modestly, but steadily, I think.'

'I'm still annoyed that you wouldn't come and run my dress department. The woman I've got is adequate but you would have made it the place to go.'

'It's nice of you, but I really love my shop, Peter. I don't think I could bear to be anywhere else; it's exactly right for me.'

He was a nice man, old enough to regard me as still young and desirable, but handsome and distinguished with his thick, greying hair and superbly cut clothes.

We entered the foyer of the opera well pleased with each other. Looking round I saw that indeed 'everyone' was there. Princess Stephanie, Rudolf's widow and the plainest woman in the Empire; Hugo von Hofmannsthal; the French Ambassador with his party. I'm good at walking up staircases – models have to be – but as I ascended, smiling at acquaintances, demurely ignoring the stares of potential admirers, I was searching for one man. And just before the bell rang for the first act I saw him.

Klaus van der Velde started life trading tobacco on the quayside in Rotterdam and now trades in sopranos, pianists and string quartets. I'd met him through Alice in the days when I worked in the shop in the Herrengasse and he'd pursued us both, along with most of the other personable females in the city. This was before I'd met Gernot and I was technically available – but not to him. He had a fierce Dutch wife who was reputed to disinfect the marriage bed every time they made love. A square-headed, thickset man; unscrupulous, even brutal – but tender-hearted men don't often become impresarios.

The first act of *Tristan* is long. The tenor staggered, the soprano tottered, and I recalled Motte-Ehrlich's *bon mot*: that the most important thing when singing Isolde is a comfortable pair of shoes.

But the interval came at last.

'Peter, you know Van der Velde?'

'The impresario?'

'Yes. Could we bump into him, do you think?'

'My dear, the way you look tonight we could bump into anybody!'

We struggled to the buffet. Van der Velde had already acquired a Wagnerian stein of beer and was standing with his wife beside a potted palm. As Peter went to procure champagne, he turned and stared unashamedly at the blonde woman in black with gardenias in her hair.

I smiled at him.

The discovery that he knew me pleased him. It pleased his wife rather less, but she followed him as he bent over my hand and tried to think who I was, and more importantly, whether I mattered.

'It's a very long time since we met,' I said. 'Alice and I often speak of you. She's still at the Volksoper. What fun we had at the Landtmann with the Schoflers and all that crowd.'

He now placed me and a flicker of surprise passed over his face for our last encounter, in a fiacre in the Prater had not been particularly friendly. I don't think I actually hit him, it is not often necessary for me to protect my virtue in so drastic a manner, but I may have used my parasol.

'Susanna! My dear, you look *radiant*!' His eyes crawled along my throat, fastened on the necklace. Had I, perhaps, become somebody who mattered?

'I'm a very grand lady now,' I said as Peter came back with my champagne. The respectability of my wealthy escort impressed Van der Velde even more. 'I have my own salon in Madensky Square.'

'Salon' is not a word I often use, but the ambiguity was serviceable.

'And a great success, I'm sure.'

'Yes, a success.' I am not a great whirrer of fans, but I thought a little whirring would not come amiss. 'As a matter of fact I've been expecting to see your auto any day now that we have our little prodigy opposite. I suppose Meierwitz has beaten you to it?'

'Prodigy? What prodigy?' His nostrils twitched with curiosity.

'Oh, a little pianist – a child of nine or so – a waif from Poland. Hardly a Chopin, but friends of mine tell me his Waldstein is remarkable.'

Van der Velde frowned. 'Did you say Meierwitz has heard of him?'

I shrugged. 'I've no idea, but that's the rumour. You know I'm not musical – better not take any notice of anything I say. But come to Madensky Square anyway – I'll make you a beautiful cravat. Excuse me, I must have a word with Count Leitenhof.'

Extremely pleased with myself, I swept away on Peter's arm – and found myself face to face with Gernot.

He was not alone. His wife, the high-born Elise, newly watered in Marienbad, walked on one side of him, his whey-faced daughter on the other. An aide-de-camp hovered . . .

Gernot's face did not alter by one millimetre. The eyes gave no recognition, the mouth remained a tight, uncompromising line. He was in uniform, unutterably distinguished-looking and, I hazarded, extremely bored. Almost tone deaf, he attends the opera strictly in the line of duty.

As we passed each other, I heard the whey-faced daughter saying: 'That woman in black velvet – her face seemed familiar. Didn't she use to model in a shop in the Herrengasse?'

And the voice of the high-born Elise, who should not have been wearing magenta satin with sky-blue lace: 'Anyone can come to the opera these days, we all know that!'

Gernot said nothing.

The second act was almost unendurable. He was here in Vienna and he had not let me know. He sat below me in his box and was as lost to me as if he was on the moon. What idiotic conceit had led me to think that I was ever part of his life? He belonged entirely to those pale haughty women to one of whom he had bequeathed his tight-lipped mouth.

Why didn't it stop, this unbearable screeching? Why didn't the audience storm on to the stage and put an end to this torture? And what a horrible man Wagner was: arrogant, promiscuous, a scrounger.

The second interval. More champagne, more acquaintances, Peter's and mine. The need to smile and be charming and make Peter proud to be with me.

'I would give forty camels for her. Yes, forty camels,' said a guttural foreign voice, and I turned round to see an Arab potentate in splendid robes staring directly at me through a jewelled glass.

And coming towards me, Gernot. He was alone. His wife was talking to the French Ambassador, the daughter was nowhere to be seen. Probably in the lavatory; she looked like a woman who had frequent recourse to toilets.

Only he wasn't coming towards me. He was going to go past me to join the party of the War Minister who had beckoned to him. I simply happened to be there.

As he drew level, he bent down briefly – and straightened to hand me my non-existent handkerchief. Then he said one word – 'Thursday' – and was gone.

We returned to our box for the last act. And how beautiful now was the music, how it purged the soul! And how ridiculous, how utterly absurd it was to criticize the personal life of a transcendent genius like Richard Wagner!

*

'I'm going to challenge him to a duel, of course', were Gernot's first words to me – and my hand went to my heart as I saw him laid out under the birch trees, blood staining the rich earth. 'It goes against the grain, mind you,' he went on. 'A foreigner, and without a commission. But no insult to you shall go unavenged.'

'What insult?'

'Forty camels, indeed! I gather it's the top price in Arabia but it's an insult just the same. Not four hundred, not four thousand camels would buy the smallest of your eyelashes.'

I managed to smile, but my pulse was still racing. Gernot hates duelling, is trying to get it stopped – but I know for a fact that he has fought one duel at least and I can't even bear jokes on the subject.

It was an afternoon meeting. Elise was still in Vienna, in the wing of the old Stoffler Palace which the von Lindenbergs use when they are in town. Gernot had to attend a banquet in the evening and I knew that after today the manoeuvres would claim him so it was important to keep things light. I am, after all, a Woman of Pleasure. But it had opened some frightful door, this image of Gernot stretched out beneath the birches. In my clothes I could smile and chatter, but out of them . . .

'What is it, my treasure? What troubles you?'

'Nothing.' I turned my face to that hollow above his collar bone that God designed especially for me. 'Only, if perhaps today Love could be "Strong as Death"? Or even stronger?'

And it could . . . It was . . .

The monks of Leck swore that the Song of Songs was a paean to Mother Church, but the monks of Leck did not know Gernot!

At half past four I was allowed to sit up and drink a glass of wine.

'Now tell me what you were doing at the opera dressed like Marguerite Gautier and unsettling so many gentlemen?'

I explained; then launched into the saga of Frau Egger and Lily from the post office which I knew would be much to his taste.

'Oh, and I wanted to ask you about those wretched buttons of hers. Her husband swears they're very rare and valuable – from a

British regiment long before Napoleon; he practically tore them off her cloak. But the Countess von Metz said they belonged to the Pressburg Fusiliers who were disbanded in '84. Who is right, do you suppose?'

I got up and fetched the button I had secreted in my purse.

'*Aggredi*,' he said. 'Wait, let me see.' Wearing only his monocle he peered intently at the crest. And then: 'Yes . . . Yes, of course.'

He was silent for some time, his face closed and brooding.

'The Countess is right,' he said. 'Look, leave this with me, will you? And don't say anything to anyone – not to anyone, please.' He put the button away in his cigar case. Then in a voice of outrage: 'What on *earth* are you doing?'

'I'm getting dressed. It's nearly five o'clock, I must go and so must you if you're not going to be late for your banquet.'

'I'm not going to the banquet.'

'Please, Gernot, I don't want you to alter your plans for me. You have your life to lead.'

'I have my *existence* to lead and I lead it. Now, however, I am living my life.' And his face creasing in a rare smile: 'I shall send Hatschek to make my excuses on a snow-white charger like the one you picked out for me at Uferding.'

He never tires of that joke, my Field Marshal!

When I had known Gernot for two years I suddenly realized that I was going to love him for ever. This happened not, as you might expect, during any particular moment of physical ecstasy, but as we sat at luncheon in a country inn and he selected, from a fruit bowl on the table, a pear which he placed on my plate.

I had been given pears and other things by men both younger and better-looking, but as he looked at me – offering the pear, but allowing by the faint lift of his eyebrows that I might reject it if I wished – a gate shut behind me with a perceptible click. The gate led to other relationships, marriage, the whole intensely agreeable world of erotic dalliance.

I confess I was both resentful and shaken, for what can be more conventional than the situation of a personable young dressmaker and her high-born 'protector'? Lightness, skill, good manners, laughter and compatibility are the ingredients of such an affair, and all these we had brought to bear on our relationship. And then he handed me this pear . . .

The first effect of this realization was a violent jealousy. It was not so much other women that I feared, or even his wife. What I was jealous of was quite simply Gernot's unknown life. Perhaps jealousy isn't the right word – I was consumed by a passionate curiosity; a desperate need to know where he lived, what paths he trod, what he saw from his windows.

It was a kind of madness and it gave me no peace. So one day when I knew the family was absent, I went in secret to Uferding.

It was a day in midsummer but misty, grey and sad. I took the train and then a cab which set me down by one of the side entrances.

The gate, splendidly carved with the von Lindenberg griffons, stood open; there was no one to be seen. I walked in, my heart thumping, passing between rows of ornate statues: of the Sabine women, their marble legs hanging from the shoulders of their seducers, of Hercules draped in pythons . . .

The path widened to accommodate a fountain of the kind I had yearned for when I first came to Madensky Square: three tiers, Poseidon with bulging pectorals, nymphs . . .

And this was only the side entrance!

Next came a series of ornamental grottos and then a group of statues which I approached with caution, and rightly, for as I passed a jet of water from the hat of a cavalier narrowly missed my shoulder. I've never been very amused by these jokey *Wasserspiele*. I'm always too aware of the work of some poor dressmaker or milliner ruined to provide a few moments of amusement for the jaded hosts.

I was approaching the east wing of the schloss now: yellow stucco, green shutters . . . and a first-floor verandah with a pergola on which I instantly saw Gernot breakfasting with the high-born Elise . . . buttering her croissant, handing her a pear. *My* pear . . .

The sun had begun to pierce the mist. Rounding the side of the house, I came upon smooth lawns stretching away towards verdant and rather bosomy hills – and in formal flower beds, a mass of pink begonias which spelled out, unmistakably, the words: LONG LIVE THE KAISER.

I must say I was terribly surprised. It would be Elise, of course, who had given instructions to the gardener, yet I had to face the fact that my lover's home was disconcertingly different from anything that I had imagined.

Passing an orangery with cages of singing birds and tubs of exotic lilies, I made my way up the terrace steps towards the front of the house.

And now I was accosted. A steward of some sort, responsible-looking and soberly dressed, approached and asked if I had an appointment to look over the house.

'No, I haven't. But if it were possible . . . ?'

My hand went to my purse; his stretched discreetly in my direction.

'Aye. The family's away. Only the public rooms, of course.'

He led me up a flight of steps into a domed entrance hall with a painted ceiling of swirling and richly endowed muses. Everything in the house was pretty, Italianate, and held no surprises.

Upstairs there were more salons, and in the main bedroom a gigantic bed dripping with brocade, the legs carved into the shape of writhing and grimacing Turks under the heel of the Austrian conquerors.

'Prince Eugene slept here,' said the steward. 'The family use it only on state occasions.'

This I could believe. But what was a state occasion? Had the midwife held up a squealing new-born child beside the carved posts of helmeted Habsburgs and said to Gernot's parents: 'It's a boy!'? Would he die in this monstrosity, my austere and ironic lover?

On the way out I looked at the stables and these too surprised me. I knew nothing about horses then, but I was aware that Gernot's life, like that of most soldiers, was largely lived on horseback.

But again I'd imagined it wrong. There were only three horses, two of them obviously carriage horses, and one which looked at me gently over the top of the door: a white horse with tender eyes. Not an Arab, I thought, nor a Lipizzaner – its back was very broad and its neck short – yet it carried Gernot and I spoke to it and stroked its nose: this quiet, domestic-looking horse who spent so much more time with my lover than I.

I said nothing to Gernot about my visit to Uferding for many months. But once when we had a whole night together, I told him that I had been to see his home.

'Good God! When?'

'Last summer. The syringa was in blossom.' I smiled. 'And the begonias.'

'Begonias? Those little handkerchiefy things in primary colours? I didn't know we had any.'

'There was a whole lot of them, in writing. LONG LIVE THE KAISER, they said.'

He came and sat down beside me on the bed. The cigar was in full flight and he was grinning. Did you like it? My home?'

I don't think I hesitated even for a second. I spoke enthusiastically of the verandah where it must be so pleasant to breakfast, and the bed with the writhing Turks in which, or so I understood, he had been born.

'Ah, yes, the bed . . . It's entirely honeycombed with mouse nests, the mattress. But go on; I'm really very interested in your reactions.'

I was by now a little hurt by Gernot's evident amusement, but I went on to describe my visit to the stables, my communion with his horse.

'My horse? Yes, of course . . . Do tell me what you thought of my horse.'

'I thought it was very nice. Very gentle and peaceful. I suppose I was a bit surprised because – Gernot, what is the matter?'

His mirth was now so extreme that he was compelled to abandon his cigar. 'Yes, a very gentle horse indeed. A milk float would strain the poor beast, though he sometimes carries their mother-

in-law round the park. She has very bad rheumatism, poor lady.'
He bent over me, his eyes tender. 'I'm glad you're so stupid, my
dear sweet love. When I first saw you, so wild and distraught in
the forest, I was overwhelmed by your capacity for grief. Then
when I met you again in the Herrengasse modelling that dress, I
thought you were the loveliest, most poised creature I had ever
seen. Since then you've given me two years of utter delight and to
be honest I was getting nervous. The fates can't mean me to have
this paragon, I thought: not a scarred, flawed, ageing bloke like
me. But now that I know you are superbly and overwhelmingly
foolish, I feel much better.'

'Why? Why am I stupid?'

He decided to explain. 'Do you really imagine, my darling
idiot, that I would allow anyone in my employ to write LONG
LIVE THE KAISER in begonias? Or anything else, come to that?
Quite apart from the fact that the poor gentleman could serve his
country best by dying as quickly as possible. Or that I would
house all those ludicrous statues – and I never breakfast on veran-
dahs because of the wasps.'

'I don't understand.'

'You went to *Schloss* Uferding. It belongs to my cousin and
he's let it to a man from Wiener Neustadt who makes saucepans.
A very good fellow – and patriotic, as you see. The horse is for his
mother-in-law: an undemanding animal. I'm so glad you didn't
like the place. It's a sort of joke; quite well done, I suppose, and
we liked the funny fountains when we were children. I haven't
been there for years. It's *Burg* Uferding that is my home.'

My lover continued to be so entertained by his supposed birth
in the state bed of Prince Eugene and his wild rides, *ventre a terre*,
on the gelding of the saucepan manufacturer's mother-in-law, that
the love we made that night was distinctly on the rococo side.
Afterwards I said: 'I promise I won't go there, I'm through with
sentimental journeys. But what is the Burg like? The place where
you *do* live?'

He rolled on to his back. 'Quite small. High up. There's a
single tower . . . wooden . . . a courtyard. The rooms are a bit

cramped . . . there's a smell of leather and wood.' He wound one of my curls round his finger. 'The stables are almost as big as the house,' he said, and grinned.

I was satisfied. In such a place I could see him and – just as important – I could see Hatschek.

The Kaiser has departed for his villa in Bad Ischl, and God help the poor chamoix which, for the next month, he will pursue relentlessly in lederhosen. They say he has run out of wall on which to stick their horns. Well, all of us have problems.

His departure is always the signal for the city to empty for the summer. Most of my clients have houses in the mountains or by a lake. Frau Hutte-Klopstock is going back to the High Tatras. The glacier named after her proved to be so small that it melted, and she and her husband are going to try and find glory by pioneering a different route.

Leah Cohen spends the summer on the Bodensee. She came to invite me to go with her, but though I shall close the shop for two weeks at the end of the month, I shan't go away. There's a lot of work to be done on the Huber trousseau, and I love these weeks of high summer: the dark trees trembling in the breeze that you can scarcely feel down below; the quietness.

'How is the psychoanalysis?' I asked her. 'Does it help?'

Leah has been getting so depressed and having such bad dreams, that her husband has sent her to Professor Freud in the Berggasse for treatment.

'Well, it doesn't help my *depression* – but then I know why I'm depressed. It's because I don't want to go to the Promised Land and dig holes for orange trees. But I must say it's simply marvellous for the feet! You know how my ankles kept swelling after Benjamin, and an hour on the couch is simply bliss!'

Professor Starsky is going to a conference on Herpetology in Reykjavik, and the English Miss will spend August on the moors near the Scottish border where her people live. A friend is going to take the setter bitch into the country while she is away which will give Rip a chance to pull himself together. Inflamed by the heat, his passion has broken all bounds. As soon as the bitch appears, he pounds across the square and weaves hysterically in and out of her legs. To see the stomach of your beloved arching high above you, as unreachable as it is desired, cannot be easy, and it is no wonder that as he lies panting in the shade of the chestnut trees, he is inclined to be short-tempered.

Herr Heller never goes away. His dusty shop is like the shell of one of Professor Starsky's reptiles. Even when he leaves his books just to go and stand outside on the pavement, he somehow looks unprotected and a little lost. He's going to have a hard time with his granddaughter, though. The Schumachers left yesterday with forty-five pieces of luggage for a fortnight in Ascona, so Maia won't have anyone to bully into making yurts.

My neighbour on the other side, Herr Schnee, has had a splendid piece of luck! The tackroom and workshops of the stables housing the horses of the Carinthian Jaegers has been destroyed by fire and he has a big order for new harness in time for a state parade in October. His nephew is a cornet in this crack regiment which puts the Cossacks to shame for style and ostentation: shakos with golden plumes, dolmanyis, breeches of white kid, and he's threatening to line up his horses outside his uncle's shop for a fitting!

'On my fiftieth birthday, this is to be –' said Herr Schnee, drawn out of his usual crustiness by this event. 'He's a wild lad; I wouldn't be surprised if he meant what he said!'

Tomorrow I'm going to do battle with Nini!

My God – you'd think I was proposing to crucify the girl. Of course I realize that no one with Hungarian blood in them can be regarded as normal but my suggestion that Nini should go away to the country and have a holiday while I closed the shop was received as if I'd threatened to do her a frightful injury.

'Why? Why should I go away?'

'Because you need a break; because you've been working very hard; because the heat is impossible.'

'I don't want to go to the country. I don't *like* the country. I never know what to do when I'm there. Walking up a mountain, walking down again, what's the point? Anyway why should I have a holiday when there are families living six to a room who can't even afford the tram fare to the Prater? I don't see what I've done to be sent away.'

'For heaven's sake, Nini, I'm offering you exactly the conditions you're fighting so hard for for the poor and the oppressed. The Cohens have offered to have you, so have the Schumachers – or I'll pay for a room for you in a pension.'

'What about Gretl? Why doesn't she have to have a holiday?'

'Gretl doesn't spend her nights in stuffy cellars planning to blow up the bourgeoisie. Anyway she's having the fortnight off to prepare for her wedding.'

'Ha!' said Nini. I saw her point; Gretl very much likes being engaged – the ring, the status – but she doesn't show the slightest hurry to name the day. 'And anyway,' Nini went on, 'something very interesting is coming up in Ottakring.'

This, unfortunately, I knew to be true and it was one of the reasons I was determined to send her away.

'Nini, I'm not prepared to argue. I'm closing on the twenty-second and you're going away.'

She flounced off in a temper, wearing white pique, to paste slogans on a railway bridge. When she returned, however, she was in an accommodating mood.

'One of the men told me about a summer camp for workers' children on the Grundlsee. It's run by an international welfare organization. Children come from all over the world, and doctors and students and counsellors look after them. They want people to wash up and do the chores, I wouldn't mind that.'

'Good,' I said. 'That's settled.'

I haven't said anything to Jan Kraszinsky about my efforts on Sigismund's behalf which is as well because there's been no sign of Van der Velde.

'We have money for six more weeks,' he said when I met him in the paper shop.

The child is practising something which seems to smoothe out everything inside one very gently, yet at the same time makes one feel as though there are bubbles inside one's nose, so I suppose it is by Mozart.

Oh God, I don't know how to write this . . .

I felt it the last time I lay in Gernot's arms; I knew it was there, the ultimate horror waiting to strike. Only it isn't I that have been struck down; not this time. It is Alice.

Two days ago, Rudi Sultzer collapsed in his office. They thought it was the heat and he was taken home to the Garnison-gasse to rest. Laura gave him vegetable juice and read to him from *Faust* and said it was nothing serious, but the doctor, when he came, disagreed with her. Rudi's heart was tired and he needed absolute rest. Then yesterday morning he had a second attack and this time an ambulance took him to the Municipal Hospital. His heart was not just tired, it was failing, and he lay propped on pillows, blue-lipped and scarcely conscious, fighting for his life.

'He looks so small, Frau Susanna,' said Edith, who had hurried in on the way home from the hospital to cancel her fitting. And almost no hair. I hadn't realized how much hair he'd lost. It's a terrible place, that hospital. Nothing prepares you.'

No, nothing. And certainly not Laura Sultzer or *Beowulf*.

'What do they say about his chances?'

She shook her head. 'They don't say much – but they don't expect him to recover, I know.'

'Is he in a public ward?'

'No, he's in a room on the second floor overlooking a dark courtyard. Oh God, it is an awful place to die, that hospital!'

I let her cry, patted her shoulder, but my mind was fixed on one thing only: how to help Alice.

For all of yesterday, all of today, Alice has sat on a wooden bench in the hospital waiting room, waiting for the moment when she could rise with the other visitors, summoned by the bell, and go to bid her love goodbye.

It never came, this moment, nor would it. Two visitors per person is the iron rule in that barrack and in case of serious illness, only relatives. Alice knew this as well as anyone, she expected no miracles, but it was impossible for her to leave the building in which he lay.

'Does he seem at peace, your father?'

Edith frowned. 'I don't know . . . it's so difficult for him to breathe. He said something to my mother . . . something about not having been worthy of her. But he didn't finish it properly . . . he seemed to lose interest as he said it . . . as though it was too difficult, or not important. Then once or twice I thought he was looking for someone. Not my mother or me. Someone else. Perhaps I was imagining it.' She picked up a pincushion and began to denude it of pins. 'No, I wasn't imagining it.'

I waited, afraid even to move.

Edith gulped and went on quickly. 'I saw a woman in the waiting room in the hospital. She was sitting there in a white dress with a flowery hat. I thought I'd seen her before once, when Father had pneumonia. She was standing down below in the street and it was raining. She just stood there – she'd forgotten her umbrella and the rain completely ruined her hat. I remembered it because it was a pretty hat, like . . .' She broke off, flushing, and turned away.

I made up my mind.

'Fraulein Edith, you love your father, I think?'

'Yes. When I was little we used to do a lot of things together, but my mother felt that . . . I mean, my father was not very spiritual,' said Edith, her voice trailing away.

'Well, listen; you have a chance to do something for your father. It's not something any young girl could do, but you have been brought up to be broad-minded and aware of . . .' Here I faltered, unable to imagine that Edith had been brought up to be aware of anything as simple as the relationship which existed between Alice and her father. 'I think that the person your father was looking for is the woman you mentioned. She is someone he has known a long time and been fond of, and I think he'd like to say goodbye to her.'

'Oh, but I couldn't! I couldn't bring . . . how could I? My mother would never—'

'This has nothing to do with your mother. Nor with you, really, Edith. You only have to mention to the doctor or the ward sister that your father has a relative who lives in the country and would like to say goodbye. It would all be over in a few moments.'

'No, I can't do that. I can't. My mother . . .'

'Very well.'

I rose and opened the door for her.

'You do understand?' The Bluestocking turned to me, mottled but obstinate.

'Yes, yes.'

I had already forgotten Edith.

It took me an hour to walk round the hospital, question the porter, get my bearings. Then I went to the waiting room.

Alice was still sitting upright on the wooden bench, shivering in her pretty dress.

'Sanna! Oh God, Sanna. What are you doing here?'

'I'm going to take you to Rudi.'

'You can't,' she said wearily. 'No one is allowed in except relatives. And they always come, both of them. It's only right; they're family. Only . . .' Her lips began to tremble. 'I thought if I could see him just once more. Just to . . . thank him . . . that then I could bear it.'

'Well, you're going to see him. I told you. Now. Get up,' I said firmly, as if to a child.

She rose, shaking her head, and picked up the bunch of corn-flowers that lay beside her. 'I brought them because when we first met . . .' But this did not seem to be a sentence that one finished.

I led her through an archway into the main corridor, green-painted and deserted but for an orderly pushing a patient on a trolley. Beneath the grey blanket shrouding the figure, one foot protruded. Now to the left, up the first flight of stairs; I'd done my homework; there was no need to ask the way.

Another long corridor, past doors open to sights I prefer not to remember. The smell of chloroform, of lysol . . . Alice, I think, was aware of nothing, her only terror that we would be stopped before she reached her love.

'Excuse me, but visitors are not allowed at this hour.' A starched sister, all bristles and authority.

I smiled. 'We're not visiting a patient, sister. We're visiting Professor Mittelheimer.'

My smile, that of a third-class houri in the red-light district of a minor provincial town, was an accident brought on by nerves, but it disconcerted the Sister so much that she let us pass. With the reputation of the poor Professor (whose name I had got off a notice board) in ruins, we went up a second flight of stairs.

We had reached the private room. (Please God let it work! Let her see him just once more.)

'I'm sorry, but nobody is allowed past—'

Beside me, Alice faltered, missed her step. It was too cruel when we were almost at Rudi's door.

And then a second nurse, senior to the first, coming out of her office. 'Unless one of you is Herr Doktor Sultzer's sister from Prague?'

I gestured to Alice.

'That's all right then. The Herr Doktor's daughter telephoned us to expect you. Only a few minutes though. He is very ill.'

(Oh Edith, how I wronged you. I will be your friend for life.)

She led us to the room where Rudi lay. I stepped aside and Alice went forward to the bed. When she bent over him and saw the unmistakable signs of death, the colour drained from her face and I moved towards her, afraid that she would faint.

Then somehow – I don't know how she did this – she re-assembled from the terrified stricken woman she had become, her charm, her beauty. Alice put up her hand to flick back the wisp of veiling on her hat. She laid the cornflowers on the counterpane. She smiled. Properly, I mean. Naturally. Then she said: 'Rudi?'

Not in a desperate way; not calling him back from limbo. She said it as you say it when someone you love lies beside you on the pillow and it amuses you to say his name.

So he came back. For lamentations and guilt he had not returned, nor had the ministrations of the doctors brought him back, but Alice called him lightly, cheerfully, and he came. Not at once . . . slowly. His eyes opened . . . focused. And when he realized that she was there, really in the flesh and not a mirage, and looked at her, she must have had all the reward that women like us can ever hope to have.

So far we could still have been watching a man taking leave of a beloved sister. The smile on the dying man's face could have been the tender smile of a fond older brother remembering childhood games. The silly pet name he now spoke softly into Alice's ear as she bent over him might have belonged to their nursery games, though it would have been an unusual nursery. But now Rudi Sultzer very slightly turned his head and as Alice brought her mouth towards him and kissed him gently on the lips, the Herr Doktor's hand moved up from the coverlet . . . sought something . . . found it.

Not her soft hair beneath the hat, nor her sweet mouth. Something that represented a more lasting sanctuary, a memory of all that was good on this earth: her breast.

'Ah,' said Rudi with infinite content.

It was only when I heard the hiss of outrage behind me that I realized that Edith Sultzer had come into the room.

Rudi never regained consciousness after Alice's visit. He died quietly in the early hours of the morning and in the evening Alice was on stage in a gold bolero and red velvet skirt singing of love and lilac blossom in *Waltzertraum*.

She was in the second row as usual. She'd put on a lot of make-up and she sang nicely and I don't know if anyone noticed anything, but I did. Something had happened to her mouth; something that can happen gradually with age or overnight with grief.

Herr Huber was beside me. He'd driven us to the theatre and been a tower of strength. It wasn't till I caught the scent of his Hungary water and saw that he had laid his snow-white handkerchief in my lap, that I realized tears were running down my face.

I hadn't cried till then. It was my business to help Alice, not to cry. But it was too much, suddenly; the glimpse I'd had of the future. My sweet and pretty friend in the back row among the village elders with her spinning wheel, singing year in year out about the spring . . .

In the last few days I've cancelled all but my most important clients and left the shop to Nini so that I could be with Alice.

This secret mourning is very hard. In the Garnisongasse, Frau Sultzer mourns loudly and in public. Her husband's colleagues come to commiserate, relatives appear. No doubt the Group, who thought so little of Rudi in his life, are busy writing poems in his praise or trailing dark sprays of ivy through the flat. Does Laura put up notices saying: *Silence! Frau Sultzer is remembering her husband*? I don't know. There has been no sign of Edith since she hissed away in fury down the hospital corridor.

Alice puts up no notices, that's certain. She sits quietly in the flat she had prepared for Rudi and does exactly what she's told. If you say 'Eat, Alice!' she eats; if you say 'Lie down and rest', she stretches out obediently on the bed. Sometimes, in the puzzled voice of a child, she asks a question.

'What do you suppose they *mean* when they say we shall meet again in heaven? *What* shall we meet? If I went right along the rows of angels would I find one with bandy legs and pince-nez? You never seem to hear about angels like that.'

And she is mystified by the behaviour of the British in India.

'They're trying to abolish *suttee*, did you know, Sanna? Why are they trying to do that? *Everyone's* allowed to throw themselves on the funeral pyre in *suttee* – not just the wives and relatives. Everyone who belonged to the man that's died.'

Then came the reading of Rudi's will. His investments were secure; his life had been heavily insured. With a little care, Laura would be able to live much as before. Nothing, of course, had been left to Alice; there was no mention of her in the will; she had not for a moment expected it. With the will, however, there was a letter, the contents of which knocked Alice out of her dangerous docility and brought on a storm of such dreadful weeping that at last it brought her sleep.

Rudi had asked to be buried at St Florian's.

'I don't understand it,' said Laura Sultzer, arriving in my shop on her way to interview Father Anselm. 'I naturally assumed that Rudi would be cremated – we were both free thinkers. I wasn't even aware that my husband knew this church existed.'

I, however, was aware, for it was in the churchyard of St Florian's that Alice and Rudi had met. It was just after I'd moved to the square. I was in bed with flu when Alice came to see me and I think I must have been running quite a high temperature because I became very agitated about the untended grave of the Family Schmidt which I had adopted. (This was before the harebells had seeded themselves.) Alice immediately offered to take some flowers and ran over to Old Anna to buy a bunch of cornflowers.

Rudi Sultzer had been visiting a client in the Walterstrasse and taken a short cut across the square. Like so many people he'd lived in Vienna all his life and never been in St Florian's, and now he paused and wandered into the churchyard. Where he saw a woman with gentle eyes laying a bunch of cornflowers on a grave . . .

'I shall of course do my duty,' said Laura and she did it. Rudi now lies in our churchyard. The hole they dug for him was small, but oh, it was deep!

'My husband had very few friends,' Frau Sultzer had told the priest. 'Hardly anyone came to the house.'

She was mistaken. There was scarcely room in St Florian's for all the people who wanted to pay their respects to Rudi's memory. He must have helped countless people of whose existence his wife was not even aware.

Father Anselm had arranged for a full choral service. Not less than twelve carriages with their black horses and nodding plumes disgorged the mourners, and the hearse was piled high with wreaths.

There was only one oversight. No one had seen fit to alter the notice on the churchyard gate. It still said: DOGS NOT ADMITTED. They had forgotten to amend it to: DOGS AND MISTRESSES . . .

By this notice, Alice stood for the length of the service. Erect, exquisitely elegant, her veil down over the black hat she had tried on that day at Yvonne's and bought now to bid her love goodbye, she waited, her hands grasping the spiked railings – the only mishap a split in the finger of one glove as the pallbearers passed with the coffin.

Rip waited with her and so did I. We heard the responses, and Ernst Bischof singing the *De Profundis*. When the bells began their dreadful tolling Rip lifted his head and howled and I bent down to caress him, but Alice saw nothing, heard nothing, that did not touch her remembered life with Rudi.

Only when the congregation came out and they took the coffin to the grave did she begin to tremble so much that I was afraid.

'Come, let me take you home.'

But her hands only fastened tighter round the railings. 'I can't . . . not till . . .'

Laura was pushed forward and laid a handful of earth on the coffin, followed by Edith. And then it began, that dreadful, relentless shovelling of the obliterating earth.

It was over. Frau Sultzer still lingered in the porch, but Edith now set off down the path towards the line of waiting carriages.

Grim-faced, alone, plainer than ever, the Bluestocking marched towards us, her hideous, thick-soled shoes crunching the gravel. Any hope that she might foil to recognize her father's mistress in her polka-dot veiling vanished as she stopped, scowling, beside Alice – and remembering the scene in the hospital I prepared to throw myself between them, quite ready to murder anyone who tried to hurt my friend.

Her face still contorted, Edith stumbled forward. Her arms went out stiffly like the arms of a puppet . . . and closed round Alice's shoulders in a clumsy, pitifully unpractised embrace.

'I'm sorry,' she whispered. 'I'm very sorry.'

They clung together, Alice released by this undreamt of gesture into torrents of tears. 'But at least you didn't miss him,' said Edith Sultzer. 'I did. I missed the whole of his life.'

Then she walked on and got into the first of the carriages and sat there, scowling again, and waiting for her mother, who had noticed nothing.

Nini departed this morning for the Grundlsee. She wore her assassination shoes – high-heeled kid with grosgrain rosettes – which were so expensive that she meant to keep them for a really important event in the Anarchist calendar, and a bronze silk faille suit with a Winterhalter blouse. A perfect outfit for washing up the dishes of a hundred disturbed children and sweeping floors.

'I still don't see why I have to go,' she said mulishly. 'You know how much work there is to do on the Huber trousseau.'

I took her to the station and saw her into her compartment, where a young man with a violently waxed moustache rose to receive her suitcase with alacrity. Poor fellow: it hurt me to see his look of expectancy. Nini's been fending for herself since she was fourteen. Long before I found her in Ungerer's atelier she'd had more experience than women three times her age – and no one can wield a hatpin like my assistant.

The flat seems appallingly silent without her. I asked Alice if she'd like to come and stay; this is the time when Rudi would have come to her and I hate her to be alone, but she needs to be in her own place, she says, and I understand that. At least the Volksoper is closed. Herr Huber has been kindness itself driving her to the theatre, seeing she has a meal afterwards.

'Na, na,' he says in his slow, rumbling voice when I thank him. 'You know what an honour it is for me to have the friendship of two such gifted women.'

If Vienna now belongs to the poor, the industrious and the bereaved, the Countess of Metz certainly fits in this category. She stays in her palace with the shutters closed and writes me petulant notes. She would like her bottle-green suit and she would like it quickly. She doesn't know what is delaying me, and to give wings to my endeavour she has sent me a pair of battered candlesticks of the kind old ladies hit burglars on the head with and a Louis Quatorze spittoon.

The choirboys have gone home for the holidays and the

Schumachers are still away so the square is as silent as the house. It is very hot now; the mornings are misty and vaporous; you know where the sun is rather than see it, and the flowers have stopped being blue and yellow as in spring; they're mostly red now: dahlias and tall gladioli, and in the window boxes a mass of scarlet geraniums that seem to shout their colour into the muted light. Rip is in an aquatic and sportif mood, clambering up the side of the fountain and very seriously thinking of jumping in, but there is the problem of his back legs. He's much more cheerful without the setter of the English Miss. Passion isn't at all good for the character; I've always known that.

My pear is well. Not exactly enormous – toe-sized one could say – but it's a late-maturing variety and I have absolute faith in its ability to swell.

Tomorrow I shall shut the shop. Nothing happens in these dusty summer days and I'm glad of that. I'm not sure that I really like 'events'.

No, I was wrong. Something has happened that has upset me very much.

Magdalena's wedding dress has gone off to be sewn with seed pearls, her blue velvet cloak is being embroidered with silver acanthus leaves. I have made her a day dress of linen the colour of sandalwood and another of pearl-grey faille striped with rose . . .

But Magdalena herself remains an enigma. She is utterly beautiful, graceful, remote . . . always polite to her fiancé whom, however, she almost never addresses directly. Certainly her engagement has achieved the result she hoped for. Herr Huber has had the twins coached for cadet college, medical treatment has been arranged for the taxidermist and he is negotiating for a better apartment for the family. But I've only seen her animated when she's in company, real or imagined, with her saints.

At least until tonight. I'd taken pity on the Countess von Metz and delivered her two-piece, and as the evening was so beautiful I walked back, taking a short cut through that enclave behind St Oswald's Church where the Jesuits have their priory. There's a little garden there that is used by lovers and old people. It's pretty and quiet, with the priory on one side and the old Krotsky Palace on the other, and the roses are famous.

It was already dusk; and I half averted my eyes from the two people standing very close together under an acacia. The man was tall and dressed in a black cloak like a student. The girl too wore a dark cloak? – but what stood out even from a distance was the intensity of their involvement. She was looking up at him, entreaty in every line of her body; he bent over her with an unmistakable tenderness and love.

Then they drew apart, and as the girl walked away past the flower beds her hood fell back and I saw, quite clearly, Magdalena's face and the long white-blonde hair.

There's nothing I can do about this, nothing I can say – but oh, that poor, kind, unsuspecting man! Is it all a sham, this religiosity of hers? For it seems clear now that she chose the butcher from her other rich suitors for the ease with which she will be able to deceive him. There was nothing of farewell in that meeting under the acacia tree.

One thing is certain: in thinking Magdalena Winter incapable of passion, I was a fool.

August

Sigismund's uncle fainted today on the stairs. Frau Hinkler told me this in her usual pleasant manner. 'He's starving himself to keep up the instalments on the piano. I didn't get a doctor; what's the use? He can't pay.'

I've never been inside Sigismund's attic; the glimpse through the window that first night was enough for me, but in the evening I put some fruit and a jar of soup into a basket and went across.

Frau Hinkler let me in with a bad grace. She longs to evict the Kraszinskys and any sign that they're not friendless infuriates her.

Oh God, that wretched room! The piano stands in the centre and I see it now as a black monster devouring the lives of those two miserable exiles; endlessly consuming the money that they need to live. It alone had been wiped clean: everywhere else, on the bare boards, on the window sill, the dust lay clotted. Sheets of music and a few tattered books were piled on newspaper on the floor – and on a trestle bed against the wall lay Kraszinsky, still wearing his rusty black clothes, with his arms by his sides like someone waiting for the undertaker.

'I've brought you some soup. Is there somewhere I can heat it up? Do you have a kitchen?'

Sigismund, who had appeared silently by my side, led me into a scullery with a dirty sink, one dripping tap, a paraffin stove. His crucifix, I noted, was once again tied with a grubby piece of string. I scrubbed out the only saucepan, disposed of a cockroach, rinsed the grease from two tin bowls.

'We are going back,' said Kraszinsky as I returned to his bedside. 'We are finished. I have written to Preszowice.'

'You'd like that?'

He shrugged. For myself, yes. Perhaps I can get my old job back. But there is nothing there for the child – nothing. I dream about my sister.'

As I was leaving, Sigismund beckoned to me from the doorway beside the scullery. It led to a windowless slit of a room with a skylight so begrimed that it let in almost no light. This, clearly, was where Sigismund slept – only what was it that he wished to show me? The rancid smelling mattress on the floor? The one cane chair with a broken seat?

No . . . something else. Against the wall, on what must have been the wooden box in which he'd brought his few possessions, Sigismund had set up an icon corner such as all pious households have in the east.

In the centre was a picture of a young woman in a leather frame. Kraszinsky was right – his sister had been beautiful. The oval face was tranquil, the mouth full. Beside the picture was a bracelet made of woven hair, now faded but still retaining the reddish tint it had had in life. Had they cut the tresses from Ilona's head as she lay murdered in the forest? It was hard to hold it and admire it as the boy put it into my hand.

The third object on Sigismund's shrine was an old cigar box and as I bent down to look at it he made a protective gesture, covering it with his fingers.

'You don't want me to open it?'

He hesitated; colour flooded his narrow face; then suddenly he turned back the lid.

Oh God! Inside was the lace-edged handkerchief I'd dropped the night I took him to the churchyard to smell the limes . . . the gold ribbon I had sent over for his crucifix, carefully coiled as sailors coil a rope . . . two shrivelled forget-me-nots from the bunch I had worn in my belt the first day I said 'Grüss Gott' to him by the fountain. And most macabre of all, cut from an ancient newspaper which some earlier tenants must have left behind, an advertisement for my shop in the days when I still had to advertise.

Crossing the square to go home, I took deep breaths of air,

trying to shut out what I had seen. Even before I reached my door, it had begun again: calm, orderly, serene – Sigismund's music. I was right about the piece. It is by Mozart. The *Rondo in A*.

The Schumachers are back. They invited me over as soon as they'd unpacked and the girls showed me their treasures: the skeleton of a fish from Lake Locarno, a thistle head the size of a plate . . . Gisi, now that she is no longer the youngest, has been taken out of nappies. She has a surprised and slightly anxious look as though she finds this sudden adulthood uncertain and draughty.

Then on Sunday we had the christening.

The godmother Helene had chosen for the baby was ill so I held the comical creature whose blemish I no longer 'see'. Even before I gave her to the priest she was not entirely pleased with events. A terrible frown appeared between her autocratic eyebrows, and she wrinkled her nose. And when Father Anselm sprinkled her with holy water and pronounced her string of resplendent Christian names, Donatella's yells of rage would have displaced a whole regiment of devils from the depths of hell.

Afterwards there was a party in the Schumachers' pretty Biedermeier drawing room and today Herr Schumacher has gone to Graz to fetch his nephew.

I was present at Gisi's christening too, and at Kati's and at that of the quicksilver Resi . . . I could recite all the Christian names of all the little Schumacher girls.

But I don't know what my own daughter is called. I don't know what names the people in Salzburg chose for her. Somehow I can never get over that. That I don't know my daughter's name.

Oh dear! I expect it will be all right but it has to be admitted that the goldfish slayer is not a pretty sight. The carriage in which Herr Schumacher brought him from the station turned in between the chestnut trees as I was crossing the square, and he ordered the coachman to stop, and introduced the boy.

'This is my nephew, Frau Susanna. Gustav, bow to the lady.'

I was surprised at this instruction. At fourteen, I thought Gustav might be able to bow without being told, but I was wrong.

Over the boy's somewhat vacant face, with its flat nose and faint tracings of a moustache, spread a look that was both bovine and puzzled.

'Take off your cap!'

This at least Gustav seemed able to do. He inclined his head and murmured something which could have been a greeting.

'We'll soon get him trained up, eh Gustav? You're going to be a great help to me, aren't you, boy?'

Gustav said something which sounded like 'Ugh', or maybe 'Agh' and put on his cap again. I don't think I have ever seen a boy with such enormous ears.

The girls' aquarium has been moved to the attic where Lisl can keep an eye on it.

Nini has been back three days and she spends a great deal of time telling me that she is all right.

She does not look all right. There are dark rings under her eyes and she is ill-tempered and twitchy. She also works the kind of hours which would make her absolutely furious if they were demanded of a textile worker in Ottakring, and there is a tendency to stare at roses. Roses, where Nini was concerned, belonged behind one ear or copied in silk to go on a bodice. Now she stares at them, and since the ones that are easily available to us are the pink ramblers separating my courtyard from Herr Schnee's, which are currently at the brown dishclothy stage, I am not particularly pleased.

I shall put up with this for a few more days, but if it doesn't improve I'm going to have it out with her.

The Schumacher girls are awed by Gustav. He is awful in an archetypal way like the monsters and ogres in fairy tales: large, slow-moving and stupid. Most of all they are awed by his appetite.

'Yesterday he ate thirteen zwetschken knödel,' said Mitzi, sitting up in bed. 'Honestly, Frau Susanna. Thirteen!'

'And he never looks at Baby. He just goes past with his head turned away.'

'He and Ernst Bischof go out at night with a catapult and kill cats. They don't just scare them; they kill them.'

I'd gone over to help Helene who has become embroiled with a complicated piece of smocking on a dress for Donatella.

Is it as bad as the girls make out?' I asked her when I'd said goodnight to the children and joined her in the drawing room.

'Well, it's fairly bad. There was nearly a nasty accident last week when the men were loading. Gustav doesn't exactly have a way with horses. But Albert is determined to succeed with him because the business *has* to go to someone with the Schumacher blood.' She poured a cup of coffee and handed it to me. 'It must be nice to be so pleased with your blood, don't you think?'

We sat for a while over our work; then the study door was opened and we heard the irate voice of Albert Schumacher.

'No, no *no!* How many times do I have to tell you – that's *sycamore!* Sycamore, you blockhead!'

'Albert's been trying to teach him how to distinguish the different kinds of wood,' said Helene. 'But he doesn't seem able to take it in.'

This certainly seemed to be the case. There was some more shouting, then Gustav shambled past down the corridor and Herr Schumacher in his smoking jacket appeared in the doorway, mopping his brow.

'Where is she?' he demanded of his wife.

'She's asleep, Albert; don't wake her.'

'She always wakes up about nine, you know that. It'll do her good to be awake before her bottle.'

He made his way upstairs to the nursery, returned with Donatella in his arms – and disappeared into his study.

Helene endured it for a few minutes; then we rose and followed him.

The baby, freed from the constraints of her shawl, was propped in an armchair. Herr Schumacher had taken a circular piece of wood from the baskets of offcuts he'd brought home from the yard and was holding it up to her face.

'There you are, my pretty. Look at that! That's oak. See how dense it is? See how it is figured?'

Donatella saw. She kicked; she crowed – bubbles of froth formed on her lips.

'And this is sycamore, my treasure. *You* wouldn't mix it up with oak, would you? You can see that it's lighter, can't you; you can see the silkiness?'

She could indeed. Made ecstatic by so much conversation after the uninspiring confinement of her cot, Donatella waved her arms with such enthusiasm that she keeled over and had to be righted.

In no way disconcerted by our appearance, Herr Schumacher extracted another sample.

'Now this one's really special, sweetheart. This is rosewood. There's nothing quite like it.' He waved the block above her head and growing quite cross-eyed with pleasure, she bared her gums in a seraphic smile.

'You see,' he said, turning to us. 'She knows already. She's got more sense now in one finger than that oaf has in the whole of his body. In one *finger* . . .'

My mother taught me to cook and she taught me well. So when Nini, at supper, pushed my excellent Kaiserschmarr'n round and round her plate with a fork and sighed, I suddenly cracked.

'All right,' I said. 'Now I'd like to know what's the matter with you? What went wrong at the Grundlsee?'

'Nothing went wrong. Why should it?'

'I don't know why, but it did. I suppose you fell in love?'

Nini glared at me, attempting outrage. Then she put down her fork and groped for a handkerchief.

'It was so unfair! I can't tell you how ridiculous he looked – well, not ridiculous, but absolutely like someone you couldn't possibly be in the slightest danger from. Hardly taller than me, with floppy hair all over his eyes, and socks that kept coming down – and a snub nose. He didn't even have eyes that were a proper colour. Not blue or brown or black . . . just bits of colours with flecks in them.'

Was he working in the children's camp?'

'Yes, he was. I didn't notice him at the beginning. There was a tall, good-looking Frenchman that I was rather interested in. Whereas Daniel came from America and that was against him – a hotbed of capitalism – and then they said he was a bank clerk. Both his parents were Austrian, but their families emigrated separately and they met in New York. So Daniel was a second-generation immigrant, but his German was perfect of course. Only as I say I didn't notice him at first. It was the children that made me notice him.'

'In what way?'

'Well, there were a lot of counsellors – about eight of them, and some had diplomas in Psychology and all that, but the kids were always round Daniel. Only, he wasn't really *doing* anything. I mean, not therapy or ploys . . . he was just looking at things. Almost *being* them . . . You know what I'm like about Nature – there wasn't any Nature where I was born, just people packed together and the smell of drains and sweat. But Daniel has this passion for pebbles . . . I mean, *pebbles*. He'd sit crouched down on this path and just look at them and it's perfectly true, they *are* all different and some of them have quartz in them and some have pale veins like jade and some – oh, God, listen to me! But the children would all crouch down too and suddenly it was incredible to be alive in a world of pebbles. He'd do it with trees, too. The other counsellors organized botany expeditions and brought little bits of branches in and the children learnt the names and drew them – but Daniel just lay under an oak tree and sort of became an oak.'

'He sounds unusual. Very much so.'

'Oh, he was unusual. Mad, really. His clothes . . . he looked as though he'd slept in them and his hair was across his face and he was quite small. I don't like small men. Mind you, he wasn't just a sort of fey Pied Piper, he was witty too. It was the children laughing you heard as often as you saw them staring at a stone. Once on a rainy day there was a meeting about the children's behaviour problems and there was a great dossier about their backgrounds and a Counsellor's Report. I wasn't really part of it, I was just a washer up. Then I realized Daniel wasn't there – he should have been but he wasn't, and I slipped out. And I found him half way up the hill with all the children in his group and some of the others, and they'd collected twenty-seven salamanders – you know how they come out in the rain – and there they were, making a grotto for them out of moss and stones, and the kid who was cradling one of the salamanders very, very carefully in his hands was the one they were doing a Case History on down in the camp. Disturbed father, alcoholic mother, two convictions for petty thieving . . . I think for Daniel the children's past didn't really exist: he saw them as though they had just been born.'

She blew her nose and now that the Kaiserschmarr'n was beyond redemption, she speared up a forkful and put it in her mouth.

'Anyway, I just joined in. There were fourteen children in his group and I became the fifteenth, I suppose, tagging along when I wasn't doing the chores. He was nice to me but nothing more and I got fond of the kids. And honestly I felt quite safe because of the way his socks kept coming down and him having a snub nose and being so small.' She paused and glared balefully at her plate. 'I should have known there was something wrong about him. I should have known.'

Everything would have been all right, Nini went on, except that three days before she was due to come home there was an accident.

'There was a counsellor there – a woman – who was terribly precise and fussy, always walking about with files and bits of paper trying to assess the children and write reports. Her children played her up like anything and whenever they could, they slipped off to join Daniel. Anyway on Sunday we all went rowing on the lake and one of the boys in her boat stood up and started fooling about and she got her oar caught and the kid fell in. It's terribly deep, the Grundlsee, and we were half way across and the child couldn't swim. The woman just shrieked and yelled and completely lost her nerve. I was in another boat with Daniel and he just dived in with all his clothes on and swam over to the boy. It was awful, Susanna; the most frightening thing I've seen. The other boats were a long way off and this idiotic woman just shrieked and shrieked. I rowed up as close as I could, but the boy in the water was in a complete panic and he clung on to Daniel's neck and I thought he was going to choke him to death. They went down three times and they say that after three times . . .'

Nini's voice broke. She retreated behind her handkerchief and I was silent, noting that for the first time she'd called me simply 'Susanna' without the 'Frau'. However unhappy the outcome of this love affair, Nini was growing up and would soon leave me, and I registered the pang this caused me without the least surprise.

'He had to half throttle the boy before he could tow him in and then when we were trying to get them into the boat, the boy came round and tried to pull Daniel under again. I thought we'd never do it . . . never.'

But the other boats had arrived by then; both of them were saved.

'They took the boy to hospital, but Daniel wouldn't go. They carried him to his room and he looked awful – he'd swallowed so much water and there were great bruises round his throat. Of course everyone was making the most awful fuss of him by then – he was a hero – so I kept away. But my room was opposite his and just before I went to bed I put my head round the door to see if he was all right. It was very late – and he said my name, and I went over to the bed.'

She broke off in a confusion I had never seen in her.

'It's so unfair,' she said, returning yet again to this theme. 'He was half drowned and there was something caught in his hair, some kind of water weed I suppose. And he didn't ask or anything, he just stretched out his arm as though I was a glass of water and he needed a drink.' Nini paused. Her black eyes were unfocused as she remembered. 'I meant just to be kind – he'd done this brave thing. And after all, since I was fourteen I've had to . . . sometimes it was the only way we could eat. But oh God . . .'

Nini is almost never still. Now she sat unmoving as the bust of Nefertiti and as sad.

'So then in the morning he said we must be married. He didn't ask me, he just said it as though it was completely obvious, and the incredible thing was, I simply said yes. I mean, marriage – that awful bourgeois thing, so respectable and hampering, but I said yes without thinking at all. Only then we began to talk. I should have known but I didn't. I should have seen there would be this awful betrayal, but I didn't think he had it in him to be so deceitful and devious and cruel. It wasn't as though he didn't know how I felt about things: I'd told him often enough.'

'But what was it? Was he married already? Had he committed a crime? What was the betrayal?'

Nini blew her nose. 'Have you ever heard of the Frankenheimer Merchant Bank?'

'Just about. It's an American bank like J. P. Morgan or Rothschilds, isn't that it?'

'Yes, that's it. Well, Daniel owns it. Or rather his father does, but Daniel's the only son and he's all set to take over. There isn't just the bank; they own some other vile capitalist consortium. I wormed it all out of Daniel – at first he didn't seem to think it mattered. They have a house on Fifth Avenue and another on that island where all these swinish people go – the Vanderbilts and all that crowd. His mother's the patroness of some music school in New York. He thought I'd like her. God, a *patroness* . . . can't you see her with her great bosom full of jewels getting out of her limousine and all the poor little children bowing and scraping on their violins and being patted on the head? And Daniel spends a month every year doing something like this: working with children, or last year he worked in an old people's home in France – and the rest of the year he's in the bank grinding the faces of the poor and making millions.'

'And what did he say when you told him how you felt?'

'He didn't think it mattered. He said I could be an Anarchist just as well in New York. He said Marx said the revolution would begin in America and if it came it meant that people wanted it and he'd hand over the bank or go bravely to the guillotine – well, he'd go to the guillotine whether bravely or not – but till then he thought there was no point in upsetting his father who'd slaved to start the bank, and anyway he said he liked figures – he liked the way they worked. And he just kept saying . . . we . . . we belonged together and it was to do with my soul and my eyebrows and when you met someone like that and let them go, it was a bad deed . . . it was *wrong*, a sin. But it's a lot wronger to own a bank and grind the faces of the poor, I think. And we argued and argued and I couldn't make him see. So I just packed my bags and went. There were plenty of people to do the washing up; a whole new lot had come from Germany. And I'm really perfectly all right. Absolutely fine. Only I would very much like to be busy, if you don't mind, so if you didn't send Magdalena's tea gown to be embroidered but gave it to me, we could save a *lot* of money . . .'

Magdalena's wedding dress is really far too magnificent for a small private wedding with only one bridesmaid in attendance. In designing it I had responded to her beauty and Herr Huber's wishes, rather than the occasion.

But it is not too magnificent for the church.

Outwardly the Capuchin Church is a narrow, faded building, squeezed in between others on the west side of the Neuermarkt. Inside, too, it is austere with only the dark brown of the marquetry work behind the altar for decoration.

But to walk down the aisle of the Capuchin Church is to walk on the whole history of the Empire, for below in the crypt lie the bodies of all the Habsburgs who have ruled over Austria. Maria Theresia lies there in a vast sarcophagus, entwined in statuary with her husband, and Leopold I who saved us from the Turks. Crown Prince Rudolf sleeps in the crypt, wept over by parties of tourists; and Napoleon's sad little son, the King of Rome whose cradle they adorned with a thousand golden bees to bring him luck and happiness, but to no avail.

Somehow it seemed to me suitable that the eerie Magdalena with her mad religiosity and her extraordinary beauty should walk to her bridegroom over the buried bodies of more than a hundred Habsburg kings.

Since the ceremony was to be small and private, a rehearsal hardly seemed necessary but when Herr Huber suggested it, I agreed with alacrity. Anything to banish the spectre of the tall, dark man who had bent over Magdalena with such unmistakable tenderness beneath the acacia in St Oswald's garden.

For once, Frau Winter, overcoming her scruples about Herr Huber being in trade, attended with her twin boys, for there was to be a luncheon afterwards provided by the butcher. And Frau Sultzer arrived with Edith. She came on the tandem, and it was nice of her for Rudi has not been dead a month and I'm not so foolish as to imagine that in her own way she does not grieve. As usual her arrival caused a certain consternation; as usual she unstrapped her briefcase from the carrier so that Schopenhauer could be assured of her attention, even in church.

But only one briefcase . . . Edith, as she followed her mother, had a naked and vulnerable look.

'Is it finished then? The essay?'

'Yes, I handed it in last week.'

The Bluestocking looked tireder and plainer than ever: a different girl from the one who had chatted so happily to Herr Huber's sisters in Linz.

Magdalena, wearing white, seemed thoroughly at home in the sombre church, talking animatedly to the priest about music for the service, lighting candles at the side altar, dropping on to her knees to pray. If only I hadn't seen what I had seen at St Oswald's, it would have convinced me thoroughly, this piety of hers.

I'd brought Nini along and the measurements for Magdalena's train. There would be no problem with the dress; there were very few steps; a girl with Magdalena's grace would manage without help.

'You'll have to stay about eight paces behind Magdalena,' I said to Edith. 'There's no need to lift the train – it'll fall into its own lines – just see, that it's clear as you come through the door and then when you get to the altar, arrange it on the steps before you stand aside.'

Herr Huber, of course, should not have been present at all. But one can hardly expect a man to pay for the trousseau and take on the care of the bride's family, and have nothing to do with the arrangements. Now he sat squeezed into one of the side pews and followed Magdalena's every movement with his eyes.

It hadn't seemed necessary to rehearse the procession, but it so happened that the organist was in the church, and at a word from the priest he went up to the organ loft and started to play the Bach passacaglia which Magdalena had chosen for her entry.

It was strangely exciting, the sudden music; it made it real. Magdalena felt it too, I think, for she lifted her head and began to walk up the aisle in perfect time to the music.

And counting carefully, making sure she kept the right distance, Edith, with her pigeon-toed gait, fell in behind her.

Herr Huber, I'm sure, made no sort of gesture; he saw nothing but his bride, but after a few paces, Edith suddenly stopped.

'No,' I heard her say in a frenzied whisper. 'No, I can't, Magdalena. You mustn't have me as a bridesmaid. You mustn't.'

Magdalena turned.

'You mustn't,' Edith repeated. 'Don't you see, it'll be a farce. You'll spoil it for him. He'll see you come and then me behind you. He'll be sick. Everyone'll be sick.'

I moved quickly towards her, expecting hysterics. But Magdalena was looking at her friend with the bewildered look of someone woken too suddenly from a dream.

'Who? Who'll be standing there? What are you talking about?'

'Herr Huber of course. Your bridegroom.' It was Edith's turn to look confused.

Magdalena, with an almost visible effort, brought herself down to earth. 'I want you to be there, Edith,' she said to her friend. 'I need you to be there.'

She had spoken with certainty and kindness. Edith steadied herself and the procession continued – but to me it was as if Magdalena had proclaimed her passion to the world. For one thing was certain: the figure she'd imagined waiting at the altar as she fixed her eyes raptly on the crucifix might be her chosen bridegroom – but it was not Herr Huber from Linz.

I've always wondered what it would be like actually to *see* the Taj Mahal. I've read so much about it, seen pictures in the *Illustrierte Zeitung*. But when one got there in the moonlight would there be an anticlimax? Can it be as white and majestic as everybody says?

Well now I know, because I have seen one of Laura Sultzer's notices. It was pinned to the door of her room just as in the legends that Alice and I have collected through the years and there was no letdown at all.

Silence! it said, *Frau Sultzer is reading Grillparzer.*

I stared at it entranced while the maid who had admitted me looked worried.

'I don't like to disturb her – she's got them all in there, you see.'

'The Group, you mean? She's reading aloud?'

'That's right. It'll be a good hour before they're through.'

But I'd come myself with Edith's completed bridesmaid's dress instead of sending Gretl, for I have decided to keep an eye on the Bluestocking, and I had no intention of going without seeing her.

'Don't worry,' I said. 'I'll take full responsibility,' and I knocked and opened the door.

Laura sat on a high-backed chair reading aloud from Austria's most famous (and some would say her only) poet. Round her, in poses of rapt attention, sat her acolytes. I took in a pair of hermaphrodite feet in open sandals and the bosom of the lady who does Croatian cross-stitch, heavily banded in red and black.

'I've come to borrow Fräulein Edith,' I said cheerfully, 'I want her to try on her dress.'

Frau Sultzer put down her book and glared.

'As you can see we are busy.'

Edith rose quickly to her feet. 'Oh, but Frau Susanna has come herself . . .'

Accompanied by stares of outrage from the ladies, she hurried to the door.

The room that Edith took me to had to be her bedroom because it contained a bed. There was, however, nothing else even mildly feminine: no dressing table, no mirror, and the wash stand looked dangerously small. Instead there were bookcases lined with dark tomes and on the wall, framed in black, the prizes Edith had won at school.

The dress was a perfect fit, the soft green not unbecoming, but as Edith's bespectacled face, the bewildered eyes, emerged, I had again the feeling that in designing for her I had missed some clue.

'Have you been attending to your diet?' I asked her, for there was a large red spot in the middle of her chin.

'Well, I try. I remembered what Herr Huber said about red meat making good blood. Of course when I'm with the Group I can't . . . but when I'm alone, Cook sometimes brings me a steak.'

'That's good. Now all you have to do is wash your hair a bit more often and your skin will soon improve. Dandruff is very bad for acne. Every three or four days with a good shampoo.'

'Every three or four days!' Edith looked at me with horror. 'But my mother . . . I mean, surely that would interfere with one's natural oils?'

'Edith,' I said firmly, 'I do assure you that there is nothing that needs interfering with so much as one's natural oils.'

As she was dressing I asked her a question I had been turning over in my mind. 'Has Magdalena ever given you a hint of another . . . attachment? Someone she is fond of?'

'No, never; never. If she's got another attachment it's to the church. To God. She's asked Herr Huber to let her go into retreat once a month here in Vienna after their marriage; just for a few days. So you see . . .'

And I did indeed see. A few days every month to be with her lover – and for the rest, her family provided for, a generous and complaisant husband. Well, why not – many people would regard it as a sensible solution to her problems, but there was something about Herr Huber's innocence that made me furious on his behalf.

I was preparing to leave when Edith touched my arm. 'I've got something for . . . your friend. If you think she'd like it? If it wouldn't upset her?'

She led me to her rolltop desk, opened it – and took out a package. Inside was a long-stemmed pipe with a blue dragon on the china bowl.

'It was my father's favourite,' said Edith and, somewhat unnecessarily, added: 'My mother doesn't know.'

'That's very sweet of you, my dear. I think she'd love to have it.'

But I'd caught sight of something else that Edith had hidden in her desk. A book that was quite different from the scholarly volumes stacked round her walls. The cover was garish, the title, in tall red letters, stood out clearly, *The Art of Pork Butchering* by Hector Schlumberger.

Alice was sitting at her table playing patience with the new pack of cards she'd bought for Rudi to use during their summer idyll, and she'd lost weight.

'Edith thought you'd like to have this.'

She took the pipe, opened the porcelain lid, closed it . . . traced the outline of the dragon with one finger.

'It was his favourite,' she said, as Edith had done. And then: 'Sanna, I've never asked you, but I wondered . . . I mean how long does it go on hurting so *much*? How long was it before it stopped hurting after you came back from Salzburg? They say that Time Heals, but how *much* time? When did it stop, the hurt about your daughter?'

I hesitated, then told the truth. 'Oh Alice, it's never stopped. I don't know what time does, but I don't think it does that. Only, after a while . . . two years . . . three, perhaps . . . the pain becomes manageable. It becomes part of you and if someone offered to take it away . . . you wouldn't want them to because the pain is the link with the person you've lost. It sounds maudlin, but I don't mean it like that.'

'Yes,' said Alice. 'I see.'

She then went to get ready for the dress rehearsal of *Wiener-blut*, which is just as bad as everyone expected. 'They've given us new outfits for once: really very smart: sprigged muslin and poke bonnets . . . but you might as well be naked when the horses are on the stage. They've hired a special man with a gold shovel to scoop up their droppings and that's all the audience will be waiting for. The man with the shovel.'

I know it's completely ridiculous, but deep down I feel a touch of resentment because Rudi left her so unprovided for. It's five years before she'll get her pension and even then it's nothing much. Yet what could he have done without hurting Laura, a thing both of them spent their lives trying not to do?

After all, the gardenias, the decollete were not in vain! Sigismund has been reprieved. With luck now his piano will turn into an Arab steed on which he can gallop away to his destiny; a three masted galleon in which he can sail to glory!

I had given up all hope of Van der Velde but yesterday he came and he is going to give Sigismund a concert!

'I've got an unexpected gap,' he said, striding into my shop in his velvet-collared overcoat. 'A soprano I booked for October has let me down, the bitch. It's a six o'clock recital in the small salon at the Zelinka Palace so there's not much at stake.'

'He's really good, then?'

Van der Velde shrugged. 'He's small for his age and he's Polish; I can probably do something with that. But God, what a hovel! Someone'll have to clean him up,' he said, looking meaningfully at me.

'Are you going to give them an advance? They're practically starving.'

'An advance! You're out of your mind. They'll get twenty per cent of the takings if there are any, and that's generous. I'll need every kreutzer I've got for advertising, and even then I'm chancing my arm. I've never seen an uglier child – and obstinate too. He won't play the Waldstein. Still, its mostly Chopin they'll want.'

He hadn't been gone for more than an hour when Jan Kraszinsky appeared in the shop and asked me to make the boy's concert clothes.

'I don't do boy's clothes, I'm afraid,' I explained. But he didn't go, just stood there in his fusty black suit and looked at me.

'Sigismund expects it. It was what he said first when Herr van der Velde said we must get some clothes. "She will make me some new trousers and I will see inside her shop!"'

'I'm sorry.'

He took a step towards me. 'Herr van der Velde said it was you who told him about Sigismund.'

'I mentioned the boy, that's all.'

He moved forward, tried to take my hand to kiss it, and I retreated behind my desk.

'Sigismund must have . . . shining knickers,' said Kraszinsky, his German not quite up to his vision. 'And a blouse . . . with rufflets.' He sketched a frenzied cascade of frills with his unwashed hands.

'No! Absolutely not! Your nephew must not be dressed up like a little monkey.' (Oh, why couldn't I keep out of it? Why couldn't I be quiet?)

'But Herr van der Velde said that Sigi must look young. He must look like a very small boy so that people think he has even more talent.'

'The child is small enough as he is; you need no tricks. Sigismund is a serious child; he must be dressed with dignity. Look, I'll send you to a friend of mine – a man I worked for for three years. He speaks Polish too.'

I wrote down Jacob Jacobson's address and still Kraszinsky stood there exuding his particular brand of obstinate despair. 'Will you make me a drawing?'

'All right. It's an informal concert so you don't need velvet. Black grosgrain trousers – not shorts on any account. A white high-necked blouse – not satin: raw silk. The neck of the blouse and the sleeves piped in black.'

I sketched as I spoke. A miniature Peter-the-Great-as-Ship-builder emerged, and did not please Kraszinsky.

'But that is how the peasants dress in Preszowice.'

'Yes. You want that look. You mustn't try to turn him into a pretty Viennese boy – you can't do it anyway. Be proud of where you come from.'

He took the sketch.

'Will he want money now, this Herr Jacobson? Will he wait till after the concert?'

I was silent, remembering my years with Jacob, the warmth, the jokes. What if the concert was not a success, what if nobody came? Perhaps it would not be the best way to repay my debt to Jasha, to leave him with an unpaid bill.

'Oh, all right,' I said irritably. 'Bring the boy in the morning and I'll see what I can do.'

He was outside the door as I opened the shop.

'*Grüss Gott*, Sigismund.'

He bowed his concert master's bow, entered; stood in the centre of the room, looking . . . At the white daisies in the alabaster bowls, at the swathed mirrors, at the fans and ostrich feathers in a glass case. His nose wrinkled as he drank in the smells: the phlox in a silver tankard on my desk; my own scent which a little man in the Graben mixes for me, Nini's shampoo . . . Best of all he liked the low round table covered in a floor-length cloth of yellow silk to match the curtains. In hands which bore evidence of recent energetic scrubbing, he picked up the material and looked underneath.

'It is like a house.'

'Yes.'

I told him about the Countess von Metz's Pekinese who'd liked to hide there and make puddles, and took him off to be measured.

'God, he's thin,' said Nini.

His legs were like sticks; a tide mark at the base of the skinny neck showed where the washing had stopped abruptly.

I showed him the design for the concert clothes. 'That's the silk for your blouse; and that's the material for your trousers. It's called grosgrain.'

He nodded and repeated 'Grosgrain', frowning with concentration. 'And what is this?'

'That's muslin.'

'And what is this?'

'That's velvet.'

He walked beside me along the bales of cloth, asking the name of each, almost touching, but not quite. Sometimes he repeated a word. 'Taffeta,' he said in his husky voice, and 'Crêpe de Chine.'

Back in the salon he lingered again by the low table covered in yellow silk. Then suddenly he crouched down, crawled underneath it, and let the cloth fall again.

'Can you see me?'

'No, I can't. You're completely hidden.'

It's the first time I've seen him behave like a child, this future Paderewski. The next time he comes I'm going to put him in the bath.

The effect of Van der Velde's visit has been extraordinary. Frau Hinkler now tells everyone that it is only her kindness and care that saved the Kraszinskys from starvation. A man came from the piano firm, extending the period of hire till after the concert and offering unlimited credit in exchange for a mention in the programme.

'I always knew the boy would make it,' says Joseph, who now offers Kraszinsky cups of coffee on the house.

I cannot say that I have ever heard Joseph know anything of the sort, but never mind.

The Schumachers are genuinely delighted. Mitzi and Franzi and Steffi are to be allowed to go to the concert, but not the mercurial Resi.

'Mama thinks she would wriggle too much and fall off her chair,' said Mitzi.

Even Augustin Heller has decided to go and hear the boy. Herr Schnee is too busy, he says. The state harness for the cavalry of the Carinthian Jaegers is to be collected the same week as the concert

– but he comes out occasionally to stand on the pavement and listen to Sigismund practising.

'He's really getting it,' says Herr Schnee, as Sigismund explodes into a bravura passage.

For we have become musical connoisseurs, all of a sudden, in Madensky Square. We all know Sigismund's programme: the Moonlight Sonata, three Chopin mazurkas, polonaises, the Waltz in F Major . . . We even know his encores (if there are any): a piece by Schumann, a Brahms impromptu . . . Joseph, who can't even hum 'O Du Lieber Augustin', can be heard discussing Sigismund's interpretations with Herr Schumacher as he serves the wine. And in her attic, Nini leans out with shining eyes.

'Listen!' she says, 'he's playing the Revolutionary Prelude!' For it is this agitating piece that Van der Velde, that astute showman, has chosen for Sigismund's last encore.

Nearly all my clients are back, following the Kaiser who returned last week to endure his birthday celebrations. Poor man, he's eighty-one and tries hard to enjoy the processions and garden parties and firework displays in his honour. Last year he bent down to a little girl who was presenting a bouquet and had to be righted by his aides: something had seized up in the small of his back. This year a shower of pink tissue-paper hearts descended on him from a balcony and got caught in his moustaches, but he endures it all.

Professor Starsky called in to greet me. He is a modest man, but he feels that his lecture on the 'Epineuria of the Rainbow Snake' was well received in Reykjavik – and the English Miss strides past again behind her lovely dog.

I've made it clear to everyone who comes to the shop that they must buy a ticket for Sigismund's recital if I'm to get paid for his trousers. For Leah Cohen this is no hardship – she is musical and has promised to bring the whole family. Things look bad for her; her husband's emigration papers have come through and there is nothing now between her and the Promised Land. 'And what's so awful is to think that Miriam is staying behind and lording it in Vienna – bringing up her children and her grandchildren here while poor little Benjamin has to grub about making holes in the desert.'

But of course poor little Benjamin is delighted.

Frau Hutte-Klopstock is back from the High Tatras. Her sister has been in Paris and says that Poiret is freeing women from the corset. All I can say is that if he was designing for the women of Vienna, he would think again. But she too has bought a ticket for the concert, for Sigismund now belongs to us all.

Only the boy himself is unchanged. He practises all day as he always did and in the evening comes out and stands by the fountain.

'Is it necessary for me to try on my clothes again?' he asks when I stop and talk to him.

So I increase his fittings to a number somewhat in excess of what is needed to try on a pair of trousers and a shirt. It doesn't matter now. Soon Sigismund will ride away on his black steed of a piano and trouble me no more.

I must try to be seemly. I mustn't stand by my bedroom window shivering with happiness when my best friend is bereaved, my assistant is pining and there is cholera in Lausanne. Only how can I help it?

Alice has gone to spend a few days with her sister. Before she left she asked me if I'd put flowers on Rudi's grave while she was away.

'Anything that's friendly,' she said – and tried to give me money.

It's too late in the year for cornflowers, but Old Anna found me a bunch of tousled pinks which were friendliness itself and after supper I went across to lay them at Rudi's feet.

It had been raining and the air was wonderfully fresh. Hardly aware of the gathering darkness, I wandered about, in no hurry to go back indoors. The harebells on the mound of the Family Schmidt haven't yet recovered from Sigismund's depredations. Next year, perhaps – but next year the child will be gone. If the concert's a success, Van der Velde means to send him on a tour of Europe.

The cathedral clock struck ten, and a minute and a quarter later, our St Florian's. It's the scents that are so marvellous at this time of night. Stocks and tobacco flowers from the sacristy garden; syringa on the Schumachers' wall . . . and close by, stabbingly sweet, a dark red rambler, L'étoile d'Hollande, flowering for a second time.

I heard Rip bark once and someone hushing him. Then silence, and I resumed my litany of smells. Lilies from the urns of the Family Heinrid, a sprig of cupressus rubbed between my fingers . . .

And one more smell . . . a smell that I couldn't believe, that had to be a mirage, a dream, it was so lovely!

Only it wasn't. It was here, it was real – the scent for which I'd trade all others in the world.

I picked up my skirts and hurried towards the light of the porch. A pebble was dislodged; the smell of onions grew stronger.

'Hatschek! Oh, Hatschek!'

'Aye,' he said. 'It's me.'

'Oh God, I'm so pleased to see you. It's so long, the summer. But he isn't in Vienna? He can't be?'

He shook his head. 'He's still away and working himself into the ground. I came with dispatches. But he sent a letter.'

A letter. We don't write to each other, Gernot and I. It's too uncertain, too dangerous. In heaven I shall be able to write to him, but not here.

Then suddenly the night became ice cold. Why a letter now? Because he has decided to be faithful for ever to the high-born Elise and accompany her to the sulphurous springs of Baden-Baden? Because the Kaiser has sent him to govern Mexico . . . ?

I broke the seal, took out a single sheet of paper.

'On the sixth of October I'm going to Trieste to meet the Colonel of the Southern Division. It's only a brief meeting – no inspections – no reviews – and after that I'll be free for three days. This is what I want you to do. Take the night train – the 18.35 from the Sudbahnhol I shall be in the front of the train with my aides, but don't look for me. When you get to Trieste go to the Hotel Europa; you'll be booked in there and as soon as I've finished I'll come for you. We shall go on to Miramare where, at long last, I shall keep my promise. I may die unshriven but you shall – I swear it – see the sea.'

I looked up. 'Oh Hatschek! I'm going to see the sea!'

'Aye. And about time too. All these years he's been meaning to take you and there wasn't ever a proper chance. It's funny you not having seen it; an educated lady like you.'

I shook my head. But I'm not allowed to mention my peasant origin to Hatschek. For he approves of me, he really does. I'm not like Serbia or Macedonia. I'm good for his master.

'I know you want me to chew up this letter and swallow it,' I said challengingly. 'But I'm not going to. When I've read it a few times I'll swallow it, but not now.'

He grinned. 'I'm to tell him "yes" then?'

'Yes, Hatschek. You're to tell him "yes".'

He took a packet out of his tunic. 'It's all there – the tickets, the sleeper reservations, the address of the hotel. He says not to miss the train, whatever you do. It's the last one out over the weekend.'

'I won't miss the train.'

No need to inform Hatschek that I shall be sitting on the platform three hours before the train is due. Let me keep my dignity. Not that I fool him. Hatschek knows perfectly well how dementedly I love his master.

The sea, people assure me, is not at all like a very large lake. It is not like the Bodensee, where Alice once sang *Fledermaus* on an enormous floating raft. You cannot see across to the other side of the Bodensee, but the sea is not like that. It is not like a whole row of Attersees laid end to end, nor like the lake into which I threw my daughter's doll, though that lake was very, very deep.

The sea is different . . . other . . . it is something else. Everyone agrees on this. There is salt in the air that one breathes, and always a little wind – and the birds that wheel above the waves are serious birds which don't sing, but mew and shriek and cry. The sea makes a hem for itself, a strand on which flowers are not allowed to grow: it belongs to the world of the water, this hem, a golden boundary. So important is the sea that it makes the sky above it different too; the clouds move faster – and suddenly when one looks up, there is a ship. Not a paddle steamer or a barge. A ship.

I fetched the Baedeker and looked up Miramare. Population 2,100. A botanical garden with interesting palm trees. The Hotel Post, the Hotel Bella Vista, numerous pensions . . .

Sappho lived by the sea. They say that when she died she flew away over a cliff and became a swan, but I shan't do that. I shall take the ocean from my lover's hands, and I shall live.

September

'But you can't,' said Nini when I told her that I was going away for three days on October the sixth and she would have to look after the shop. 'It's the day of Sigismund's concert.'

I had forgotten this. I had simply forgotten.

'It can't be helped,' I said. 'Someone will be glad of my ticket.'

'He'll be so upset.'

'No, he won't. He won't even notice, so many people are going.'

Nini snorted and I glared at her, but she can't be reprimanded too severely at the moment because she is still very unhappy about the American boy who 'betrayed' her on the Grundlsee. Far from relaxing her Anarchist views, Nini is throwing herself with an even more fanatical intensity into her work for the cause, and next to the poster above her bed which says *Property is Theft* she has stuck another saying *Blood Shed for the Revolution is Blood Shed for Humanity* under which, I suspect, she cries herself to sleep.

Today I met Frau Egger coming out of a shop in the Fleischmarkt. I cannot say that she is my favourite client, but it is my habit to greet all my customers with politeness, so that I was amazed when she flushed bright red and scuttled away, still in the loden cloak I had made for her. Is she perhaps becoming unhinged from the strain of receiving the Hof Minister's attentions every Tuesday and Friday afternoon? Certainly there seem to be far fewer barrel organs about these days.

I love September; even as a child I think it was my favourite month. The little Schumacher girls are making corn dollies and wreaths of Michaelmas daisies for the church just as I made them with my mother when I was a child. And of course it's the most exciting time of the year for the shop: you can see the whole panorama of the coming season in the orders I receive. Frau Hutte-Klopstock has been reading a life of Pocahontas and thinks it would be nice to go to the races in something *fringed* and the Baroness Lefevre must have got tired of sitting on ortolans, for she has forsaken Chez Jaquetta and ordered a skating costume lined with fur.

But let me not fool myself. I know why this September is so magical. It's because I'm going to see the sea with Gernot. I'm going to have three days and nights with him and the waves will lap at our feet and his right arm will embrace me.

Magdalena's trousseau is finished. Gretl will take the wedding dress to the Winters' apartment; the rest of the things are to go down to Linz for there is to be no honeymoon: the couple are going straight to the villa with the bird table that is not a bird table framed between dark trees. On Monday Herr Huber will come to settle his account, but before that he has arranged a party – the last before his wedding.

At the end of September there is always an Operetta Night in the Stadtpark Kursalon. Singers come from the Volksoper; they have electric lights now, strung between the trees, and after supper (which is taken out of doors if the weather is fine) there is dancing to an orchestra which plays on the bandstand from which Strauss himself so often conducted with his fiddle.

For Alice the evening means hard work projecting her voice over the sound of rattling crockery and burghers enjoying their food, but for Herr Huber the occasion is all he could ask for to celebrate his coming bliss.

He looked so happy when we set out. I've blamed myself since for letting my own affairs swallow me up during those minutes in which I might have prevented what happened. But that's foolish. I was up against the lying sweetness of music that tells you no love is ever unrequited, no passion unfulfilled, while it is playing.

I may be the best dressmaker in the city, but I'm no match for the Viennese waltz.

Herr Huber had secured a table beside the dance floor with a vacant place for Alice when she could join us. Frau Sultzer had tried to prevent Edith from coming. 'She's still in mourning,' she said, but her own mourning did not prevent her from cavorting through the Vienna Woods telling the Group how to recite Grillparzer, and Edith now sat beside Magdalena consuming, without even the faintest tremor, a substantial portion of Tafelspitz.

I had come reluctantly, but I found I was enjoying myself. Herr Huber's exuberance, his intense enjoyment of the food – above all his melting and voluptuous pleasure in the music, was somehow infectious. I even managed to feel some pity for Magdalena. The bargain she had made might be a shoddy one, but it was hard, none the less, for the butcher's endearing sensuality – so evident to Alice and myself from the beginning – was entirely beyond her comprehension.

'Wien, Wien Nur Du Allein', sang the soubrette above the chorus, and yes, it was true. Only Vienna, only being here under the chestnut trees was what we wanted. The women whose men were present stretched out their hands across the table; those whose men were absent or dead (but not absent tonight, though dead) looked into their glasses and smiled.

The meal was cleared. More wine was brought. It was time to dance.

'Would you like to try, my dear?' said the butcher shyly to Magdalena.

'No, thank you. I don't dance.'

Edith too shook her head though Herr Huber was polite enough to ask her. Beneath the table I could see his feet in their white spats, tapping, tapping . . .

'Well, perhaps we'd better show them,' I said – and he beamed and rose to his feet, wiping his hands carefully on his handkerchief.

He was an extraordinarily good dancer; one rested on his stomach with the greatest comfort. As we spun and reversed to

'Voices of Spring' we attracted – for the floor was still fairly empty – some approving nods, and from a group of army officers, a smattering of applause.

'Won't you try, Magdalena?' I said as we returned to our table. 'The orchestra's so good.'

She looked for help to her friend, but the Bluestocking was talking to Alice who had joined us, and with the lightest of shrugs she let herself be led away by her fiancé. And of course she could dance; what Viennese girl is unable to waltz?

'May I have the pleasure, Madame?'

I looked up to find one of the soldiers who had applauded us bending over me. A Captain, rather older than the rest. It was an impertinence: I was with friends – but as I was about to refuse he held out his hands in a gesture that was curiously familiar and said 'Please?' – and I got to my feet.

The feeling of familiarity persisted as we circled the floor. He was about my own age, with dark eyes, a touch of grey in his moustache. I asked him the usual things: did he come here often, where was he stationed, was he married?

Yes, he was married. 'And you?' he asked, glancing down at my hand. 'You never married?'

Even then, in spite of the strange form the question took, I wasn't sure.

'No, I'm not married.'

'But you've done well. You're so elegant. So lovely and—'

At this moment all the lights went out. A deliberate ruse on the part of the management or an electricity failure? I don't know. But as soon as it was dark, I knew who he was. When I could no longer see his face, I remembered everything else: the way he used to hold out his hands, knowing that the good things of the world would come to him, the feel of his skin . . . and I was back in the attic of the fruit market, learning how simple love was – how unalarming.

'Karli! Oh, Karli!'

'I came back, Sanna, I came back,' he said, pulling me closer. 'It was a long time, I know . . . they sent us all over the place, but

I want you to know that I came back. On my wedding night when I should have been upstairs I sat down and wrote you a letter – only there was nowhere to send it.' The orchestra, by the glimmer of their desk lights, played on. It was the 'Destiny Waltz' and in the darkness I was seventeen again. 'I didn't realize how special you were, Sanna; I was so young, but later . . .'

I stroked his hair. 'It's all right, Karli. I managed. I'm fine now; I have a good life and so do you. It was so long ago.'

'Yes, it was so long ago. But I never forgot. It was like being in the sun all the time, being with you. You think it's always going to be like that when you're young . . . you don't realize. I thought that's what love was like, but it was you. It seems so awful that it's all gone – that there's nothing to show for it.'

I nearly told him. Oh God, so nearly! I wanted to say it so much: 'We made a golden child out of those weeks together, you and I. I have seen her and she is unparalleled, and though she is lost to both of us, she lives!'

But I didn't say it. I sent him back untroubled to his life. If he'd been happier I might have told him, if he'd spoken of his wife with pride – but I know what it cost me to leave our daughter where she is, and I did not think he had the strength.

Then the lights went on again, the past vanished, and I saw not my young lieutenant, but a tired man with broken veins on his face and disappointed eyes. Karli too came out of his dream, and as the music drew to a close he led me back to my table, bowed formally, and gave me his card.

'If I can ever be of service,' he said – and I watched him walk away to join his friends.

Only then did I notice that I had returned to a calamity. Alice and the Bluestocking had risen to their feet, both with a look of horror on their faces. I followed their gaze.

Herr Huber was standing in the middle of the empty dance floor. Blood from three long scratches ran down his cheeks, and he was crying.

I don't think I shall ever forget the sight of that huge, wretched man, unaware of the glances that were thrown at him, mopping and mopping with his large white handkerchief, now at his bleeding cheek, now at his streaming eyes.

Of Magdalena Winter there was no sign.

For twenty-four hours we heard nothing. Magdalena did not return home, she sent no word to Edith. Then, just as the police were about to be called, a message written in her own hand was delivered to her parents. She was safe; she was well; she was not to be searched for – and that was all.

Safe in the arms of her lover, I was sure, but held my peace. 'It was my fault,' said Herr Huber, sitting in my armchair. His kind face destroyed by grief, he stared blindly into his coffee cup. 'I behaved like an animal. An animal.'

He had arrived in my shop as promised to pay for the trousseau which Magdalena now will never wear.

'It was the music,' said the butcher. 'The music and the sudden dark. It overcame me.'

'But what exactly happened, Herr Huber? What did you do?'

He put down his cup. 'I kissed her on the mouth,' he said, and blushed a fiery crimson.

'Good God! Is that all? But you were to be married in less than two weeks. Is that so terrible?'

'Yes it is, Frau Susanna,' he said solemnly. 'I broke my oath.'

'Herr Huber, I think you'd better explain what kind of marriage you had in mind. I have often been puzzled by certain aspects . . .'

'Yes . . . yes. Only it is necessary to speak intimately.' He paused to wipe his eyes. 'You will of course have asked yourself why such a beautiful girl should agree to marry a man like me, especially when so many other people had proposed to her.'

'I wouldn't have put it like that. But go on.'

'It was because I agreed to her conditions. A pure marriage. A marriage of companionship. Well, not exactly companionship because naturally she did not want to spend too much time with me. But she agreed to live in my house and share my meals and let me adore her. Just to see her move about, to look at her, that was all I wanted. It was a privilege for which I would never have ceased to be grateful. To wake and know she was there . . . to see her moving across the lawn with a watering can . . .'

'And what was she proposing to do in this extraordinary menage?'

'Well, she had the benefit of knowing that her family was cared for – she's extremely attached to her brothers – and she was going to devote herself to work for the church. You could say that she was going to marry Jesus and I was going to marry her – only not carnally.'

'Herr Huber, you are a grown man, a man of the world. Did you seriously imagine that this bizarre arrangement would work?'

'I have to say to you, Frau Susanna, that I hoped . . . yes, secretly I hoped . . . I thought that if I was very patient . . . *very* patient . . . that one day perhaps she would lean her head against my shoulder, just for a moment . . . and I would touch her hair. Not stroke it . . . not at once, not for many months . . .' He had begun to cry again and, aware that I was about to lose my temper, I busied myself with the coffee cups. 'Then perhaps very, very slowly . . . perhaps in a year . . . she would let me brush her hair or sit beside her on the bed and hold her hand . . . And, yes, yes; I admit I dreamt that the time would come when she would come to me and smile that divine smile of hers and say, "I've been silly, Ludwig; of course I'd like to be like other married women".' He paused and looked at me like an enormous, desperate child. 'I loved her so much, you see. So terribly much.'

'Well, I think the whole thing is disgusting,' I said furiously. 'Obscene. You're a healthy man with an interesting profession—'

'No, no! I never spoke of it to Magdalena. It distressed her.'

'Well it doesn't distress Fräulein Edith and she's a great deal more intelligent.'

But the poor Bluestocking didn't exist for the lovesick butcher.

'How can you say that?' I had deeply offended him. 'How can you talk of obscenity? It was the purest, the most—'

'It wasn't anything of the sort,' I snapped. 'It was loathsome. An insult to human love. You've been saved from the most appalling unhappiness and so has your fiancée. I can't imagine how a man of your intelligence could come up with anything so sickly. You ought to be ashamed.'

'Ashamed! Of wanting to be pure! Of trying to embrace high ideals. Of being like Parsifal!'

'Parsifal. Ha! What do any of us really know about Parsifal? As for the opera it lasts six hours and in the first act absolutely nothing happens except someone waiting to have a bath. Furthermore, if Parsifal was so pure how did he manage to father Lohengrin – answer me that!'

After he left I regretted my sharpness. The poor man is half demented not only with grief but with anxiety. Where can a girl with no money have gone to? Is she hungry? Is she in need? All the same, it's odd how low purity comes on my list of priorities. From my earliest youth I have wanted to be successful, warm-hearted, generous and rich – but pure, no. Even when there was still a chance of it, I can't say I ever wanted to be *that*.

I wish there was someone other than Jan Kraszinsky to supervise the child's work for the concert. Surely he shouldn't be working so ceaselessly? It isn't just the way he plays that Kraszinsky is bullying him about.

'Don't make faces', we hear him yell. 'Don't screw up your mouth!' The child isn't even allowed out now in the evenings for his airing by the fountain. It's understandable, I suppose, Kraszinsky's agitation, so much depends on this one night. He's borrowed money on the strength of it and given up so much, but he's a fool. He'll break the boy's health if he goes on like this.

This morning I met Rip coming out of the paper shop and because we're old friends, he let me take the *Neue Presse* briefly from his jaws. Opening it at the concert page, I found Van der Velde's advertisment: a pen and ink drawing of a romantically coiffed waif who looks about six years old with the caption: *In 1842 – Anton Rubinstein! In 1887 – Ignace Paderewski!! In 1911 – Sigismund Kraszinsky!!!*

The child's debut is attracting a lot of attention; nearly all the seats are sold and the critic from *Tageblatt* is said to be coming, and the man from the *Allgemeine Zeitung*. Van der Velde took the boy to the hall to show him where he was playing.

'What was it like?' I asked Sigismund.

'It is a very fine piano,' he said seriously. 'A Bosendorfer – and I don't have to sit on books; there is a special seat.'

'And the hall itself?'

He looked at me, puzzled. I don't think he saw anything except the piano. His concert clothes are finished. I've made him an extra pair of trousers for every day and Nini, unasked, has stitched him a handkerchief embroidered with his initials. With his hair properly cut, he looks now what he is: a plain and serious little boy – but tired, terribly tired. Van der Velde, who surely should be keeping an eye on him, has gone to Paris.

Mitzi Schumacher, that gentle soul, has her own anxieties.

'Should I marry Sigismund, do you think, Frau Susanna, when I'm grown up?'

'Do you want to, Mitzi?'

'No, I don't. He's too thin and small. But someone should look after him if he's going to be a famous pianist and see that he eats enough. Maia won't – she says that pianists only go to boring towns, not interesting places like the Amazon, and Franzi doesn't like to cook.'

'If he's going to be famous perhaps he could get a housekeeper,' I suggested – and took Mitzi out to look at my pear.

But the pear affected this motherly person much as Sigismund had done.

'It's not very big, is it?'

'It'll grow,' I said firmly.

Though I do wonder . . . The first frosts are expected soon. Perhaps I should simply cut my losses and pick the thing?

Alice has received a letter which has troubled her. It's from a bank in Switzerland and full of mysterious and pompous language. They want her to travel to Zurich bringing evidence of her identity, and she's convinced that she has committed some misdemeanour of which she is unaware.

'I think that's most unlikely, Alice,' I said. 'I can't imagine a more law-abiding person and Switzerland isn't really a very frightening place. Also they say they'll give you back your fare – and I shouldn't think they'd do that if they're going to arrest you. Anyway Swiss gaols are probably lovely: all scrubbed and hygienic with cow bells to summon the warder.'

It doesn't seem to get any better for her, Rudi being dead.

'If only there weren't so many small bandy-legged men with gold pince-nez,' said Alice, trying to laugh. 'I see them everywhere.'

The search for Magdalena continues. I take no interest in it – where the girl has gone with her lover is no concern of mine – but Herr Huber seems to be shrinking inside his skin. Sometimes I wonder if it wouldn't be wiser to tell him what I saw at St Oswald's: one short, sharp blow might be better than this long-drawn-out distress. I have told Edith, but the Bluestocking in her own way is as obstinate as her mother and she doesn't believe in Magdalena's elopement.

'I don't think she'd do that,' she said. 'It doesn't sound like Magdalena. She never wanted anything to do with men.'

Ah, I wanted to say, if you'd seen her with this man. If you'd seen the yearning, the way she leant towards him.

But I left it. I can't do anything now about Magdalena, nor about the little Count of Monte Cristo preparing for his big day as I prepare for mine. For it's less than a week before I take the train to Trieste. I'm making myself a dress of corn coloured shantung – very simple, very Greek. Fluted like a pillar I shall stand with my lover on a promontory licked by the azure water – and I shan't only look like a temple, I shall be one. Yes, it's true. The thoughts I have, the gratitude, the worship will be the kind of thoughts that they must have had in the dawn of time, those men and women who lived so closely with the gods.

'Physical love is completely unnecessary for you,' Gernot once said to me. 'A work of supererogation. You're in love with the whole created world. I'm competing with every idiot sparrow chirping on a window sill, with every tree that bothers to put out a leaf.'

If only it were true! If only he knew how the sparrows would fall and the leaves shrivel if I lost him.

But he shall know. I'm not ashamed that I mean to make of this journey a kind of sacrament. If either of us smile on our death-bed, it shall be because we are remembering our days and nights beside the sea. So move over, Oh Shulamite, for I assure you that the best bedroom of the Hotel Post or the Hotel Bella Vista (or even of a pension with an asterisk, hard as it is to imagine Gernot in such a place) shall be the setting for my 'Song of Songs'!

I've bought a new sponge bag too.

October

I woke early this morning, the day before my voyage to the sea. The weather has been misty and autumnal, but I don't mind that – indeed it makes it better. For once you go through the Mallnitz tunnel and come out on the southern slope of the Alps, the sun always shines, Gernot told me that. Just one tunnel and you are among the lemon trees and the blue skies, in the country that the songs are about. 'Kennst Du Das Land Wo Die Citronen Blühen', wrote Laura Sultzer's Goethe, and tomorrow I too shall know it.

At seven thirty I slipped out to the apothecary in the Walter-strasse to fetch the special shampoo that Herr Frieberg mixes for me, for the dress of corn-coloured shantung in which I shall stand like a pillar on a promontory demands the echoing gold of my coiled hair and though Nature has done what she can, Herr Frieberg's Special Mixture is undoubtedly a help.

When I had washed my hair and buffed my fingernails I wandered peacefully through the shop. Everything is ready for to-morrow's journey. My hats, nested in tissue, rest in their boxes, my case is dusted, the shoes already packed. The most reliable cab driver in the Albertina Platz will come at five o'clock, a good hour before I need to leave to catch my train, but I love stations and hate rush.

Across the square I could see Jan Kraszinsky come out of the apartment house looking dishevelled and agitated as usual, and hurry off towards Joseph's café. I haven't seen Sigismund for days.

'Let it go well for him tomorrow,' I prayed – and forgot him.

In the long mirrors I saw myself, my hair loose, my eyes bright, and felt a surge of gratitude to God for letting me have a little longer, still, to summon beauty. He could so easily have smitten me with a spot on the chin, a cold in the nose, but He had seen into my heart and stayed His hand.

Kraszinsky had left the café and was running across the square. He was hatless, his coat-tails flapped – he was coming towards my shop and I was instantly angry. I wanted nothing of the Kraszinskys and their problems on the morning of my waiting day.

'He's gone!' said Kraszinsky almost falling across the threshold. 'Sigi's gone!'

'Nonsense! He'll have gone out for a stroll.'

'No, no! He never goes out now, I forbade it because of the boys.'

'What boys?'

'Herr Schumacher's nephew and the other one who sings in the choir. They throw stones at Sigi and shout things.'

Oh God, poor Sigismund. I had known nothing of this. 'When did you last see him?'

'In the night. I woke up and I thought I must tell him to change the fingering in the polonaise, so I went in and he was there then.'

'You woke him in the middle of the night to tell him that?'

'Yes, yes . . . Often I have ideas in the night and I tell him. The concert *must* be a success, it must! I have borrowed so much money! Oh God, what shall I do?'

The man was quite out of control, shaking . . . a little mad.

'Did Frau Hinkler not see him go out?'

He shook his head. 'He must practise still – he must practise! Yesterday he made a mistake in the last movement of the sonata.'

'I'm not surprised he made a mistake. I'm surprised he can still play at all. Look, you'd better tell the police, but I'm sure he can't have gone far. He may even be back now; he could have slipped in through the courtyard.'

I almost pushed him out of the door, but my lovely, quiet day of anticipation was shattered. Nini came out of the workroom and I told her what had happened.

'Poor little scrap; I saw him yesterday at the window and he looked terrible; really ill. No wonder he's run away.'

'He hasn't run away,' I said crossly. 'Where would he run to?'

Strange that I never thought of the obvious thing. Even after Nini gave a little squeak and said: 'Oh! There's something moving there, under the table', even then I didn't think.

But of course he was there. He must have crept in while I was out at the chemist . . . come for sanctuary to the 'little house' of yellow silk he'd hidden in when he came to be measured for his clothes, and fallen asleep.

For he slept still; he had only stirred briefly. He lay curled up, his arms crossed over his chest. I saw a human embryo once, in a jar in Professor Starsky's lab; a waxy white, curved little creature with slits for eyes who lay as the boy lay, seeming to protect itself from birth, from life.

We pulled him out, helped him on to the sofa.

'I can't,' he said, still not quite conscious. 'I can't. I don't remember how it goes any more.' And then something in Polish which he repeated. 'Sleep,' said Sigismund. 'Please can I sleep?'

I could have murdered Kraszinsky at that moment.

While Nini locked the door and pulled down the blinds, I pushed the hair away from Sigismund's face and found a bloodied graze on his temple. A stone thrown with venom would have made such a mark.

'He won't be able to play, will he?' whispered Nini.

'I don't know.'

With twenty-four hours to go it seemed impossible. Even if they could get him to the hall what kind of performance could be expected from this weary little wreck? But it wasn't the ruined prodigy I saw in Sigismund's hollowed cheeks and stricken eyes; it was a sick and ill-treated child.

I sent Nini for some milk and a croissant, and while the boy ate and drank I tried to think what to do. I'd kept the day deliberately free of clients; most of my packing was done. And suddenly I knew . . .

'Sigismund,' I said, 'we're going away for a little while. Just you and I. We're going to play truant.'

He put down his cup. 'I don't have to practise any more?'

'No. You don't have to practise ever again if you don't want to.'

'And it doesn't matter if I screw up my mouth?'

'It doesn't matter in the least.'

He was on his feet; he put his hand in mine. He was ready.

I gave Nini her instructions. 'I'm going to slip out at the back. Give me half an hour, then go and tell Kraszinsky that the boy is safe. I'll bring him back this afternoon.'

Only when we were in a cab bowling down the Walterstrasse did Sigismund ask: 'Where are we going?'

And I answered: 'To the Prater.'

The words were hard to say.

I had not been in the Volksprater – the Wurschtlprater – since I went to try out for my daughter the dappled horses on the roundabouts, the coconut shies, the swings. That day, twelve years ago, when I had been so sure that she and I were about to begin our life together, had been one of the happiest of my life. She was with me all the time in spirit, driving a miniature carriage pulled by white llamas, throwing hoops over bobbing celluloid ducklings, clapping her hands when I won for her a cross-eyed, fluffy dog. And at the end she led me, my lion-hearted daughter, towards the giant wheel with her blonde head tilted to the skies.

So it was not easy now to drive through the gates with this alien child.

Sigismund, as we got down from the cab, stood looking around him in bewilderment. There must have been fairs even in Galicia, but the boy seemed overwhelmed and his cold hand fastened tightly on mine.

But in any case I wasn't going to let him choose what to do first. I knew. The treasure I'd discovered when I came here with my little phantom daughter was still there: I could see the brightly coloured sign above a clump of bushes. GROTTENBAHN, it said – and I moved resolutely towards it, paid, led the child into the first of the wooden coaches, painted a brilliant red and blue.

'What is it?' he whispered.

175

'You'll see.'

Only a few people got in behind us; it was late in the year for the Prater. The bell rang and we lurched forwards into the darkness. There was time to be properly afraid – and then the train stopped.

We were opposite the first of the lighted caves. It showed Cinderella stooping by the embers, her golden hair brushing the hearth. Everything that would later transform her life was there: the pumpkins, the mice . . . One baby mouse playing beneath the dresser was half the size of the rest, with tiny crooked whiskers. The clock ticked in the corner, hams and salami hung from the rafters. She was utterly forlorn, poor Cinderella, and as we leaned out of the train (which we were not supposed to do) we could see the tears glitter on her cheeks.

'Who is she?' whispered the boy beside me, and I realized that he had never heard of Cinderella; never in his life.

Yet he was transfixed, as I was too. For we were entirely in the kitchen, sharing her loneliness, her rejection – but at least I knew the future as did the children in the coaches behind me. That the old woman visible through the window was coming . . . that as soon as the train moved on she would be there, the fairy godmother under whose cloak one could see the glimmer of silver.

The train surged forwards and beside me Sigismund sighed. It was too soon, always too soon, that jerk of the train, one never had time enough. Another journey into the darkness, and then we stopped once more.

Snow White this time, and the glass coffin and the dwarves clustered round in mourning. And how they mourned! They held their heads in their hands, they clutched their handkerchiefs, one lay prostrate among the lilies of the valley on the ground. White doves hung above the bier, white roses sprouted from the earth and she lay with her raven hair streaming across her face.

And again for the other children in the coaches the sadness was almost pleasurable because they knew, as I knew, that the prince would come (one could see his painted horse, his handsome head on a distant hill), the poisoned apple be dislodged, the grief-stricken dwarves rise to their feet and dance.

But not Sigismund. 'Why is she dead?' came his hoarse little voice beside me. 'Who killed her?'

'I'll tell you later. But it's all right. She comes alive again.'

Another plunge into the darkness and the giant Rubezahl, our special Austrian giant and wholly benevolent. He was holding a cow in the hollow of his hand and chiding it for not giving milk while tiny people in the field below looked pleased.

And on again to the Sleeping Beauty. She lay back in a swoon holding her spindle and she had the richest, fattest plait of flaxen hair you have ever seen. A great hedge of thorns grew across the window and all around her lay the palace servants overcome, as she was, by sudden sleep. There was a sleeping dog, a sleeping chef in a tall hat – and a sleeping kitchen boy still holding aloft the cutlet he had been about to eat.

'A sleeping chop!' said Sigismund, pointing, and for the first time since I had known him, I heard him giggle. He had made a joke.

There were twelve stories depicted in the Grottenbahn and Sigismund knew none of them. The Little Mermaid, walking on her sore new feet towards her prince, Mother Holle trying to shake down the sky, Little Red Riding Hood carrying her basket between marvellously spotted toadstools while the great wet tongue of the wolf lolled between the pines . . .

The last but one of the lighted grottos was almost the best: Thumbelina landing in Africa, held in the beak of her swallow. And what an Africa! Swirling scarlet lilies, fruit hanging from palm trees – and in the petals of a flower as golden as the sun, Thumbelina's tiny princeling awaiting her.

In the last of the caves, Hansel and Gretel lay asleep in the forest, pillowed on leaves, while above them an arc of angels in white nightdresses with pink bare feet and glittering halos, held out protecting hands.

And here at last Sigismund was able to make a connection

through his music, and in his husky voice he hummed the theme of the 'Angel's Ballet' from Humperdinck's opera.

Then we were out in the daylight, blinking, trying to adjust to the shock of daylight and ordinariness.

The train stopped. The other people got out. Sigismund made no move whatsoever.

'Where would you like to go next?' I asked.

A stupid question. He sat absolutely immobile, grasping the rail in front of him.

'Again,' he said.

I bought two more tickets. We went round again. Cinderella, Snow White, the great giant Rubezahl . . . When we got to the Sleeping Beauty he made his joke about the sleeping chop, when we got to Hansel and Gretel he crooned the ballet music from Humperdinck, and each and every time the train moved on, he sighed.

'What about one of the roundabouts?' I suggested when we were out once more.

He shook his head. 'Please, again,' he said.

You can believe it or not, but we went seven times round the Grottenbahn. Seven baby mice, seven benevolent giants, seven jokes about sleeping chops, seven golden princes waiting for Thumbelina . . .

Then I struck and pulled him out of the car and we went to look for something to eat.

The sun had pierced the mist. We found a place where we could sit under a chestnut tree, but Sigismund was not very interested in his Wiener wurstl. He wanted to know the stories. All the stories.

'I can't tell you all of them, Sigismund. Choose one. I'll tell you the rest some other time.'

He chose 'Snow White'.

'Once upon a time,' I began, 'there was a woman who longed and longed for a child. She wanted a daughter more than anything in the world . . .'

I had stopped, fighting the lump in my throat. But it was she herself who urged me on; the golden-haired phantom who had travelled with us on the Grottenbahn and who is now – perhaps I'd better face this once and for all – old enough to have children of her own.

'One day she sat beside her window which was framed in darkest ebony; outside, the snow was falling and as she sewed she pricked her finger so that three drops of bright red blood fell on to the ground . . .'

He moved closer and his mouth parted. What had been done to this child, or left undone? Even in a Polish forest, surely, they had heard of Snow White? But of course it is women who tell these stories to their children. There seemed to have been no women in the boy's short life.

'I will get you a book, Sigismund,' I said when I had finished. 'All the stories are in a book.'

He shook his head. He wanted me to tell them, and of course he is right. The stories are for telling.

We went then to the roundabouts. He chose to ride not on a dappled horse – I had noticed already his dislike of horses – but on a swan. He enjoyed it, but he didn't want to go round again. It was an experience complete in itself.

Then came the *Wurschtlmann*. He's so famous the Prater is named for him and you can see why. A hideous rubber man with a red nose who, for a few kreutzer one can thump and pound and wallop to one's heart's content, knowing that he will right himself undamaged and come up for more. Give him a name – that of your mean-minded boss, your bullying commanding officer – and you can punch him insensible and walk away, purged.

'Would you like to have a go, Sigismund?'

Even before he shook his head I saw him instinctively shield his hands, hiding them behind his back – and that was the first time I remembered the concert.

In the end, though, the Prater is about the ferris wheel whose fame has spread throughout the Empire. It towers over everything else, its carriages take you a hundred metres into the sky. To be up there and look down on the city is to ride with the gods.

So I asked him: 'What about the giant wheel? Would you like to go on it?'

His hand tightened in mine. A tremor passed over his face. She had not been frightened even at six years old, but the boy was scared.

'The view is very beautiful from the top. You can see all Vienna.'

He stood still in the middle of the path. He tilted his head and gave a small sniff.

'I want very much to be brave,' he said in his low, cracked voice. 'I very much want it.'

And suddenly it all dissolved – my long antagonism, my restraint, the resentment that I felt at being asked for what belonged only to my daughter. I saw him sitting beside his dead mother in the Polish forest, waiting for her to wake . . . Saw him wobbling on the *Encyclopedia of Art*, playing and playing because he could no longer talk. I remembered the silent patience with which he'd endured his uncle's bullying, saw the graze on his forehead of which he'd said no word.

And I knelt beside him and took him in my arms.

'You are brave, Sigi. You're very brave, my darling,' I said – and kissed him.

So now I can tell you this. They are entirely exact descriptions of what happens, those ones in the fairy tales which tell you what occurs when you kiss an ugly frog, a hairy beast, with proper love.

Sigi didn't kiss me back or cling to me. He just straightened his shoulders and then in a calm, almost matter-of-fact voice, he said: 'Now we will go up', and then led me to the brightly painted carriages swaying high above our heads.

It is evening now and I am sitting at the window waiting for my lovely day. Sigi is asleep in the house opposite; he will play tomorrow and play well, I know it. Kraszinsky has had enough of a fright to leave him alone. I went in with him and helped to put him to bed; he was asleep as soon as his head touched the pillow.

And he made no fuss at all when I told him I wouldn't be at the concert.

'I have to go on a journey, but I'll be back on Tuesday and then we'll go to Demels and have a splendid *Jause*!

'Can we eat Indianerkrapfen?', was all he wanted to know.

'Yes, Sigi. Lots of Indianerkrapfen.'

All the Indianerkrapfen in the world he shall have when I have been with my lover by the sea.

I haven't written for over three weeks. I couldn't. I was too wretched.

It was because of Herr Schnee's horses that it happened and who could have foreseen that? His nephew, the cornet, kept his promise. At five o'clock on the day of Sigi's concert and my journey to the sea, he trotted into Madensky Square at the head of his troop. They were splendid horses, cavalry chargers, each ridden by a trooper in full regalia of the Carinthian Jaegers: dolmanyis, shakos, swords . . .

It was a kind of joke. It is not easy to remember that. A sort of birthday tribute to Herr Schnee – a salute – but a jape really. Horses do not need to be fitted for their harness, but the cornet was very young.

The day was misty, if I remember. Dusk fell early, but the lamps were not yet lit.

When the horses came I was standing outside on the pavement with my suitcase waiting for the cab to take me to the station. I saw how fresh the horses were; how mettlesome. One in particular, a black ridden by the soldier who was next in line to the officer.

The cornet shouted, 'Halt!' and dismounted, and gave his reins to the man behind him. Herr Schnee came out, smiling and bowing, and walked along the line of horses which stretched past my shop also, and then he and the cornet went inside.

In the apartment opposite, Sigi and his uncle came out on to the step to wait for Van der Velde's limousine. I was hidden from him by the horses but I saw how proudly he held himself in his new clothes.

Then . . .

I know what he saw. I know exactly what he saw in the dusk. He was four years old again in the forest in Preszowice. I know the word he screamed though it was in Polish:

'*Cossacks! Cossacks!*'

And he went mad. He raced across the square to the horsemen who had come to kill me as they had killed his mother.

Rip, barking, followed him.

The boy couldn't see me as I stood pressed against the doorway of the shop. He threw himself at the leader of the troop, he tried – this midget – to wrest the man's sword from its scabbard, and all the time he screamed abuse in Polish.

The trooper was amused at first. 'Hey, hey,' he said, reigning in his horse, controlling the cornet's charger.

Then Rip arrived. In a paroxysm of barking, he ran between the horse's legs.

I shouted to Sigi. 'It's all right, Sigi. It's all right!'

He didn't hear. Still yelling abuse in Polish, caught in his time warp, he started to tug at the bridle.

The soldiers were no longer amused. One of them dismounted and grabbed Sigi. He wriggled free and cut across behind the black charger.

'You must run, you must run!' he shouted, tugging at my skirt.

And Rip followed. Sigi, after all, was a member of his house and he barked defiance at the stamping horses . . . managed to rise on his vestigial hind legs . . . to nip the black charger in the fetlock.

Oh God, those seconds that pass so quickly that one cannot believe, one cannot call them back and undo the horror they contain.

He was a good horse, the black; there was nothing vicious in him. He only reared up to escape the irritation of the yapping dog – and brought his forelegs down again. Not really very hard, but hard enough. Rip only had time to yelp once, and then he lay still.

There was so much blood – so unbelievably much blood for such a little dog.

The accident changed the soldiers' mood. Their faces turned ugly, sullen, foreseeing trouble. And all hope of quietening Sigi's madness vanished.

'You see! You see how they kill!'

I had pulled Rip's body clear; I wanted to cover him; I did not think it was fitting that he should lie there so mangled, so . . . exposed, and I took off my travelling cape and laid it across his body.

Then Van der Velde's limousine turned into the square. Kraszinsky rushed up to him, and the impresario strode over to the horsemen.

'Get hold of that boy,' he ordered. 'Take him to my car. Hold him down till I come.'

They responded at once to the authoritative voice, the velvet-collared overcoat. Two men dismounted and grabbed Sigi, still clutching my blood-stained skirt, and dragged him away.

Then my cab came. I seized my suitcase. Delivery, the end of the nightmare – Gernot and the sea!

I was pulled back savagely, my arm wrenched behind me. 'Oh no!' said Van der Velde. 'You're coming too. You landed me with this hysterical little tyke and you're going to take the consequences.'

'I can't. I have to go. I have a train to catch.'

Van der Velde laughed and twisted my arm tighter. He was enjoying himself. 'You can go when he's played – because he's going to play if I have to tie him to the piano stool.'

The soldiers were on his side. I was linked with the boy in blame for the accident. 'Want any help sir?' one of them shouted.

Van der Velde marched me across the square, pushed me in beside the child, slammed the door. As he started the engine I saw a misshapen figure in a grotesquely flowered hat come out of the apartment house: Frau Hinkler dressed for the concert. She stood for a moment on the steps, then began to walk towards the soldiers . . . to run . . .

*

I was very quiet in the motor. My suitcase had been left on the pavement, but I still had my purse with the tickets. Nothing else mattered; my blood-stained skirt, my missing cloak . . . not even the sobbing child on the seat beside me. As soon as the car stopped in a crowded place I would get out and run for a cab. Van der Velde would not dare to pursue me where there were people. There was still time.

We came to the busy section by the opera. The car stopped. I reached for the handle of the door.

Van der Velde was in front, but Sigi saw what I was doing. 'You'll be all right now,' I whispered to him. 'You can see no harm has come to me.'

He didn't answer. He had stopped sobbing; he made no noise at all, but he had begun to shiver. It was bad that time in the square when his uncle didn't come home, but this was far, far worse. His whole body shook as if with a frightful fever.

If he had tried to pull me back, or screamed, I'd have made my escape, but he made no attempt at all to stop me. He just sat there, looked at me – and shivered.

So I stayed.

I suppose I must try to describe the concert, but the truth is, I don't remember much.

In the artist's room we tried to wash off the blood and tidy ourselves. Van der Velde led me to one of the press seats in the front row. Then he made an announcement: there had been a traffic accident on the way to the hall; he craved the audience's indulgence for the child.

It was a good move, of course. There were sighs and whispers, a fluttering of programmes: the poor little waif. Then the impresario came down to sit beside me and make sure that I wouldn't try to escape. The idea was that Sigi would be able to see me and know that I was safe.

What a joke!

He came on to the platform, bowed his concert master's bow, began to play. He played the Beethoven sonata, the Chopin mazurkas, the waltz in F . . . There was not one moment, between the pieces, when he even glanced my way. For this child, who an hour ago had been completely mad, nothing existed except the piano.

I could have left in the interval; even Van der Velde saw that the child had forgotten me, but it was too late. The train had gone.

The concert ended in an ovation. There were cries of 'bravo' and 'bis'; he was recalled again and again; a woman in a silver fox plucked a rose from her bosom and threw it on to the stage. My last glimpse of Sigi was of a dark head appearing briefly between the circle of well-wishers that surrounded him – newspaper men, autograph hunters, agents – and then vanishing once more.

That was three weeks ago and I haven't seen him since. When the Kraszinskys returned to the apartment house, Frau Hinkler screamed such abuse at them, holding Rip's body in her arms, that Van der Velde took them back to a hotel. He smells money now and is prepared to see the Kraszinskys decently housed. The cheque for Sigi's concert clothes came through the post and now he is on a concert tour of Germany.

There's one thing I still don't know; whether the fuss, the acclaim, was because he looked so young and there had been an accident, or whether he has a proper and lasting talent. I didn't hear him, I was too wretched – and anyway I wouldn't know.

No, I'm lying. After the encore that Van der Velde had specified, there was a fourth. Sigi chose that: it was the Mozart *Rondo in A* and I heard that.

I heard his music.

I think I have lost Gernot.

We do not telephone, but this time, for something so important, he would surely have phoned? If he still loved me he could not be so cruel as to deny me a chance to explain. Or he would send me a letter telling me where I could get in touch with him. But in all the weeks since I missed the train there has been no word.

So I think that something was damaged permanently when I failed to come to him. I have never before not kept an assignation, you see. Once I had a broken ankle, but I still came. Once, in a blizzard, I was ten minutes late, but I have always come. And I think that he cannot forgive me. For I have no illusions about myself and Gernot von Lindenberg. In the eyes of God we are equals, and perhaps in bed (where God, so strangely, often seems to be present) but in the eyes of the world we are desperately unequal. There must be a hundred women waiting to step into my shoes.

Alice guesses that something is wrong. 'Is it the little dog, Sanna? Is that why you're sad?' she asked me.

No, it is not the little dog. I miss Rip very much – we all do in the square – but he was ten years old and died in an instant. Each time I look out of the window in the early morning I wait to see him come down the steps to fetch the paper and then remember he is not there – but it is not the little dog. What has happened to my face cannot be laid at Rip's door. How do the cells in my skin, the follicles of my hair, know that I have lost Gernot? 'A woman is as old as her elastic tissue', a pompous friend of Professor Starsky said once, and my tissue has become profoundly inelastic. Nini has taken to bringing me hot milk at bedtime. Soon, if this goes on I shall be wearing navy blue with touches of white.

Oh God, no. Not that. Gernot will write, he will phone, he will send Hatschek. I *cannot* have to live without him!

Meanwhile I'm not the only person with problems. Gretl's fiancé, who is now in charge of his own fire engine, has given her an ultimatum: marriage within six months or the engagement is off. Gustav Schumacher has jammed the master switch in the saw shed and fused the electricity supply to two apartment houses and a laundry, and Leah Cohen's husband has bought the tickets for the Holy Land.

'Promise you won't dress Miriam when I've gone, promise me,' she begged. 'That's the only thing I can't stand, the idea of Miriam swanning about in your lovely clothes.'

Edith Sultzer has just telephoned to say she wants to see me.

She arrived with her briefcase so full that the lock did not shut and she had to hold it under her arm.

'Goodness, Edith, what have you got in there?'

The Bluestocking threw me an agitated glance. 'Could I come through into the workshop?'

'Of course.'

The cutting-out table was clear. Edith asked for some newspaper, which Nini brought. Then she opened the case. Plaited into four strands, fastened by twine, the lengths of white-blonde hair tumbled out in incredible profusion.

'Good God – what is it?'

'It's Magdalena's hair. I told you it belonged to The Christ. She's cut it right off and she wants to sell it. She said one could get a better price if one sold it privately. Only I don't at all know where to go.'

I ran my fingers along the marvellous silky stuff, feeling quite shaken at this heroic butchery.

'You've found her then? But where? Where is she?'

'She's in the Convent of the Sacred Heart. She's going to be a nun. That's why she wants me to sell her hair; to get money for the order.'

'I see. And the man I saw her with?'

'He's a Jesuit priest – Father Benedictus. He was her confessor when she was being confirmed. She went to ask him if she could be released from her engagement – she went several times, but he wouldn't let her. He said to be offered a pure marriage and a chance to help the church financially was a fine opportunity. They're very practical, these Jesuits. But of course when Herr Huber broke his side of the bargain, Magdalena felt free . . . and she ran away and took refuge with the nuns.'

'How did you find her, Edith? Did she send you a message?'

Edith shook her head. 'I packed some toilet things and went round to all the convents saying I'd brought some things for her and would they give them to her. In the first three they said she wasn't there, but in the fourth they just took them and asked if I'd like to see her. She's only a postulant still, she's not walled up.'

'You seem to have been very resourceful.'

Edith shook her head. 'I just remembered what she said when

she was little. Again and again she said it. "I'm going to be a nun because I love Jesus more than anyone else in the world." I think he was so real to her she couldn't bear anyone else even to touch her. She wanted to make the sacrifice for her family, but she just couldn't.'

Then she asked if I would come with her to the convent. 'She looks so different – it isn't just the hair, it's everything. You know how dreamy she was; not quite in the world. Well that's all changed. And if you saw her, Frau Susanna, you could help me to tell Herr Huber.'

'He doesn't know yet?'

Edith shook her head. 'I told her family, but they just weep and wail though Herr Huber gave them quite a big sum of money even after she ran away. You're so good at making people feel better, and I don't know how to say things . . . only in essays, not to real people.' She gave a little sniff. 'I'm going to miss Magdalena. We were both misfits – she was too beautiful and I was too ugly.'

So I went with her to the Convent of the Sacred Heart. There was no difficulty about seeing Magdalena. The woman who admitted us was Sister Bonaventura who had made the silken rose on the rich cream dress I wore to the Bristol, and we are friends.

The convent adjoins a group of almshouses with a small hospital, and the nuns are responsible for this.

It was there that we found Magdalena. She wore an apron and a cap over her shorn hair, and was swabbing down, methodically and carefully, the stomach of an ancient lady who lay on an iron bed. Nothing could have been further than the image I had had of Magdalena rapt in prayer and communicating with her saints. Rather she looked – as she dried the old lady and rolled her over like a strudel – like a satisfied housewife attending to her daily tasks. And it occurred to me that Magdalena's love affair had ended rather better than Alice's or Nini's – or mine: in a busy and contented marriage.

We exchanged a few words, but Magdalena had started on a second patient, cutting the toenails on a pair of gnarled and yellow feet, and we soon took our leave.

There seemed to be no point in delaying over breaking the news to Herr Huber. On the way to his shop in the Graben, we called for Alice. She was packing for her journey to Switzerland but she agreed to come with us. The butcher has a special fondness for her and I felt we needed help.

We found Herr Huber supervising a display of knackwurst, and the way he looked when we told him that Magdalena was safe – the relief, the tenderness on his face, the sudden hope we had at once to extinguish – is best forgotten.

'She was on her knees as when I first saw her?' he asked eagerly. 'She was in prayer?'

'No. She was swabbing down an old lady's stomach,' I said firmly.

'And she has cut her hair,' said Edith. 'She has given it to The Christ.'

'Like Cosima Wagner,' put in Alice.

Herr Huber's bewildered round eyes went from one to the other of us. 'Did Frau Wagner give her hair to The Christ?'

'No. To Wagner. She cut it off and put it in his grave. He was The Christ to her. Well, God . . .'

But poor Herr Huber was quite unable to deal with a shorn Magdalena swabbing the abdomens of ancient ladies. We carried him off to lunch at the Landtmann, but he was a broken man, able to swallow only a couple of schnitzels and a slab of oblaten torte.

'I'm giving up my room at the Astoria,' he told us. 'And I'm putting a manager into the shop here. There's nothing in Vienna for me now.' He brightened for a moment. 'Fortunately I've had a good offer for the villa. A very good offer.'

I didn't ask if the bald Saint Proscutea was included in the fittings.

'You'll be living in the old house by the river, then?' said Edith, and Herr Huber nodded.

I suggested that Magdalena's trousseau should be sent to her convent for the nuns to sell, and he agreed to that.

'Of course I shall be coming to say goodbye. You have been

such good friends to me.' He dabbed his eyes. 'And everyone is welcome in Linz. My sisters would be so happy.'

'How soon are you leaving?' asked Edith.

'In about three weeks. Earlier perhaps.'

Edith put down her knife and fork. 'Really?' she said. 'So soon?'

I have told myself that I have lost Gernot and I have believed it. Yet deep down there has been a glimmer of hope. After all it is not sense to think that one broken assignation – even such an important one – could have such consequences. My fears could have been due to the time of year, the shortening of the days, the cold which so easily extinguishes hope.

But now I know that it is true. I have to live without him. I know because of Hatschek.

This is what happened.

The Baroness Lefevre, the one who got tired of sitting on ortolans, lives in a grace and favour apartment in the Hofburg. She's had influenza and I said I would call and fit her for her skating costume.

I was walking through the gate from the Michaeler Platz into the first of the palace courtyards when I saw Hatschek coming out of a door on the far side.

He saw me. There was not the slightest doubt about it. He was coming directly towards me and when he caught sight of me, he smiled his slow, stupid smile and touched his cap.

Then he must have remembered his instructions for he flushed a fiery red and turned on his heel.

It was absolutely unmistakable: the recognition and the rebuff, but I couldn't believe it, I couldn't take it in – and I called to him and hurried after him. I was quite without pride; all I wanted was just a few seconds to explain – just a few seconds, nothing more.

He increased his pace – then, just as I was catching up with him, he veered to the right and turned in through the archway where the Swiss Guards stand on duty.

That part of the Palace is sealed off to everyone who does not have business there. Hatschek knew the password; some of the offices of the Ministry of War are there, and they let him through, but not me of course – not a distraught woman carrying a cardboard box – and I stood there waiting helplessly while he hurried down a flight of steps and vanished.

So it's true, you see. It's over. Hatschek has been forbidden to speak to me. I'm like Serbia now, and Macedonia – bad for his master.

I must have loved Hatschek too, just a little bit, for somewhere in the agony of losing Gernot is this other foolish grief for the Bohemian Corporal who was my friend.

November

All Souls' Day was a suitable one for a day given over to the dead: murky, dark and chill.

The bereaved came to St Florian's all the previous evening bringing candles and coloured lanterns to burn through the night. Professor Starsky, whose wife lies there, brought a wreath of artificial poppies, and this year as in all the years since I've been here, the grave of the family Heinrid was tended by a hired crone who sat all night mumbling liturgies. They're all over Vienna, these frightening old women muffled in shawls who, for a few kronen, will guard the graves on the night of All Souls, munching fat bacon from their baskets and calling on the Holy Ghost for the lost souls in purgatory. Herr Heinrid (who is eminent; he's Egger's second-in-command at the Ministry of Planning) rents the same one every year and then arrives himself, after a good breakfast, to fill the family urn with flowers.

I don't know where Rip is buried. I'd have liked to pay my respects to him but Frau Hinkler will speak to no one since he died.

I had lit candles by Rudi's headstone because Alice is away in Switzerland, but on the day of All Souls I do not stay in the city with its flickering lanterns and its Masses for the Dead. On All Souls I have business elsewhere. I go to Leck.

The monks are generous. Everyone who has served the abbey can lie within its walls. No grave here is untended, for a lay brother keeps the flower beds bright and the grass cut. It's a sunny churchyard on the slope of a hill; one could grow vines there, but the church grows souls instead.

On All Souls' Day, though, there is seldom any sun. As I walked from the station with my basket, the rain bit my face and flurries of wind whipped at my cloak.

I went first to the grave of the old monk who had told me about Sappho and her songs. He doesn't need anything – he never did, even in life – but I say a prayer for him and leave a white rose because of what he told me: that in the valley where she lived they grew wild, the hyacinths and the roses, and she used to make garlands of them for her friends.

Then I went to see my father.

I never went back to see him after I eloped with Karli. He knew nothing of my daughter's birth. I meant to write to him when I was settled, but I imagined Aunt Lina gloating over my disgrace, seizing any letter that came.

Actually I was wrong. She fell ill soon after I left and found it increasingly hard to look after my father. Who knows, she might have been glad of someone young and strong to help her. For my father grew cantankerous and difficult as he grew older. In the end she went home to die and my father lived on alone.

It wasn't till the year after I left my daughter under the walnut tree that I returned to Leck. My father was pleased to see me; he wanted me to give up my job in Vienna and come back to keep house for him, and I refused.

So it never went right after that. I came a few times, and I wrote, but I wouldn't do the one thing he wanted. The guilt was bad – it still is – but that's the trouble with guilt: it can make you suffer like nothing else but it can't change what you do.

It always seems wrong to put flowers on my father's grave: an awl, a chisel, is what he would have wanted there; it's his hands I remember – planing, sawing, measuring . . . So I left my candles and asked his pardon for letting him die alone (though I was there actually, during his last illness, trying to undo the neglect of years with my assiduous nursing).

And then to the grave that would call me back from the furthest corner of the earth.

My mother lies in her own place beneath a tombstone that says only: *Elisabeth Maria Weber 1841–1887*. She *was* the beloved wife of Anton Weber; she was, God knows, the beloved mother of Susanna Maria Weber, but it doesn't say so. When we buried her, my father and I, we felt no need to state the obvious.

The bells toll and toll always on All Souls' Day, the solemn chant of the prayers for the dead goes on from dawn to dusk, and there is always a wind. Yet the day I spend with my mother, muffled like those graveyard crones so that the cold won't drive me away, is never sad.

We talk, you see. We talk and talk, my mother and I. I tell her everything that has happened through the year and she listens (God, how that woman listened!) and then she tells me what she thinks. I was twelve when she died but even now there are thoughts that come to me only in her voice.

Mostly she approves of me, she really does. There are certain pettinesses she doesn't care for, and she thinks there's no reason for me to carry on the way I do about Chez Jaquetta who also has to live. But my mortal sins – the conception of my daughter without benefit of clergy, my relationship with Gernot – for those, out of her great compassion she forgave me long ago.

But this time she was not entirely pleased with me. She was sorry that the little dog died, sorry that Sigismund had gone without a word and very, very sorry that I had lost Gernot for she knew, if anybody did, how deeply I had loved him – but did I not still have my shop, my work, my friends, the beautiful square in which I lived? What about the sparrows, my mother wanted to know? What about the autumn leaves? She did not really want a daughter to whom a Hungarian Anarchist felt compelled to bring hot milk in bed.

'It's the only bad thing, Sannerl,' said my mother in her soft, warm dialect. 'Turning your back on the created world. Not seeing, not touching, not hearing. It's what we can't be doing with up here, that kind of waste. You've had twelve years of good living. Don't whine, my darling. Because it is a kind of whining: getting bags under your eyes and not tasting the butter on your bread.'

I listened. I wept a little and I remembered how I'd lost my *Lebensmut* after my daughter was born and how everything goes wrong when you lose courage. Then I gave her the flowers that Old Anna always saves for me to bring to Leck – and went home.

And the next morning the letter came.

It was thick, white, with my name typed in black letters and the seal of the House of Habsburg on the back.

I took it with such eagerness. I knew it was from Gernot: he was going to forgive me: he was going to explain Hatschek's strange behaviour: the nightmare was past!

Then I opened it.

The official language confused me so much that I couldn't at first take in what I was reading. I had to go through the pompous cold jargon of bureaucracy twice before I understood the contents.

It was not Gernot who had written to me. It was the Hof Minister Willibald Egger.

What I remember next is Nini bending over me asking if I was all right.

'What is it, Frau Susanna? Has something happened?'

I motioned to the letter on my lap.

'But he can't!' said Nini when she'd read it. 'He can't do that. He's insane!'

'The Walterstrasse *is* narrow,' I managed to say.

'So it's narrow; that doesn't mean he can pull down the whole side of the square. He *can't*! Not your shop and Herr Heller's and Herr Schnee's . . . He can't!'

'Ah, but he can, Nini. He can.'

I took the letter from her. The kind man had provided a map to show the extent of his depredations. The chestnuts would come down and General Madensky on his plinth. Joseph would lose his terraces. The new road, veering westwards through the demolished side of the square and the presbytery garden, would leave St Florian's as an island surrounded by traffic.

'What does he mean you won't get any compensation?'

'I only rent the shop, you know that – he can give notice

without paying me a kreutzer, and he has. April the first. Herr Schnee's in the same position. Heller owns his shop so I expect they'll have to pay him something, but it'll be a pittance; Egger will see to that.'

'It's unbelievable. A swine like that, a man with a disgusting Little Habit able to destroy people's lives . . .'

Gretl had come through from the workshop and the girls went to make me some coffee. I had begun to see what the loss of the shop would mean to them, but they only thought of comforting me. Then Herr Heller came past the window and knocked on the door of the shop. His white hair was on end; he looked grey with shock. Heller is sixty years old; his shop has been his life.

Helping him to a chair, pouring some coffee, steadied me a little. As he was drinking it, Herr Schnee arrived from the other side.

'Isn't there anything we can do,' said poor Heller. 'An appeal? A petition?'

'Waste of time,' said Herr Schnee tersely. 'No one can do anything to stop Egger. Heinrid's been trying for years: he'll have opposed this scheme, with his family buried in St Florian's, but he's only the second-in-command and Egger's got them all in his power. You'll see – this place'll end up as the Eggerstrasse with motors hooting down it all day long and clouds of dust and fumes. That's probably why he's bricking up the fountain: to make a place for his statue.'

We looked at the plans again. What was left of the square would be a travesty, that was certain.

Joseph came next from the café.

'I told you . . . I told you. No one believed me. They're all in league against us, the bureaucrats.'

'At least you'll still have a roof over your head,' said Herr Schnee. 'You can still run your café.'

'What's the use of that? It's the terraces that brought the custom. My mother's taken to her bed.'

All morning people came. Frau Schumacher hurried across and took me in her arms and cried.

'I can't bear it, I can't bear it if you go! Albert says he won't stay, not in what will be left of the place. And poor Father Anselm – when you think how he struggled to make a garden in spite of the boys. He's gone to see the Church Commissioners, but they'll never find a place like this.'

Then my clients began to arrive. Egger's plans had been published in the morning papers. There was no way of keeping the news from them.

Frau Hutte-Klopstock tried to hearten me. 'You'll find somewhere else, Frau Susanna. You won't be beaten.'

I don't know. I don't think I can do it again; not what I made here.

Leah Cohen arrived without an appointment and with a hamper which she unpacked on my yellow table, urging me to keep up my strength and eat.

'When I think that Egger came to Heini only last month about his insomnia . . . I could so easily have told Heini to kill him with a little morphia – not that he ever listens to me!'

In the afternoon an extraordinary thing happened. The English Miss halted, tied the setter to the lamp post – and came in to the shop. Close to, the long-legged, high-breasted Amazon was a shy woman with gentle eyes the colour of her blue-green misty tweeds.

'I wished to say how sorry I am,' she said in excellent German. 'It has been such a pleasure walking past here each day . . . it was like a garden – always something interesting and right for the season.'

She is not the daughter of a lord with horses in Rotten Row as I'd imagined. Her name is Norah Potts and she's a paid companion.

Professor Starsky called with a bunch of roses. I was alone when he came and stupidly inattentive, for when I came out of my thoughts I found that he was again offering me, in my homeless state, his hand and heart. Well, who knows, perhaps I shall come to it. There may be worse things than being a Frau Professorin with access to herpetology conferences in Reykjavik.

Old Anna's visit was almost the hardest to bear. She came with her basket as she'd come that spring morning when I decided to keep this journal, and there were tears in her eyes. 'They want to take away everything that's good, don't they? They want to destroy everything that's quiet and belongs to the past. Thirty years I've sat under those trees . . .'

'Oh, Anna, you'll find somewhere else. We can't do without you.'

'No, I'm through. I'll have to go down and stay with my son. He doesn't want me – no one wants an old woman – but he'll have to put up with me. It doesn't matter; my life is past. But it's you. Such a lovely place you've made; it's like a fairy story in here, the light and the prettiness of it all! And the way you've taken that wild Hungarian girl and given her a home. Oh, I could spit!'

I went to bed at the usual time, but of course I couldn't sleep. Hour after hour the anxieties ran round in my head. How could I get my stock cleared and my orders fulfilled in so short a time? What was to become of Nini? Where could I go?

I got up and stood for a while looking down at the moonlit square. Each of those five chestnut trees were like people to me; entirely distinct. General Madensky had been cleaned only a few weeks before; his domed head was devoid of pigeon droppings and we had all admired him.

How could one man with a few pieces of paper destroy all this? Presently I put on my cloak and let myself out through the workroom and into the courtyard. It was very cold but my pear tree stood proudly in the light of the full moon. This time next year it would be gone, its roots covered in asphalt.

'Whom the gods love die young,' I said to the little tree, and touched its bark.

Then I looked more closely. The light was very bright; I could see the branches clearly.

My pear had gone. Only two days ago I had seen it hanging securely from its bough. I'd made a resolution to pick it on Sunday, it was already absurdly late.

I bent down and searched the paving stones. There was no sign of it. I fetched a lantern to look more thoroughly, and now

I noticed that the stem holding the pear had been cut. There was no doubt about it; it was severed cleanly in a way that could only have been done by scissors or a knife.

And this suddenly was too much: this shoddy and pointless theft. I had lost Gernot, I had lost my livelihood and still kept some measure of control. Yet now, standing there in my night-clothes, I sobbed like a child because of a tiny, unripe and probably uneatable pear.

If only people weren't so kind it would be easier.

Actually I'm lying; everyone hasn't been kind. I met Chez Jaquetta in the Kartnerstrasse, all dyed lovelocks and battleship *poitrine*, and there's no doubt about it – she smirked.

But everyone else . . .

Herr Huber called in his motor and said he'd heard of a shop in the Graben three doors down from him which was becoming vacant. I went with him to inquire, but the rent was way above anything I could reasonably afford.

I've just managed to stop Nini from going to Ungerer to ask for her old job back ('Only in the evening, just to help out a bit with money') and Gretl is threatening to postpone her wedding yet again. She's told her fiancé that she must stay and help me pack, as though seeing her safely settled isn't the thing I need most.

Peter Konrad has offered me the job of running the dress department in his store. This is a serious possibility and I must think it over carefully. The salary is good, I'd have a chance to travel – he even said he'd take Nini. It's not what I want: I want to make dresses not buy them for other people, and I'd find it hard to work for someone else after being on my own for so long – I'm really very opinionated. But I don't think things will ever come together again for me the way they've done here: the shop, the square, the people.

And Alice . . .

I'd left a note for her and as soon as she was back from Switzerland she hurried round. She wore the kind of pretty, silly hat she hadn't worn since Rudi died and she was almost her old self, but her first concern was for me.

'Your lovely, lovely shop – it's insufferable. Only listen, Sanna, you know there's room in my flat for both of us, don't you? Lots and lots of room now that Rudi doesn't come any more. You could stay as long as you like – for ever if you wanted to. And there's nothing to pay – it doesn't cost me any more to have you there.'

I hugged her and thanked her, but it wouldn't work. We're not girls any more; those times are past.

Then she told me why they'd asked her to come to Zurich. 'It was because of Rudi, Sanna. He's left me some money. Quite a lot of money!'

'Oh, Alice, I'm so glad!'

'It isn't just the money,' said Alice. 'Well, it's that too, of course – but mainly it's knowing that he thought of me. And all that time! Ever since we were first together he's put some away each month into the bank in Zurich. It's so like him – thinking it out so that it wouldn't upset his family, doing it so quietly. And do you know what was so marvellous? Being there in the National Bank talking to the manager and . . . being known as belonging to him. Being able to admit to a total stranger how much I loved him and everyone treating me like . . . his wife.' She broke off and dabbed her eyes. 'It was so lovely, Sanna, being able to hold up my head and . . . sort of declare myself. All those pieces of paper to sign, linking me with Rudi.'

Then last night I had supper at the Schumachers.

I didn't want to go, I wasn't in the mood, but Mitzi told me the occasion was special, there was to be a surprise, and at the last minute – I don't know why – I put on the rich cream dress with the self-coloured rose. It wasn't easy to take it out of the cupboard and it was slightly too grand for the occasion, but some instinct prompted me and I was right for the little girls clustered round me full of compliments – and still with this slight air of mystery. Maia was there too, spending the night with Mitzi, and Gustav growing even fatter and more vacant-looking. The saga of his disasters at the timber works is becoming quite Homeric.

It was necessary, of course, to admire Donatella, holding court in her cot, and Kati and Gisi who were too young to be allowed to stay up for supper, and then we sat down to one of Helene's excellent meals: mushroom soup, roast goose . . .

Then Lisl came in with the desert.

I have never been particularly fond of knödels: it seems sad to me that fresh fruit should be covered in potato dough, rolled in breadcrumbs, fried . . . But it was clear that the knödel that was to be served to me was special. Mitzi and Maia took it from Lisl, it was on a Meissen plate all on its own, liberally doused in vanilla sugar – and a slightly unexpected shape.

'It's for you,' said Mitzi, beaming. 'It's a surprise.'

'We both thought of it,' said Maia firmly. 'Both of us had the *idea*, but Mitzi cooked it.'

I picked up my fork, hoping to rise to the occasion, whatever it might be.

'Shall I cut it right through?'

'Yes,' said the girls, clearly relieved. 'It would be best to do that first. You don't just want to swallow it without looking.'

So I cut it carefully into two. In the middle of a very thick ring of dough was something brownish and small and just a little de-composed.

'Goodness!' I said, playing for time.

'Don't you see what it is? Don't you recognize it?' Mitzi's blonde head and Maia's black one were bent over my plate. And then, thank heaven, recognition came.

'Oh,' I said. 'It isn't . . . it can't be . . . but it is! It's my pear!'

'Yes, yes,' cried the little girls sitting round the table, and nodded and beamed.

'We made it for you because we thought you wouldn't get enough to eat the way it was. So we picked it,' said Maia. 'We did it secretly at night so that it would be a surprise!'

So you see my mother was right. It's all still there: sparrows and leaves, knödels and friendship. Even without Gernot, it's all still there. Somehow I'll manage. Somehow I'll find a way.

Egger has wasted no time. Men appear continually in the square: those men in brown overalls with hard hats and tape measures and furtive faces. The chestnut trees are to be cut down next month: already they've made white crosses on the bark. There's always one tree – the one closest to Joseph's cafe that I worry about: its leaves fall earlier than those of the others and its buds come out later. Maybe its roots, below the pavement, have encountered some obstacle, and I have the absurd idea that the white cross will kill it even before the felling: that it is a kind of evil eye.

Herr Schnee is being businesslike about clearing his premises. He's morose and terse and says there's no point in shillyshallying; the sooner he's out and in a new place the better. He has a chance of a workshop on the other side of the town and is not inclined to be sentimental about the square.

Augustin Heller's a different matter. He's a broken man, wandering about his shop, putting things in piles and then forgetting where he's put them. I can't imagine how he will ever manage to get away. His daughter in Wiener Neustadt has 'agreed to take him in' as he put it. This is Maia's mother – a woman as bossy as her daughter, but without her daughter's imagination. No wonder that Heller has aged by ten years since Egger's letter came.

Now I had better put down what happened this afternoon.

The Countess von Metz arrived in her creaking carriage and asked me to make her an evening dress. She was as rude and decrepit as ever but I had the feeling that she was concealing some kind of triumph.

'I've come to ask you to make me an evening dress.'

'I'm afraid that's impossible, Countess. As you may have heard, my shop is closing and I can't take any new orders.'

'Ah, Egger.' She banged on the floor with her cane. 'Yes, I've heard. But you won't let a parvenu like that stop you. You'll start up somewhere else.'

'No, I don't think so. I've been offered a job in a department store.'

I hadn't yet decided what to do about Peter's offer but whatever else happened, I was going to get rid of the Countess von Metz.

'I wouldn't approve of that,' said the incredible old woman. 'I would not be pleased.'

I said nothing. She'd paid me for her green broadcloth with a piece of arsenic-impregnated wallpaper sandwiched between glass. It came, she'd informed me, from Napoleon's house on St Helena and was the undoubted cause of his demise.

'Nevertheless, I must insist that you make me an evening gown immediately,' she went on. 'It is a matter of considerable importance.' And unable any longer to conceal her triumph, she said: 'I have been invited to a house party at Burg Uferding.'

Strange how nothing *shows* when one's heart races and one's mouth becomes dry as dust.

'Burg Uferding?' I managed to say. 'Isn't that the home of Field Marshal von Lindenberg.'

'It is.' But she was not at all pleased that I – a mere dressmaker – had heard of Uferding. 'They're having a house party next week and I have been asked to join them. The Field Marshal wrote himself at the bottom of his wife's letter, so you see I must have something new to wear. It might be an advertisement for you; I'm quite prepared to mention your name.'

But now I did have to turn away. She was going to Uferding, this horrible old woman. She would sit in his hall by the great log fire and his dogs would lay their heads in her lap. Perhaps Gernot himself would tuck the wolfskin rug round her knees, settling her in the sleigh the von Lindenbergs used to take their guests to church – and in the candlelit dining room she would watch his hand stretch out to the silver fruit bowl. Perhaps for this selfish, ancient creature he would select a pear and—

No. *No. . . !*

'Well?' came the irritable voice of the Countess.

But I couldn't turn round yet. I was in agony. Yes, I, a healthy woman, not hungry, not cold, experienced agony – and only those who have never been in love will quarrel with the word.

Then I got myself under control – and what I did next I did because of the absurd and foolish notion that at least something of mine would go to Uferding. That perhaps she would keep her word and speak my name in Gernot's presence and he would hear that I was losing my shop and—

And then, nothing. Gernot had probably known long ago what was going to happen. I could see now that he had been trying to warn me all along of Egger's plans.

'I can't make you a dress in so short a time,' I said. 'But I have some evening dresses belonging to a trousseau that has not been claimed. I could alter one for you.'

Magdalena's dresses were laid out in the workroom, ready to send to the nuns to sell; they would not miss one. The Countess was shorter than Magdalena but her measurements were not dissimilar.

And as always, just when I hated the old woman most, she disarmed me. She walked among Magdalena's gowns with a kind of eagle-eyed reverence – and when she picked the dress she wanted it was not the Renaissance gown in cloth of gold, nor the burgundy velvet with a tabard, but the simplest of Magdalena's evening dresses: a soft georgette in misty blue, high necked and gently draped, on which Nini and I had worked for countless hours – and which was, quite possibly, my masterpiece.

We hear about Sigi only from the papers. The tour of Germany and Switzerland was a success and he is bound for Paris. Helene brought me an article from the *Wiener Musikant* with a picture of him. The critics have been enthusiastic: only old Hasenberger, the veteran musicologist, and Busoni who heard him in Berlin, said his talent shouldn't be forced, he should be put to a good teacher and have time to study and mature. But there doesn't seem the slightest likelihood of that happening now that Van der Velde has got hold of him.

The attic flat across the way is still empty. Frau Hinkler has been so morose since Rip died that I don't suppose anyone can get past the door and now, with the dirt and noise of the demolition to come, it will probably be impossible to find a tenant.

Sometimes at night I imagine I can hear him practise.

We have had a drama: Gretl's fiancé has become a hero and she has agreed to marry him at the end of January. There was a piece about him in the paper, three girls wrote and asked if they could meet him, and that was too much even for my dozy Gretl. Father Anselm will perform the ceremony – so she at least is taken care of.

And the goldfish slayer has been sent back to Graz! I'd better begin at the beginning.

Of late, Gustav, egged on by Ernst Bischof, has been in search of his manhood, and in pursuit of this elusive quality, he managed to smuggle a cigar and a box of matches into the timber yard.

During his lunch hour three days ago, he retired to the loft above the stables where Herr Schumacher's dray horses are kept, and proceeded to light up.

The experience was not what Ernst Bischof had told him it would be. Gustav choked, spluttered . . . and dropped his burning cigar into the straw!

At first the boy was more terrified of his uncle's wrath than of the flames. By the time he emerged, screaming, into the yard, the loft was ablaze, and the horses stamping with terror.

Herr Schumacher is a fool, but he behaved well. With the help of his men he led the horses to safety out in the street, but by the time the fire brigade arrived the flames had ignited a pile of saw-dust and spread to the open-sided shed where the sawn planks were put to season. And beyond that were the workshop with its valuable machinery . . . the barn with the wagons . . . the offices and store of figured hardwood for the cabinet trade . . .

That all these were saved were due to the energy and foresight of Gretl's fiancé. While the men in the first engine started to douse the stables, he drove his machine up the alleyway at the side of the yard, leapt the fence and hacked down the far wall of the blazing shed, pushing it inwards in spite of his blistered hands, so as to contain the blaze until his men could follow with their hoses.

Herr Schumacher is insured of course. Rebuilding of the stables has begun already – but the day after the blaze, Gustav was put in a carriage and returned to his parents. The little girls are delighted; the aquarium has been brought down from the attic – but the problem of the inheritance remains unsolved.

What is going to happen now about Herr Schumacher's blood?

December

I suppose I should have known. Nini wasn't just wearing her assassination shoes when she went out, she'd made herself a new velveteen jacket and her eyes were shining with excitement.

But they do so often. With her fervour, her belief in 'The Propaganda of the Deed' whatever that may mean, she often goes to her meetings looking like that.

It was her half day so she left in the afternoon.

'I'll be late,' she said – but she is often late, and I went on with my stocktaking. Peter Konrad has found someone who'll take my cloth at valuation.

In the evening I went out to buy a newspaper. On the front page was a picture of what looked like a moustachioed slug, but was apparently Herr Engelbert Knapp, the German arms manufacturer and steel magnate who was arriving in Vienna as a guest of the Austrian Ministry of Trade.

Even then I felt no disquiet. I had heard Nini rage about Knapp, who is said to treat his workers abominably and recently called in the army to put down a strike in his factory at Essen – but who have I not heard Nini rage about: archdukes, cabinet ministers, financiers?

There had been some threats to his life by subversive bodies; an extra contingent of police had been detailed to guard his route from the station to the Hotel Imperial . . .

I don't wait up for Nini. When I first took her in I set myself the task of leaving her free, so I went to bed at the usual time, but when I woke I knew at once that she wasn't there. Her bed had not been slept in; her room was bare and tidy. Between the two

Anarchist posters, she'd pinned a picture of a candy-striped pinafore cut from a fashion magazine.

I told myself that she'd found a boy she liked and spent the night with him – not unlikely in view of her determination to forget Daniel Frankenheimer. But for all her wildness Nini is considerate. She's come in in the small hours, but never as late as this.

So by the time the pounding on my door started, I was prepared. But it wasn't the police; it was Lily from the post office, tear-stained and frantic. Her father's a revolutionary, that's how she and Nini met.

'They've got her, Frau Susanna! They've got Nini! They've rounded up everybody in the group – as soon as Knapp died they went to the cellar and took everyone.'

'What happened to Knapp?'

'Someone threw a bomb at his car as he was coming down the Ring.'

I took the paper from her. *Assassination Horror* screamed the headline. A young man dressed like a student had stepped out from behind a tree as the car slowed down to take a bend, and thrown a bomb. Herr Knapp died instantly, as did his chauffeur. His secretary was seriously injured and so were a number of by-standers. The assassin made no attempt to escape. '*Long live the poor and the oppressed*', he'd cried, and biting on a cap of fulminate of mercury which he had in his mouth, he fell lifeless to the ground.

'You must tell me exactly how far Nini was involved,' I said to Lily. 'That's the only way I can help her.'

'I don't know exactly, Frau Susanna. Honestly I don't. I know she had to go to a hat shop in the Neuermarkt at three and pick up a message. It was part of a chain of messages, I think. But she couldn't have been there when the bomb was thrown because she was in Ottakring when the police came and that was miles away. They were all there.'

Oh yes, I thought wearily. Naturally. They would all assemble afterwards so as to save the police the trouble of rounding them up one by one.

'Where have they taken her, Lily? Have you any idea?' Lily's face was grim. 'She's at Pechau. They've taken her to Pechau.'

It's the worst of all the gaols in the city: ancient, rat-infested, notorious. I packed a shawl, some washing things, a basket of food – quite without hope that they would let me see her.

It takes an hour to drive to Pechau and you can tell that you're approaching it because even the surrounding streets are dank and squalid and the muffled people who walk in them seem blighted by the proximity of that awful place.

I had dressed carefully, I spoke carefully, I smiled. This got me past the outer office and into an inner one with a desk and a chair – and an official of the kind I remembered from the days when I had pleaded for particulars about my daughter. A stone-waller, a no-sayer, a cipher whose bumbledom was itself an act of cruelty.

'I have come about my assistant. A dressmaker. A girl I have adopted. I think she was arrested last night in Ottakring.'

He drew a dossier towards him.

'Name?'

I gave Nini's name which is long and very Hungarian. He consulted his papers.

'There is no one of this name here.'

Oh God, Nini – did you have to give a false name as well as everything else?

'Herr Lieutenant,' I said, elevating the oaf to officer status, 'the girl is just twenty years old. She is a minor. Would you allow me to see the prisoners you took last night? That's all I ask. Justice must be done, I entirely see that; she must take her punishment. But I am, in effect . . . her mother. I only ask to know where she is.'

I made no attempt to bribe him. The sums involved, the procedure, the donations to the Prison Officers' Welfare Fund, were out of my reach. I could only entreat.

'You may look at the female prisoners taken last night. Three minutes only. And leave the basket here.'

I followed a janitor into the basement.

It's the smells that tell you first that you are in a place without hope. Unwashed bodies, urine, vomit . . . Then the sounds; moaning, keening, a raucous laughter that is worse than the wails . . . A monotonous, endless banging of something against iron . . . And the cold.

We had passed through a steel door into the women's quarters. A series of cages, each the size of the lion's cage in Schönbrunn Zoo, but filled with women. Some stood by the bars, hanging on with their hands as Alice had stood at Rudi's funeral; some lay huddled on the ground, rolled up as if to make themselves as small as possible and minimize their wretchedness. A few sat with their backs to the wall, gossiping, not ashamed. These, I supposed, were the prostitutes who were picked up and released at the whim of the police. Nini was not in the first cage, nor in the second, on the floor of which lay a woman so old that it was impossible to believe she was still capable of wrongdoing. In the third cage I saw her at once. She had lost her jacket and her blouse was torn, one spiky shoulder protruded from it. There was a bruise on her forehead and a patch of dried blood. She still wore her assassination shoes.

'Nini.'

She lifted her head, came towards me. Best not to remember her look as she saw me; I have done nothing to merit that. 'Oh, Frau Susanna! How did you know?'

'Lily told me. Don't worry, Nini. I'll find some way of helping you.'

She shook her head. 'The others are all in the same boat. They're all my companions. I mustn't get anything they don't get.' She pushed her hair out of her eyes – prisoners are not allowed hair pins. 'But we did it,' she whispered, 'we killed the swine!'

'Yes. And a number of other people too. Listen, Nini, you know you mustn't admit to anything – not even taking messages. Nothing. Not for your sake – you wouldn't mind being martyred – but because you'll make trouble for someone else.'

'I know. Don't worry, they can cut out my tongue.' Then suddenly her eyes filled with tears. 'They don't let us go to the lavatory,' she said. 'I didn't expect that. We have to go in a bucket in here. With everyone watching. I expected the beatings, but not that.'

'I'll get help, Nini; we'll get you out.'

But the janitor had had enough. 'Time's up. No more talking.'

I was led back to the office. 'The sanitation in this prison's a disgrace,' I said furiously. 'I'm going to see that questions are raised in Parliament.'

He shrugged. 'No one'll spend the money. Did you find the girl?'

'Yes.'

'Well, they'll be charged next week. Nothing to be done till then.'

'I'll be back with a solicitor,' I said, and left.

I drove straight to the lawyer who had helped me when I rented my shop. He did not deal in criminal cases, but recommended a colleague in the Borse Platz. The colleague kept me waiting an hour and said he would find it very difficult, on ethical grounds, to defend an Anarchist. Even if he could overcome his scruples, the fee would be very high.

'How high?' I asked, and blenched as he told me.

'Don't you have a friend in Important Places?' he asked, leering at me. 'They're worth all of us poor lawyers put together, these important friends.'

'No,' I said. 'I don't.'

Not any more. Not now.

Then I drove to the main post office and found Lily behind her grille, and she helped me to send a cable to New York.

Somehow I've crawled through the last three days. I've left it to Gretl to explain to my clients what has happened and most of them have been patient and understanding. The Baroness Lefevre even offered to ask her husband to plead for Nini, but when it came to the point the Baron didn't feel able to intervene on behalf of a girl who wanted to destroy the fabric of society.

Meanwhile I've gone backwards and forwards between the prison and the offices of anyone I thought might possibly help me: lawyers, welfare workers, priests, but nothing has happened – nothing.

And there's been no answer to my cable. I hadn't really expected it.

I've been allowed to see Nini for a few minutes each day. She still holds her head proudly, she still, even in her rags, keeps that extraordinary style, and she's admitted nothing. There hasn't been much actual cruelty on the part of the prison staff – it isn't necessary. The filth, the horrendous sanitary arrangements, the haphazard mingling of sick and deluded women with young girls does its own work. There are bruises on Nini's face which were not there when she was admitted, but when I asked her how she came by them she only shook her head.

I've decided to swallow my pride and beg that slimy lawyer in the Borse Platz to defend Nini. If I hadn't been so distraught I'd have realized at once that I only had to sell The Necklace to get his fees. But when I called there this afternoon, he had left for the assizes in Graz.

This morning I went to the prison early and for the first time found Nini looking frightened. At the back of the cage sat three women, huddled and weeping, with white cloths round their heads – and on one of the cloths, bloodstains.

'It's typhus,' she whispered. 'They've found a case of typhus and they're shaving everybody's head. They came and did them this morning and the rest of us are going to be done in batches. You should see the wardresses – they have these cut-throat razors and they just shave you to the scalp. They love doing it because it's what the women mind most of all.'

It is that that Nini fears: losing her hair – but I know about typhus. I saw our neighbours' little daughter die of it at Leck.

Upstairs, the prison officer told me to stay away. The women are now in quarantine.

I drove back, utterly sick at heart, as near defeated as I remember being. As the fiacre stopped at the corner of the square, I looked out, amazed. It has been snowing for days; the fountain is frozen, there are icicles on St Florian's head. People hurry across, their footsteps muffled. No one lingers.

But the square was full of children. I'd heard their shouts before the cab turned in through the chestnut trees and now I saw them in their mufflers and fur hats, bright spots of colour on the whiteness of the snow. They were running and calling out to each other, some were crouched low beside piles of snowballs – one, a ragged little boy I don't ever remember seeing before, had climbed on to St Florian's shoulders as a lookout and, even as I watched, was brought down by the arrow of an attacker.

For it was a battle that was being fought – but a battle with rules. The fountain was the stockade in which the besieged American pioneers bound for the Golden West defended their kith and kin. The children's toboggans had been piled up like covered wagons and from behind them the intrepid settlers fired on their attackers.

But the Indians were brave too. Screaming their uncouth war calls, they leapt from General Madensky's plinth, charged from between the chestnut trees . . . Maia's imagined horse was shot from under her and a Red Indian chorister from the presbytery pulled her on to the back of his saddle and galloped on. Among the settlers I saw – but could scarcely believe my eyes – Ernst Bischof allowing little Steffi to provide him with bullets of snow.

The door of the Schumachers' house opened and Helene called the girls in to lunch.

She might have saved her breath. Mitzi, inside the stockade, was tending the wounded; Resi, who had strayed from the safety of the wagons, was being dragged off to be scalped.

A prosperous-looking couple crossed the Walterstrasse with a fat little boy in ear muffs.

'Can I play?' he shouted – and ignoring the protests of his parents, he ran to Madensky's statue and instantly became an Indian brave.

I had never seen a game like this. There were scarcely any props: the Indians had no feathers, the settlers no guns – yet so engrossed was each and every child in his part that I could have told exactly what they were doing.

But now a boy, older than the rest, in a corduroy cap and outsize muffler appeared from behind the statue of St Florian. He must have died earlier, perhaps the better to mastermind the game – and taking heed perhaps of Frau Schumacher's pleas, he suggested to the settlers a heroic demise, en bloc, and to the Indians a triumphant ride off into the hills.

Not a boy, I realized as I looked more carefully: a young man. At the same time Nini's voice sounded distinctly in my head: '*It was the children that made me notice him*'.

Impossible. I had sent the cable only three days ago. Then he bent down, beat the snow from his trousers . . . and pulled up his socks.

He had never had my cable. His mother was travelling to Paris on business and he came with her for talks with the European branches of the bank, and because he wanted to see Nini.

'I've bought her a Christmas present,' he said, stamping his boots clean in my hall.

I couldn't believe it. I began to tremble, so great was the relief.

'What is it?' he asked as he followed me upstairs. 'There's something wrong. She's had an accident? She's ill?'

I told him.

'Oh,' he said. 'I see. That was to be expected, I suppose.'

'Can you help, Daniel? I don't know what to do. I've tried everything.'

He put an arm round my shoulder. Nini had described him exactly. He was small, he had a snub nose, his eyes were no particular colour and sock suspenders seemed to be foreign to his nature, yet I felt instantly comforted.

'I think we'll have some lunch,' he said. 'I'm staying at the Bristol – they're supposed to keep a good table. Will you come?'

'No . . . if you don't mind, not the Bristol. I could make us something here. An omelette?'

'Yes, I'd like that.'

I was upset that he wanted to have lunch. I wanted him to start at once doing whatever can be done. But when I came to eat I realized that I had been very close to collapse, and perhaps he realized it too, for he watched me closely and made me open a bottle of wine though he himself drank little.

Not till we had had our coffee did he push back his chair and say: 'Right. I'd better get going. There's just one favour I'd like to ask of you. I'd like to see Nini's room. You see, even if I can get her out, I think she'll turn against me. She'll say it was just privilege, the rotten system and so on. So I'd like to be able to imagine her when I've gone.'

'I'll show you. But you won't be able to imagine her for long. The shop is being pulled down, you see, and most of the square.'

'My God!'

I took him upstairs. He walked over to the poster which said *Property is Theft* and the one that said *Blood Shed for the Revolution is Blood Shed for Humanity*. He touched briefly the lace-edged pillow and the picture of the candy-striped pinafore she'd cut out of *Damenmode*. He looked at the pile of leaflets urging the textile workers of Ottakring to strike and picked up the silver-backed brush I'd given her last Christmas.

'She's very tidy,' he said. 'Somehow I didn't expect that.'

Then he wound himself in to his strange muffler, ready to go to the Bristol. At the door he turned and took both my hands. 'I promise I'll refer back to you as often as I can, but this is something that has to be traced out step by step. And it can't be hurried. Everything has to be just so. If the bribe is too big they get suspicious, if it's too small they get insulted. If you offer membership of the Jockey Club to someone who wants a permanent box at the opera you've wasted a whole round of talks. And bribes alone are no good – there has to be pressure as well. It can take days . . . weeks . . .'

'How will you start?'

'With the American Ambassador. Thank God he's in town – and what's more, he knows my father.'

'But how can you interest a man like that in a girl who wants to blow everyone up? An avowed Anarchist?'

'I'm not going to interest him in an avowed Anarchist. I'm going to interest him in my intended. For I intend to marry Nini, you know. What she intends is nobody's business.'

I didn't tell him about the typhus. He doesn't have to have *all* my nightmares.

Daniel has been at the Bristol for five days. The ship on which he was due to return sailed from Genoa and he let it go. Each day he comes and tells me what he has done. He never gets ruffled and if he gets discouraged he keeps it to himself, but it seems to me that his nondescript eyes, the freckles on his nose, are growing darker.

The children are a trouble. When they see him coming they run out of their houses, pursued by the irate voice of Father Anselm from the presbytery, of Helene Schumacher forbidding her girls to go out inadequately dressed into the snow. Daniel only speaks to them for a few minutes and then they are off. Once they became vile slavers on the Gold Coast, dragging the captive Africans to their ships, only to be overcome in their turn by pirates and forced to walk the plank. Once they set off in canoes to find the source of the Rio Negro, beating off crocodiles, piranha fish and savages, and claimed new territory for the Austrian flag. I never saw children play together as they played with Daniel Frankenheimer in the doomed square. I think Maia would have gone through fire for him.

When he could stay a while we talked and I learnt about his family. He was proud of his father's achievements, but impatient of some of his attitudes to his workers. 'He's too paternalistic; he won't see that times have changed. Unions are here to stay – people want things by right, now, not by the gift of their employers. But he's got the most terrific flair.'

'And your mother?'

Daniel grinned. 'She's an obsessive. Little and mad; looks like a wolverine – and acts like one too when she's after something.'

'What's she obsessive about?'

'Well, the family partly – Dad and me and my older sister. But mostly her music school. She was trained as a pianist, you see. And I must say she's made a marvellous job of it. People are auditioning to come there now from all over the world.'

'It's for exceptionally talented children, isn't that right?'

Daniel nodded. 'Her people came from Russia originally and she's based it on the ideas of the Imperial Ballet School in St Petersburg. Incredibly hard work, the top teachers, but a chance for the children to perform as they go along and be part of the world they're going to join. When Gustav Mahler was in New York he came to see it and he wrote my mother a letter saying he wished he'd been trained there instead of the Vienna Conservatoire!' Daniel laughed and cut himself another slice of Herr Huber's latest leberwurst. 'Last month the fire alarm went off in our house in Fifth Avenue. My father pulled all the documents out of the safe and the maids rescued my mother's jewels – but my mother came down in her nightdress and all she was holding was her letter from Gustav Mahler!

Then he went off to the next round of meetings and dinners with recalcitrant and obstinate officials. As he crossed the square, the little ragged boy I'd seen first climbing on St Florian's shoulder, stepped out from behind a chestnut tree and took his hand.

He has done it! Daniel has performed the miracle! Nini is out; she is free!

I had no warning. I was fitting a customer when a black limousine with a flag on the bonnet drew up outside. The chauffeur got out, opened the door, handed Nini out – and drove away without a word.

She wore the clothes she'd been arrested in and there was a blood-stained bandage round her head.

'Oh, Nini!' I said, embracing her. And then: 'It doesn't matter about your hair – nothing matters except that you're safe.'

She winked. Yes, really; this half-starved, exhausted girl

winked at me. Then she pulled off her bandage and her hair, uncut, abundant and filthy tumbled round her shoulders.

'Good God, Nini! How?'

'I tricked them. I borrowed the bandages from one of the women who'd been shaved and when they came to me I said I'd already been done. They were in such a muddle most of the time, and drunk into the bargain.'

She went to the bathroom and spent an hour there, and then she slept. She slept till early evening and only then, sitting in her dressing gown drinking the broth I'd made for her, did she ask: 'How did you do it, Frau Susanna? How did you manage to get me out?'

'I didn't, Nini. I tried and tried, but I failed. It was Daniel Frankenheimer who got you out.'

She put down her spoon. 'Daniel? But how? How could he, in New York?'

'He isn't in New York, he's here.' And I told her the full story. 'He's at the Bristol and he'd be glad to see you when you're rested, but not before.'

'I am rested,' said Nini. 'Actually.'

She then went upstairs to attend to her toilette, which took some time for she chose to regard her bruises as a fashion point needing to be offset by an olive green silk scarf (mine) knotted just so, and this in turn caused other problems.

Which she solved, I do assure you . . .

Did I look like that when I drove off to the Bristol – my eyes so bright, my hands touching my hair almost as though they were the hands of someone else, the man who soon now . . .

Yes, I suppose that's how I looked, but it doesn't matter. She left an hour ago and I think – yes, really, I think – it's going to be all right.

No, I was wrong.

Is it because she doesn't believe in God that she's so savage with herself and the world? So obstinate and stupid? Can the woman in Salzburg be going through what I'm going through now: the anger, the frustration at seeing happiness thrown away? Surely my daughter can't be such a fool?

Daniel lost his temper. I don't blame him; it's foolish to imagine that the power he exerts can't have a darker side. I can see why he acted as he did, but he has lost her. He knows this. He left yesterday to catch the *Lusitania* in Cherbourg.

Nini stayed all night at the Bristol. Perhaps it was the happiness I saw in her face when she returned that set her off. I've never known anyone so convinced that happiness is not for her. I could see it all begin – the guilt, the questions.

Daniel came to lunch. He wanted to make the practical arrangements for her to join him in the States, but she began almost at once, bragging about Knapp's assassination, about the blow struck for the proletariat. It was twenty-four hours since she'd come out of prison, but she seemed already to have forgotten what it was like.

'I shouldn't have come out,' she said. 'I should have insisted on waiting till everyone was released. It's only because the system's so rotten that you could get me out. It's not till all the swine like Knapp are dead that the People will be free.'

'Ah, yes, the People.' Daniel put down his knife and fork. 'You don't think it might be possible to help the people without blowing them up? In some more modest way, perhaps? By using democratic means? By working for the eight-hour day and better housing and paid holidays, without bloodshed and carnage. Or is that not dramatic enough?'

'No, it's not. You have to make the world see. Kropotkin said blood shed for the revolution is blood shed for humanity, and he's right. If you're mealy-mouthed and afraid nothing gets done. You have to be strong and not have scruples, and destroy the Enemies of the People without hesitation.'

I saw the exact moment when Daniel lost his temper; there was this apparent darkening of the eyes and skin, which is his response to trouble.

'I've got something to show you, Nini,' he said. 'Now. Come with me.' He pulled her out of her chair. 'Get your coat.' And to me, without any of the respect he'd shown me up to now, 'You'd better come too. Perhaps you can make her see sense.'

He bundled Nini downstairs, waited, glowering, whilst she put on her coat. We strode out into the snow and down the Walterstrasse. God knows what it is about that boy in his extraordinary muffler that makes the cab drivers stop for him, but he only flicked his fingers as we crossed the road and the driver turned and reigned in beside him.

'Get in,' he said, and gave the cabby his instructions.

I hadn't been in the Municipal Hospital since Rudi died. The same corridors, the same smell of lysol as we followed Daniel. Nini was very pale now, but he didn't even look over his shoulder.

No one stopped us this time; it was visiting hour. The corridors grew a little lighter, a little less sombre, and we entered a ward with pictures on the wall and a rack of well-worn toys.

And so neat, so clean, so small in their iron beds – the children. Nini faltered and turned away, but Daniel took her arm and led her to one particular bed over which two nurses were bending.

They straightened, recognized Daniel.

'Ah, Herr Frankenheimer.' The sister lowered her voice. 'He seems a little better. He liked the engine you sent, but of course he doesn't really know much yet; we have to keep him so heavily drugged.'

The boy turned his head on the pillow. Seven years old, perhaps. A grey-white face, fair hair darkened by perspiration. For a brief moment he opened his eyes.

'Would you like to see?' whispered the nurse. 'The surgeon's made a beautiful job of the operation; there's a good chance that he'll pull through now.'

She drew back the bedclothes. The child moaned once. There wasn't anything to see, actually. Only that he had no legs.

Daniel lifted his head.

'Meet an Enemy of the People, Nini,' he said quietly. 'His name is Heini Fischer. His mother took him to town to look at the shops. They didn't buy anything because his father's unemployed, but they like to look in the windows. When Herr Knapp drove by, she pushed him forward so that he could see the important gentleman in his fine car.'

Nini showed no emotion. She didn't gasp or turn faint. She just walked away down the ward, down the corridor, out of the hospital. I followed her, but she said nothing, and when we got home she went to her attic and I heard her pull the chest of drawers across so as to block the door.

She came down in the morning to do her work, but still she wouldn't speak and when Daniel came she went upstairs again and refused to see him.

It has been her life since she could think at all: the revolution, the movement, the cause. It was what sustained her in the slums of Budapest and the tenements of Vienna: the danger, the romance, the ideology. I think it has all gone, banished by those small, blood-soaked stumps in Heini Fischer's bed.

But of course in destroying her beliefs, Daniel has destroyed the part of her he loved the most: the wild, brave, passionate girl who wanted anything except to live an everyday, unthinking, un-committed life.

He knew at once, even in the hospital, what he had done, but he waited for a few days in case she would see him. Before he left he gave me a card.

'It's the name of our agent in Vienna. If ever she changes her mind he'll fix everything up for her: passports, tickets, money.'

I embraced him, and there were tears in my eyes. At the door he said something unexpected. 'Of course if he's dead, it's different. But if it's not that, if he's alive still, I'd have thought it would come right. I'd have thought you were almost impossible to leave.'

Then I let him out at the back because the children were waiting for him in the front, and he had to catch his train.

Herr Schnee has gone. The van came two days ago and his belongings were piled into it.

'No point in hanging round,' he said gruffly, coming to shake my hand.

I'll miss him; already the empty shop next door makes my rooms seem colder; it's incredible how quickly a place looks neglected and forlorn. I think it has shaken everybody, his departure – we can see that it's true now, that it's going to happen, the destruction of the square.

Poor Augustin Heller is ill; he sits in his dressing gown and coughs. It may be the dust as he moves piles of books that have been undisturbed for years, but I think it's exhaustion and fear of the future. I'd feel afraid if I was going to live with Maia's mother in Wiener Neustadt.

'He's so messy in his habits,' she complained when I took him some soup, not knowing she was there, and Maia scowled. She loves her grandfather, I think.

I've decided to accept Peter Konrad's offer. I looked at two more shops, but they were dark and gloomy places without any accommodation, and the only one that was at all possible was ludicrously expensive. Peter and I understand each other, it should be all right, and at least Nini will be looked after; he's offered to employ her as a vendeuse – though personally I'd rather be served by a cougar than Nini in her present state. Fortunately there's so much work to do now, finishing orders, clearing the stock, packing, that she goes to bed thoroughly exhausted. What she does when she gets there is another matter. Much what I do, I suppose.

It now becomes necessary to celebrate Christmas.

I shall do my best. I've ordered my carp from the fishmonger and asked Old Anna to keep me the smallest Christmas tree that she can find. Usually I decorate the shop, but we are at the packing case stage now and there would be no point.

What has not been easy to endure have been the visits of all the people who work in the square: the dustmen and lamplighters and window cleaners who come for their Christmas bottle of wine and their tip.

'It's a crying shame what's being done to this place', they said one by one, 'it's a sin', – and the roadsweeper became so lachrymose that we had to have recourse to Gretl's uncle's eau de vie.

In the café too there is little rejoicing. Joseph's mother has shown no inclination to leave her bed; she used to start baking her poppyseed beiglis in the first week of December and the smell was always part of Christmas for me. And Father Anselm's Adam's apple seems more prominent than ever as he sets out the crib in the vestry and pins up the notice of the services for Holy Night. The new presbytery to which he'll move the boys at the end of January is a gaunt red-brick building without a garden, and far too far from his beloved church.

But there's one household where this loveliest of festivals is secure. The Schumacher girls each have their advent ring, their gingerbread house (Donatella has already eaten the cotton wool smoke from her chimney). Their painted clogs went out punctually on St Nicholas' Day so that the saint could bestow his silver coins, and their tree has arrived on a dray from the timber yard; the tallest, loveliest tree in Vienna.

Herr Egger may have blighted the rest of us, but not Mitzi and Franzi, not Steffi and Resi or Kati and Gisi – and certainly not Donatella – as they prepare to celebrate the birth of Christ!

Well, I did it! Christmas is over and until midnight, at least, nobody actually cried!

It's no good pretending that Alice and I were in the best of spirits as we lunched on my excellently roasted carp. Christmas is never the easiest time for Other Women, but in previous years there was the hope that January would bring the men we loved back in to our lives. Nor was Nini, gloomily chasing her food around her plate, exactly a social asset. But I had invited Professor Starsky to join us and there was plenty of wine. There are times when a well-informed dissertation on aphagia in the reptiles of South America can be of real benefit, and Christmas Eve in the year 1911 seemed to be one of them.

We had scarcely finished the meal when Herr Schumacher called and asked me to go for a drive.

'Now?' I said, amazed. Alice and I were going over later to see the lighting of the tree and the children opening their presents.

'Please,' said Herr Schumacher, unaccustomedly humble.

'Helene said you might be so kind. There is something on my mind.'

It was a strange drive I took with him, almost in silence, through the deserted streets, past windows where families still sat at table, past wreaths and ribbons hung on the doors. Then we turned in at the timber yard.

I shivered as I stepped out into the slush and picked my way past the piles of timber and the scaffolding on the stable block. The place was far bigger than I had realized.

'I wanted you to see for yourself,' he said. And in spite of myself, as he began to show me round, I became interested. On every other subject Herr Schumacher's conversation is to be avoided, but as he explained the function of each of the machines, ran his thumb along a particularly finely seasoned plank, or outlined his plans for expansion, he spoke with energy and sense.

'My father was a carpenter,' I said. 'It's one of the first smells I remember, the lovely smell of wood.'

The tour ended in his office and here at last, Herr Schumacher came to the point.

'Frau Susanna, I asked you to come because I know you have run your own business for a number of years. And very successfully.'

'Yes.'

'And you are a woman.'

To this also I agreed.

'Now what I want to know,' he said, leaning towards me, 'is this. Have you ever found yourself at a disadvantage on account of your sex? When a rep comes, for example?'

'No. Never.'

'And your accounts? Have you had difficulty with them?'

'Certainly not. Why should I? I can add and subtract and multiply. On good days I can even divide.'

Herr Schumacher put up a hand to indicate that he had intended no disrespect. He paced to the noticeboard, rearranged the position of the calendar, turned.

'You see, I have been in great trouble over the inheritance,' he said, sitting down again. 'It's natural for a man to want everything he's built up to go to his own kind.'

I pulled up the collar of my coat. The office was unheated and the topic not one that excited me as it should.

'And then I thought . . . it came to me in a flash,' said Herr Schumacher, his eyes glittering. 'Yes, in a flash! It isn't only Gustav who has the blood, I thought. Someone else has it. *Someone else has the Blood*, Frau Susanna! My daughter, Donatella!'

'All your daughters have the Blood, Herr Schumacher. Mitzi and Franzi and Steffi . . . all of them.'

'Yes, but they'll marry. Whereas Donatella . . .'

'I should think she'll marry too,' I said. 'With that personality and those eyebrows no one will worry about her cheek.'

I had said the wrong thing.

'No no, I shouldn't think she'll marry. I should think she'll want to stay with her father. So I thought, *why don't I train her up to succeed me?* But the question is, can she do it? And that's what I want to ask you, Frau Susanna. Do you think a girl could manage all this?' He swept a hand towards the window and his domain. 'Could she?'

'Of course she could. Without the slightest difficulty, if she wanted to.'

I appeared to have conferred an invaluable gift on Herr Schumacher. He became wreathed in smiles, he pumped my hand. He opened his cigar case to offer me a cigar, recalled himself, and closed it.

'Thank you, Frau Susanna. Thank you. You've taken a weight off my mind. That's what I'll do then. She can start quite young. Lisl can bring her round sometimes just to get the feel of the place. Oh, yes – it won't take me long . . . she can already tell sycamore from oak, you know. There's not the slightest doubt about it.'

Two hours later I was in the presence of the timber heiress herself as she sat on a white damask cloth beneath the glittering Christmas tree, obstinately ignoring her presents and passionately consuming a piece of wrapping paper.

Nothing can really describe the Schumachers' drawing room on Christmas Eve: the candlelight, the blissful little girls and Helene's eyes as she watched them. I'd stitched a lace-edged bed jacket for each of them and they came one by one and thanked me and curtseyed – but the spontaneous shrieks of appreciation were reserved for an afterthought I'd brought along in a pudding basin: a dozen muscular-looking water snails which Professor Starsky had got for me, promising that they would keep the aquarium free from slime.

Alice and I stayed to supper and went with the Schumachers to Midnight Mass, so it was one in the morning before I let myself into the house – to find the salon ablaze with light, and standing in the centre of the room, revolving slowly before the gilt-edged mirrors, Nini.

She wore her nightdress and over it, unbuttoned, a fur coat.

I'm not a person who goes in to ecstasies over valuable furs; I've seen far too many priceless pelts ruined by indifferent tailoring. But this coat was a miracle. It might have been made for Catherine the Great, or Anna Karenina . . . or Nini.

'Daniel's Christmas present?' I asked.

She barely nodded. She was too busy revolving, looking, touching . . . turning the high collar up to frame her face, watching the fall of the hem as it caressed her bare feet.

And all the time, steadily, the tears ran down her cheeks. But it didn't matter of course. You can cry on a Russian sable. There's nothing you can't do to a coat like that.

Edith has won the Plotzenheimer Essay Prize in Anglo-Saxon studies. I saw the announcement in the paper and meant to write her a note of congratulation, but as it happened I saw her the next day. Professor Starsky had persuaded me to come to a lecture in the university given by an eminent philosopher, and I was taking my seat among his colleagues, pathologists and physiologists mostly, when I felt a kind of tremor pass along the row, heard a few muttered oaths – and looked up to see that Laura Sultzer had swept into the room.

The intrepid rescuer of rats looked whiskery and well, but poor Edith, trailing behind her, was a doleful sight. Her face, beneath the dead-cat beret that she wore, was paler than ever, her shoulders were hunched in weariness.

When the lecture was over I excused myself from the Professor and went to speak to her as she stood in the foyer, guarding her mother's briefcase and waiting for the tandem.

'I heard about the prize, Edith; that's wonderful! You must be very pleased.'

'Yes,' said Edith listlessly. 'My mother is pleased. She's arranging for me to stay on and take my doctorate. I'm to investigate the ideas of Theophilus Krumm in greater depth.'

'And you? Do you like the idea?'

Edith shrugged. 'I suppose it will be all right. I'm very busy really. I'm secretary to the Group now and I have to take notes at all the meetings.'

'You haven't seen Magdalena again?'

'No, but she's very happy, I think. Her brothers have passed their exams for cadet college.'

'And Herr Huber? Are you in touch with him?'

Edith shook her head, found an ink-stained handkerchief, and blew her nose. 'I don't have any reason to see him – he's hardly ever in Vienna now.' Then suddenly she turned to me and said: 'Frau Susanna . . . it isn't true, is it . . . what they say about clothes? I mean, that they can transform people? That they can turn an ugly duckling into a swan? Or make the wrong person into the right one?'

'No, Edith,' I said sadly. 'They can't do that. It's more likely to be the other way round. They're more likely to turn a swan into an ugly duckling.'

Then the tandem came and Edith mounted, getting oil on her skirt, and wobbled away.

But that night I had an idea.

*

First I consulted Alice. She was doubtful, she thought it would be too difficult technically. All the same, she wanted to be involved – Edith, after all, is Rudi's daughter.

'I'll help behind the scenes,' she said. 'You might be glad of some sort of headgear.'

Nini too thought it wouldn't work, but she can never resist a challenge and soon she was busy with calico and pins, looking out discarded materials and almost her old self as she prepared for the charade.

'We could use the oi-yoi-yoi dresses,' she said. 'They're still in the storeroom.'

The oi-yoi-yoi dresses were brought to me by a poor widow years ago to sell and I was always meaning to throw them away. (They're called that because 'oi-yoi-yoi' is what Leah Cohen said when she first saw them.) Then we made a list of Edith's good points (her waist, her ankles) and her bad points (practically every-thing else) and settled down to our task.

Next I telephoned the Bluestocking and told her that I had some beautiful dresses which I was selling off cheap.

'I'd like you to come and try them on; they're just right for you.'

'Oh, I don't know. I mean, my mother . . .'

'Edith, I'm not talking about your mother, I'm talking about you. Your father left you an allowance, didn't he? You'd be doing me a favour. I have to clear my stock.'

'I see? . . . Yes . . . Well, in that case . . .'

'Come to lunch first and be prepared to spend some time. I'm going to invite Herr Huber.'

I then contacted Herr Huber and said I needed his advice about suitable removal firms and we arranged for him to come on Wednesday when he was in town.

The luncheon party was a success. Edith had washed her hair, asked warmly after Herr Huber's sisters in Linz, and made intel-ligent suggestions about the franchise for supplying charcuterie on the boats of the Danube Steamship Company.

When the meal was over, I took the butcher aside.

'I wonder if you'd do me a favour, Herr Huber ? You see, I have some clothes I want Fraulein Edith to try on and I remember what excellent taste you have. Could you possibly stay and give us the benefit of your advice? She has great confidence in your judgement and her mother isn't quite . . .'

'Really? Well, of course. Certainly. It will be a pleasure. Such a well-informed girl, such an excellent brain.'

Not a propitious beginning, but I was determined to proceed.

We put him down in the oyster velvet chair and I took Edith to the fitting room where I removed her spectacles, loosened her hair and instructed her to change into a broderie Anglaise slip I had brought down. 'Some of the dresses are very close fitting,' I said, firmly confiscating the Croatian petticoat which smelled faintly of camomile tea.

Poor Edith. She looked at me with such trust.

Then Nini brought the first of the dresses.

It was an oi-yoi-yoi dress of brown moiré, but we had improved it, slashing the neckline so that Edith's salt-cellar collar bones jutted out above the zig-zag edging, and turning the puffed sleeves round to form two listing protuberances on her shoulders.

I led her out to where Herr Huber sat.

'What do you think?' I asked the butcher.

'If you forgive me, Frau Susanna, I think it is not at all a good choice. That brown is quite wrong. Fraulein Edith has quite nice grey eyes.'

I shrugged. 'I know,' I said as Edith scuttled back into the cubicle, 'but I have to think what would be acceptable to her mother. Frau Sultzer is not noted for her taste.'

We removed the mud-coloured moiré and substituted a half-stitched frock of emerald satin, and Nini grinned for it had been her idea to add a bustle which started half way up Edith's back and ended disastrously on the most prominent part of her behind.

Once again we pushed her out and revolved her in front of Herr Huber who shook his great head from side to side, wondering, I suppose, if I had taken leave of my senses. An oi-yoi-yoi coat and skirt which Nini had dyed an unspeakable shade of puce came next.

'Oh, please, Frau Susanna, please don't make me try that one. *I know* it won't suit me.'

'Now, Edith, don't fuss,' I said briskly, bundling her into it. 'You can't tell till you've tried it on,' and I jammed Alice's contribution, a frilled lampshade of the same vile material, over one eye.

Herr Huber this time was in anguish. 'No no! Fräulein Edith must have soft colours and gentle curves. That is all wrong!'

The last dress, Nini and I had tacked together the night before, and it was our masterpiece. Red and purple spotted silk left over from an order for a fancy dress party, straining over Edith's hips, hugging every bulge on her stomach. Not only that, but the twelve hooks and eyes which fastened it at the back were almost impossible to undo. I tumbled her hair over her bodice and made sure that her spectacles were out of reach.

'Well, if you really don't like it,' I said, managing to sound offended, 'you can take it off. Nini and I'll go upstairs and see what else we can find.'

Then we left her. But we didn't go upstairs; we stayed behind the door in the workroom and eavesdropped.

'Oh God!' Edith was becoming increasingly desperate as she pulled and tugged, trying to free herself. The humiliation of being seen in those awful clothes, the disappointment, was bringing her close to tears.

'What is it?' we heard the butcher ask in worried tones. 'What's the matter?'

'I can't get out of this horrible dress. I'm stuck, I'm completely stuck. I want to get out of here! I want to go home!'

She was really crying now as she struggled with the recalcitrant hooks. It was hard not to go to her aid, but we waited, peering through the crack in the door.

'Oh God, why was I born!' sobbed Edith. 'I never wanted to be clever and give my toys to the poor; all I ever wanted was to be ordinary and now I have to be mocked and made a fool of. I'll never get out of this dress, *never*!'

Herr Huber rose, took a few steps towards the fitting booth, flushed and retreated.

'Can't someone help me, *please*?'

Herr Huber rose once more, looked at the door behind which we were hiding. 'They seem to have gone,' he said. He approached the cubicle again, hesitated. Then: 'If you will allow me,' he said, and disappeared inside.

For a few moments we heard only low murmuring – then a sudden and violent tearing of cloth as Herr Huber lost patience.

'Oh dear! It's torn. They'll be so angry!'

'Nonsense! Such a dress needs to be torn. Now we'll just take the nasty thing right off and then you'll soon be more comfortable. There, that's better, isn't it? Now don't distress yourself, my poor girl, let me wipe your pretty eyes.'

Edith was still crying, but the sobs were muffled. She was crying *into* something.

'I'm spoiling your coat.'

'No, no . . . not at all. I have plenty of coats. Only don't be sad, my little one. See how pretty you look in your petticoat. And see how soft your hair is . . . Look how it likes to fall over my hand . . .'

The truth is, I'm a genius, and clairvoyant too. But when the happy pair had left arm in arm and I told my helpers about the vision I'd had of Edith bouncing on a bed beside a wide grey river, they were not impressed.

'Obviously Herr Huber had already described his house by the Danube,' said Alice. 'All you did was to sense that they would make an excellent couple.'

But as I pointed out, there was nothing 'all' about sensing that!

January

The boys are due to move out of the presbytery in three weeks and today there was a concert in St Florian's in aid of equipment for the new building, which as it stands would do nicely as a workhouse or penitentiary. Ernst Bischof sang two Mozart motets and 'I know that my Redeemer Liveth', and though Helene and I have been waiting for his voice to break for the whole year, I think that if he had cracked or faltered then, we could not have borne it.

As I was leaving the church I felt a hand on my shoulder and turned to see Van der Velde, fatter and more prosperous-looking than ever.

'I was just going to call on you,' he said, bending over my hand.

'Good God! What brings you here?'

'I came to hear the choirboy. They said he was good and he is, but he's too old for me. By the time I'd built him up he'd be finished.'

He suggested a cup of coffee and I led him to Joseph's. Somehow I didn't want him in my flat.

'And Sigi?' I asked when we'd been served.

'Well, you'll have read about him. He did the German tour . . . Berlin, Frankfurt, Dresden, Dusseldorf . . . Then Switzerland and Paris . . . He gives a concert every few days and they do well.'

'You're pleased then?'

'Yes and no. Mostly no. He's insatiable. Wants more and more concerts – he'd play every day if I could get a hall. And he has to be paid in cash. This skinny infant insists on payment in gold coins. He screws them out of me after every performance – won't wait till the end of the month.'

'You've met your match, then,' I said smiling.

'It isn't so funny,' said Van der Velde angrily. 'The critics are beginning to turn on me – this heartless impresario dragging the poor child round Europe. He ought to have time to study, to mature, they say. Well it isn't me, it's him. Oh, I admit I do all right out of him, but I'm not stupid. I know if he plays too much they'll tire of him. But you tell that to the boy. His contract's up in a fortnight and if he asks for any more money I'm going to turn him over to Meierwitz – he's a Jew, he can deal with a kid that haggles like a stallholder in an Arabian souk. And I'm sending Uncle back to Poland.'

I asked a question that I regretted as soon as the words were out of my mouth.

'Does he ever mention me?'

'No,' said Van der Velde. 'Never. But he knows about the square. I showed him a newspaper.'

As we rose he said, 'He's coming back to Vienna, you know. Playing at the Redoutensaal on Friday. If you want a seat just mention my name at the box office.' He bent over my hand again, then turned it so that he could kiss the inside of the wrist . . . that old tired trick. But I let him. It seems that these days I have nothing to defend.

I have decided not to go to the concert. It is over, Sigi's story and mine.

I decided it – but when Friday came, I went.

That he was playing at the Redoutensaal shows how important he has become since his debut. It's the most beautiful of our concert halls, in a wing of the Hofburg itself, and perhaps the best loved by the Viennese.

I thought there would not be a seat; I've never trusted Van der Velde to keep his word, but when I gave my name I was handed a ticket straight away.

The hall was full. Many in the audience were the usual

fashionable, gushing women in Chez Jaquetta's clothes, but not all. I found myself next to an old man with a full beard like Brahms, and remembered that I'd had him pointed out to me as Hans Klepstedt, the Director of the Liszt Academy of Music.

Then Sigi came on to the platform. I thought there must be some change, but he was just the same. His hair was a little longer, his concert master's bow a little deeper, but that was all. Van der Velde had followed my lead over his clothes: the high-necked blouse, the dark trousers were a copy of the ones I'd made for him.

I bent my head, not wanting to be seen, and he began to play. Mendelssohn, Schumann, Hummel . . . and Chopin, of course. I doubt if he will ever be allowed *not* to play Chopin. Then the interval, and prolonged applause, but beside me the man with the beard frowned.

'You didn't enjoy it?' I asked him.

'Yes, yes. It was enjoyable. But he plays too much. The Mendelssohn was not prepared. They say he only learnt it three days ago.'

'But he has talent?' I asked as sharply, as anxiously, as any doting parent.

'Oh yes. Undoubted talent. Exceptional talent. But he should have time to study, to reflect. Van der Velde will ruin him if he goes on driving him like this.'

'They say the boy himself wants to keep on playing.'

The white eyebrows rose, the great beard waggled to and fro. 'Really? That surprises me. He is a genuine musician, he must know what he is doing to himself.'

Sigi came back and played the rest of the programme. The applause at the end went on and on; he was recalled for one encore, for two, for three . . . The women in particular would not let him go and clapped their gloved hands; bunches of flowers were brought in from the wings.

I slipped away, certain that I had not been seen. It was snowing, but I turned my collar up and plunged my hands deeper into my muff, needing to walk through the lamplit streets, needing the air.

A number of carriages passed me; then one which slowed down in front of me, stopped . . . The door opened and someone jumped down: someone muffled and very small.

'Why did you hurry away?' asked Sigi. 'Why didn't you wait?' And as I looked at him, finding no words, he said: 'We have to eat Indianerkrapfen, don't you remember? You said in the Prater that we would.'

'Yes, Sigi. I remember.'

The carriage had driven away. In search of chocolate eclairs, at eleven o'clock on a winter's night, we went to Sachers.

They recognized him – from the posters, from the concert, I don't know. The head waiter bowed and addressed him as Meister Kraszinsky and a fat lady in a mink coat came over and asked him for his autograph.

'Is it nice being famous?' I asked him.

He shrugged. 'It is necessary if I am to make enough money.'

'Why do you need so much money, Sigi? Why so much?'

'Why?' He looked surprised. 'So that I can buy for you a house, of course. A house with a shop in it because you have lost yours.'

Thank heaven the waiter came then for our order. It gave me a few moments, at least, to control myself.

'Wait, Sigi. Is that why you've been working so hard and giving so many concerts?'

'Yes. But it doesn't matter because it will be so beautiful, the house, and the shop will be beautiful too.' He leant across the table. 'It will be by a lake and there will be a balcony so that you can look over the water and see when I am coming home in the boat from my concerts. And on the other side, not by the water, will be the shop with yellow curtains like you have now. I saw such a house in Switzerland – ah, it was beautiful! It was like looking in a cave in the Grottenbahn. And Nini can come too if you wish it, and I will buy you a dog like . . . like Rip but with proper legs.'

I saw it as he spoke. I saw the house as he did, lit like a cave in the Grottenbahn and I tell you this: I wanted it. I wanted to live with him in a house by a lake with a dog with proper legs. I wanted to stand and watch him come home across the water to a meal I had made for him, and a glowing stove. I wanted it very badly.

Our order came and as the waiter set down the round, cream-filled puffs doused in ink-black chocolate, I knew that never in my life would I eat another Indianerkrapfen. And all the time my frantic thoughts went round and round. How could it be done? How could I set him free for his life without hurting him unbearably? How could I cut the shackles from this child whom life had already dealt the most terrible of blows, and not reject him. It was impossible.

Or was it?

I lifted my head. 'Sigi,' I said. 'I can't come and live with you in your house. In any house. I can't.'

He had started to eat. Now he put down his fork.

'Why can't you? Why?' The husky croak was very faint now, scarcely audible.

'Listen,' I said. 'I'm going to tell you something that nobody else knows – not Nini, not anyone in the square – and you must tell no one. You see, I have a daughter.'

And as the café emptied, I told him the whole story. To this foreign child whom I now loved, I spoke as I had spoken only once before, to Gernot von Lindenberg that first time in the rain-swept hunting lodge. I told him of my daughter's birth, her loss, the agony of seeing her once again in Salzburg and leaving her.

'I don't know where she is now, Sigi, and she's not small any more, but I still hope . . . I still wait for her to come back to me. And if she came . . . if she needed me . . . and found you there instead, it would hurt her so much. She might come one evening to the window and see us having supper together and she would say "My mother doesn't need me, she has another child."'

He understood. His dream died and he grew pale, but he understood. 'If it was your mother, Sigi . . . if she had lost you when you were little, she would wait always, wouldn't she?'

'Yes, she would wait.'

Then . . . listen to this . . . he felt in his pocket and he handed me – *he* handed *me* – his handkerchief because I was no longer in control. So I've done something, haven't I? Surely, God, you can say I've done something for this child whom I found so ragged and unkempt? I've hurt him, I've handed him over to an unscrupulous man – but I've taught him about handkerchiefs!

I seem to have stumbled on another impasse. Marie Konrad came to see me this afternoon.

I've always liked Peter Konrad's wife. A good mother, a good wife, pretty and entertaining. I've been to her villa in Schünbrunn for dinner, and we meet sometimes in theatres or restaurants.

Still I was surprised when she asked if she could speak to me alone. We're acquaintances rather than friends.

'I'm sorry to come like this,' she said when we were settled upstairs. 'I feel ashamed . . . but . . . I'm frightened. Yes, to tell the truth, I'm frightened and I came to ask if you could help me.'

'I'd like to help you,' I said, mystified. 'But how?'

She had begun to fidget with her reticule, to smooth down her perfectly smooth collar. Then she lifted her head and I saw that she was blushing.

'By not taking the job my husband offered you in the store,' she blurted out. 'That's how you could help me, Frau Susanna. That was what I came to ask you to do.'

I didn't at all understand what she was trying to tell me. 'But why? How would that help you? Have you someone else for whom you want the job?'

She shook her head. 'It isn't that.' She was dreadfully ill at ease and I was becoming increasingly puzzled. 'It's Peter. He's a good husband – a very good husband – but he looks so distinguished, and well . . . he's susceptible. There have been affairs, of course, but they didn't last. But if you came to work with him, if he saw you every day and stayed behind with you to consult and so on, I know . . . I just know how it would end. And this time it would be serious.'

'Frau Konrad, I assure you, on my honour that I have never and would never—'

She interrupted me. 'No, no – I don't mean you. I'm not accusing you of anything. I know you would do what you could to stop it – but you're not like the others and he has always . . . felt attracted to you. You should have heard how he spoke of you after he took you to the opera. The way you walked up the staircase . . . the Arab who wanted to buy you with camels. And a Field Marshal in full uniform – a Field Marshal – picking up your handkerchief.'

I winced as the knife went in, but Marie noticed nothing.

'He doesn't know yet; he thinks it's just admiration. But I know – and I'm afraid. Seeing you all the time, sharing your interests . . .' Her head was bent; she laced and unlaced her fingers. 'You can't help it – you're so beautiful.'

'Am I?' I said, suddenly flooded with bitterness. 'Are you sure? Am I still beautiful?'

She looked up, staring intently at my face. 'Yes,' she said quietly. 'You look tired now, but it doesn't matter. It's your bones and the way you move . . . and your smile.' She wiped her eyes. 'Oh God, it's really so awful isn't it, this love.'

'Yes, it's fairly awful.' I walked to the window, looked out at the square I've loved so much, turned. 'All right,' I said. 'I'll tell him no. I'll refuse. But he must still take Nini if she wants it.'

'And you won't say that I've been?' she begged.

'No, of course not. Don't worry, I'll find an excuse.'

'You're so good. So *good*!' She tried to take my hands but I shook my head and freed myself. I was good once, in a village behind the hill in Salzburg, and it has nothing to do with something so trivial as this.

All the same, I don't quite know what is to happen now, or where I shall go.

At eleven this morning a carriage stopped outside my shop and a woman got out. She was in early middle age, slim and small, with an unremarkable face which nevertheless seemed familiar and a look of purpose and intelligence.

She greeted me, gave no name, removed her furs – and I gasped. 'I'm sorry,' I said, 'but you must tell me. Who made that dress?'

She smiled. 'It's good, isn't it. So simple . . .'

'Yes, but that kind of simplicity . . . And I've never seen worsted used like that; only in clothes for men. It's French?'

'Yes. Her name is Coco Chanel. She makes hats in the Avenue Gabriel and a few dresses privately for people she knows. She's only a girl still, but there's no doubt she's a genius.'

The perfection of the beige wool dress so hypnotized me that it was a while before I realized that I had a wealthy customer with impeccable taste, but alas too late. My stock is practically exhausted.

'I'd like to see some evening dresses. Is there anything you could show me?'

'Very little, I'm afraid.'

I explained the situation and she nodded. 'Yes, I've heard. I'm so sorry, it's such a delightful square. Still, now that I'm here I'd like to see what you've got.'

'There's a green taffeta and a white silk. I'll fetch them and—'

She interrupted me. 'I'd like to see them on the model, please.'

'Very well.'

I found Nini and told her to put on the green taffeta, and in spite of her troubles she swept into the salon with her beaky nose in the air, handling the rustling train with her old bravura.

'Yes, I like it. Could it be altered quickly? I leave tomorrow.'

Nini had been revolving in the centre of the room. Now she wheeled round, walked over to the woman in the gilt chair and addressed her with a sudden and most disconcerting rudeness.

'Did he send you?' she asked, at her most Magyar and insolent.

She had met her match. The woman in the Chanel dress drew together eyebrows that were only slightly less arrogant than Nini's.

'Nobody sends me,' she said icily. 'I am here on business.'

'But you're his sister, aren't you?'

239

The change was remarkable. The woman's face puckered up in a smile, the eyes shone. 'Ah, that was beautiful,' she said appreciatively. 'I shall dine out on that!' Her voice now was gentle, she had seen the wretchedness in Nini's face. 'I'm his mother, actually.'

'Oh. How . . . how is he?'

Frau Frankenheimer shrugged. 'He's back in New York and working very hard. His father's pleased to have him back; he's put through some useful deals already. So are the eligible girls of our circle. Invitations pour through the letter box . . .'

She broke off deliberately and, ignoring Nini, said: 'Actually I didn't come here primarily to buy a dress and certainly not to talk about my son. I came to ask you about a child who used to live opposite. A pianist, Sigismund Kraszinsky. I was told that you knew him well, that he owes his career to you.'

'No, not that. But, yes, I know him.'

'Well, the problem is this. I heard him in Paris a few weeks ago and offered him a place in the school I help to run in New York. It seemed to me that he was exactly the sort of child we want: highly talented but in need of a very thorough grounding in musical techniques. And in need of a stable background in which to develop – the school is residential; any child who enters it is cared for till he's ready to make his debut. However, the boy refused. He said he had to make money, a great deal of money. He seemed to be obsessed by that.'

'Yes,' I said, 'I see.'

'So I left it – in any case we have far more applicants than there are places. But a few days ago, just as I was leaving Paris, I had a cable. Apparently the child has changed his mind and he now wants to come. I've talked to Van der Velde and he'll let him go – he knows by the time we've finished with him he'll be worth a fortune and he can take some of the credit. But . . . I don't know how to put this without sounding priggish . . . though we offer a highly technical curriculum, we do try to develop the idea of a talent as a gift from God, something that carries certain obligations. And if there's something money-grubbing in the child himself – if money is the prime objective, which would be perfectly natural given his background – then I don't think he'd fit in.'

'No, no, no!' I came towards her; I think I was wringing my hands. 'No, he's not like that at all! Listen, please listen. Let me tell you why he wanted money.'

Once I began to talk I couldn't stop. I told her everything about Sigi – our first meeting by the fountain, the day at the Prater, the accident – and the last evening at Sachers. 'That's why he wanted money, you see. Not for himself – never for himself.'

When I finished she rose and laid a hand on my arm. 'I won't tell you that you are going to be proud of him because I know you are already. I won't even tell you that the world will hear of him, because you know that too. I'll just tell you that we'll look after him as you would have done . . . you or the red-haired angel.'

Then deliberately shrugging off emotion, she became practical.

'Now the only question that remains is how to get Sigismund to New York. I'd like him to go at once because term begins next week and I've lured Leschetizsky over to take a master class. But I'm not going home yet – I'm on my way to St Petersburg; I still have grandparents there, they're in their eighties and I've promised to visit them before it's too late.'

'Sigi's too young to travel alone,' I said.

She nodded, holding my eyes.

'Yes, definitely. Daniel will meet him and take him to the school, but I'll have to try to find someone to go with him on the boat. The uncle's going back to Preszowice, and anyway he's useless. Well, no doubt something can be arranged.'

There was a rustle of taffeta as Nini stirred in the green dress.

'I could take him,' she said gruffly. 'If you like. Just take him over and maybe stay for a short time, if Frau Susanna can spare me. Just for a visit.'

'Would you?' Frau Frankenheimer was entirely matter of fact. 'That would certainly solve the problem.'

And she began to discuss the alterations to the green dress – but it was at this point that I remembered something Daniel had said. Something about wolverines . . .

It all happened so quickly after that.

Less than a week after Frau Frankenheimer's visit, I stood on the platform of the Westbahnof saying goodbye.

Nini was shivering in her cloth coat. She has sold the Russian sable and given the money to the family of the little boy who lost his legs.

'You'll be cold on the boat,' I said. 'Let me lend you my shawl.'

She shook her head. 'I'll wrap a rug round me,' she said, and I saw her swaggering round the deck, starting a new fashion for steamer-rug cloaks.

'It's only a visit,' she said. 'I'll be back.'

'Yes,' I said. 'Of course.'

'And anyway you'll come. It would be a marvellous place to have a shop, New York.'

'Yes, marvellous.'

We've said these things to each other a hundred times since Frau Frankenheimer's visit. We had to.

The guard came along the platform, calling to the passengers to take their seats.

'Goodbye, Nini.'

We hugged each other quickly, and then she climbed into the train and waited for the boy.

A stupid, concert-going lady had presented him with an outsize bouquet of hothouse flowers. As I bent down to him, his face was almost hidden by the outsize blooms.

'We'll meet again, Sigi. We won't lose each other. Not you and I.'

He said nothing. This child of all children knew how easily people are lost. As I kissed him I heard for the last time that husky, almost inaudible croak.

'I hope she comes soon.'

'Who, Sigi?'

'Your daughter.'

'Yes, I hope so too.'

But she could have come running down the platform with outstretched arms and I wouldn't even have seen her, as I stood watching the train go out and waving, waving . . .

There were a number of things I needed as I came back from the station: oblivion, a hot bath, a large glass of Gretl's uncle's eau de vie – but not, God knows *not* – Frau Egger pacing dementedly between the packing cases.

'Oh there you are, Frau Susanna! Thank heavens! I've been so distracted . . . I don't know what to do. I'm at my wits' end!' But this was too much.

'Frau Egger, your husband has destroyed my livelihood and made a great many people most unhappy – I really cannot discuss any more intimate details of—'

'No, no. It isn't that! It's far worse! I know I shouldn't come to you, but I have no friends, and it's all to do with the buttons he says, and now he's gone completely mad. He's going to fight a duel!'

'A duel?'

She nodded. 'This afternoon, in that meadow by the Danube Bend where they used to fight – except that I think it's a corporation dump now, but that wouldn't stop Willibald.'

I sighed and removed my coat. 'You'd better come upstairs. And try to be calm – just tell me what happened, quietly.'

It had begun just before Christmas, she said, with the arrival of a mysterious stranger late at night asking to see her husband.

'He didn't give his name, but he was the kind of person one admitted,' said Frau Egger.

The man was closeted with Egger for an hour and after he left, the Minister was in a dreadful state, white, shaking, hysterical. And the next day he said he had to go abroad on urgent business.

'He wouldn't tell me what it was or why he had to go, but from the way he packed all the valuables, even my pearls, I knew he meant to flee the country.'

'But what about his work at the Ministry?'

'I don't know about that. He went on going to his office, but I don't know what he did there. He was quite wild all that week

– furious and frightened at the same time. And then just before he was due to leave Vienna, something extraordinary happened. We were having lunch and a military parade went by outside the window. It was the Carinthian Jaegers marching with a full band and you know how smart they are.'

'Yes.' I had good reason to know that.

'And Willibald went to the window and suddenly I found he was standing to attention and saluting! And then . . . he went upstairs to the attic and when he came down he was wearing a military uniform. It was much too small for him – he's put on weight and he couldn't get most of the buttons done up, but they were the same buttons I found, with *Aggredi* on them. And then he saluted again and said: "Herr Lieutenant Willibald Egger at your service!"'

'I see. So he had been in the army.'

'Yes. And after that he became quite different: calm and almost dignified and yet . . . sort of mad. He said things about dying for his regiment and bringing down the traitor who had betrayed him and so on. I really feared for his reason and I began to . . . spy on him and to ask the servants to watch him.' She flushed. 'They aren't very fond of Willibald and they're always ready to listen at keyholes and so on.'

Two days after he had put on his uniform, Egger had driven to a secret destination and when he returned he was more exalted than ever. He fetched his sabres from the attic and he began to make telephone calls to his acquaintances.

'I heard him talk to Heinrid on the phone – that's his deputy at the Ministry – to ask if he'd act for him, but Heinrid hates Willibald – he's opposed him all the time over the plans for the square, and he wouldn't. But the chiropodist said he would.'

'I can't believe this, Frau Egger. No one fights duels anymore.'

'It's true, Frau Susanna. I know it's true. And then yesterday afternoon Willibald made me . . . you know . . . come up to the bedroom. And it wasn't Tuesday or Friday which is when he does it. Well, you know . . . it was Wednesday. And he kept saying he forgave me.'

'Forgave you for what?'

'I don't know – the buttons perhaps – but he forgave me and he said he'd left me well provided for – though actually the money comes from my side of the family. And why I know it's serious is because of . . . The Habit. He didn't try it once, he didn't even *think* of it, he was so lit up. And I'm terrified, Frau Susanna; I don't know what to do! I don't want him to be killed. I wish he'd never been born but I don't want him to be killed and I certainly don't want him to kill anyone else. He's a good fencer in spite of his stomach – he goes to the salle d'armes once a week . . .'

'It will be just some harmless quarrel from his student days, perhaps.'

'No, no, you don't understand. It's a Field Marshal he's challenged.'

I didn't hear any more, but I wasn't hysterical, I promise you. I put on my coat, but before I left the house I went down to the workroom and cut off a double length of black veiling which I fixed under my hat so as to conceal my face. It was only then that I ran into the street to find a cab.

It was not the corporation dump – on the contrary. There was a notice saying *It is Forbidden to Leave Litter* and a smell of gas from a nearby gasometer.

But the rest of it was the exact landscape of the nightmare I'd had when I lay in Gernot's arms and he'd joked about challenging the man with the camels: the birches, the snow, the carriages of the seconds drawn up by the road – and I knew for certain that the creeping wretchedness of the last weeks had led me to this moment: to Gernot lying dead, his blood staining the ground.

Yet I managed to walk (or rather to stumble, for my double layer of veiling made it almost as difficult to see as to be seen) as far as a tree to which I clung.

At the end of the field on which I stood was a narrow belt of birches, then a meadow beside the river. It was there that they were assembled. I could make out two men in uniform – Gernot's seconds – and a little round man in a brown overcoat, the chiropodist, perhaps. Another, a tall man in a frock coat and top hat, was bending over a black bag: the doctor. The principals were further off. I just caught a glimmer of Gernot's scarlet and blue and then it was gone.

I'd intended to throw myself between the combatants, to scream, to threaten to call the police – God knows what I'd intended, but it didn't matter because all I was able to do was hold on to the tree. Then one of Gernot's seconds caught sight of me and hurried across: a Captain of Dragoons.

'Frau Egger! This is terrible. You must leave at once – at once! This is no place for a woman.'

'I . . . can't.'

'My dear lady, I assure you there's nothing to be anxious about. It's just a routine matter. The duel was forced on . . . the gentleman for whom I'm acting but he has everything under control. They're only fighting to first blood – the most your husband will receive is a scratch on the cheek. Now please return to your carriage.'

He left me. I heard someone counting out the paces, heard a word of command. The tree to which I clung was an oak; they're strong trees, neither of us fell down. I couldn't see the combatants, but I could hear . . . Hear the clash of the sabres going on and on . . . then an oath . . . a scream . . .

The doctor, his coat tails flapping, began to run.

I didn't faint. I would have liked to, but I didn't, and when they brought the stretcher through the birches, I saw that the blanket shrouding the still figure covered also the face.

It was the little fat man they sent to tell me.

'Madam, we have the gravest news. You must be brave. Your husband is dead.'

'It was his own choice.' The Captain of Dragoons who had followed spoke tersely. 'There's no doubt about it. Both parties are agreed.'

The little fat man nodded. I was sure he was the chiropodist: he looked kind, like someone acquainted with ailing feet. 'Herr Egger impaled himself on the Marshal's sword.'

'Nonsense,' snapped the Captain. 'If he'd done that the Marshal would have been able to pull back. He deliberately failed to beat off an intended feint attack that was only meant to keep him at a distance. It was not the action of a gentleman.'

The chiropodist looked shocked. 'Frau Egger, your husband died a glorious death by his own will. You must accept his choice.'

'Yes . . . thank you. And the Marshal?'

'Very distressed,' said the Captain. 'Naturally.'

Gernot von Lindenberg now appeared between the trees. He did not look distressed. He looked tired, angry – and alive!

'This is a bad business,' he said. He pulled back a corner of the blanket, let it drop. 'You'd best take him straight to the mortuary.'

'But sir, if we are going to hush this up—'

'It no longer amuses me to hush things up, Captain. I shall make my report direct to the Kaiser.' And to the chiropodist and Egger's other second, who had just been sick behind a tree: 'This matter is entirely my responsibility, gentlemen. Your names need not appear.' Then he caught sight of me, approached, bent over my hand. 'Madame, I am sincerely desolated. I did everything to avoid the conflict and everything to avoid serious bloodshed, but your husband was a skilful fencer. If I'd guessed his intention I could have thwarted it, but it never occurred to me. I trust you will allow me to see you safely home?'

I bent my head, allowing it. We walked some way in silence, his hand under my arm. When we were out of earshot he dropped my arm abruptly and turned me round to face him.

'Are you mad, Susanna? Are you absolutely out of your mind? What do you mean by coming here? I've spent three interminable months keeping away from you so that I could tie this business up without involving you and now you come here like a madwoman in a novel and—'

'I'm veiled,' I said crossly. 'How did you know me?'

'How did I know you? How did I *know* you? Dear God grant me patience!'

We had reached his carriage. The man in the driving seat

jumped down, saluted – and grinned at me. Another person un-
deceived by my disguise.

'Hatschek,' I said, 'oh, *Hatschek*.'

The carriage was closed and snug. Gernot drew the curtains and
we drove slowly back towards the city.

'It was bad when you didn't come, Susanna,' he said quietly.
'It was very bad.'

'Oh God, darling, it was bad for me too – you can't imagine
how bad – but I couldn't help it.' And I told him about Sigi and
the accident.

'Yes. I know. I trusted you. I knew you'd come if you could.'

I hung my head. I hadn't trusted him. 'I thought that you no
longer . . . that because I had failed you . . . you didn't want . . .'

'You thought *what*?' he said furiously. 'You were capable of
that . . . meanness . . . after twelve years of knowing me? My God,
don't we have enough difficulties in our life without that kind of
rubbish? Every meeting is like wading through shifting sand to an
oasis. Don't you ever do that again, Susanna. Don't you ever dare
to doubt me!'

Then he told me what he had been doing.

From Trieste he'd been sent straight to Potsdam for another
useless conference with Wilhelm's lackeys. It was the end of October before he got back to Vienna, to find that Egger had got his
way about Madensky Square at last.

'And I just saw red. That swine isn't going to lay hands on her
shop, I thought. I'd suspected there was something disreputable in
his past ever since you showed me that button, so I planned a
quixotic little enterprise: confronting Egger, offering him a chance
to cancel his plans and leave the country, or face exposure and
ruin.'

'Blackmail you mean?'

'What words you use! Anyway if I'd known what was to come
I'd have let your shop go hang and set you up in a villa in Hitzing
like all good mistresses. First of all I had to get evidence that he
was the man I thought he was and that meant going off to Mor-

avia and searching the records in the barracks, and tracking down people who might have known him. I'd never have done it without the Countess von Metz. Her brother was Colonel in Chief there and she was indefatigable. Incidentally I wish you could have seen Elise trying to get the name of her dressmaker out of the Countess! You'd have enjoyed that.

'It was December before I had what I wanted – and all the time I kept away from you – it only needed Egger to connect my interest in the square with you and I lost any leverage I had. He'd have dragged you into the mud in no time. Anyway, I went at night to confront him and it all seemed perfectly straightforward. He was obviously terrified and he said he'd rescind his plans and go. And then a week later he suddenly arrived and challenged me. I thought he'd gone completely mad, but there was no way of shaking him off. I suppose in his way he loved the army and preferred death to dishonour.'

'But what had Egger done? What did you find out?'

Gernot opened his cigar case.

'Listen,' he said, 'and I'll tell you.'

In the year 1882 the Pressburg Fusiliers were stationed at Gratz-islek, in Eastern Moravia. There was only one other detachment stationed there: the 19th Imperial Uhlans under the command of Colonel von Metz, the Countess's brother who was a martinet and unpopular with his men. Nor was the social life of the garrison town exactly scintillating. There was one café, one hotel . . . and as far as the eye could see, flat country which in summer became a dust bowl, and in winter a desert of ice.

Into this unprepossessing place there moved a merchant who had acquired the local schloss, a run-down gabled monstrosity in which he proposed, by painstaking bribery, to ennoble himself and his wife.

The wife, who was pretty, was even more bored than the soldiers. The merchant was frequently away in Prague or Budapest or Vienna, and she began to flirt her way through the garrison's officers. Most of the men seemed to have taken her measure, but one fell seriously for the lady and a proper liaison began.

'You can guess who it was, can't you?'

'Egger?'

Gernot nodded. 'Only he had a different name then.'

The lady was expensive. She didn't so much want furs or jewels as to get out of Gratzislek as far and as fast and as often as she could. Lieutenant Egger spent his free time wining and dining her, ran out of money . . . saw a rival begin to gain on him. Even then, it seems, he had a head for figures. He was in charge of the mess funds . . . he began to borrow money. A little at first, then more and more.

'It's an old story. It happens in every mess at some point. One minor crook. They're found out, sometimes they shoot themselves, sometimes there's a duel. Mostly they're just removed one night, stripped of their rank, not seen again. But Egger was cunning. He managed to frame his corporal, the chap who helped him with his accounts. The man he accused was a poor devil – a Jew from some obscure place in Ruthenia who lived for the army, but was never really accepted – oh, read the Dreyfus case; it's all in there. The corporal was confronted with his crime and went back to his hut and cut his throat. Which of course was seen as proof of guilt. Everything would have gone on as before, but the lady came to see the Colonel. She knew Egger had been borrowing money and the corporal had been engaged to one of her servants. There was an investigation but before he could be brought to trial, Egger vanished. A couple of years later the regiment was disbanded and no one heard of him until he reappeared under a different name, married a wealthy woman and started to crawl his way up the Ministry.'

'I see. And you got proof of this?'

'I and the Countess. She remembered a man in her brother's regiment who'd known him and we managed to track him down. It's to her you'll owe your shop, Susanna, as much as to anyone.'

'Are you sure Egger's plans will be cancelled? Will the square really be safe?'

He nodded. 'Heinrid will leap at the chance. There'll be some kind of face-saving manoeuvre about unexpected expense and so on, but it'll be all right, you'll see.'

'And the duel? Will it mean trouble for you?'

Gernot shrugged. 'I may have to resign.'

'Oh, *no*!'

He took my hand, decided I didn't need my glove, removed it. 'There's no need to look like that, my love. I can live without the army. If I'm right about what's coming I'd a great deal rather be in Uferding planting trees than sending men half my age out to be slaughtered. And it would be easier for us to meet.'

We jolted on towards the lights of the town. 'You know, Susanna,' he said, 'it isn't warm, passionate women like you who make the Great Lovers of this world. It's cold-hearted devils like me who are generally bored or discontented and frequently both. When it all stops for us, the ennui, the frustration . . . when we find a place of sanctuary, then we're totally caught. Yes, we're the ones to watch where loving is concerned.' He leant his head against the back of the seat and I saw the weariness in his face. 'It isn't every day I kill someone,' he murmured. 'One loses the habit.'

'You could sleep, Gernot. Close your eyes. I'll wake you when we're there.'

His head turned. He frowned.

'Try not to be stupid,' he said – and took me in his arms.

31 March 1912
Madensky Square
Vienna

I woke early today, just a year since I started to keep this journal. Looking out of the window I could see the pigeons stirring on the General's head and hear the plash of the fountain into which people have started throwing coins, for it is becoming known, our square. When Alice moved in next door, using Rudi's money to start her millinery business, the fashionable world really took notice. The best dress shop and the best hat shop side by side – outfits that could be designed, *in toto* – brought the carriages smartly to our door. We're being sensible, Alice and I, keeping our businesses separate, not knocking down the wall between us, but knowing what friends we are makes life agreeable for our customers. And oh, it is lovely having her so close!

The door of the apartment house opposite opened and the red setter bitch walked regally down the steps and sat yawning in the sun. She is no fetcher of newspapers and frankly she is losing her looks. When the English Miss agreed to model in my shop, she moved into the attic flat and asked Frau Hinkler whether, for a suitable fee, she'd mind the dog. Frau Hinkler made it clear that no dog could be of the faintest interest to her after Rip, but in three months the bitch has acquired the stomach of an alderman and the smug expression of someone whose lightest wish is someone else's command.

The English Miss, of course, is a sensation. Is it being brought up on an island surrounded by heaving water that gives the British that look of dreamy unconcern? I could put her in a shroud and my customers would clamour for it.

The choristers were out early, walking across to sing the morning service in St Florian's. Ernst Bischof's voice broke at last; he is no longer there. The new soloist is fat, solemn and good, and frankly Helene and I are finding this a little dull.

Joseph, wiping the tables on his terrace, looked disgruntled as well he might for his mother, who retired to bed when Egger's plans for the square were published, liked it so much there that she has not got up again and he's had to pay someone else to work in his kitchen.

The church clock struck the half hour, and punctual to the minute the door of the Schumachers' house opened and Lisl handed Herr Schumacher his walking stick and hat. It was clearly one of the days on which the timber heiress was to accompany her father in order to soak up the necessary impressions in the yard, for her bassinet was loaded into the carriage, and then the nursery maid hopped in beside the coachman.

Professor Starsky came next, looking up at my window. A menagerie owner is deluging him with goitrous axolotls which he sends 'Express' from Pest, but not 'Express' enough. At least Laura Sultzer no longer brings terror to the poor man's heart. Laura was so angry when her daughter insisted on marrying a pork butcher that she took the Group to the villa in St Polten where she discovered she had healing powers, and is now becoming an expert on herbal remedies, particularly worts.

The Professor raised his hat; I waved. He's coming to supper next week and so is Alice, but though Alice has been so wonderful, understanding how much I miss Nini, offering to mind the shop whenever I am called away 'on business' (but she has guessed, of course; she guessed years ago) she has not been entirely cooperative about the Professor.

'I'll come to supper,' she said, seeing through me as usual, 'but I have to make it perfectly clear, Sanna, that the Professor is *yours.*'

I dressed quickly and went downstairs. There were two letters. One was from Leah Cohen who is standing up well to the hard work and simple living conditions, but badly to a Madame de

Rubin on a neighbouring settlement who gets her orange-planting clothes sent out from Paris.

The other was from New York. It was very thick and when I opened it I found three sheets of music paper covered with notes. I've become a kind of Razumovsky, you see, for Sigi has started to compose and though I can't read the music and certainly can't play it, I'm exceedingly honoured. With the new étude inscribed to me was a note from Nini who is putting Daniel through the maximum inconvenience by suggesting that they live in sin in a cold water apartment in the Bronx. Personally, in this struggle, I back the wolverine who wants an official daughter-in-law to show off to her friends, and wants her soon.

Have you asked her yet? was the P.S. on Nini's letter, and the answer is, no I have not. Frau Egger has adapted well to widowhood. She has resumed the petit point which she used to enjoy as a girl and I am about to be presented with a footstool cover depicting two pheasants and a deer. But no, I have not found the opportunity to ask this burning question and I doubt now that I ever will. Nini and I are destined to go to our graves, I fear, without learning about Herr Egger's Nasty Little Habit.

The salon was bright with sunshine; the narcissi that Old Anna brought me yesterday were bunched in their alabaster bowl. I went through into the workroom where the dummies of my regular customers greeted me like old friends. Frau Hutte-Klopstock's was draped in the white muslin that is to make her look like Debussy's Melisande. Edith Huber's was clad in a grey alpaca dress which might have been worn by that low-spirited English governess, Jane Eyre.

It didn't take Edith long to understand the point of my charade that day in the fitting room, and when Herr Huber proposed, she came at once to see me.

'You must tell me what to do about clothes, Frau Susanna, please. I mustn't disgrace him.'

'You won't disgrace him, Edith, but I'll tell you what to do about clothes. Nothing. Forget them. Dress as plainly as you can, ignore fashion – be seemly and nothing more – by day. But at night . . . !' And I scribbled down for her the address of the woman who makes lingerie for the girls of the Opera Ballet.

And it worked, of course. Inspired by that great gift, a secret wife, Herr Huber, within a month of his marriage, had patented the Huberwurst which is causing a sensation in the world of charcuterie.

It was almost time to open the shop, but I went out first into the courtyard because they're so magical, these hesitant first days of spring. Mitzi had spent the night with Maia and they were playing next door.

'We're in an igloo,' came Maia's voice over the wall. 'You can't cook in an igloo.'

But Mitzi is growing up. 'Yes I can. I'm going to heat some seal oil and fry strips of penguin meat.'

The buds on my pear tree are already showing white. This year I feel sure will be its annus mirabilis. It will give two pears or even three – but if not it doesn't matter for I have plenty of time. When you plant pears you plant for those who come after you, for your heirs. And I have an heir . . . an heiress. No one ever had such an heiress as I. I know her name now. She's called Elisabeth. They gave her the name I offered her in the hospital – my mother's name. I found this so amazing, so unbelievable, but Gernot said it just meant that the nun who was on duty that night, the one who gave me the baby to hold, had told them what I wanted. He's not at all keen on miracles, yet it was a sort of miracle he performed for me.

Because I've seen her – I've seen my daughter! Oh, only from a distance, but I've seen her, and it was because of him!

Gernot was right about the square. There were some fulsome obituaries about Herr Egger who had died so tragically in a shooting accident; then Heinrid came to lay a wreath on the family grave, and two weeks later the plan was dropped.

But he was wrong about having to resign from the army. The Kaiser was displeased about the duel, but a great deal more displeased at the idea of losing Gernot. 'Don't be silly, my dear fellow,' he said – and immediately sent him to Albania to calm King Ferdinand.

When he came back we met at the Bristol and he asked me if I'd like to go to a wedding.

'You'd have to go incognito – in one of your famous veils – and watch from a window. But I'll take you if it would make you happy. If there are no tears.'

'Your daughter's, you mean?'

He shook his head. 'The whiskery young man in the Diplomatic Corps got away. I was afraid he would. No, not my daughter's wedding. Yours.'

I was sitting at the dressing table, brushing my hair. I knew he was watching my face so I took some deep breaths and managed to speak steadily (I think).

'How do you know she's getting married?'

It was his turn to pick his words with care.

'Since you first told me about her, I gave instructions to . . . certain people to keep me informed about her.

'You can call it spying,' he said, anticipating my words, 'but I thought of it as keeping watch. You were in fact perfectly correct in that assessment you made in Salzburg. The Tollers have been excellent parents, your daughter has grown up in peace and happiness and she is marrying the man of her choice. But if it had been otherwise – if anything had happened to her adoptive parents – I would have been in a position to let you know.'

'My God, Gernot, all those years.' I was humbled, overwhelmed.

Then he handed me a newspaper in which Herr and Frau Toller announced the wedding of their daughter Elisabeth in St Peter's Church, Salzburg, on 16 March.

'Well, do you want to go?'

'Yes, Gernot, I want to go.'

But he was irritable and edgy as we drove from the station in Salzburg to St Peter's Square, wondering, I suppose, if I was going to collapse and make a scene. Though now I think of it, men often look like that at weddings. He was in mufti and hates hard hats.

He had arranged everything. Opposite the church is a row of ancient houses, once part of a friary. We were admitted to one of these, taken to the first floor, led to a bare room where two chairs were placed by the windows. Gernot handed me his field glasses.

Down in the street the carriages were assembling, dropping the guests. Some came on foot, solid-looking burghers in their best dirndls and loden suits. Then a carriage, smarter than the rest, the horses in white rosettes, out of which stepped two young men. One was slender, tall, in a well-cut grey suit with a carnation in his buttonhole and a dark, sensitive-looking face. The bridegroom, I was sure. The other was a fair man, stocky, with a blond beard: one of those dependable friends who makes a perfect best man and never drops the ring.

The bells had grown silent, the last of the guests moved into the church. Somewhere, just inside, I knew, the woman waited, in the place where I should have been, to set my daughter's dress straight and send her up the aisle. Had she spent the night in tears or was she proud and pleased? Did she like the young man?

It was a grey day, blustery. I realized that I had thought of my daughter as existing in perpetual sunshine.

Then she came. The carriage was decked with flowers, and she sat beside the water engineer with her white veil blowing in the wind. Beside me, Gernot frowned and I sat up very straight in my chair. No scenes, no tears; I had promised.

The water engineer got down and helped her out. A small man with a goatee . . . My hand tightened round the glasses. She descended gracefully, walked up the steps, erect and slender, managed her train with skill.

Of course. Of course.

The church door closed. I followed the service in my mind. The introit . . . the blessing . . . the moment of communion . . . Till she came out at last with her veil thrown back and I could see her face.

God, she was beautiful! My daughter was, is and always will be the most beautiful creature that exists on earth.

Then I saw that there had been a disaster.

'Gernot, she's married the wrong man! Look – she's on the arm of the stocky fair one. The one she's got is hardly taller than she is!'

My lover does not often laugh. A twitch of the cheek to indicate a brief amusement is generally as far as he goes, but now he almost choked on his cigar.

'Oh splendid, splendid! You obviously have the right idea already. Heaven forbid that the poor girl should choose her own husband.'

'No, honestly, Gernot, the other one—'

Then I too began to laugh. Would I really have been one of those mothers speaking always 'for her daughter's good'? '*Of course* I like Paulchen, my darling, I like him very *much*, but I do feel you should tell him to come in earlier at night. It's not fair on you when he stays out so late . . .'

Gernot was still in a state of high amusement when we arrived at the Hotel Winkler and booked in for the night, but later he paid me a compliment that I value very much.

'No one,' he said, 'absolutely no one who has not been to bed with a mother-in-law can be said to have truly lived.'

I was thinking of her still, my newly-wedded heiress, as I stood in the sunlight beside my little tree. I may never see her again in this world, but to her I bequeath everything I have learnt, and am, and have experienced. For you, my Kleis, my Elisabeth, the pale green tips of the larches, the overtures of operas, the alpenrosen . . . For you the filigree of spiders' webs, the giants and angels in the Grottenbahn, the garlands and the songs. I haven't lived for you – I wasn't able to – but I've lived *at* you – and for the last time, my darling, I'm sorry, so very sorry, that I wasn't brave enough.

It was a long day in the shop and among my clients, alas, was the Countess von Metz whom I shall dress now, I suppose, until she dies. But tomorrow is Sunday and when I have been to church I shall go down to the workroom and make a dress. The material is waiting for me and it's ravishing: aquamarine watered silk as blue and green and silver as the sea which now, perhaps, I shall never see.

And when I have made it, I shall put it on and float through the streets of the Kaiserstadt and Franz Joseph will drive by in his gold-wheeled carriage and decide to live a while longer, poor old man, because there are such lovely dresses in his town. The little girls will stop playing with their hoops and ask their mothers if they too could, please, have such a dress when they're grown up; and the hussars in their scarlet and blue, and the young men about town in their silk hats will stare at me and wonder whether perhaps I could be persuaded . . . Yes, even though I have had another and quite unnecessary birthday, they will wonder it. But I shall float on unregarding in my sea-green dress, for there is only one man in the wide world, only one ageing, irascible man, who may say the words which will reward me for all my labour:

'Take it off, my darling. Quickly, please. Take it off!'

PAN
HERITAGE
CLASSICS

Bringing wonderful classic books to a new audience.

MURDER AT
THE OLD VICARAGE
A CHRISTMAS MYSTERY
JILL MCGOWN

THE HILLS
IS LONELY
LILLIAN BECKWITH

THE GROVE
OF EAGLES
A NOVEL OF ELIZABETHAN ENGLAND
WINSTON GRAHAM

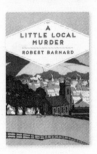

A
LITTLE LOCAL
MURDER
ROBERT BARNARD

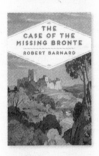

THE
CASE OF THE
MISSING BRONTE
ROBERT BARNARD

MARRYING
OFF MOTHER
AND OTHER STORIES
GERALD DURRELL

THE
ENCHANTED
PLACES
CHRISTOPHER
MILNE

MURDER IN
ADVENT
DAVID WILLIAMS

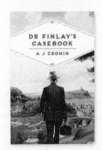

DR FINLAY'S
CASEBOOK
A J CRONIN

Bello:
hidden talent rediscovered!

Bello is a digital only imprint of Pan Macmillan,
established to breathe new life into previously published,
classic books.

At Bello we believe in the timeless power of the imagination,
of good story, narrative and entertainment and we want to use
digital technology to ensure that many more readers
can enjoy these books into the future.

We publish in ebook and Print on Demand formats
to bring these wonderful books to new audiences.

About Bello:

www.panmacmillan.com/imprints/bello

About the author:

www.panmacmillan.com/author/evaibbotson

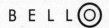